That Second Chance

"With each book I read by Meghan Quinn, I become more in awe of her writing talent. She truly has a gift! *That Second Chance* was simply perfect!"

—*Wrapped Up In Reading*

"A sweet, sexy, swoon-worthy, *must-read* romance from Meghan Quinn—I would *highly* recommend it! I fell head over heels in love with the quaint and charming small town of Port Snow, Maine, and all of its residents."

—*The Romance Bibliophile*

"I'm basking in the happily-ever-after goodness of *That Second Chance*, which gets five stars."

—*Dog-Eared Daydreams*

"I adored the small town of Port Snow and the fabulous, tight [bond] the Knightly family has not only with each other but with their community as a whole."

—*Book Angel Booktopia*

That Forever Girl

"A terrific read."

—*Once Upon a Book Blog*

That Secret Crush

ALSO BY MEGHAN QUINN

All of her books can be read in Kindle Unlimited.

New Releases

The Secret to Dating Your Best Friend's Sister
Diary of a Bad Boy
The Locker Room

The Dating by Numbers Series

Three Blind Dates
Two Wedding Crashers
One Baby Daddy
Back in the Game (novella)

The Blue Line Duet

The Upside of Falling
The Downside of Love

The Perfect Duet

The Left Side of Perfect
The Right Side of Forever

The Binghamton Boys Series

Co-Wrecker
My Best Friend's Ex
Tangled Twosome
The Other Brother

Stand-Alones

Dear Life
The Virgin Romance Novelist Chronicles
Newly Exposed
The Mother Road

Box Set Series

The Jett Girl Series
Love and Sports Series
Hot-Lanta Series

That Secret Crush

MEGHAN QUINN

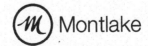

Text copyright © 2020 by Meghan Quinn
All rights reserved.

Published by Montlake, Seattle

www.apub.com

Amazon, the Amazon logo, and Montlake are trademarks of Amazon.com, Inc., or its affiliates.

ISBN-13: 9781542018432
ISBN-10: 1542018439

Cover design by Letitia Hasser

Cover photography by Rob Lang Images

Printed in the United States of America

*To all the readers who've harbored a secret
crush for so long*

PROLOGUE

REID

What the fuck was that?

Did I just experience real-life witchcraft? Whatever it was, I'm pretty sure Neptune and Uranus collided in space, because that shit was crazy.

Stunned and nervously laughing at each other, my brothers and I hurry to a more populated part of the city. We're soon threading our way through crowded cobblestone Bourbon Street toward a partially broken neon sign advertising *huge* pretzels.

"She was scary as shit," Brig whispers into my ear, reaching for my hand. I swat the idiot away.

Out of all my brothers, Brig is by far the most sensitive, but holding hands—come on, dude, self-respect.

Although I can't blame him for quivering in his jeans.

It might be all the alcohol I consumed, but damn . . . I'm feeling a little uneasy and a whole lot terrified.

Why, you ask?

Because I'm pretty sure an old crone who surfaced from Satan's lair just cast some weird-as-shit curse on us. She pointed a crooked finger and laid it all out: we'll have nothing but broken love for life.

And before you scoff at such a blasphemous occurrence, you have to know this: There was fucking *wind* whipping us in the nuts as she spoke. And on this still, muggy New Orleans night, where the fuck did that wind come from? There were no fans in sight, and there was zero traffic down the narrow cobblestone side road.

Confused? Okay, here are the Cliff Notes.

Baby Brig turned twenty-one, and the four of us Knightly brothers very intelligently chose New Orleans as the place to celebrate because we didn't want to be cliché and go to Vegas—although I'm kind of wishing we had right about now. We were in the middle of having a great alcohol-fueled night on the town. But, not paying any attention to where our wobbly legs were taking us, we ran into some old palm reader's table, and Brig's fat ass broke it. To make up for the destruction, Brig paid her to read his fortune.

Well, she did a shit job.

Oooh . . . you have brothers. They're going to get you into trouble one day—thanks, lady, tell us something we don't know.

Her prediction was a load of crock, and because of that, we might have, you know, vocalized our intoxicated opinion on her subpar storytelling. That's when the crazy shit went down.

Not taking a liking to our constructive criticism, the old bat started flinging her cloak-draped arms around while her evil eyes turned a shade of petrifying yellow, and a huge mole grew on her nose out of nowhere. Pop! Just like that, the mole . . . with accompanying thick black hair.

Okay, maybe the mole isn't true, and her eyes didn't change color, but she did wave her arms around, and she said some pretty traumatizing shit. Things like *Your dicks are going to fall off* and *You'll forever have sensitive nipples.*

Hmm . . . that doesn't seem right.

Did she say that?

Confused, I break the silence hanging over all of us. "Did she say our dicks were going to fall off?"

Panic rises in Brig's voice. "Shit, did she? Did I miss that part?" He grabs his crotch with both hands as he continues to walk. "I can't afford to have my dick drop dead."

"As if we can?" Rogan, the group pessimist, says, ducking around a rowdy bachelorette party. "Pretty sure we all need our dicks, dude."

Griffin, the oldest and most sensible despite his alcohol intake tonight, speaks up. "There was no mention of dicks falling off. She just said we'll be cursed with broken love."

"Okay, so broken *dicks*," I clarify.

"Like, I'll never be able to get it up again?" Brig steps in front of all of us. "Quick, take me to a strip club. I need to make sure that's not what she meant."

"She didn't mean that, you idiot." Rogan wraps his arm around Brig's neck and continues down the street, giant pretzels in sight.

"That lady was a fucking whack job. Clearly she has some kind of mental health issue. It's best if we just forget about everything and move on," Griffin says.

Sage advice from the brightest out of all of us.

And even though I'm not as freaked out as Brig—I mean, I'm not clutching my dick and praying to the good Lord right now—I have to admit whatever happened back in that alley didn't seem entirely kosher.

What did she say again? Something about having broken love, and it won't be until our minds have matured that the curse will be cured? What the hell does that even mean? Not that I'm looking for love, not when my restaurant is my life right now, but it would be nice to know that I still have the option.

When my best friend, Eric, and I were getting through culinary school, pretty much every instructor told us that we weren't going to have any time for relationships. The only love of our lives would be our knives.

That's turned out to be true. Betty, Beverly, and Barbie are my girls. Every night we have a foursome, and weirdly, they're the best I've ever had. They enjoy my hands, and I enjoy their cutting edge—fuck, I'm hilarious.

So even though that lady was weird, I don't think I have anything to worry about.

Broken love.

Curses.

Yeah, okay, you old crone. Go tickle someone else with your mole hair— we're not interested.

Together, we step inside the crowded, noisy pretzel bar and take a seat before putting in our order. Brig sits next to me, bouncing his knee and scanning the restaurant, its garage doors tucked up into the ceiling, used for closing time only. Everything about this place—selling giant pretzels in the heart of the French Quarter for all the drunk tourists—is genius. Despite the sticky bar top, peeling walls, and dirt-encrusted floors that probably haven't seen a mop in a few years, there's no doubt in my mind that it makes a killing . . . on just pretzels. Brig leans in and whispers, "I think she followed us; I can feel her here, staring at me."

"Dude, you're fucking paranoid right now. Chill, man."

"Did you not hear her?" Brig seethes with worry. "She said we would never have dicks again."

Christ.

I drag my hand over my face. We are way too drunk to be dealing with something like this. "She said we would have broken love. Your dick is fine."

"That's what you think? Have you looked at yours yet? What if she turned them green or something? And broken love . . . that's even worse. You know my goal in life is to be a husband. How can that happen if I'm cursed with broken love?"

Luckily, at that moment, my phone vibrates in my pocket. I reach for it and see Eric's name flash across the screen. He knows I'm in New Orleans celebrating Brig's birthday, so this must be important.

I hold up the phone to my sweating, hysterical brother. "Have to take this. Talk to Griff—he'll hold your hand."

"Really? You think so?"

I don't bother to reply and take off toward the hallway that leads to the employee entrance at the back of the bar, trying to gain a little bit of privacy and to get away from the loud, pounding music.

Straight from culinary school—and after working multiple jobs and saving every last penny we ever earned—Eric and I were able to scrape enough money together to start our own restaurant in Boston, which we named Bar 79 after Harbor 79, our favorite place to fish in our hometown, Port Snow.

After six months of tireless menu prep, designing the space, and marketing the hell out of our New England–inspired cuisine with a twist, we opened our doors. And we're only three months in, but we're killing it so far. The food blogs love us, and three major articles have been written about our impeccable flavoring and our incredibly close bond.

I accept the call and bring the phone up to my ear. "Hey, man, what's up?"

"Hey, I know you're out with your brothers, but I, uh . . . I have a problem."

"What's going on? Is it the restaurant, or is it something with Janelle?" Eric has been dating our business manager for the past three months, ever since we opened. I told him it was risky and maybe not the smartest idea he's ever had, but he was gung ho on making a move, and there was nothing I could say or do to stop him.

"Uh . . . yeah."

Still drunk, but not so much that I can't help out with any restaurant issue, I lean against the wall. "Walk me through it."

Eric has always been the big picture guy, the dreamer, the extravagant one, while I'm more grounded and work out the fine details. So when he calls with a problem, I'm usually pretty confident in my ability to help him work through whatever it is.

"Uh . . ." His voice shakes, a crack in his usually even-keeled persona. Cue the worry. This can't be good. "Did you recently ask Janelle to make a transfer?"

Janelle has been handling our business for the past five months, ever since Eric confronted me about not being able to juggle everything as we were gearing up for the opening. I was dropping the ball on multiple responsibilities, like managing our funds, paying vendors, and getting all our orders in on time while still trying to cook and develop the menu, so he found Janelle and brought her into the mix to help manage everything. With her MBA and businesslike confidence, she was doing a good job, I thought—well, until this very moment.

"A transfer of funds?"

"Yeah."

"No. Why? Did she?"

"She did."

"Okay, so what's the problem?"

"She, uh . . . she kind of transferred *all* the funds."

I press my hand to my forehead, wishing I wasn't drunk right now. "Dude, spell it out for me, okay? I've been drinking all damn day, I just got my dick turned green, and I'm hungry for a pretzel. What the hell is going on?"

"She took it all, Reid. She fucking took it all."

"Took what? Our money?" That can't be right.

"Yeah. Took every last penny and just disappeared."

"Wait. What?" I pinch the bridge of my nose, trying to comprehend what Eric is telling me. "She took all of our money? Where did she go?"

"No fucking idea."

"So . . . we don't have any money in the joint account?" I think back to how much was in there. After all our expenses and the cost of the opening, we were at about twenty grand, I think. *Okay, don't panic.*

"No, man. She took it all, out of *all* of the accounts."

My heart seizes in my chest as my breath comes out in gasps. Confusion and understanding collide in my brain, sending my stomach into a nauseous roll.

"What the fuck are you telling me right now?"

"The restaurant . . . fuck, man, it's broke."

My head falls back against the wall, my body going limp as I slide to the sticky ground that hasn't seen a mop in a decade.

Broke.

As in, no funds?

There has to be a solution. The police, lawyers . . . this shit isn't legal.

"Did you report her?"

"Yeah, but because she's a partner, there isn't much we can do. She had access to everything. She fucked us over."

I rub my hand across my forehead, eyes shut, preparing for the worst. "So what the fuck are you trying to tell me?"

"We were already behind on bills. Janelle apparently wasn't paying them but was still paying herself. Rent is two months overdue, vendors want their money, contractors still need to be paid. We're fucked, Reid. Utterly fucked." He lets out a long breath and says the last thing I ever expected to hear. "We have to close."

No fucking way.

◆ ◆ ◆

I pace the sealed concrete floor of Bar 79's kitchen, still trying to comprehend what the hell happened while I was gone.

I told Eric to meet me here in the morning after I got back, but he has yet to show up. I'm seriously starting to worry that he's stood me up when the back door bangs open. I glance up to see Eric stumble inside, a bottle in his hand, a hitch in his gait. What the ever-living fuck?

"Are you drunk?"

"I can't believe you're sober." He makes his way to a prep table and hoists himself on top of it before taking another swig of what I can only imagine is a bottle of scotch.

"How the hell am I supposed to have a conversation about our restaurant when you're drunk off your ass?"

"Just a wee bit twisted," he says, holding his fingers up. "And there's nothing to talk about. We're fucked, Reid. She took it all. We put every ounce of our savings into this place, and my parents' money . . ." His face twists in grief before he takes another swig.

"We have to be able to find some investors, some partners. We have great reviews; we're up and coming on the restaurant scene. We have options."

He shakes his head. "News is already spreading. No one is going to want to work with two idiots who don't know how to manage a business."

I run my hands through my hair, tugging at it. "This can't be it. There has to be something we can do."

"We owe vendors a shit ton of money, Reid. We are so far in debt that even if an investor likes our talent, they're not about to scoop up all the debt we owe. Face it, this is over." He leans back on one hand and takes a sip of his drink.

"Fuck!" I shout and kick a garbage can across the kitchen. "Fuck! I told you not to date her. I told you it was a bad idea."

Gaining a little clarity, Eric sits tall and jabs at his chest with the hand that's holding his bottle. "Are you blaming this on *me*?"

"She worked you, man. She used you and took what she wanted— that was her plan all along. I never should have let you hire her."

"I never would have had to hire her if you didn't drop the fucking ball on all the business shit. Don't blame me, Reid. When we went into this partnership, you said you could handle the business end while I took over the big picture planning. I did my part. You were the one who fucking failed on his end. I stepped in and tried to find the solution."

"With a pair of tits," I shoot back. "You hired her because of her tits, not her qualifications."

"Fuck you." He slides off the prep table, the slap of his sneakered feet reverberating through the kitchen. "We never would have been in this situation if you didn't fuck us over to begin with. Don't blame this shit on me, not when you're just as much at fault. Face it, Reid, we might be good in the kitchen, but when it comes to running a business . . . we both just destroyed our careers."

I don't want to admit that he's right, and I don't want to take blame for this, even though a heavy weight is pressing down on my chest, reminding me over and over that this very well might be my fault.

I should have asked for help.

I should have interviewed Janelle.

I shouldn't have been so lazy when it came to decisions.

But . . .

"I trusted you," I say, hands on my hips, staring at Eric. "I trusted you to make the right decision for the business, and you thought with your dick instead of your head."

He tosses the bottle to the side, the glass shattering as it hits the floor. "Yeah, well, I trusted you to hold up your end of the bargain, and you didn't, so looks like we're both shitheads." He shakes his head and starts to walk toward the back door. "Good luck with your life, Reid. Just don't ever try to run a business again. Anything you do is guaranteed to crash and burn, just like Bar 79."

CHAPTER ONE

REID
Three years later

Muscles screaming, back aching, I haul the lobster cage over the edge of the boat and fall backward on my ass from the weight.

Christ.

Catching my breath, I wipe the sweat off my brow with the collar of my flannel shirt. I shucked my puffy vest an hour ago, despite the chilly February air.

Six lobster traps, all full of plump brown crustaceans eager to pinch my cock off. I see it in their eyes, in the way they snap at me with their meaty claws.

Too bad, fuckers, you're not getting out.

Leaning back on my hands, I take in the rising sun as it lights up the sky, bathing it in a beautiful shade of orange.

Peace.

On the water, floating in my rickety boat, smelling like a corpse—this is the only place where I can find any peace. Away from my invasive family, far from the never-ending gossip in town, and a good distance from the life I fucking despise.

Once a top chef, now a poor fisherman who has to work for his parents to make ends meet.

Put that on my dating profile.

Ladies will be swiping right in the blink of an eye.

Lives on a houseboat, smells like crabs—but doesn't have crabs, win—interfering brothers, and exceptionally nosy older sister. Used to cook but now eats soup from a can, willing to split the check with you but not willing to pay in full—sorry, but there's only dust in these pockets—rocket of a cock, great fingers, and will eat you for nourishment.

I'm a real fucking catch.

Not that I'm looking for love. No, that boat sailed three years ago after an unfortunate incident in New Orleans.

But on the plus side, at least my dick didn't turn green. Perfectly peach, at least that's what Brig likes to tell women. What a fucking douche canoe.

I stare down at my haul, each lobster with a dollar sign hanging over its antenna, a little *cha-ching* sounding off in my head with every little bulgy-eyed bastard I count.

"You know, I used to look at you fellas differently," I say, forgetting myself as I speak to the lobsters trying to claw their way out of their boxes. "Instead of seeing you as a cash crop, I used to enjoy thinking of all the ways I could break you down and serve you." I stare at one lobster in particular—he's got a bit of feistiness in his eyes. "I used to make one hell of a lobster bisque with your aunts and uncles. The people in Port Snow say the Lighthouse Restaurant makes the best lobster bisque in town, and yeah, that shit is good, but then again, they've never tried mine." He snaps his claw at me. "I get it, fella, it's barbaric of me to talk about your death, but hey, money is money, and even though you look like a kind crustacean, you're still getting the pot. Daddy needs funds, and that's where you come in."

I stand from where I've been sitting on the deck, thankful for my yellow slicker pants—or else my ass would be soaking wet. I secure the traps, get behind the wheel, and roar the engine. Time to head home. I have fudge duty today.

Fucking shoot me.

What makes working at the Lobster Landing a nightmare is not just the nosy locals or the needy tourists but the perpetually lecturing father of mine.

Every time he sees me, his eyes light up, and he makes a beeline to where I'm working.

"Reid, how's it going? Have a good catch this morning? Have you thought about my offer to work with Willy Kneader up in Pottsmouth? Have you picked up your knives lately? Did you see that recipe I emailed you?"

And the worst question of them all . . .

"Have you thought about your future lately?"

No.

No, I haven't.

Thanks for reminding me almost every day how pathetic I feel, though.

Yeah, I know, I sound like a martyr, and in all honesty, I know my dad has good intentions—he only wants the best for me—but the best thing for me right now is to be left alone. Let me figure things out on my own.

The ride back to the harbor is not nearly as thrilling as when I'm driving out toward the sea, nothing but waves in front of me, and as I get closer and closer to Port Snow, the same sense of dread that hits me every morning fills me.

I'm the laughingstock of the town—the fuckup, the failure, the boy who had to come crying back to his mommy and daddy because he was a dumb-ass and trusted a complete stranger with his business.

My family has told me more times than I can even remember that the town doesn't see me that way, but who the fuck are they kidding? Damien Turtle came back to Port Snow after his wife was found in bed with his best friend. The locals gossiped about Turtle's turtle and its supposed insufficiencies nonstop for months! Can you even believe that?

Poor fucking guy.

I can only imagine what they're saying about me.

I take a deep breath. At least it's not a green dick.

Thank God for small miracles.

I spend the next hour lugging the lobsters out of my boat and into my truck, then hauling them up to the Lighthouse Inn. I drive around back and am just stepping down from the truck when Eve, the restaurant manager and Eric's twin sister, strides out of the employee entrance to meet me.

"Jesus, Knightly." She wrinkles her nose and comes to an abrupt halt. "Did you take a shower in the past month?"

I scratch the side of my jaw, my unruly scruff grating against my nails. "Splashed some water on my face last week. Are you saying I smell good?" I take a step toward her.

She quickly retreats and plugs her nose. "I'm saying you smell like death," she says, her voice coming out nasally.

"So, that means you want to give me a hug, right?" I hold out my arms, and before she can move even farther away, I snag her and hold her tight against my chest and wet slicker pants.

She squirms against me, but she's no match for this honed physique. "Oh my God, I'm going to throw up."

Chuckling, I let her go, and she bends over to the side, gasping for air. I lift my arm and take a whiff. I'm not *that* bad—just a little sea life on these bones, that's all.

"You know I don't have all day, Roberts. As much fun as it is staring at your ass bent over like that, I need to get paid, and I need to get to the Lobster Landing in thirty." I hold out my hand. "Pay up."

"Please tell me you're going to take a shower before you go to cut up fudge."

"No, I plan on horrifying tourists with my putrid stench," I deadpan.

"So you admit you smell putrid." She digs into her pocket. "At least we can agree upon that."

"Hey, there are other things we agree upon."

She holds out a few bills, which I snatch, fold up, and stick into my flannel shirt pocket.

"Yeah, and what would that be?"

I nod at her shirt. "How great your tits look in that maroon collared shirt."

She rolls her eyes. "Never going to happen, Knightly."

I hold up my hands in defense. "Slow down there, Eve. You act like I want to fuck you or something. That's far too presumptuous. You're my best friend's twin after all, so that would be like fucking Eric with a wig on."

"We're fraternal."

"You sound the same."

"He's a man."

"Yeah, it's really unfortunate that you have such a baritone voice coming out of such a hot body."

She swats at me. "Get out of here. I'm done with you." She calls through the back door, "Joe, lobsters are here," and then turns back to me, a smile on her face. "I told you to get out of here, Knightly."

I take a few steps backward. "You want me—you know you do."

"It's disgusting how confident you are."

"Confidence is sexy in a man."

"Confidence is annoying in you," Eve says as Joe pops out the back door and gives me a nod before taking in the lobster. "I'll catch you later, Knightly."

"See ya, Eve."

I hop back into my truck and make the drive down to the harbor to my houseboat, which I rent from Rogan. The small two-story boat caught my attention when he was first remodeling it. With its perfect location out in the harbor, it's as far away from the town gossip as I can get. Rogan was going to use it as another tourist rental property, but I convinced him to let me rent it from him, though the fucker doesn't give me a cut on rent. Well, a little cut, but not as much as I was hoping.

With not much time to spare, I take a quick shower and put on my signature white shirt with the Lobster Landing logo plastered on the front. I throw on a matching baseball cap and worn jeans before heading out the door.

The walk to my family business is short but just long enough to give me some unfortunate time to think.

I claim Eric as my best friend, but in all honesty, I can't remember the last time I spoke with him. He's still living in Boston, where he found a job as a line cook at a three-star restaurant, and he's still trying to chase the dream—one I gave up on a long time ago, probably the moment I walked back into town with my tail tucked between my legs. After we lost the restaurant, we had a falling-out, a big one. I blamed him for bringing Janelle into the mix. He blamed me for not keeping up on the books in the first place. I blamed him for not helping with managing the finances. He blamed me for not helping out with promotions. We pointed fingers, we swung fists, and we planted a giant stake into our friendship, dividing us and sending us our separate ways.

I occasionally send him a text about some stupid local gossip, and he sends me GIFs on my birthday. It's nothing like it used to be, and I don't think it ever will be.

Eric and I used to be attached at the hip, but Eve and I have a better friendship at this point.

But that's life. You lose friendships; you gain some.

I lost a big one, and I only have myself to blame.

CHAPTER TWO

EVE

"Are you doing anything special tomorrow?" Harper, my best friend, asks, bringing her drink up to her lips.

Victoria, our good friend from grade school, rubs a napkin over the bar before resting her arms on its peeling top. The polish has worn off over the years, and instead of sanding down the bar and refinishing it, the owner has decided to let the bar top "show its character." The Lighthouse Inn is one of many places to rest while you're visiting Port Snow. The food is subpar, and the accommodations could use some work, but the scenery is epic and why it's a sought-after tourist destination.

"I was just about to ask that," Victoria says, stirring a lemon in her water. Uppity and very particular about everything in her life, Victoria runs the town library and the historical league, is a published historian, and owns way too many dresses from the 1850s. But she has a kind heart, and we love her for that.

"Just the usual." I shrug, mindlessly wiping down the bar top with a wet rag, not really cleaning anything in particular but giving myself something to do on the slow night.

I hate this bar. I hate wiping it down every night, serving the same old locals and helping tiresome tourists when they ask for sightseeing information. This wasn't exactly how I envisioned my life turning out: me serving up outdated cosmopolitans and bottom-shelf vodka cranberries. But when you sacrifice your dream for someone else, this is what happens. Good thing I was never taught to wallow in self-pity, though. No, I've been proactive with my life choices, and I always strive for more. I can taste it, my freedom, and it's come from nothing more than sheer hard work and determination. Seven years of juggling my time, seven years of long days and even longer nights spent studying, but graduation is around the corner, and I have plans to use my degree.

Exciting plans.

"Do you want company? Rogan and I can come with you." After years of being separated from her high school sweetheart and enduring one of the most tragic breakups I've ever witnessed, Harper finally got back together with her longtime love, Rogan Knightly, a few months ago. And they are sickeningly cute together.

I'm not jealous of their love. Not even a little.

Okay, maybe a tiny bit.

But my happiness for her definitely wins out. Even though Harper is two years older than me, she took me under her wing when we were young. We bonded over the insufferable Knightly brothers and were always running into each other over at the Knightly house. We spent many nights hanging out in the living room while the boys were forced to clean the kitchen after a big meal, talking about everything and anything that came to mind and solidifying our bond for life.

I shake my head. "No, that's okay. I'll just be a sobbing mess anyway."

"You shouldn't have to go alone."

Yeah, I agree—Eric should be there with me, but when I asked him if he was coming home this weekend, he said he couldn't get the time off. I want to believe him—I truly do—and most of me does. But a small part of me believes that if he asked, if he actually spoke to his manager about the importance of this weekend, he would be here.

But like always, Eric just pushed the hard stuff under the rug and walked by without a second glance. Despite being twins, we sure do have different ways of dealing with the unfortunate and devastating moments in our lives. While I take situations head-on, Eric hides.

It's why he and Reid barely speak anymore.

It's why he avoids my phone calls and texts.

And it's why he hasn't been home since Dad passed.

Losing Dad and then, only a few months later, losing the restaurant put a pretty big rift between the two of us. Yeah, we still talk and support each other, but I can tell Eric can't bear to see me face to face, not after the promise he broke, the promise that was supposed to set our future . . . my future. Unfortunately the night they closed Bar 79 was the night I lost my confident brother forever, and I know him well enough to understand that seeing me just reminds him of everything he's lost.

"It's really okay. I'm good. But thank you."

Victoria frowns. "Well, I think Rylee was planning on having the girls over tomorrow night. If you need a drink or three, you should come join us."

Rylee is the local romance author; she met a guy at a wedding she was crashing for research and ended up marrying him. Beck Wilder . . . sigh, the rebel from out of town. Superhot with a heart of gold. They have triplets, and every month, Beck takes them over to her parents', which lets them host a blessedly kid-free get-together with friends.

"Who's going to be there?"

"Ren, Harper, Zoey, Rylee, of course, and myself." Victoria brings her hand to her chest. "And I think Jen Knightly."

"Ruth isn't going?" I ask, thinking of the local coffee shop owner, who's become a key member of our growing group.

"I think she has a date," Harper says with a smirk.

"Oh yeah? With who?"

"She wouldn't say, but I'm pretty sure it's a guy she met online. She's been messaging back and forth with him for a bit. She's pretty excited."

"Good for her," I say. "She's been hung up on Brig Knightly for a while, so I'm glad she's finally venturing out."

"Poor thing has no idea everyone in town knows. Well, everyone but Brig. And I agree; she needs to move on. Sure, Brig's going to be my brother-in-law soon, but he's a blind idiot when it comes to love."

"Which is so strange, don't you think?" Victoria asks, taking a small sip of her drink, fingers poised on the straw, one pinkie sticking up in the air. "That man is living out his very own romantic comedy, and yet he can't figure out how to find love and hold on to it."

"Don't you get it, Victoria?" I lean across the bar and glance around the room to make sure no one's listening. "It's *the curse*."

"Oh good gracious," she huffs with an accompanying eye roll. "The Knightly curse, can't ever forget about that."

"It's so real, according to Brig," Harper says, chuckling. "He lives and breathes by that thing. Didn't you hear about the witch doctor he went to the other day to 'expel' the curse?"

"He did *not*." A snort pops out of me. "Oh shit, that's amazing. Did the doctor say anything?"

"Sent him home with some oils and bundles of sticks to burn, apparently to clear out his aura. Griffin took the sticks. He said that, as a volunteer firefighter, he couldn't in good conscience let his brother burn those things in his house."

"Thank God for Griff. With how chaotic and intense Brig is about the curse, I could easily see him burning down his apartment."

"Easily." Harper laughs.

"So," Victoria says, "are you going to come tomorrow? I think Rylee is serving nonalcoholic beverages as well per my request, if you're not up for drinking."

"Oh, I'll be up for drinking; there's no doubt about that. And yeah, I think I'll stop by later on. Better than wallowing away in my apartment, right?"

"Exactly," Harper says with a smile. "And if you change your mind about going alone, we're only a phone call away. All of us."

It's a nice gesture, but that's exactly what I don't want. All of my friends to be there. Even though living in Port Snow has given me a second family, I really wish I had my first family. My mom, my dad . . . my twin brother. But we can't always get what we wish for, especially when one of those family members doesn't follow through.

◆ ◆ ◆

With a deep breath, I look out my car window and stare down the double grave site that rests thirty feet away. Though one headstone is a bit older than the other, they both bear loving words about being a great parent, a wonderful partner in life, and a beautiful soul.

Hands on the steering wheel, I close my eyes and will back the tears that already threaten to spill over.

Dad passed three years ago today, and the wound he left behind still feels raw. We lost Mom the year before Dad passed, and I always think he died so soon after because he didn't want to spend another year on this earth without her. Their love was magical, what movies are made about. High school sweethearts, they became wildlife photographers, traveling around the world and getting to see some of the best sights I could only dream of until they settled down and decided to have a family in their late forties. But they couldn't get pregnant, despite many years of trying.

That's when they pursued adoption and got a call about Eric and me. Our birth mom signed the papers right away, asking for nothing financially, only that we would live a stable, happy life. My parents made that happen. They gave us a community, a loving home, and every opportunity we could imagine, even if we didn't take it.

Losing Mom was hard enough, but losing Dad . . . it still rips me to shreds, knowing I'll never hear his deep, raspy voice again or feel his big arms wrap around me. I put my life on hold to take care of the both of them while Eric went off to pursue his dreams. It was a decision we made together, one I don't regret because I was there when the cancer finally took Mom, and I held Dad's hand when a stroke took him shortly after. I brought them comfort and peace when no one else could. And through it all, the good days and the bad, the stories they told me, the wisdom they imparted to me, and the sly smiles I would gather every once in a while when they were feeling well made everything worth it. But even though the last few years are ones I'd never regret for a second, I assumed the dreams I put on hold would pick back up, and Eric and I would join forces. But when the time came to claim my future, Eric wasn't mentally or physically there for me.

It was a tough pill to swallow, realizing just how alone I was, how alone I am in this world, but it hasn't stopped me. It might have been a small speed bump in my pursuit of making something of myself, but it wasn't a roadblock. My journey is slower than others', but I refuse to let any circumstance that comes my way stop me from accomplishing my dreams.

Dark clouds are rolling in, and according to the forecast, we're supposed to get a blizzard within the next twenty-four hours. The temperature will drop, and standing next to a cold gravestone will become unbearable soon, so I open my car door, grab my keys, and bundle deeper into my wool coat as I walk toward my parents' grave site.

Dead brown grass and patches of leftover snow from the last storm crunch beneath my feet as I approach. Given the time of year, I don't bother with flowers or anything that could be buried in snow. Instead I think of all the pretty colors I can plant in the springtime. Mom loved pink tulips, but Dad was always buying her daisies, claiming they were understated, beautiful in their own right. I plan on giving them both. That way, Dad will have to deal with Mom's tulips planted next to him, and Mom will have to put up with Dad's daisies.

A small smile pulling at the corner of my lips, I reach their headstones and squat down, grateful that the engraved words are still pristine despite the harsh Maine winters.

"Hey, you two," I whisper. I lean forward and press a kiss to each of their stones with my hand. "God, I miss you." I take another deep breath. "Three years today, Dad, and I still can't get rid of this sick feeling deep in the pit of my stomach from losing you. And Mom, I could really use some of those endless nights where we stayed up talking, *gabbing*, as you liked to say. But I bet you two are having a blast being together again." I chuckle. "Do you do all the haunting that you promised when you were in hospice? I specifically remember you saying something about scaring the white hair off Mrs. Davenport. I can only imagine the kind of fun you two would be having with her."

I twist my hands together and roll back on my heels, still squatting. "I'm sorry Eric isn't here. He couldn't get out of work, but I guess you guys know everything that's going on, right?" I sigh. "I wish he would come back to Port Snow, recharge, get out of the mindless line cook job, and start fresh, but he feels too guilty. After losing both of you, then the restaurant—all the money you invested after selling the house—I'm pretty sure he can't bring himself to show his face. Not to mention the tension between us. It's a tension I never thought we would have, but you don't need to worry; we will figure it out." I smile softly to myself.

"Anyway, enough about Eric. I'm finishing up school right now. It's taken some time, but once I have my business degree wrapped up, I'm going to attempt to make something of myself. There are a few businesses in town that I know could use a little help, and I'll be more than qualified. Melanie over at Sticks and Wicks mentioned needing some help with her books, and Ruth at Snow Roast was talking about a new business venture she wanted to pursue but was too scared to attempt on her own. I thought I could offer her some help." I pick at the dead grass below my feet. "Working with some of my friends in town would be fun, different, not what I had planned in life, and it makes me feel a little uneasy switching gears from what I thought I would be doing; but when faced with adversity, I always seem to make things work out for me. Still"—I sigh—"between us, it's scary not knowing my next steps. I thought I had everything planned out, I thought I had a support system by my side cheering me on, but that was all taken away, and now I'm figuring things out on my own, by myself." A small tear tips over and rolls down my cheek. "The unknown is hard for me to accept, and the loneliness is even harder. I don't have many people to turn to. Avery is making a life in the city; Harper is back with Rogan, and they're super in love; Eric barely speaks with me out of pure shame; and I don't have you two to hold me anymore when the fear of the unknown starts to creep in. And honestly, I'm still having a hard time dropping the dream Eric and I shared, the one we would talk about over the dinner table with you. It felt so real, like it was all going to happen when Eric opened Bar 79. I guess you can never truly count on anything, though, and as you taught me so skillfully, we are not ones to dwell." I take a deep breath. "So, once I graduate, I'm putting together a résumé, and I'm going to go business to business and blow this small town out of the water with my intelligence." I lean in a little closer. "Wouldn't you just dance in your graves out of pure joy if I started an empire like the Knightlys? Remember that talk we had over s'mores that one night, Dad, when I snuck you out of the nursing home? When you said I should take over Port Snow just like the Knightlys did? I could only be so lucky. Whatever I end up doing, though, I know I'm going to make you proud. I promise."

A second tear rolls down my cheek, and I wipe it away before leaning forward and placing another kiss on their gravestones. "I love you both, miss you terribly, and will keep working hard to get what I want like you always taught me. Hard work and determination, right, Dad? It might have taken me seven years to get to the point of finally graduating from college—with a broken dream under my belt already—but I wouldn't have changed the path I took because it meant spending more time with you two, and it gave Eric the opportunity he needed to pursue his goals, at least try to pursue them. And don't worry, I'll spruce up these headstones once spring comes."

I give them a quick wink even though they can't see it and wipe away one more tear before straightening up. With a brief wave, I turn around and almost jump out of my skin when I find a man leaning against my car, hands stuffed in his worn jeans pockets, a flannel shirt hugging his massive shoulders, and a baseball hat hiding a pair of brilliantly blue eyes I've known ever since elementary school.

Reid Knightly.

The sadness of the day, the tearful conversation I just had with my parents, and now seeing Reid standing there, waiting for me—it's all too much. A wave of emotion hits me as I walk toward him. Burying my face in my hands, I step up into his open arms and let him pull me into a calming embrace, his arms like an impenetrable shield protecting me from the outside world.

One arm is wrapped around my back as the other grips the back of my head, keeping me in place as tears stream down my face and onto his flannel shirt, sorrow and relief escaping me all at once. Sorrow for losing two of the best people I've ever known, relief for not having to do this alone.

"Shh," he says softly. It's rare that Reid shows an ounce of sensitivity. Going through life with a chip on his shoulder—a rather large one—he's a sarcastic ass who spends his days mouthing off and hiding behind his jokes. But today is different; this moment is different. "I'm here, Eve," he whispers into my ear, sending an onslaught of chills down my right arm.

Fresh from the shower, he smells like soap with a hint of sandalwood, a scent I've grown to associate with his adult self. When he was young, running around the backyard with Eric and getting into every bit of trouble they could find, he smelled like a sweaty boy having entirely too much fun. Back in middle school, when he and Eric really got into cooking, he constantly smelled like garlic, his favorite food to work with. And in high school before they left for culinary school, he smelled like Axe body spray because at that point he realized smelling like a douche was better than smelling like garlic.

But now . . . now he smells like a man.

Calming myself, I lift my head off his chest and look up at him. The bill of his hat throws a shadow over his eyes, but this close, those blue irises still sparkle. "What are you doing here?"

He shrugs. "Didn't think it was right for you to be by yourself."

"How did you know?"

"I knew what today means, and I knew you'd be here . . . and Eric wouldn't." He reaches down and brushes away the tears that have pooled under my eyes. "You would do the same if it were my parents."

I would.

"Well, thank you. It means a lot to me."

"I also thought it would be a great opportunity to squeeze a hug out of you—you know, since you're vulnerable and all."

And there he is.

Scoffing, I push at his chest, trying to put some distance between us, but he just laughs and pulls me in closer. "Oh yeah, give me the good stuff. Just like that, run your hands up my back."

"Shut. Up," I say, a laugh popping out of me.

"All this wiggling is getting me hot and bothered. Want to do it in your car?"

"You realize you're sick, right? A sick bastard taking advantage of a grieving daughter."

"And as the scum of the earth who is well aware of that, if you need me to hold your boob in this time of need, I can lend a hand . . . even two."

Impossible.

Stepping away and crossing my arms over my aforementioned chest, I say, "You wouldn't even know what to do if I said yes to that offer."

"How little faith you have."

I shrug. "Word on the street is you fumbled so badly with Lydia Samson that you thought her armpit was her vagina."

"Jesus Christ," he moans, dragging his hand over his face. "Can you stop bringing up Lydia Samson? It was dark, I was drunk off my ass, and she kept saying, *Yes, right there, right there.* She was the sick fuck, letting me pump my dick into her armpit. We were in a closet on a boat, for fuck's sake."

I burst out in laughter at the infamous story, which I got second-hand from little old Mrs. Davenport of all people.

He points his finger at me, a stern look in his eyes. "You see? *This* is why I don't do nice things, because ungrateful people like you bring up situations like Lydia Samson."

"You tried to screw her armpit, Reid. That will go down in history as the best story of my life."

"Then you need to get out more, because that shit is *stale*."

I shake my head. "Never. All I have to say is *Lydia* around our friends, and everyone laughs."

"Because they're all sick fucks like you. I was sixteen, it was the first time a girl told me to push my pants down, and I was a little overzealous. Everyone should just be happy I was out of my room at that point."

I cover my mouth just as a snort pops out of me. Oh, Reid. Everyone knows he had his hand perpetually on his penis the minute he found out he could have fun with it—whenever he wasn't hanging out with Eric or cooking. The Knightly clan would blast him for constantly being in his room to the point that he stopped caring and would actually announce what he planned on doing. His poor parents.

"The horniest of the Knightlys."

He shrugs unapologetically. "When you're the most well endowed, you have to do something with all that extra testosterone raging through your veins. It was better to take care of business than go on Hulk-like smashing sprees."

"Most well endowed?" I roll my eyes. "Please, everyone knows that's Griff."

False, everyone knows it's Reid.

I can remember back in high school when all the girls would talk about the Knightly boys and rate them based on sex appeal and the rumor mill. I would never tell Reid this—why inflate his cocky ego more than necessary?—but Lydia Samson was terrified of how big Reid was when he pushed down his pants and spread it around that he was *huge*. She really made him screw her armpit because she was too nervous to let his willy anywhere near her lower half. His size was later confirmed by Diane Rebar and Heather Maker, then Nancy Vaughn, who swore she would never go near another Knightly brother after her sexual encounter with Reid.

If the legend is true, then Reid Knightly is a force to be reckoned with in the bedroom.

Do I believe it?

Maybe, but then again, word spreads like wildfire around here, flamed and wafted far past the truth, making every story you hear less and less believable.

"Griff." He laughs and shakes his head. "Okay, Eve, keep telling yourself that." Reaching out, he tugs on a lock of my long brown hair. "Want to grab a bite to eat?"

My stomach aches at the thought of food. I'm starving.

"What were you thinking?"

"Franklin's Deli. His new homemade mustard makes my nipples hard."

Just because I can, I reach out and rub my hand over his thick pecs, feeling the sharp nubs beneath my palms. He stands there, chest puffed out, almost proud to prove that in fact his nipples *are* hard from thinking about mustard.

"Not lying. Hard as fucking stones."

I pull my hand away. "There's something seriously wrong with you."

"Yeah, you've known that for over fifteen years now, and yet you still hang around me." He rocks on his heels, grinning.

"Because it's either you or Mrs. Davenport. Options are slim around here, Knightly. Don't think too much of it."

He steps up and pulls me into another hug.

"A leg up on the Daven-ator, that makes me one lucky son of a bitch. Come on, my treat."

CHAPTER THREE

REID

Typical Eve.

Whenever I say *my treat*, she really makes sure to go all out with her order. Two different sandwiches with the specialty mustard that Franklin, the dickhead, upcharges now—"Supply and demand," he likes to point out to grumbling locals—two different soups, a bag of sea-salt-and-vinegar chips, and three cookies, not to mention a bottled water and a bottled iced tea.

With her smorgasbord spread before us, I didn't even bother ordering anything, knowing full well she's not going to eat all of this. I pick up a sandwich half and take a large bite.

Shit . . . this mustard is so fucking good.

We're sitting in the front window, the deli's prime spot, where every passerby can see us. I swallow my bite and whisper, "Why is this mustard so goddamn good? I swear, I would drink a whole goddamn bottle if I could."

She leans forward as well, making sure Franklin—the worst gossip in town—can't hear us. "I think he puts crack in it, legit stirs it in." She twirls her hand in the air, stirring a fake bowl.

"A crack den posing as a deli." I snap my fingers. "I could see it."

"There's some gossip we should spread around. I can see the headline in the newspaper now." She holds up her hand and waves it across the imaginary paper. "*Crack Den Deli. Flamboyant Mustard Extraordinaire at the Helm.*"

"Catchy. I'd read that."

At that moment, Franklin steps up to our table, a sly smile on his face, hands folded. "Enjoying yourselves?"

Eve coughs up a piece of bread.

"Yeah, thanks," I say, keeping my reply short. No one likes to talk to Franklin because the guy loves to play your conversation on repeat to whoever cares to listen.

"Oh yes," Eve chimes in, recovering. "These chips are supreme."

His eyes narrow. We both know what he's looking for—he wants a compliment on the mustard. It's like an unspoken rule in town that we don't let on to Franklin how good the mustard is, though we keep coming back for it.

"Very well," he says, spinning on his heel and walking back to the deli counter. "If you need anything, holler."

When he's out of earshot, Eve says, "Think he heard us talking about his crack den?"

I glance back at Franklin, whose eyes are still narrowed at us.

"I wouldn't be shocked if he bugged this table so he can hear what everyone is saying."

"Sounds about right."

She leans back in her chair with a cup of chicken-noodle soup. "Thanks for being there for me today," she says sincerely.

I pop a chip in my mouth. "That's what friends are for, Eve. No need to thank me unless you want to sit on my lap; then I'll take that as a thank-you."

"Never going to happen, Knightly. It's sad that you keep trying."

"Hopelessly optimistic."

And that ass of hers is so fucking fine. Sure, we're just friends, but I don't think I would ever give up staring at it—or asking for it. It's fun, constantly having blue balls around her—every man's dream.

"Ha!" She laughs and swallows a spoonful of soup. "*Hopelessly optimistic* would be the last way I'd describe you. More like sarcastically pessimistic."

She has me there. Optimism runs through the Knightly blood, but I'm pretty sure I've forgotten how to access it.

"Sounds about right." I nod and stick another chip in my mouth. "What are you up to tonight? Are you working? I was planning on bothering you at the Inn tonight."

"Not working but probably drinking with the girls. Rylee is having everyone over."

"If I put a wig on, think they'll let me join?"

"Only if you wear a hot-pink skirt too."

"Done." I wink and pick up the iced tea we seem to be sharing, taking a swig and then handing it over to Eve. She presses her lips on the rim where mine were two seconds ago and downs the liquid without a second thought. I watch her throat contracting as she swallows, sending my imagination into overdrive as I picture my cock at her lips rather than the iced tea.

Yeah, okay, so I have a fucking crush on Eve.

It's been impossible not to, but I've known the girl ever since I've known Eric, since we were ten years old and they moved to Port Snow from Pottsmouth the summer before fifth grade. Eric and I instantly hit it off after we were put on the same baseball team that summer. Eve, on the other hand, was just a tagalong—until I started noticing her on another level. Then I wanted to hang out with her a lot more. It started off with just thinking she was pretty, but when she started to gain confidence and sass me anytime she had a chance . . . fucking hell, I started to crush really hard. To the point that I was the idiot who would tease and make fun of her because I didn't know how to control my emotions. And it only made her push back.

The tension between us built for years. Eric was oblivious, but I wasn't. I knew I wanted her, but I never knew how to go about asking her out.

And I missed my opportunity in high school when we had our first dance. It had been my plan all along to ask her to be my date. I wanted to be the guy who stood an arm's length apart from her and shuffled back and forth, but before I could strap on my balls and ask, Cory Morris stepped up and took her. He was about five inches taller than me at the time—I was a late bloomer in height, though not in the penis—and he won Eve over quickly.

A jealous fool, I spent most of high school pushing her buttons, and she pushed mine right back until we both placed each other squarely in the friend zone. She dated other guys while I dated other girls—and did stupid shit like fuck a girl's armpit—then went on my merry way to culinary school.

And though we're both single and living in Port Snow again, the opportunity for romance has passed. We're destined to be friends for life.

Which is fine, truly. I have no problem ignoring my pesky feelings and staring at my friend's ass. Well, I mean, I *act* like I have no problem with it. But there are times when I'm lying in bed, alone, wondering what she's doing at night, what she's wearing, if there would ever be an appropriate time for me to let her know about my "pesky feelings." Probably not.

"I'd give you twenty dollars to show up at Rylee's in nothing but a hot-pink skirt, wig, and bra."

"Twenty bucks?" I mull it over, crunching down on a chip. "Nah." I pat my stomach. "These abs are worth at least thirty dollars on their own."

"Abs." She snorts. "Please, don't you mean whiskey gut?"

My eyes pop open as I sit straight up in my chair. "Excuse me? Did you just say I have a whiskey gut?"

"I mean . . . don't you?"

"No. Where the fuck did you hear that?"

"Tony Larkin."

"Ton—" I take a deep breath and lean in closer. "Tony Larkin has been trying to get into your pants since freshman year. He would say just about anything to make his unibrow seem more attractive."

She smirks. "Prove it."

Exasperated, I grab the hem of my shirt and lift it up, showing off my six-pack, one I work on every night. Unlike Rogan, who was born with an eight-pack, I actually have to put in some effort to make mine pop.

I watch carefully as Eve's eyes roam my exposed stomach, taking in every inch, one divot at a time, until her eyes meet mine. Head tilted, she finally says, "Damn, you're pale."

Jesus.

I toss my shirt down and grab another half of a sandwich. "We live in fucking Maine—what did you expect?"

"Not to be blinded." She blinks a few times. "Warn a girl to put on her sunglasses before you go flashing that around. You're basically translucent. I think I saw your intestines."

"Think you're a regular Kevin Hart, don't you?"

She fluffs her hair. "No, more like an Amy Schumer. More badass."

Can't argue with her there.

"Mom? Dad?" I call out as I enter my childhood home and kick off my shoes.

"Kitchen, dear," Mom calls back. I follow the scent of homemade marinara sauce down the hall to the kitchen and the attached dining area, which overlooks the bay.

My parents have lived in this house for over twenty years, and even though the pictures hanging on the walls are from the nineties, it's been updated and renovated throughout the years. Brand-new hardwood floors throughout the main living space, a fresh coat of paint on all the walls, and a state-of-the-art kitchen for all the fudge making my dad conducts on a weekly basis. Thanks to Rogan, they haven't had to do much of the work themselves. Pretty sure Rogue and Griffin are tied for favorite child.

Dad is at the stove, stirring a giant pot with a wooden spoon, while Mom hovers around him, holding a bowl of homemade dough and glancing over his shoulder. Neither one of them can give up control in the kitchen, which is why we were fed so well as kids.

I press a kiss to my dad's partially balding head and one to my mom's cheek before reaching into the fridge for a water and sitting on the counter.

"To what do we owe the pleasure of your visit?" Mom asks, keeping her eyes on my father.

"Just stopping in. Had the day off, so I thought I'd see what you two are doing."

"You took the day off?" Dad asks, a pinch to his brow. "Since when do you take days off?"

They both know I'm trying to rebuild my savings, trying to make sure I don't ever end up hitting rock bottom again. I may have replaced my knives with a lobster cage, but I'm still determined to make sure I never have to live with my parents again, even if it means working at the Lobster Landing until I'm fifty.

"I still went out to sea this morning but asked for a day off from the Landing. Griff was cool with it." Griffin has recently taken over the family business from Dad, working his ass off to prove he can run it and make it just as successful as when my parents were in charge. He loves working there, selling fudge and baked goods. I, on the other hand . . . no fucking thank you. Dealing with sweaty, grouchy tourists during the summer and entitled locals during the off-season—yeah, I'd rather be out on the boat. And now that Dad has handed over the crown to the family business, he's no longer training Griffin, which gives him more time to pester me about what I want to do with my life, where I want to take my "talents." What's even more annoying is that he speaks to me in such a loving and caring manner that when I get pissed every time he brings up the future, I end up feeling like an even bigger asshole later.

"Why did you ask for the day off? Just needed some time to rest your brain?" Mom asks.

My parents weren't great friends with Eve's parents, who were quite a bit older, but they were still cordial and kind and would have them over for dinner on occasion. So when Eve and Eric lost both their parents, they were there for my friends, but I wouldn't expect them to remember the days they passed.

"Today's the anniversary of Jay's death."

"Oh dear, how could we forget?" Mom says just as Dad turns around to face me for the first time.

"Is Eric in town?"

I shake my head. "No, but I did go out to the cemetery. Eve was there by herself. I gave her privacy while she talked with her parents, and when she was done, I took her out to lunch so she wasn't by herself."

A look of pride washes over my mom's features. "That was very sweet of you, Reid. Where is she now? Would she like to come over for dinner? I would hate for her to be alone tonight."

"She's getting ready to go over to Rylee's. They're having a girls' night over there. I'm going to head up to the LI after dinner, just in case she decides to show up. I don't want any dickheads trying to take advantage of her right now."

"Is that what the hip kids are calling the Lighthouse Inn now? The LI?" Dad asks.

"Yup. Dare you to say it in front of the town elders." I wiggle my eyebrows, trying to entice him.

He doesn't fall for it. "And risk getting my ass handed to me? I'll pass." Stirring the pot again, he says, "Did Eve say why Eric didn't come back?"

"Work, I guess. But I doubt that was the truth."

Silence falls in the kitchen as a big pink elephant comes stomping into the small space, blowing his trunk and announcing his entrance.

The restaurant.

The failure.

The broken friendship.

The reason why Eric Roberts really isn't back in Port Snow.

Because of me.

Mom clears her throat. "Have you spoken with him lately?"

I lift the bottle of water to my lips, stalling for a few seconds. "Nope."

A year ago, my parents would have followed up my answer with encouragement to reach out to him, to mend the broken friendship. But by now they know it's a lost cause, and they let my answer slowly float through the air.

"Well," my mom says, taking some flour and tossing it on the center island. "Why don't you help me make some biscuits then?"

I hop down from the counter and press a kiss to her cheek. "You know I don't cook anymore, Mom. I'll be upstairs if you need me."

With a parting glance at the spaghetti sauce—just from the scent, I know it needs a touch more basil—I speed out of the kitchen, make my way up the old set of stairs that I've climbed far too many times to count, and take a quick glance out the window, where light flakes of snow start to descend to the ground. Will this snow ever end?

My parents always try to get me involved in the kitchen in a not-so-subtle way. They want me to jump back into my old life, and I always turn them down. Those days are behind me.

I'm a different man now, with a different path. But despite my vow to never make another meal, every fiber of my being longs to chop a fresh crop of vegetables, to smash herbs between my fingers and take in a deep whiff.

My heart craves the kitchen, but I just can't bring myself to feed it.

CHAPTER FOUR

EVE

"Want another?" Rylee asks, wobbling up to me with a pitcher of piña colada in her hand. She's gone with the whole tropical theme tonight—Hawaiian shirt, steel drum music, and blow-up palm trees included.

And I would be remiss not to mention the tiny umbrellas that garnish our drinks.

"I'm good." I hold up my hand, feeling a little tipsy. I want to hold on to that feeling, but I don't want to get wasted; I just want to ease the ache in my stomach. I might put on an act, force a smile, and show everyone that everything's okay, but in reality, the burn of my dad's death, of this day, has set a fire in the pit of my stomach. Even though the company is nice, I'm at the point where I'm ready to just be alone. At least I think that's what I want.

"You sure? I bought lots and lots of booze, so feel free to drink it all."

I chuckle as her words slur. Good luck, Beck. "Not concerned about drinking all your booze."

"Well, it's here if you want it. You know Beck doesn't drink, so someone is going to have to make a dent in it."

Harper comes tottering over to me, wearing her bikini top and a pair of sweats. "Wowee, these drinks are *strong*. Wouldn't you say?"

"Please tell me Rogan's picking you up tonight."

"Oh yeah, I told him we could do it on the counter again after I was done here."

Lovely.

She holds up her phone. "He keeps texting me to see if it's T-minus naked time yet." She leans in, rum heavy on her breath. "I FaceTimed him in the bathroom and flashed him a boob. Let's just say . . . he's on his way."

"Flashed him a boob, huh? Classy." I wink.

She flips her red hair. "That's me, pure class." She stares down at my cup, hooks her finger on the lip, and pulls it closer. When she sees it's still halfway full, her eyes widen. "Hey, how come you didn't get a refill?"

"I want to be able to open my eyes tomorrow without wearing sunglasses."

"What are we talking about?" Ren, Griffin's girlfriend, asks. As a new-to-town algebra teacher, she was driven off the road by a wayward moose, but Griffin came to her rescue. It was a long and interesting courtship, especially since Griffin had to get over losing his wife, but they are adorable together, and I'm so glad Ren is a part of our little group.

"Eve here wants to be able to see tomorrow," Harper says, jabbing her thumb in my direction.

I shake my head. "I'm just not getting super drunk, that's all."

"Griffin sent me a text asking if I was drunk and if I wanted to get frisky later." Ren giggles. "I sent him back a GIF of an old lady humping the ground. Gave him the green light."

"Wow, looks like the Knightly boys are getting lucky tonight."

"Maybe Reid can get lucky." Harper nudges me with her pointy elbow.

"Stop that." I swat her away. "That's never going to happen. He's a good friend. He actually . . ." I swallow hard, wondering why I'm about to say this, blaming the alcohol. "He actually surprised me at the cemetery today. Told me he didn't want me to be alone and then took me out to lunch. It was nice."

Ren clasps her hands to her chest. "See? I just knew that boy had some of that sweet and kind Knightly blood inside of him. He isn't always a smart-ass."

"Oh, you should have known him growing up," Harper says, taking another long sip of her drink, her cheeks puckering before the reminiscing begins. "He was always getting on Rogan's and Griffin's nerves. It was like he was born with this special knack for driving his brothers crazy. A negotiator, a poke-the-bear kind of guy, a weasel when he knew what he wanted. The number of times Griff and Rogan had to pay him off not to rat them out to their parents . . . you know, I think that's when he really started saving for the restaurant. Funded by his brothers."

I wouldn't doubt that.

"Yeah, he would come over to our house and brag about banking another twenty from his brothers for not tattling. I mean"—I shrug—"you have to hand it to him: he knew how to mine his brothers for cash and did it well."

"Ahh, you're just saying that because you've always had a crush on him," Harper says with a wave of her hand.

"I *don't* have a crush on Reid. He's one of my good friends. And yeah, he's hot; I would be stupid to say he isn't, but we're just friends." That might be a lie, but we won't go there right now.

"That's what they always say." Harper bumps my shoulder with hers just as Rogan comes through the door. "Gah, look at him. That jawline, God, I just want to nip at it."

Rogan scans the room. When he spots Harper, his face immediately lights up, and he makes his way to his girl.

I'm not going to lie—having someone in my life who would look at me like that, like I'm the center of his universe, it wouldn't be the worst thing. I've dated here and there but never had anything too serious. I haven't had much time, especially when I was taking care of my parents, and now that I'm finishing up my degree, any and all romance has been put on hold—and I'm okay with it.

But there's one thing I wish I had—the companionship, the intimacy my parents once shared. I always admired how deeply in love they were and thought I'd have the same kind of relationship. I know, I know, I'm young, and there's still plenty of time, but that doesn't make me want it any less. And I guess I get some companionship with Reid, but intimacy—not so much. Yeah, he flirts and talks about my ass probably too often, but I know what I am to him: his best friend's sister, the girl he grew up with, pulling on her pigtails and pushing her into rain puddles. He's treated me more like his tomboy friend than he's ever treated me like a woman, and that's fine, because that's our relationship. At least that's the way everyone in town, including him, sees our relationship. But deep down—so deep I can barely admit it to myself—I've been harboring a crush on that boy for as long as I can remember.

Rogan bends at the waist and presses a slow, languid kiss against Harper's lips. I stare, though I feel a bit like a creeper, watching as their hands lightly caress each other, as he whispers something into her ear that makes her cheeks flush, and as he groans quietly when she plays with the small hairs on the nape of his neck. They're in love, so much in love that it does make me a little envious.

Living in a small town where the only new people are tourists makes it pretty difficult to meet someone, and since I'll be earning my degree soon, I'll finally have some free time on my hands. Maybe it's time I join one of those dating apps Brig's always gushing about, despite never having much luck.

After giving his bride-to-be a lot of attention, Rogan directs those Knightly blue eyes at me. "Hey, Eve, how are you?" It's not a generic statement—there's feeling behind his question, actual concern, and I truly appreciate it. I might not have a family here in town, but my second family is just as good.

"Doing okay. I'm about to head out, actually, up to the Inn to check on some things."

"Want a ride?"

I shake him off. "That's out of your way."

"It's not a problem at all, gives some time for Harper to sober up a little bit."

"I don't need to sober up! I'm the perfect mix of coherent and loose."

Rogan chuckles and takes Harper by the hand, pulling her to her feet and wrapping his arm around her waist. "Let's get you home. Come on, Eve. It's no problem. Plus Walter is on a warpath tonight—you don't want an Uber ride from him."

I never want a ride from either of the two—yes, two—Uber drivers in town, but walking in this weather isn't an option either, so I take Rogan up on his offer.

It takes a few minutes not only to say bye to everyone and explain why I'm leaving but also to get Harper in the car. She keeps dancing with everyone she hugs goodbye and awkwardly thrusting her hips into Rogan's leg. When we finally make it outside, the snow is really starting to fall, so she plops herself down in Rylee's yard and starts doing snow angels.

Good luck tonight, Rogan. I'm not sure he's going to be able to wrangle her the way he wants.

Once in the car with everyone buckled, Rogan takes it slow on the freshly snow-covered streets.

"It has to be at least six inches already," Rogan says, the car barely moving forward.

I furrow my brow as I look out the window. "I can walk. You don't have to drive up the hill."

"He's a pro, aren't you?" Harper says, rubbing the back of his neck. "Don't worry, we got you. In the meantime, why don't you tell Rogan about how his brother surprised you."

"Who? Reid?" Rogan asks, eyes trained on the road, hands at ten and two.

"Yeah, he met her at the cemetery without even being asked. Wasn't that sweet?"

"He's always been considerate when it comes to the Roberts. Our family, on the other hand"—he chuckles—"it's like he was put on this earth to make our lives difficult."

"Don't let him fool you—he makes my life difficult most of the time too, except for today." I stare out the window as large, quarter-size snowflakes rapidly fall from the sky. "Today he was exactly what I needed—a friend."

"He has his moments. I'm glad he was there for you." Rogan clears his throat. "Eric wasn't able to make it into town?"

"No, couldn't get off work, and honestly, I don't think he even tried."

Instead of digging deeper into the complexity that is Eric, Rogan says, "Going to the Inn? Not to your apartment?"

"To the Inn. Just going to check on a few things, make sure the place is still standing, and then walk to my apartment." It's just a street away from the Inn, so it won't be a big deal. "Kind of hoping Karaoke Night is still going on. Kevin Yodel swore he would be there, and that guy puts on a show."

"Shit, Kevin is something else," Rogan says. "Babe, we should go in and see if he's performing. He has this whole Elvis impersonation that will have you keeling over in laughter."

"I thought we were going to do the counter sex." Harper pouts. "If you make me watch Kevin, I can't guarantee I won't pass out."

I pat Rogan on the shoulder. "You don't want to miss out on that counter sex."

"Yeah, I sure as shit don't. We'll catch the next one."

◆ ◆ ◆

KARAOKE CANCELED.

Figures.

Not wanting to be alone in my apartment on one of the loneliest days of my life, I decided to stop at the Inn, see if they needed any help, maybe catch a song or two from some of Port Snow's finest.

I stare at the sign on the door that leads to the Inn's bar. Instead of locals hitting up the mic with some of the worst voices you'll ever hear, they've lit up the karaoke area with multicolored flashing lights and a tiny disco ball that doesn't even spin. Over the speakers, dance music plays, bumping and thumping loudly against the walls, setting a club-like mood.

Not a single person is dancing. They're either hunched over at the bar or safe in their homes, away from the freezing weather that's rolling in.

This was a bust.

But probably for the best. I should get back to my apartment before I have to hike through feet of snow to get there.

I spin on my heel and smack directly into what feels like a brick wall, but when my shoulders are steadied by large, sturdy hands, I look up to see Reid smiling down at me.

"Hey." I rub my nose, which was just smashed against his left pec. "What are you doing here?"

"I heard Kevin Yodel was making an appearance. It's rare these days." He nods toward the sign. "Kind of wish I knew it was going to be canceled."

"Yeah, me too." I glance out the window at the snow that's building and building on the sidewalks and parking lot, spreading a blanket of white as far as I can see. "Are you going to head home? It's getting pretty bad out there."

He glances over his shoulder. "Nothing I haven't dealt with before." He nods toward the bar. "Grab a drink with me."

Since I have nothing better to do, I follow him to the bar, where we take a seat at the end. Barb is working tonight. She's probably the worst bartender you could ever hire. She doesn't ask you what you want but just serves you what she feels like serving. When Barb is at the helm, there's never a huge turnout.

"Here," she says, plopping two shot glasses in front of us, the clear liquid splashing on the chipped bar top. "Bottoms up. I'm going to the bathroom."

I bring a shot glass to my nose and cringe—straight-up vodka.

Reid lifts his glass. "Bottoms up." He raises mine too, his hand wrapped around my fingers, clinks them together, and then pushes the shot glass toward my mouth before dropping his hand back down to the bar top. He downs his shot in one smooth motion and then waits for me.

"Don't be a pussy, Roberts. Down that."

"Don't call me a pussy—that's so crass."

He barks out a laugh. "When did you become the polite police? I'm pretty sure you told me to eat my own shit the other day."

True.

"Well, we're in public."

He rolls his eyes. "We're always in public. Stop stalling and down the drink."

"I don't want a headache."

"Eve, drink the goddamn thing."

"Why?" I ask, my fingers tightening around the small glass. "Are you trying to take advantage of me, Knightly?"

"No, I wouldn't have to take advantage. I'd just give you the go-ahead, and you'd be all over me."

"Oh fuck off, I would not."

He turns on his stool and leans against the bar, his arms propping him up as he stares out at the derelict dance floor. He tilts his head to the side to talk to me.

"Please, you've had a giant crush on me ever since middle school. I know you want all of this." He gestures up and down his body. For a brief moment, my heart catches in my chest, wondering if he actually knows about my crush . . . that is, until I see the wicked teasing in his eyes.

I snort, spilling a little bit of vodka on my jeans.

"Yup, you figured me out. I've been pining after you all this time," I deadpan. "Been saving myself too. Only want one penis, and it's yours."

"You don't have to tell me. I know you've been. Read it in your diary two weeks ago. So drink up, and I'll get you another shot." He's such an ass. I don't have a diary.

"We are not having another," I say right before throwing back the shot, the burn down my throat making me shiver. Why I did that I have no idea, but when I open my eyes, Reid is reaching over the bar, grabbing a bottle of tequila, and pouring us each another.

Okay, tequila I can do.

But drunk and alone with Reid . . . not sure about that just yet.

"Here."

We tap our glasses, tip our heads back, and chug, both our shot glasses making a clink on the bar top together. They barely have time to settle before Reid pours us one more and puts the bottle back.

"Seriously, what are you doing?" I ask when he hands me the glass.

"Trying to get you out on the dance floor." He wiggles his eyebrows. "You have to loosen up, Roberts."

"You don't have to get me drunk to dance." I take the shot and slide off my stool. "I dance on my own." Walking backward, I do a pretty lame attempt at a moonwalk, twirl, and start shifting back and forth to the music.

Reid pulls on the bill of his hat as he scans me from my boots up my denim-clad legs to my simple long-sleeve black T-shirt. His hungry eyes eat me up right before he tosses back his shot and stands too. I've seen those eyes before but only on occasion, and they usually come out to play when he's had a drink or two. Wearing a gray henley shirt and worn-out hat, he looks like the perfect country boy, ready to stir up some mischief.

Just like the boy I met so many years ago, the same boy who once froze every single one of my bras, thinking it was funny.

It was not.

I quirk my finger at him, and for once he takes direction, striding across the dance floor and taking me by the hands. He pulls me into his chest and lowers one hand to my back while the other clasps our palms together. As "Love Shack" plays through the speakers, he guides me back and forth across the dance floor, surprising me with just how good he is at dancing.

He spins me out, then back in and continues to glide us around as a laugh falls past my lips. The tragedy of my father's death fades away. The annoyance of my brother not coming home disappears. And instead, a new memory is made on this dreary day, a moment I think I'll carry with me for a very long time, because this is the moment Reid Knightly danced with me.

"We need some new tunes," he says, looking around. "This old stuff is fun, but I want you grinding on me."

"Excuse me?" I laugh out loud, wondering if I just heard him right.

"Hold on," he says, letting go of my hand.

Not really sure what I should be doing with myself, I sidestep in time with the music and snap my fingers at my sides. Yeah, I dance like a middle-aged woman at a wedding, and I'm okay with it.

Reid disappears behind the bar and heads to the back while the lights reflecting off the stagnant disco ball pass over my body, lighting me up. If there were more people in the bar area besides Marv, the local drunk, I would be feeling pretty damn stupid at this point. Don't get me wrong: Marv is one of Port Snow's own, and we take care of him when he needs it, but I don't think he can even remember his own name. I have nothing to worry about.

The music stops, so my feet do too, but before I can go take a seat at the bar again, a club mix fills the speakers, and a familiar song starts to play. It's sexy and far more modern than what we were just dancing to.

What's this song again?

I twist my lips to the side, trying to figure it out, just as Reid comes bursting onto the dance floor. He spins me around and pulls my back to his front, then leans forward, his breath tickling my ear.

"Let me see what you've got, Roberts. Give me that good hip action?"

His hands grip me, and before I can figure out what the hell has gotten into Reid, my ass is plastered to his crotch, and we're both swaying to the music, his hand sliding to my stomach, where my muscles contract from his touch, as my hand slides up to the back of his neck, where I anchor myself.

This is . . . new.

And I know he's just having fun, but a small part of me can't help but get lost in this moment, in his touch, in him.

Feeling awkward, I ask, "What song is this again?"

"'Body,'" he answers, splaying his hand across my stomach.

Good.

Lord.

His palm is huge against my stomach and sends a bolt of electricity to my very core as his fingers curl around the fabric of my shirt, lifting the hem to just above my waistline.

Something inside of me stirs awake . . . a strange sense of hope. Hope for something I'm not sure I ever truly allowed myself to want until this very moment, as Reid presses up against me, his strong chest, his lips so close to my skin that goose bumps spread down my arm.

As we dance together, our hips synchronized, everything fades away: Marv, hunched over the bar; Barb, who's returned from the restroom and is now leaning against the wall, arms crossed, staring at us;

and the few visitors who peek their heads into the room. None of that matters because right now, I'm in Reid's arms.

I spin, loop my arms around his neck, and take a chance, looking up at him—and that's when I see it, his signature cocky smile.

Slowly his hands move from my upper back down my spine to just above my backside. He keeps them there for a few seconds before sliding one large palm down to my ass. He cups it, pulling me even closer, so I can feel every inch of him.

And I mean . . . every . . . inch.

I gasp and glance up at him, at his completely unapologetic face.

He's hard.

Hard as a rock.

And huge.

"What's happening right now?" I say, confused and turned on all at the same time.

Tilting his head forward, he brings his lips right up against my ear. "We're dancing."

That's obvious, but what's happening between us? This is the most intimate I've ever been with this man. We've hugged here and there, but our bodies have never been pressed together like this, nor have we ever put our hands on intimate parts—a.k.a. we've never grabbed each other's asses before.

But maybe this is a new level of friendship, one I could get on board with right about now.

Since he's changing the "rules," I'll go right along with it.

My hand moves up to the nape of his neck, my fingers playing with the short strands of his hair as he finds the hem of my shirt and slips his hand underneath. A thumb passes over my skin, back and forth, back and forth. A blaze of heat speeds up my back straight to my neck. I can't ever remember feeling this good with the opposite sex.

Swaying, he brings his nose to my ear, and he runs it down my jaw and then back up, his lips barely brushing against my earlobe. My stomach somersaults, rolling with nerves over what's happening and anticipation of what might happen next.

"Fuck, you're killing me," he says, almost so softly that I can't hear him. I'm killing him? Uh, how about the other way around? My heart and my brain are colliding, creating a confused and very turned-on cacophony.

When I pull away to look up at him, he lightly licks his lips and stares down at my mouth. Intent written all over his face.

Oh Jesus.

Does he want to kiss me?

Right here?

With Barb and Marv a few feet away, in this cheesy disco light? Is that what's really happening? Are we really going to cross that line?

I don't think I could allow myself to get kissed like this, not when it could be written in the gossip newspaper for the whole town to read tomorrow morning.

But to feel those lips on mine, to know what it's like to be held completely by Reid Knightly, to feel him lose control? That's something I want.

Desperately.

I glance past his shoulder to the window behind him, to the mounting snow, and consider my options. I could continue to dance with this man, driving myself crazy until I'm about to combust, or I could call it a night and invite him back to my place.

The first option is appealing until I make out with him in front of Barb.

The second option makes me break out in a sweat, but it's the most exciting as well.

What if he says no, though? What if I'm reading him completely wrong, and this is just another one of his jokes? What if the subtle touches, the small grunts, the thickness of his crotch—what if it's all just a ruse?

What if he really doesn't want anything more than to be friends?

Then my invite is dangling out there between us, hanging around with a rejection that I don't think I'll ever get over.

Indecision racing through my mind, I try to figure out where to take this night as his hand travels from my back down to the waistband of my jeans, and in one deliciously smooth motion, he slips his fingers past the fabric and under my thong to my bare ass.

Well.

Ahem.

Okay . . . I think I might have my answer.

Taking a deep breath, I bring his head down to mine. "It's getting pretty bad outside," I whisper into his ear. "Want to just head back to my place?"

He pulls away, and the surprise I see on his face makes my entire stomach drop.

He wasn't expecting me to say that at all. Not even in the slightest.

And when he removes his hand from my backside, I realize he wasn't expecting me to take our little dancing moment in that direction.

I'm such an idiot.

What a huge mistake.

CHAPTER FIVE

REID

Remove your hand from her pants.

Remove it right this fucking minute.

What the hell are you thinking?

Your hand is in your best friend's sister's pants.

Remove.

It.

Clearly I'm not thinking about consequences today, and I've lost my mind completely. From the moment I saw her walk into the Inn, some primal part of me took over my entire body and decided to make one bad decision after the other.

Bad decision number one: shots.

Then dancing.

Then grinding.

Then letting her see how fucking turned on I am.

Then sticking my hand up her shirt.

And the worst decision of them all: sliding my hand down her pants and over her bare ass.

Jesus Christ, I'm as good as begging to be featured in the town newspaper. Front page: *Reid Knightly Stupidly Feels Up Friend's Sister.*

Subtitle: *He's Crushed on Her for Years.*

Second subtitle, if that's even a thing: *Obsessed with Her Ass.*

Sponsored by Marv the Drunk and Barb the Voyeur.

Still pressed tightly against me with my cock like Italian marble trying to poke through my pants and jab her in the stomach, she lowers my head and whispers, "It's getting pretty bad outside. Want to just head back to my place?"

I pause because I swear on Marv's hairy back that my dick just tore a hole through my pants and is joining this two-person party on the dance floor.

Back to her place?

Like . . . *get naked* back to her place? *Continue dancing* back to her place? *Crash on the couch with a boner while she sleeps in her room* back to her place?

Even though option three is the most sensible, my heart and my body are aching for option number one.

Fuck, to be with Eve—it would be every childhood and adulthood fantasy come true. This woman has had a hold on my balls for over a decade now, and no woman I've been with has ever compared to her, not even close.

My dream girl, my fantasy, the most untouchable woman to ever walk into my life.

But in this moment, it feels like she's actually within reach, and for some reason, I find myself swooping in, one interaction at a time, when I know I should be peeling away.

Shocked, I put a little distance between us, wanting to see if she's coherent, or if the alcohol we consumed is controlling her thoughts. But her eyes are still lucid, and I know she's serious. Hell, she's really inviting me back to her place. So the only question is, What kind of invitation is it?

I must be taking too long to answer—she caught me off guard, thrusting my horny fantasies into reality—because her eyes suddenly harden, and she blows past me, heading right for the door and out into the snowy landscape.

Oh no she doesn't.

She's not getting away without an answer to that invitation.

Not when I was so close to making a dream a reality.

I quickly toss some money at Barb, who doesn't even move as the bills float to the sticky bar floor, and then make my way outside into the blizzard, where I can barely see a few feet in front of me. The snow thickens the air like a curtain closing on my unexpected but fantastic night.

In the light of the streetlamps lining the road, I catch a glimpse of Eve power walking through the snow toward a small apartment complex. Her head is tilted down, determination in each step.

Following in her tracks, I jog after her and catch up in no time, no thanks to the insanely large flakes of snow whipping through the air. Something washes over me—the realization that I'm not sure I can end this night without at least knowing what it feels like to have this woman's lips on mine. Instead of grabbing her shoulder or her wrist to get her attention, I do the only thing that comes to mind: I tackle her.

Right into the fresh powder.

Because I'm a good guy, I twisted in the air, bringing her on top of me rather than crushing her against the ground with my weight, but even as the cold encases our bodies, I make sure to have a firm grasp on her so she can't escape.

"What are you doing?" she squeals, squirming in my arms.

"Where do you think you're going?" I ask as snow pelts my face, making it impossibly hard to open my eyes.

"Back to my place," she grunts, still trying to free herself.

"Without letting me answer your invitation?" I roll her to the side and bury her in the snow. She squeals some more, her face full of shock.

"Reid." She pushes on my chest. "Get off of me."

"Where's the fun in that?" I lean down and nuzzle my nose against hers, and her defensiveness starts to fade away as she laughs. I roll us again, and this time she's on top of me again.

"There's snow in my pants."

"Want me to replace it with my hands?" I ask as I reach out, grab a handful of snow, and shove it down her jeans.

"Ah!" she screams, swatting at my chest and shimmying her body up and down mine, doing nothing to calm my erection, which doesn't seem to be fazed by the cold weather.

Somehow she escapes my grasp and runs down the sidewalk—but not before gathering up a ball of snow and chucking it right at my chest.

Bull's-eye.

Snow splatters up to my face, but I don't let it deter me as I swoop in like an eagle homing in on its prey. I run at her, Eve playfully screaming the whole time, and tackle her into the snow again. But this time, I'm not as nice and let her go face first. We twist our bodies around, and she ends up back on top of me. And when she looks down, her face covered in snow, I let out a bark of laughter.

Her eyebrows, eyelashes, hairline, and lips are all covered in the heavy snow, making her look like she was just rescued from the Arctic.

She swipes one hand across one eye and then the other, her eyes on fire, ready to murder. I love feisty Eve, so I brace myself.

"I'm going to get you," she warns right before scooping up a pile of snow and shoving it up my shirt and onto my exposed skin.

A sharp wave of winter races up and down my abdomen, cooling my raging erection slightly—though not enough because I quickly reciprocate, shoving snow up her shirt, and when my knuckles brush against her bra, I'm aroused once more.

It takes very little, apparently, when it comes to Eve.

"Reid, stop it!"

"You stop," I shoot back just as she flings snow at my face. She laughs and takes off again.

I'm buried in even more snow, so it takes me longer than expected to get out of the hole we've created, and by the time I catch up to her, she's heading into her basement apartment. Before she can shut the door, I slip inside with her and close the door behind me.

Both covered in snow, we stare at each other, our faces red, our hands frozen, the warm apartment already making the snow fall off us in large, wet clumps.

Her lips twist to the side as she looks me up and down. "I have snow in my crack thanks to you."

"Better than the stick you usually have shoved up there."

Her eyes widen, and a rueful smile passes over her lips before she takes a step forward. "Lord knows you've tried to pull it out several times with zero luck."

"Unclenching would help a guy out a lot."

She rolls her eyes and turns so her backside is facing me. "If you're so upset about the stick, then why are you here?"

"Uh, because I was invited."

"I had a weak moment."

Hands stuffed in my pockets, seeking any kind of pseudowarmth I can get, I rock on my heels. "Look at me and say that."

Turning to face me again, she brushes a piece of hair that was plastered to the side of her face behind her ear. "It was a weak moment."

"I don't believe you."

"Not my fault." She nods to the door. "You know how to see yourself out."

"Yeah," I drawl. "I'm not going anywhere." I kick off my boots and push them to the side, my socks getting soaked in the puddle of fallen snow. "Sorry, Eve. I'm here for the night."

Eyes narrowing, she crosses her arms over her chest. "You're so stubborn—it's annoying."

"You're the one who invited me back to your place. I don't see how this is my fault. I'm just taking you up on your offer. Now, what kind of food do you have? I'm famished." I dust the snow off my clothes, every inch of fabric sticking to my skin, and walk to her small kitchen, where I peer into the fridge.

Yikes, she has nothing in here.

"Help yourself. Pretty sure I have a jar of minced garlic and barely a squeeze of ketchup."

Yup, that just about sums it up.

"Not even eggs? How do you live?"

"Just fine. If you're hungry, I suggest you put your boots back on and head over to the Inn. Barb will fix you up something really nice."

"We both know she's abysmal in the kitchen."

Eve shrugs.

I take that moment to step out of the kitchen to where she's still standing in the entryway. I reach for her hips, but she steps away before I can get a firm grasp on them.

"What are you doing?"

Trying to romance you, but clearly I suck at it.

"Dancing?" I reply, wincing at the uncertain question in my voice.

"The night is over, Knightly. Either leave or park it on the couch."

Motherfucker. That was the least-appealing option. Figures. Maybe the snow fight was the wrong kind of foreplay. I mean, I practically cooled her loins with a fistful of snow down her pants.

Real fucking smooth.

Talk about a broken-love curse—my dick may as well have fallen off at this point. I hold my back and feign soreness. "You know, I would love to sleep on your seventy-year-old couch." I glance at the dilapidated thing that's seen better days. "But I'm afraid I have a bad back. Wouldn't want my sciatica to flare up. I think it's best I sleep in your bed."

She rolls her eyes. "Either the couch or the floor. Up to you, Knightly. As for me, I'm going to take a nice, hot shower."

I'm about to answer back when—as if in slow motion—she grabs the hem of her shirt and pulls it completely over her head, revealing her simple white cotton bra.

I've seen her in a bikini before—I've lusted after her in a bikini—so this really should have no effect on me, except that it does, and in the worst way possible. The entire night comes piling on top of me. Her roaming hands; our close, thrusting bodies; my lips caressing her ear; her fingers running through my hair.

In an instant, I'm harder than ever, and my body heats up from the inside out, threatening to burst into flames.

It's impossible not to stare at her sleek curves and her smooth skin. I make no attempt to divert my gaze, and instead I eat her up inch by inch, starting at her navel, spending an adequate amount of time on her breasts as they rise and fall rapidly beneath my gaze, and finally ending with her eyes, which bore into mine.

I bite my bottom lip. "So . . . just peeling clothes off now?"

Not my smoothest line, but Christ, I wasn't expecting to be in Eve's apartment with a raging boner while she stands in front of me, shirtless.

"Yeah, I am." She reaches behind her, spins on her heel, and, smoothly popping open the clips in the back, removes her bra. I watch the fabric slide down her toned arms and to the floor as she disappears into the bathroom, leaving the door slightly ajar.

Fuck.

I drag my hand over my mouth and shift in place as I try to figure out what the hell I'm supposed to do now. I wrench my eyes from the fallen bra and shift them back up to the bathroom, where I can spot a small portion of her exposed back reflected in the mirror.

Why is the door ajar?

The shower turns on.

Did she do that on purpose?

The curtain slides open.

Does she want me to join her?

Christ, what if she does? Showering with Eve? That's definitely an entry on my list of things I've only dreamed of doing with my best friend's sister. Shower sex, wall sex, missionary sex, dirty fucking, sixty-nine sex, kitchen sex, boat sex . . . hell, fucking on a boat. My dick presses hard against the zipper of my jeans, begging for release.

But what if she doesn't want me to join her? What if I walk in on her naked and showering, and she screams bloody murder and throws bars of soap at my head?

I waver about what my next move should be: park it on the couch and ignore the white bra on the floor or charge through the partially open door and take what I've wanted for years.

Fuck.

Well, I know what my dick wants, that's for damn sure—he's nearly leading the charge.

Hand gripping the back of my neck, I consider texting my siblings for help, but that will only bring more questioning and ridicule, along with a hefty dose of inappropriate and useless GIFs.

I'm going to have to be a big boy and figure this one out on my own.

My gut churning with indecision, I peek through the cracked-open door and stare at Eve reflected in the mirror. From my vantage point, I can see the smooth curve of her hip—only her thong still present—and about an inch of side boob.

Christ.

Side boob.

The death of any red-blooded male's self-control.

Beyoncé is wrong: Girls don't run the world. Side boob does.

Side boob runs the world.

My will slips, and before I can stop myself, I'm charging like a bull just released from his cage into the bathroom, banging open the door and tearing off my shirt at the same time.

She doesn't flinch, nor does she jerk away at my entrance. Instead, she keeps her back turned, presenting me with her thong-clad ass as she peeks her beautiful face over her shoulder. "Took you long enough." A wicked smile plays at her lips as she hooks her fingers through her thong and steps out of it, tossing the small scrap of fabric to the floor, leaving nothing to the imagination.

Holy fucking shit.

Talk about dreams coming true.

Without a second look back, she pulls the shower curtain to the side and steps in, keeping her back to me the entire time. Steam billows out from the top of the shower and fills the small space, stealing some of the air I'm desperately trying to suck into my lungs.

Unsteady, knees a little wobbly, I undo my jeans and thrust my briefs down to the ground, my cock springing forward. Excitement and nerves weave together as I take a deep breath.

This is really happening. I'm about to shower with Eve Roberts . . . you know, naked.

CHAPTER SIX

EVE

What the hell has gotten into me?

I'm shaking in the hot shower, not from the snow that was shoved into every crevice of my body but from my complete brazenness—thank you, tequila shots.

I don't do things like this, strip in front of men out of nowhere and offer up a little shower time. And definitely not with Reid.

Ever.

Yeah, we flirt, we joke, we tease, we occasionally touch, but that's as far as anything has ever gone between us.

Getting naked in front of each other . . . yeah, never done that before. We're facing brand-new territory here.

I run my face under the hot water, busying myself so I don't lose my mind from nerves. Is he going to join me? I mean, I made my intentions quite clear.

Hey, Reid, let's look at each other's private parts. Doesn't that sound like a nice, wintery thing to do?

I press my hand over my eyes, absolutely despising myself right now. What's taking him so long? Is he ever going to join me?

If he does, oh God, he'll be naked. I'll see his penis, the legendary Reid Knightly penis that's been discussed, ad nauseam, all over town.

I don't think I'm ready, because after I felt it press against me, I can tell you one thing: I'm pretty sure the legend is true.

On the other hand, he'll also see me naked. I mean, he's seen my backside, but a front side is a completely different story.

It's apples to oranges.

Nipples to butt cheeks.

Everyone has butt cheeks, but not everyone has nipples . . . well, I guess everyone does have nipples, but it's different. Nipples are sacred; butt cheeks can easily be exposed during a drunken night and a dare for a full mooning. But nipples, in my world, are saved for intimacy.

So, are we about to get intimate? If he hops in this shower and starts doing a buddy wash, I think I might die of absolute humiliation.

A buddy wash. Pass the soap, pal. Coming your way, comrade.

Just drown me now.

I can't have that. I can't stand here and soap up my privates with Reid only to high-five afterward and hit the hay. No way in hell. With my thoughts spiraling, I'm about to call the whole thing off when a cool breeze filters in, and Reid steps into the shower.

I keep my back to him, feeling my whole body stiffen.

He's here.

My breath catches in my chest, my emotions swinging from over-the-moon excited to wanting to disappear down the drain.

That's until his hand lightly travels over my shoulder down my side to my hip, where it lands softly. He holds it there for a few heartbeats before he tugs, signaling for me to turn around.

I swallow hard, my heart about to beat out of my chest as my hands shake.

This is Reid. Why am I so nervous? I've known him since before his voice started cracking. This is the boy who always stole my attention, who teased me some days and stood up for me on others.

But then again, this is Reid, the boy I've watched grow into a devastatingly handsome man. He's the man who's been there for me through thick and thin.

My friend.

My crush.

My brother's best friend.

When I turn around, everything is going to change. The relationship we once had will either morph into something amazing or be thrown away for one crazy, albeit sexy, moment in the shower.

But even now, there's no turning back—and only one way to find out where this is all going to lead.

"Eve," he says, his deep voice sending a wave of chills over my skin. "Turn around. Let me see you."

This is happening.

My pulse roaring in my ears, drowning out the pitter-patter of the shower, I shakily turn around and look up into his mesmerizing eyes. Thick black eyelashes frame those matching blue pools, and instead of a sly or wicked smile curving his lips, all I can see is true yearning and desire as he reaches down and pulls me in closer.

My hands fall to his brawny chest, and a light smattering of trimmed hair tickles my fingers. Too nervous to look down, I stare up into his eyes, and he returns my gaze, never glancing any farther down than my neck. Instead, he explores with his hands.

And it's the sexiest thing I've ever felt.

His teeth nip at his bottom lip while his hands travel up my ribs, straight to my breasts, and he takes one in each hand. His calloused thumbs swipe over my hardened nipples, and his eyes glaze over when he takes each nipple between his fingers, pulling a gasp of pleasure from my lips.

"Shit," he mutters, eyes still trained on mine. "Eve . . ." He doesn't finish his sentence, instead, he keeps one hand on my breast as the other starts to travel south. That's when I stop him—because it's my turn.

I take his wrist and move his hand back up to my breast before trailing my fingers down over his pecs and then farther down, reveling in the thick divots of his abdomen, exploring each and every one of them, still holding his gaze.

Smooth skin twitches beneath my fingers as his breathing picks up. I glide my hands lower and lower until I reach the V in his waist. I drag my fingers along the deep valley that leads straight to his lower half.

"Fuck," he says through his teeth, practically hissing when my fingers dance close to his erection.

His hand travels down my body again to just above my pubic bone, where he swipes his thumb lower. I spread my legs slightly wider, my eyes never leaving his.

I move my hand lower.

He does the same.

My fingers glide so close to the root of his cock that he hitches forward.

His fingers swipe across my slit quickly, and that's when my gaze breaks and my eyes shut.

I count to three, mentally preparing myself right before I close the rest of the distance and wrap my hand around his cock.

Thick.

Hard.

More than I anticipated. So much more.

I can't take it anymore. I glance down, and all the air escapes my lungs as I take him, all of him, in. Perfectly sculpted stomach, powerfully strong quads—probably from all the balancing he has to do out on the boat—and his cock, unlike anything I've ever seen before.

When I look back up at him, his eyes are glazed over, his gaze heated as he stares down at me.

His hands trail back up my body, and he lightly cups my breasts, testing their weight, seeing them for the first time. I use that moment to glide my hand up and down his length, testing his sensitivity with a little pressure and then a whole lot. When I squeeze the top, his eyes practically roll to the back of his head as he leans past me and shuts off the water.

"Wh-what are you doing?" I ask, a shiver running through me.

"Not here—in your bed," he says, his voice heavy.

He whips the shower curtain open and throws two towels over the both of us before scooping me up into his arms and hauling me to my bedroom. It's dark with only the smallest amount of streetlight bouncing off the snow and through the sliver of windows in my basement room. Reid leans over to the nightstand and flips on the dull light, illuminating the room in an orange-and-yellow glow. It's perfect, just enough light so I can see every sculpted inch of Reid's body.

Hovering above me on the bed, he parts the towel and stares down at my body, his eyes roaming, taking their time, until he says, "How drunk are you?"

I blink a few times, caught off guard. Is he drunk? Honestly, I don't even feel the slightest bit tipsy—I think the situation has sobered me up.

"I don't think I'm drunk at all."

"Are you sure?" I nod. "Good, because I plan on doing some dirty things to you tonight, and I want you remembering every single lick, every kiss, every thrust."

If I wasn't already turned on, I would be now. In the back of my mind, I always figured Reid would be good in bed, maybe even a little more adventurous than me, and from that sentence alone, I know I was right.

He leans down and runs his nose along my jaw. "Just to clarify, you want me to fuck you, right?" he asks, his voice a soft tickle against my skin. "You want me to taste that sweet pussy of yours and then spread your legs and bury my cock so deep inside of you that you don't think I could fill you any more . . . until I go that extra inch." He bites down on my earlobe, making me gasp. "You want that, right, Eve?"

"God, yes," I moan, surprising myself with how desperate I sound.

"Good." He presses his lips across my jaw to my cheek and then to my mouth, connecting our mouths for the first time. He takes his time, molding our lips together but never going any farther past them. He keeps it sweet, just exploring the surface as his hand gently trails down my ribs and between my legs, which I spread for him.

Mouth still on mine, he lowers himself to the bed, resting on his side so I can spread my legs even farther, before he takes one finger and rubs it up and down my slit, over the sensitive nub that's already throbbing and yearning for release.

"So wet," he murmurs against my lips. "So sexy." His tongue flicks across my mouth. "Open up for me."

My lips part, and his tongue dives in; this time his kisses have a little bit more urgency to them, a deep need guiding our tongues together. His mouth and his fingers work in tandem, sliding in and out with such precision that my orgasm is already blooming, climbing from the tips of my toes past my shins to my knees, up my thighs . . .

"Oh God," I moan just as he removes his fingers and slides down my body, his mouth tracing a path. For a few brief seconds—entirely too short—he pulls my nipples into his mouth but quickly moves farther down until he's planted between my legs, his mouth hovering above me.

I try not to think about how my friend is about to go down on me, and instead I revel in the fact that he's the man I've wanted for so long. This truth sings through my brain while he hikes my legs up and over his shoulders, and I relax, falling into the bliss of his touch.

He spreads me with his fingers and then lowers his mouth; the scruff of his jaw deliciously scrapes along my inner thigh as he brings himself to my center. He presses his tongue flat against me and very slowly drags it up only to return, repeating the movement.

I've never in my life felt anything like it before—the pressure, the rhythm, the possessiveness in his grip on my hips, the feel of his jaw, rough against my delicate thighs—it's like he knows exactly how to push me higher and higher, and he's pressing every button.

Tongue flat against my clit, he moves it back and forth, gliding rather than flicking, and it's like he's fully massaging me as he holds my hips in place. White-hot bursts of pleasure shoot through me with every twitch of his tongue, and before I know it, my orgasm is building up, coming from so deep inside of me that I can't seem to feel anything from the waist down besides where he's pressing his tongue.

Hands grip my bedding.

Chest shoots up.

Heart about to break my ribs from beating so fast.

A gasp.

A moan.

And then it hits me; pure pleasure rips through my body, tearing through every defense I've ever erected and exposing me, raw and real, for Reid to see.

Vulnerable.

High off of him.

And when he looks up, he sees it. He can see what he just did to me, how he tore me down and revealed the real me. Not the sassy Eve or the witty Eve or the Eve who's constantly teasing him. No, he sees the down-to-earth, sometimes fragile, and completely genuine Eve. The same Eve he comforted at the cemetery.

Two times in one day. I very well might be lost to this man.

Pressing a kiss against my stomach, he works his way back up to my face, tenderly brushing his thumb over my cheek as he stares down at me.

I'm at a loss for words, unable to formulate any sort of response. I feel so beyond vulnerable that all I want to do is bury my head in his chest and avoid looking into those eyes, those comforting, endlessly sexy eyes.

"Hey," he says quietly before leaning down and pressing a gentle kiss to my lips. "Are you okay?"

"Great." I return his chaste kiss and then run my hand down his rock-hard body to his solid erection, which is lying flat against my leg.

In one smooth motion, he rotates us so he's on his back, and I'm on top. Smiling, I slide down his body, letting his skin glide against mine until I reach his cock. I take in a deep breath and stare down at his length. It's more than ready, aching for any sort of release, so I wrap my hand around the base and squeeze.

His eyes shut, and the veins in his neck pop as he tries to hold on to control. I squeeze again but this time move my hand up a few inches and then back down. His chest muscles contract, his hands search for something to hold on to, and when I lower my mouth down to the tip and flick my tongue across the head, his entire upper half lifts from the bed, and his hand is cupping my chin.

"Fuck, Eve, you can't do that. I'll come in seconds. And when that happens, I want to be deep inside of you."

Desperation laces his face, and I know I want that just as much as he does. I want him to claim me, to possess me, to take everything I have to give and make it his.

So I roll to the side and pull out a box of condoms from my nightstand. He frowns at the stash and then looks back at me.

"How many—"

"Don't even finish that sentence." I press my finger to his lips. "This is just you and me."

Still frowning, he eyes the box.

Ugh, men.

I soothingly rub my hand over his corded chest. "It's been a while for me, if that makes you feel better, but I like to make sure I always have something on hand, just in case."

Still not happy, he hops up from the bed and walks out to the bathroom. My stomach drops when I hear him pick up his jeans. Is he really leaving?

But then he comes back with a strip of condoms and rips one off, and my stomach returns to its rightful place.

He hops back on the bed and pushes the box away. "Those won't fit me."

Hmm . . . I guess they won't.

"And I suggest you get rid of them because you won't need them anymore." He rolls the condom on and sweeps me onto my back, placing me beneath him again. My heart flutters, and I can't contain the smile that's lifting the corners of my mouth.

You won't need them anymore.

Just like that, in an instant, Reid Knightly is claiming me. There's no talking about it, no awkward conversation, just one statement that speaks louder than any other long talk about where this might be going.

You won't need them anymore.

The best five words I think I've heard in a long time.

"Spread your legs, Eve," he says, his voice gruff, just about to lose control.

I do as he says, and the tip of his cock dances with my entrance as he leans down and greedily takes my mouth with his. And there's no more soft, teasing exploration this time around. No, something passes through us, a carnal need to be as close to one another as possible.

Tongues clash.

Teeth collide.

Lips fight for more.

And the tip of his cock slowly enters me, stilling my mouth and pulling a gasp straight from my lungs.

"Relax," he whispers, moving his lips to my ear and then down my jaw while his hand travels up my stomach to my breast. Barely inside me, he rolls my nipple between his fingers, and immediately my lower half relaxes, allowing him to slide in a few more inches. He continues to roll my nipple over and over, lighting me up inside, sending wave after wave of thrilling pleasure through my veins.

"Fuck," he mutters, pushing in farther. "Shit, Eve, you feel too damn good."

His mouth travels back to mine, and this time the crazed man who, just a moment before, took over my lips has turned his kisses to soft, passionate ones. Long, slow strokes with his tongue match the slow roll of his fingers over my nipples. His hips lazily move in and out, pushing deeper with every thrust. When he's fully inside, he stills, letting me adjust to his thickness.

He's so much more than I expected. From his broad and sculpted body to the feel of his rough scruff against my sensitive skin to his dirty mouth, being with Reid by far exceeds any fantasies I've ever had.

The real man is addicting, intoxicating, consuming.

I get lost in his touch, in his pulses, in his sweet and tender kisses.

In the span of one snowy evening, on a day that brings sorrow and pain, Reid Knightly has easily destroyed me for all other men.

A thick pressure builds at the base of my spine, and with each thrust, it builds higher and higher until my impending orgasm starts to ripple through my body.

"Reid," I gasp, surprised at how quickly that happened. "I'm going to—"

"Me . . . too," he growls right before he picks up the pace and sends us both over the edge, our moans mingling together, his deep, mine a high, breathy gasp.

His thrusts dull until he presses his body against mine and buries his head in my neck. We're panting, both catching our breath as our pulses skyrocket, our hearts beating wildly against each other.

My hand strokes his back; his lips caress my neck until he pulls up and stares down at me, greeting me with an irresistibly devastating grin.

"I'm pretty sure things just changed between us."

I laugh and nod. "Yeah, you could say that."

"Do you regret it?" he asks, his smile faltering.

I shake my head. "Not even a second of it, but I'm still mad at you for shoving snow down my pants."

He kisses my nose and then hops up off the bed. "You'll get over it."

"Where are you going?" I ask, sitting up.

When he turns around, his eyes land on my breasts and then travel up to my eyes. "Taking care of the condom. Don't move, because I have plans."

"Yeah? What kind of plans?"

"Cuddle plans."

"Big dick *and* likes to cuddle. Wow, Knightly, you should have been advertising that a long time ago."

His laughter trails down the hallway as he calls out, "Looks like I have to make up for lost time then."

I flip back on the bed and get under the covers, trying to warm back up as I contemplate this strange new reality. Reid Knightly and I just had sex—but not *just* sex. No, we had mind-blowing, life-changing, earth-shattering sex. And after all of that, he wants to cuddle.

I don't think it could get any better than this.

CHAPTER SEVEN

REID

Smack.

I shoot off the pillow and blink the sunlight away from my blurry eyes as my ass cheek stings.

"What the—"

"Rise and shine," Eve's voice chimes. I look to the right and find her standing beside the bed in an oversize shirt and holding a cup of coffee. I rub my palm against my eye, sitting up and trying to comprehend what time it is.

"Did you just smack me on the ass?"

She nods. "Yup. I couldn't help it. Sleeping naked was a bad decision because your tush was just hanging out in the open, waiting for me to pop it."

I reach out and take the coffee from her. I press my lips against the edge, test the temperature, and down a large gulp before putting it on the nightstand and pulling her down on the bed with me.

I wrestle her onto her back. "I'm pretty sure me sleeping naked last night came in handy when I found you between my legs, playing with my junk in the middle of the night."

"I wasn't playing with your junk—ugh, why do you have to say it like that?"

I slip my hand up her shirt. "Then what would you call it?"

"Examining the goods, seeing how fast it could rise."

I shift my hardened cock against her leg. "Fast, as we discovered multiple times."

Moaning, she spreads her legs and melts into the bed. I swear to Christ himself, never in my life have I ever met a woman more responsive to my touch than Eve. If I found out anything last night, it was that I was meant to be with her like this. Intimate and close.

Staring down at her, I say, "Morning."

She smiles. "Good morning." She reaches up and strokes my hair. "Are you hungry?"

"Yeah, spread your legs more." I go to duck under the covers, but she laughs and holds me in place.

"I meant real food."

"Um, I saw your fridge; there's no food in this place."

"I have protein bars."

"Hmm." I look to the side, contemplating my options. "Let's see, I could have a protein bar, or I could eat out Eve's pussy. Wow, this is a tough one. Protein bar or Eve's pussy—how do I even decide?"

"Stop it." She swats at my chest. "They're good protein bars."

"Nah, I'm good." I try to dive under the covers again, but she clamps her legs together.

"Uh, do you have a problem with my mouth on your clit?"

"No, I just thought . . . you know . . ."

Oh hell.

"You want to talk," I finish for her. Her cheeks flush as she nods.

"I think it might be best, you know, since things are complicated between us."

"They're only complicated if we make them."

I reach for her legs again, but she chuckles and pushes me away. "Keep it together, Knightly. You had me four times through the course of the night—you can wait until we're done talking."

Brows lifted, I look down at my dick. "Not sure waiting is an option here."

"It's not my fault you're so horny."

"Uh, as a matter of fact it *is* your fault. Exhibit number one: your hard nipples." I point at the nubs poking against her shirt. Her face turns a deeper shade of pink. "Exhibit number two." I drag my hand up her thigh. "You're not wearing any underwear. Do you really think that's fair for me, knowing I have such easy access right now?"

She pats my cheek and scoots a few feet away from me. "You'll survive. Now, come on, have a serious conversation with me."

I roll my eyes and lean back against the headboard, letting the comforter fall over my poor erect and untouched penis. "Fine. Conversation and then I get to have you any way I want." I jab my thumb toward the window. "We're snowed in, so what better way to pass the time than fucking each other?"

She pretends to give it some thought. "Well, you do owe me shower sex, so we can start there."

"You drive a hard bargain, Roberts, but being the gentleman that I am, I'll acquiesce."

"Wow," she deadpans. "What a hero."

Chuckling, I reach out and take her hand in mine. I turn it over and fit our palms together; hers is much slenderer than mine, but the connection is still perfect. "Okay, what do you want to talk about?"

"Well, you know, the annoying 'what does this all mean' kind of stuff," she says in a funny nasally voice. "The stuff guys hate."

"What the hell are you talking about? We love awkward conversations that take time away from having sex."

"I should have known this was going to be torture."

"Hey, you knew what you were signing up for the minute you invited me back to your place. This really is on you." I tug on her arm. "After all these years, you made the first move."

"I did not." Her brow pulls together. "You did."

"Uh . . . you were the one inviting me back to your place and taking your clothes off in front of me. Pretty sure my clothes stayed on until I was beckoned into the shower."

"You made the first move before that."

"When?"

"Do you not remember the Inn, the dance floor? You were rubbing your body all over mine."

"Nope." I shake my head. "I was dancing, you were the one—"

"You stuck your hand down my pants and squeezed my ass."

I wag my finger at her. "I can see how that could be construed as damning evidence, but I'm pretty sure I saw something fly down there and wanted to make sure it wasn't a spider or anything."

"You're absurd. *You* made the first move; there's no question about that. Want me to call Barb and Marv and get their opinions?"

"I'd rather you not. I still can't get rid of the image of those two watching us as we danced." Fucking creepy shit. "Okay, let's just call it a mutual first move and get on with this conversation. I want to get between your legs."

"Is that how this is going to be—all about sex?"

"Yes," I answer, and when she scowls, I add, "Plus all that fun talking shit." I prop my chin up with my hand and stare at her intently. "Please, let's gab."

She palms my face and pushes me away. "Why did I think I could have a grown-up conversation with you?" She starts to move away, but I quickly pin her to the bed and hover over her.

"Because you can. Come on, hit me with your worst."

"Fine," she says, succumbing to my strength. "Are we seeing each other now?"

"Yes."

"Are you going to see anyone else?"

"No." I press a kiss to her nose. It's cute that she's worried, but I'm not that kind of man—never have been, never will be.

"Are you going to take me out on a date?"

"Do you want me to?" I counter, seeing how serious this is for her.

"Yes."

"Then yes, I'll take you on all of the dates."

"What about Eric?" she asks, worry filling her eyes.

"What about him?"

"Are you going to tell him?"

"Well, since I haven't seen him in years, and he never comes back to Port Snow, I'm going to say no. Not right now, when I'm trying to fuck you every chance I get."

"Is that all this is to you? Fucking?"

With that question, I straighten up and sit back a little. "No. It's not."

"You're making it seem like it is."

"Because you fucking rocked my damn world last night, Eve," I answer honestly, realizing it as the truth comes pouring out of my mouth. She did: she took me by the balls and flipped my life upside down in the best way possible. And the fact that I can actually be open with her about that is probably even more startling than the revelation itself. I don't talk emotions, and I sure as hell don't admit to having them, but Eve somehow pulls them out of me. Enraptured by how beautiful she is, I tuck a strand of hair behind her ear, letting my fingers linger on her soft skin. "Last night meant more to me than just fucking my friend—it meant connecting with someone in a way I never have before. You made me feel shit, Eve, and I don't let myself have feelings. But it felt good. Fuck, it felt so damn good. It's why I want to sink myself inside of you all over again, because I want that feeling of euphoria to take over me, that feeling of comfort, of belonging. This isn't just about fucking, at least not for me. This is about starting something new."

She stares at me, her mouth slightly ajar, as if I'm a completely different person.

"Wow," she finally says. "I knew you were going to make me scream in bed, and I knew you were going to be irresistible, but I had no idea you were going to bowl me over with your words."

I wiggle my eyebrows at her. "Is that a good thing?"

"It's a very good thing." The smile in her eyes promises some more good things to come.

Very good things.

"So then it's settled. We're seeing each other, we're not seeing other people, we're going out on dates, and we're creating something—not just fucking."

"And we're not telling my brother or anyone. Just keeping this on the down low for now."

"Yeah, no need to get him involved or anyone right now." Eric hasn't truly been a part of my life for years. Sure, we shoot each other the odd text messages, but when it comes to my love life . . . yeah, he can fuck off for now.

"And that's not going to backfire?" she asks, heavy concern in her voice. "I mean, we do live in a gossipy town where everyone knows everyone. He could find out, and what would he say to that?"

I think back to all the times he told me to stop checking Eve out, to the times he would punch me in the arm every time I stared at her in a bikini, to the small moments he would catch me just talking to her. He warned me, told me not to mess with her, to stay away because friendship with her should always be my number one priority. He didn't ever want to lose me as his best friend because I fucked something up with his sister.

Well, we're no longer talking—at least not as much—and not because of Eve but because of our own stupidity. I might have told him a long time ago when we were young that I would never go after his sister. But that was then; this is now. I can't hide the feelings I have for her, and yeah, maybe this will backfire on us, but that's a chance I'm willing to take when it comes to exploring what Eve and I could have.

Continuing, she says, "You know how all of those movies and stories go: the brother accidentally finds out and then blows up, the couple breaks up, and heartbreak takes over."

"You've been watching way too many Lovemark movies." I laugh her off, holding back the niggling fear that tries to make itself known. Eve doesn't need to shoulder any more thoughts, secrets, or responsibilities. "No, that won't be us because when the time comes, we'll let Eric know. But for now, let's just get to know this new development in our lives. Deal?"

I lean over and press my forehead to hers, still in awe that this girl is beneath me, running her hands up and down my back.

She tilts her chin up and presses a kiss against my hungry lips. "Deal."

◆ ◆ ◆

Reid: Dude, I have to tell you something.

Brig: Jesus, my mouth is frothing just from reading that text. You know I love juicy gossip. Give it to me.

Reid: You can't tell ANYONE.

Brig: Yeah, sure, lips are sealed. Give Daddy the deets.

Reid: I'm not fucking kidding. You have to keep this between us.

Brig: Come on, who would I tell?

Reid: Literally everyone.

Brig: I've grown up.

Reid: In the last twenty-four hours?

Brig: I've sprung a new leaf.

Reid: That makes no sense whatsoever.

Brig: Why are you fucking with me? Why text if you're just going to run me through the gauntlet? You either tell me or you don't. You either trust me or you don't. I have better things to do than wait around for you to stop dicking me around.

Reid: You're right, I'm sorry.

Brig: Thank you, now tell me your news. My lips are sealed.

Reid: Eve and I had sex two days ago. Lots and lots of it. And we're dating now.

. . .

. . .

. . .

Brig: WHAT????

Brig: Wait . . . WHAT??? With Eve Roberts? Eric's twin, Eve? The girl you've had a secret crush on ever since I can remember? That Eve?

Reid: Yeah, that Eve.

Brig: Call Griff. I'm pretty sure I'm having a heart attack. Paramedics to the garage, stat.

Reid: Stop being dramatic.

Reid: Are you there?

Reid: I'm not calling Griff.

Reid: Seriously, Brig. What the hell are you doing?

◆ ◆ ◆

Four Men and a Witch Text Message Group

Griffin: So . . . Reid banged Eve.

Rogan: What? Eve Roberts?

Reid: WHAT THE ACTUAL FUCK, BRIG!

Brig: What? **Fans Face** I had no idea. When did this all happen?

Reid: I told you not to tell anyone. What the fuck, man?

Rogan: Is anyone else picturing Reid's face getting super red right now?

Griffin: Like the Lobster Landing logo. Yeah, I see it.

Brig: I must have been texting in my sleep again.

Reid: You're dead to me.

Brig: If that's the case, I might as well tell everyone else.

Reid: I will murder your penis.

Griffin: That sounds sexual.

Rogan: Super kinky. I think Harper said that to me one night.

Griffin: Ren said the same thing.

Brig: Did Eve say that to you, Reid before you guys did the nasty? **Said in girly Eve voice** Get over here, big boy. I'm about to murder your penis.

Rogan: Oh I heard that really well.

Griffin: I could see Eve saying that.

Reid: SHE DIDN'T FUCKING SAY THAT.

Brig: I think she did.

Griffin: It's pretty likely that she did.

Rogan: Scale of one to ten on likeliness, it's an eleven . . . until he pulled his pants down and she was massively disappointed.

Reid: Not that it's any of your business, but her jaw actually hit the floor when she saw my penis.

Rogan: Because she couldn't find it, right?

Reid: Why are you like this?

Griffin: So you can dish it, but you can't take it?

Reid: I think we all know that by now.

Brig: So tell them, tell them you're dating.

Reid: Why do I need to when you do it for me?

Brig: Fine. **Takes deep breath** The curse is broken! Reid finally matured and poked Eve with his penis. He's free!

Reid: You and that GD curse. Let it the fuck go.

Jen: If you're going to include me in these texts, can you please refrain from talking about your penises? Unless you want me talking about my vagina after giving birth to children. **Rubs hands** Then game on, boys.

Reid: I just threw up in my mouth.

Brig: Flappy vagina talk—NEVER AGAIN!

Griffin: **Slowly backs away**

Rogan: Yeah, I have a meeting to run to.

Jen: My work here is done.

CHAPTER EIGHT

EVE

"Hello?" I answer in a groggy voice.

"Hey, sis."

I spring out of bed, all thoughts of sleep forgotten. I wipe at my eyes and clear my throat as I check the time on my clock. Six in the morning. Why is Eric calling me at six in the morning?

For a brief second, a wave of nerves rolls through my stomach at the thought of Eric knowing about Reid and me. Did Reid sticking his hand down my pants on the dance floor somehow get back to Eric? Barb and Marv aren't the gossiping types, but I would say that's pretty juicy information for someone to spread on a bored wintery day.

"Eric, is everything okay?"

"Yeah, sorry about calling so early. I couldn't sleep." He pauses. "How are you?"

Seriously? It's six in the morning. A *how are you* question isn't exactly what I want to be answering right now, not after working a late shift. But I would never say that to Eric—not when things are this uncomfortable between us.

"Good. You know, just working and finishing up school."

"Yeah? How much longer until you graduate?"

"Last semester. I'm almost done." As he mulls that over, I obsess over how random this phone call is. It's completely out of the blue, and I'm nervous to find out what brought it on.

Reid seemed unfazed at the prospect of not telling Eric about our new development. And it makes sense, since their friendship has dwindled over the past few years. But Eric is still my brother, and a small piece of me feels like he should know.

And I mean a very small piece of me.

"Damn, Eve, that's amazing. I don't know how you do it all. School, studying, being the manager at the Inn, and practically running the entire operation. Do you have any spare time?"

Just enough to have a wild affair with your best friend.

"I find time." I yawn and try to smother it, but Eric is too quick.

"Man, I should have waited to call. I'm sorry, but I had to get something off my chest."

Oh boy. Here it is. The reason. I brace myself, waiting for him to call me out on hooking up with Reid.

"Uh, what's that?" I ask, holding my voice still, trying to hide my nerves.

"I wanted to apologize."

Huh? Wasn't expecting that.

"Apologize for what?"

"For not coming back to Port Snow on Dad's death anniversary."

Oh.

A wave of emotion hits me all at once. Sadness, appreciation, awkwardness. It's all there.

"It's fine—"

"It's not fine, Eve. It's unacceptable. Ever since we lost Bar 79, I haven't been the brother you deserve; I've dropped the ball on many things, especially when it comes to our parents. I shouldn't let you be by yourself on those days."

"I wasn't. Reid was with me."

Why did I just say that? Maybe because he's on my brain. Maybe because I feel a little guilty about keeping Eric in the dark. Or maybe because Reid was truly there for me, and I want Eric to know that.

"Reid was there?" Confusion laces his question. "Wow, that's really nice of him."

"Yeah, well, he knew it was a tough day." And then we totally did it later that night, but I'll keep that to myself. "It was nice to have someone to lean on, but I know you were busy. You didn't need to call to apologize."

He's silent for a few breaths, heightening the tension between us. It didn't used to be like this; we weren't always so awkward and clumsy with each other, but a lot of time and space have settled between us, almost too much. I wish he would move back, live out the dream we once shared, but after Bar 79 went under, so did the rest of our plans.

"I'm still sorry," he finally says. "Really fucking sorry, Eve."

I sigh and close my eyes, hating the pain I hear in his voice. "I know, Eric. I know."

I've been to Reid's houseboat a few times. It's simple. A house on floats, seafoam green on the outside, and two stories tall, with a loft upstairs and a rooftop deck. Refurbished and the perfect bachelor pad for a guy who is trying to hide from the world. It's just another place, and yet a wave of nerves hits me all at once as I step up onto the deck that leads to the entrance. The outside lights illuminate a path where the snow has been knocked away into the harbor, and salt has been dusted over the slick surface, giving me a straight shot to his home, like a shining invitation.

I make my way to the front door, and before I can knock, the door swings open, revealing Reid standing on the other side, wearing a pair of sweats and a *Port Snow, Maine* shirt that clings to every contour of his chest. His hair is damp, and there is a light in his eyes I haven't seen in a long time.

"Took you long enough—get in here."

He pulls me by the hand and slams the door shut before tipping up my chin and kissing me.

It's been a week. One week of us "seeing" each other, and every time he goes to kiss me, it's like he doesn't even have to think about it. His kisses still startle me—but in the best way.

When he pulls away, he loops our hands together and walks me farther into his quaint little home. "I'm starving. Sit. Take your shoes off."

He ushers me to his two-person dining table, which bears a small bud vase with one fresh daisy flower sticking out of it.

Oh my God, how cute. That's when I take the time to glance around the houseboat. It's different—fresher, more grown up than the last time I saw it, as if he gave it a quick makeover before I came for our date. There are curtains—mind you, they're plain navy blue, but he still hung some—there are rugs and dish towels. No more posters, and . . . is that a *coaster* on his coffee table?

"Did you spruce the place up?" I ask, trying and failing to hide a smile.

He shrugs. "A little. Didn't want you to think you were dating someone who doesn't even know how to hang curtains." He pulls a pizza box out of his oven.

"Reid, you adulted your place."

"Yeah, so? Don't make a big deal out of it." He places two slices of pizza on each plate and then brings them over to the table, where there is also a chilled bottle of wine and two glasses.

"But it's so cute. You got matching dish towels."

"I liked the stripes," he answers nonchalantly while pouring us each a glass of wine.

He's trying not to make it a big deal, and I shouldn't either, but this is a side of Reid that's still so new—and almost as surprising as his dirty side. This is his sweet side, the same man who came out and comforted me on the anniversary of the day my dad died.

I'm so used to his sarcastic wit and joking jabs that I need to realize there's more to Reid than just the friend I grew up with; there's a depth that I'm going to guess most people don't know about.

"It looks good in here," I say before taking a bite of my pizza.

He glances up from his pizza and smiles. "Thanks, Eve."

And just like that, my heart squeezes in my chest. Even though I like the boy I grew up with, and I love teasing and joking with him, there is something about this new, sensitive man that I'm growing to like even more.

After another bite, I say, "When you invited me over for dinner, I almost expected you to make me some kind of gourmet meal."

A mozzarella string drips from his mouth. He slurps it up. "I don't cook anymore. You know that."

I tilt my head to the side, trying to understand him better. "You mean, you don't cook at all?"

He shakes his head. "Nope."

"Why?"

"No need. I either eat at my parents', eat out, or eat something that's premade. And leftovers from my parents usually last me awhile, too, since they like to make meals for what seems like the entire town."

"But cooking was your life."

"And it's not anymore, so let's not start out the evening with a fight, okay?"

"I wasn't fighting with you, but if you want to fight, we can fight."

He shakes his head and smirks. "I'd rather not, unless it's followed by makeup sex. Then put on your gloves, Roberts; we're duking it out." He throws a few cute little jabs in my direction.

"It always comes back to sex with you, doesn't it?"

"For all guys, babe, all guys." He winks.

"Babe?" I ask, surprised at how effortlessly the word fell from his lips.

"Yeah, babe. Have a problem with that?"

"Seems like you're moving pretty fast. What's going to happen next week? Are you going to get down on one knee and propose?"

"No, but I'm going to go down on one knee, throw your leg over my shoulder, and eat you out."

I roll my eyes and lean back in my chair. "Seriously, try to go five minutes without talking about sex."

"Impossible."

"You're not even going to try?"

"Nope." He smiles broadly and takes a brief sip of wine. And *oh my*, seeing Reid drink wine is sexy, the way he quickly takes a whiff of it, swirls his glass—he doesn't just drink it; he appreciates it. "So how was your day? Marv give you any trouble?"

"No, he was good. Tipped well, left at a decent hour, and I didn't have to shove him out with a broom. It was a win. What about you?"

He plucks a pepperoni from the pizza and pops it in his mouth. "Nothing too special, just the normal shit." He stares at me for a few moments and then says, "My family knows."

"As in . . ."

"As in they *know*."

My body immediately heats up, and I don't know if it's from nerves, embarrassment, or anger. Maybe all three. The last thing I need right now is the Knightly family knowing that I'm doing it with their son.

Plus when the Knightlys know, the whole town soon finds out.

"How? Why? I thought we weren't telling people."

"Yeah, about that." He looks out the window to the harbor. "I *might* have told Brig."

"*Brig?*" I shout. "Why on earth would you tell Brig? Out of all of your siblings, you told Brig? Rogan would have been your best bet. He doesn't care about shit like this. Why on earth would you tell Brig? He's almost as big a gossip as Franklin." I'm hysterical—I can hear it in my voice—but the last thing I need is for someone to tell Eric and for him to finally come back to Port Snow . . . angrily.

"I don't know, maybe because I'm closest to him," Reid answers, irritation edging into his voice. "He just told my siblings. I went down to the garage the other day and threatened his life if he told anyone. He won't say anything, so don't worry, princess, your secret is safe."

"Whoa." I push back from the table. "Excuse me, but I thought this was going to stay just between us for a bit. Sorry if I'm upset about four people already knowing. And since Ren and Harper are attached to your family, I'm going to guess they already know too."

"What if they do?"

"Are you kidding me? Reid, it would be nice to know that I could date you without the entire town watching us. It's been a week, and I haven't even seen you that much. This is supposed to be our first date, and instead of having a nice time, we're fighting."

"Because you're getting defensive. What's really going on? Are you embarrassed of dating me?"

What is happening right now? He can't possibly be serious.

"Why on earth would I be embarrassed?"

He waves at our surroundings. "I don't know, maybe because I'm not what you probably expected when it comes to a boyfriend? A poor fisherman who lives on a houseboat, scores leftovers from his parents, and sells fudge to rabid tourists."

Completely caught off guard, I jump up from my chair and head to the door. A week. It's been a week, and we're already at each other's throats. Maybe this was a terrible idea. I knew Reid had a temper, I knew losing the restaurant was a blow to his self-esteem, but him turning that all on me is not fair.

"Where are you going?" He stands as well and strides across the room, beating me to the door. I reach for the handle, but he presses his palm against the wood to stop me.

"Reid, I suggest you step away and let me out."

"No."

I look up at his determined face, and a cold anger grips me with each second that passes. *Fine,* I decide. *If he wants to talk about this, then we're gonna talk about it.*

I fold my arms over my chest and face him. "Do you really think I care about what you do or where you live? I've known you forever, Reid. Your life isn't a mystery to me. It's not like I'm just starting to get to know you." I poke his chest. "I *know* you. So it's insulting for you to accuse me of being embarrassed of you. I'm not embarrassed. I just wanted this to be between us for a bit before we have to start dodging all the town gossip. I wanted time with just you."

His face softens, and he lets out a long breath before pushing both hands through his hair. On an exhale, he mutters, "Fuck," and then pulls me into his chest, his strong arms spreading warmth through my body. "I'm sorry, Eve. Fuck, I'm sorry." He presses a kiss to my forehead, and I start to thaw from our fight. "I'm not good at this shit. I'm sorry."

At least he's good at apologizing.

I cling to him. "Please don't accuse me of thinking poorly of you again. It's hurtful. My opinion of you is so much higher than you could even fathom, and it has nothing to do with what you do or where you live but everything to do with the heart that beats inside your chest."

"Damn, Eve, that's some serious talk." He chuckles but then pulls me in tighter and lifts my chin so he can press a sweet kiss against my lips. "Thanks, babe."

"Back to *babe,* huh?"

"Yeah, and since we just had a fight, you know what that means, right?" He raises his eyebrows, and I'm about to roll my eyes when he sweeps me up into his arms and carries me up the narrow staircase to his bedroom loft.

He tosses me on the mattress and reaches behind him to pull his shirt up and over his head. The fabric drops to the floor, and my eyes sweep over his sculpted body, taking in every glorious inch, every corded muscle, and every ripple in his abdomen.

Maybe he's right.

Maybe we really should fight more.

◆ ◆ ◆

"I like that you don't wax your chest." I run my fingers through the trimmed hair scattered over his brawny pecs. It's minimal, the perfect amount, and super sexy, topping off the masculine appeal he seems to carry so easily.

"Don't have time for it. Do you know who does?"

"Brig." I don't even have to consider my answer. I think that deep down inside, Brig considers himself a hero in a romance novel and attempts to embody that role every chance he gets—and waxing his chest is just one of the necessary tasks in achieving his Fabio aspirations.

"Yup," Reid answers, his hand plastered against my ass, keeping our naked bodies as close together as possible.

Reid Knightly has always been devastatingly handsome. From his blue eyes to the swagger in his step to the curve of his jaw, he's never failed to make my heart skip a beat whenever he stepped into a room.

But Reid Knightly in the bedroom takes it to a whole new level. The dirty talk, his naked body . . . his penis. God, just thinking about it makes my stomach flip with excitement. He commands control, handling me with care but also with an edge of possession, and when he sinks into me, his face shifts to pure bliss. It's beyond fulfilling, knowing I can take down such a strong man.

"Brig is something special."

"He lives in another world." Reid laughs. "I always wonder what it would be like to live his life, live in his head. He's a smart motherfucker and has built an amazing company, and I think a lot of it has to do with the land he lives in."

"The land?"

"He doesn't worry about real things. It's like he lives in a land where unicorns deliver mail and cupcakes grow on trees. The real world is tinted by the rose-colored glasses he seems to wear all the time. The only true worry he has is whether he's going to die alone. He's told me he's had nightmares about it."

I giggle. Oh, poor Brig. "That's a valid concern. But hey, if Griffin and Rogan can break the curse, there's hope for you two."

"Jesus," he mutters. "Can we not talk about that shit?"

"Come on, do you really think you're cursed?"

He's silent for a second, just the smooth sound of his breathing filling the calm as his hand slowly strokes my skin. I'm surprised he even has to think about it.

"Do you know that happened the same night I found out about the restaurant?"

"When what happened? The curse?"

He nods. "Yeah. Right after, actually. We were at a bar, getting pretzels, still kind of reeling over the encounter." He presses a kiss to my head. "It was weird, Eve. I still don't know what to make of the whole thing. We were drunk, so the incident feels a little fuzzy to begin with, at least the before part, but I still can't get over the look in that lady's eyes. It felt so *real* in that moment, like something was really shifting in our lives."

"And what about after?"

"We blew it off. Yeah, it was some coincidental timing with the wind and all that shit, but who really wants to believe in a curse? At least I tried to not believe in it."

"So you think you have a love curse?" I ask.

"No." The tension in my shoulders eases at his words. Though I don't believe in curses, I still don't want to be dating a man who believes his love life is doomed. That's just setting up our entire relationship for failure. "But I do believe I'm cursed," he adds.

Okay, wasn't expecting that.

"What do you mean?"

Staring up at the ceiling, he places the hand that's not gripping me behind his head and props himself up a bit. I hold on tight as he shifts and gets comfortable. "It was right after we ran into that lady that Eric called me. And that's when I lost everything. I've tried telling myself the two are unrelated, but fuck"—he blows out a long breath of air—"it just feels like ever since that night, I've been stuck in a weird sort of purgatory."

"How so?" I ask, not wanting to push too much but also taking advantage of this moment, this rare glimpse of Reid dropping all the sarcasm and actually opening up.

"All my siblings seem to have something going for them. Jen has her amazing family, and even though she complains about her hellion children, I know they're her life and everything she's ever wanted. Griff has the Lobster Landing now and his volunteering. He's in heaven, so add Ren to that, and his life is made. Rogue practically owns Port Snow. He's built a small empire and has refurbished the rundown houses in town, bringing out their beauty again. And then Brig, who's the baby of the family and the one who isn't supposed to have his shit together, is fucking thriving. He's built a business the town desperately needed and then branched out from there with restoring cars, renting out old classics to tourists, and even turning his garage into an event space. Everyone has their shit together but me."

"You opened a restaurant at twenty-three, Reid."

"Yeah, and I failed, horribly. I failed so fucking badly that I had to come crawling back home. And on top of that, I lost my best friend, I'm stuck trapping lobsters every goddamn day of my life just to make ends meet, and I'm forced to work at the family business where I despise each and every shift. I'm fucking miserable, Eve, and I have nothing to show for all the hard work I put in when I was younger. All the things I missed—the dances, the football games, the dates I could have gone on—I pushed everything aside to chase a dream I ended up massively failing at."

I bite my bottom lip, really unsure of what to say. How do you tell someone they aren't worthless when that's what they truly believe? How do you tell someone that failing doesn't mean you quit, that failing is just a stepping stone to achieving what you want in life?

I know I could easily say all of that to Reid, but he wouldn't listen. I know him. He's so set in his beliefs that anything I say in this moment will go in one ear and out the other.

So instead of trying to fix how he sees himself, I need to help him see himself the way I do: strong, loyal, and caring.

"I don't think about it that way." I sit up so I can look him in the eye. Instead of shying away, he brings his hand to my cheek and rubs his thumb across my face. I lean into his touch, into his wide, large hand. "I see you as a man who went for his dreams, a man who loves his family, who adores his friends, who strives to help his town, and who continues to move forward despite his setbacks."

"You see all that?" he asks, a lazy smile dragging across his face.

"Yes, I do."

"Nothing else? Nothing at all?"

And just like that, Reid ends the serious conversation and deflects with humor as he thrusts his hips toward me. For a brief moment, it makes me sad because I wanted to dive into his feelings, to move past the thin veil of sarcasm the two of us seem to depend on. But I shouldn't expect anything else when it comes to Reid; I should be grateful for the small moment he just gave me, even if it barely skimmed the surface of the complex man he is beneath all the humor.

And I don't want to be that girl, that girl who tries to pry every last feeling out of him or who spends morning and night attempting to "fix" him. It will only drive us apart. We are so new, just trying to figure everything out, and I don't want to ruin that by trying to dive too deep right off the bat.

But I will be the girl who tries to show him his worth, because he is worth so much more than what he believes.

"Are you done with the innuendos?" I smile despite myself.

"Just want to make sure you acknowledge my dick."

He's so ridiculous. I've never in my life met a man more obsessed with his penis than Reid Knightly. At least he has a good reason for the obsession.

I reach down and cup him, pulling a hiss from between his teeth. "Don't worry, I'll always acknowledge your dick."

"Damn right."

He rolls me onto my back, and with a perfect almost-evil grin, he moves down my body and parts my legs. I sink into the mattress and catch my breath as Reid presses his mouth against me, one possessive kiss at a time.

CHAPTER NINE

REID

Why do all these candles smell like burnt ass?

I put the brown three-wick back on the shelf, pick up a jar of coffee beans, and take a big whiff. According to Melanie, the owner of Sticks and Wicks, coffee beans cleanse your nose so you can have a clear sniff of the next candle. I was skeptical at first, but after "cleansing" the first go-around, I became a supporter of the beans.

I like Melanie. She's a sweet girl, but after spending ten minutes sniffing candles while she interjected with facts about every last ingredient used in the wax, I thanked her for the coffee beans but told her I needed some privacy to sniff on my own. I couldn't care less what's in the candle—I just need it to smell good.

Visiting Sticks and Wicks is the last thing I want to fucking do right now, but I know Eve really likes candles, and since the harbor carries a pretty dangerous old-man-ballsac smell sometimes, I thought it might be beneficial to get some scented candles for the houseboat in case the smell of the harbor bothers her. Not that she's said anything, but I like to be preventative.

And you know, candles set the mood and shit.

Setting the mood means sex.

Sex with Eve is out of this goddamn world. And I would obviously like more of it, so this means candles.

I'm buying all the fucking candles.

If I happen to find a candle I like, maybe I'll get one for her too. That's what boyfriends do: buy crap for their girl. Plus, it's buy one, get one half-off in the store, and Daddy loves a good BOGO. I spotted the sale ad in the newspaper when I was scanning it for anything about Eve and me. Luckily, my family members have kept their mouths shut. Surprising, since Brig has sent me texts every day "gushing" about my newfound relationship.

Pretty sure he's trying to live vicariously through me.

Weirdly, I let him and give him details that his "nipples get hard" over. He and his goddamn hard nipples. Such a fucking weirdo.

I pick up a green candle, liking the color, and glance at the label—*Flannel.*

Huh, interesting.

How does one capture the smell of flannel? In my head, it's going to smell like a man who's been chopping up wood for two hours.

Tentatively, I pop open the lid and take a deep breath.

Big mistake.

"Oh fuck." I cringe and put the candle right back where I found it while blowing air out of my nose, trying to expel the scent. Clutching the coffee beans, I bury my nose inside the mason jar and reconsider the whole candle thing. Flannel just about singed every hair in my nose.

"Reid?"

Crap. Spotted.

Turning on my heel, coffee beans still clutched to my chest, I find Ren, Griff's girlfriend, with a small basket in hand and a confused look on her face. I don't blame her; I wouldn't be surprised if I'm caught in the newspaper tomorrow with the headline *Abnormal Spotting: Loser Knightly Sniffing Candles* with the subtitle *Has He Finally Hit Rock Bottom?*

I give her a small wave and then stick my hand in my pocket, all of a sudden feeling awkward as fuck. "Uh, hey, Ren. What's up?"

"Hey, I've never seen you in here before." With a conspiratorial look, she says, "Trying to avoid your dad again?"

It's a known fact Ren is obsessed with Sticks and Wicks. Griffin has bought her so many things from this quaint little shop, which is nestled in the heart of Main Street. It's full of candles, incense, and all good-smelling things, so you're likely to find any number of Knightly women perusing the stock on any given day, which I should have taken into consideration when coming in here.

"I'm always avoiding my dad, but this time I thought, you know, I might check out some candles."

She glances over my shoulder. "You tried Flannel?"

"Pretty sure they captured twelve pairs of sweaty balls and added a hint of mint to it."

"That's quite accurate." She walks up to me and bops me on the nose. "You've got a good sniffer. You're in the wrong area, though. These are on sale for a reason. No one ever buys them." She takes my arm. "Come on, I'll show you the good stuff."

"But is the good stuff included in the sale from the newspaper?"

She winks at me. "The ad didn't specify, so when you go to check out, tell Melanie, and she'll have to honor it."

"You know, Ren, I don't think we hang out enough."

She throws her head back as she laughs and guides me to the left of the store, where all the candles are color coordinated. I didn't come over here because it looked too fancy. "I'm pretty sure Griffin would hate it if we hung out more."

"Why? Because I know all of his secrets? He should be scared, and since he's not here right now, what do you want to know?"

Ren glances around before leaning in. "How about a candle for some intel? Is that a deal?"

"You don't even have to get me the candle. I'll tell you whatever you want."

"But then I would feel guilty. Come on, tit for tat."

I raise an eyebrow. "If Griffin knew you were offering me your tit for my tat, I'm pretty sure he'd lose his mind."

She shoves my shoulder. "You know what I mean." She holds out her hand. "Is it a deal?"

I'm not a stupid man, and I want a nice candle, so I shake her hand, ready to throw my brother under the bus. Hey, I'll do whatever it takes to impress a girl. I mean, Eve did say that I was adulting, and she noticed my matching dish towels, so imagine her reaction if she sees a candle burning the next time she comes over.

"Deal." I rub my hands together. "Candle first, though. I want something that smells fresh and clean, maybe a little manly . . . nothing flowery."

"I got just the one." She reaches for a candle and holds it out. "Mahogany Teakwood. Trust me, it's perfect for you."

"Yeah?" I open the lid and breathe in the candle. "Smells like an expensive cologne."

"Exactly. It's perfect. If, you know, you have a girl over"—Ren raises her eyebrows—"she'll love it. And I happen to know one girl in particular who really likes this scent."

Jesus Christ. Could she be any less subtle?

"Griffin told you," I deadpan.

A grin spreads across her face, and she clasps my hands in hers, practically gushing with glee. "Oh my gosh, he made me swear I wouldn't say anything, but *gah*! Reid, I am so excited. You two are so cute together."

"Shhh." I look around, thankful no one is paying attention. "For the love of God, don't go spreading it around. Eve is already pissed I told the boys and Jen. I can't have anyone else finding out."

"Oh, don't worry," she says. "I haven't told anyone, but just so you know, Harper knows as well. Seems like your brothers aren't good at keeping secrets from their significant others."

"Figures." I drag my hand over my face. "Okay, just don't say anything to anyone, okay? Especially not to Eve. Just pretend like you know nothing. Do you think you can handle that?"

"Of course."

I definitely don't believe her, but there's only so much I can do. I never should have told Brig in the first place—that was mistake number one. Then again, who else could I have told? Griffin and Rogan both are connected to Harper and Ren, who are Eve's friends. Jen is also Eve's friend, so that left Brig. It's really not my fault. It's actually Eve's fault—for being friends with everyone.

"But can I just say, you two are adorable. Oh my God, I just keep picturing what your babies would look like."

For fuck's sake.

"You need to stay away from Brig—he's getting to you. Let me guess, you also think the curse is broken."

"Oh no." She waves her hand, dismissing the notion. "I've never believed in that stupid thing. From the moment I heard about it, I knew it wasn't true. But why do you ask? Do *you* believe in it?"

I shrug and stare down at the candle. "So teakwood, huh?"

"Oh my God, Reid Knightly, you do not believe in it, do you?" I shrug, and she continues, "So you're telling me that even though you were drunk at the time, you can one hundred percent verify every detail about that story—the yellow eyes, the wind, and everything else?"

I point at her. "You weren't there; you don't get an opinion."

Chuckling, she shakes her head and reaches for another candle. "You Knightlys are deranged." She hands me the candle. "Bergamot Waters should be your second one."

I smell the candle when she removes the lid, and I have to admit that one is just as good. "Damn, that smells amazing."

She takes both candles and puts them in her basket.

"The deal was one candle."

"And the sale calls for two. Since I invaded your love life, we'll call that one."

"Well, if you're offering . . ." I pull a second set down of the same scents and hand them over. "For someone special."

Ren lights up but keeps her mouth shut as she sets them in her basket.

"Now for my payment," she says, getting back to business. "Why does Griffin refuse to eat anything with eggplant in it? He just says he doesn't like it, but I swear there's something he's not telling me. Am I right?"

My lips turn up as I nod. "Oh yeah, there's a story."

"I knew it." She steps closer. "Tell me."

"Well . . ." I draw out the moment, savoring the anticipation on her face. "It was his senior year in high school. He went out with Rogan, Harper, and Claire to some Italian restaurant where he had the best eggplant parm of his life—at least that's what he said at the time."

"Oh no. Food poisoning?"

"Nope." I chuckle. "After dinner they went to the carnival up in Pottsmouth."

"Oh no, did he get on one of those scrambler rides?"

"Nope." I shake my head. "He went on the Ferris wheel and got stuck up at the very top. It was windy; he got nauseous and threw up all over the place."

Ren covers her mouth and shakes her head. "Oh, poor Griffin."

"That's not even the worst part. He wasn't good at deciding where to throw up, so he wound up getting the mayor right down the back. It was in the newspaper for at least a week."

"Oh no." She laughs some more. "He threw up on the mayor? That's horrible."

"Yeah, and the mayor at the time was a real dickhead and made Griff's life hell. And as you know, to this day, he won't have anything to do with eggplants."

"Well." Ren grips my shoulder. "This was a very wonderful and educational bump-in. Thank you."

"Anytime."

"Now let's go pay for these candles so you can impress that lady of yours."

I roll my eyes. "You sound like an eighty-year-old woman."

"I'm okay with that." She loops her arm in mine and leans her head on my shoulder. It feels good, like family, and that's exactly what she is.

Griffin: You fucking told her?????

Rogan: Ooo, told who what?

Brig: Must be bad if Griffin used five question marks. Don't you know, dude, one is sufficient. Text messaging has truly butchered the English language.

Reid: I'm not even sorry.

Griffin: You sold me out for CANDLES. What the fuck, man?

Rogan: **Leans in**

Brig: **Salivates**

Jen: Oh damn **cups ear**

Brig: Tell us, tell us what you did.

Griffin: He told Ren about the eggplant story in exchange for candles.

Reid: For the record, her idea, not mine.

Rogan: Oh damn.

Brig: Is that when you puked on the Ferris wheel?

Jen: Onto the mayor?

Griffin: That's the one. I was doing pretty damn well avoiding that story until Reid.

Reid: I don't have any regrets. I got some candles and it serves you right for opening your mouth to Ren about Eve. Let this be a reminder to all of you, I do not hold back.

Rogan: Sooo, if I told Harper, what would happen to me?

Brig: I vote kick him in the crotch. Kick him in the crotch!

Jen: ^^ I second that.

Griffin: It's only fair.

Rogan: Shut the fuck up, Griffin, you don't get a say.

Griffin: Eggplant story. He told my girlfriend the eggplant story.

Rogan: It could have been way worse.

Griffin: How so? Now she probably thinks of me as the guy who threw up on a Ferris wheel . . . when it wasn't even moving.

Reid: Whining doesn't look pretty on you, Griff.

Brig: Doesn't go well with your complexion.

Jen: You guys should see his face right now, bright red.

Rogan: Are his nostrils flared too?

Reid: Yes, can we get a nostril check?

Brig: Dying to know about the nostrils.

Jen: Nostrils are flared, I repeat, nostrils are flared. And that vein near his temple is throbbing.

Griffin: I hope you all enjoy hell together.

Reid: Let this serve as a reminder to all of you: don't fuck with me.

CHAPTER TEN

EVE

"I can't believe you actually returned my call," says Avery, one of my best friends from high school, her voice filtering through my phone. "Have you become a celebrity in Port Snow without telling me? Are you so inundated with autograph requests and appearances at Snow Roast that you couldn't possibly call your best friend back?" I can't help but smile. Typical Avery. I miss *one* phone call, and she acts like I never talk to her.

Walking down the hill where the Lighthouse Inn is situated, and toward Main Street, I secure my earbuds. Snow is piled up on the edges of the sidewalk, and the roads are slick with a fresh flurry from this morning. "Yup, I'm the queen of Port Snow. They have me living up in the mayor's house, and I have my own assistant who brings me afternoon tea every day. It's a grand life."

"You bitch, and you didn't tell me?"

We both laugh. "What I wouldn't give for an assistant who brings me afternoon tea every day. That would be the life," she says wistfully.

"How is the job, by the way? Loving it or hating it?"

Five years ago Avery moved from Port Snow to New York City to pursue her acting career. She was a huge theater geek growing up, was the lead in every Port Snow play, and even dabbled in some commercials here and there when she had a chance. But she didn't become completely serious until she finally dropped out of community college and fled to the city. Her parents were furious, and there was a moment, right around when my dad died, when she tried to toss away her dream, but I stopped her from calling it quits and coming home. She's meant to act.

But she hasn't had her big break yet, so her new job consists of singing show tunes and waitressing at a kitschy cabaret restaurant in Manhattan, where the special every night is a house-made meatloaf with cheesy mashed potatoes.

"Hating it," she groans. "Because I have blonde hair, my costume consists of lederhosen made from old drapes, and I spend every night singing songs from *The Sound of Music*. I mean, I should be honored, but every time I break into 'Do-Re-Mi,' I truly want to pistol-whip my own face."

A loud laugh rumbles up and out of my throat. "Oh, *please* send a picture. I really want to see you in that outfit."

"There will be no photographic evidence of this job. It's paying the bills until I hear back about a big audition I just had."

"Oooh, tell me about it."

"It's for a movie."

"What? Seriously? What kind?"

"Romantic comedy, of course. You know this all-American girl wasn't born for anything else." It's true—she's the perfect lead for any romantic comedy. Bubbly, sweet, energetic. She reminds me a lot of Reese Witherspoon.

"That's so exciting! How did the audition go?"

"Pretty well, I think. I mean, I'm trying not to get super excited about it, but I left feeling good. I'm hoping for a callback in the next few days."

"I'll have my fingers crossed." I make it down the hill, turn left onto Main Street, and head straight for the giant white building with red and teal accents: the Lobster Landing. The building is iconic in Port Snow, sitting right at the end of Main Street, which is a tourist mecca with a picnic-table courtyard, the Jake's Cakes food truck, and harbor-tour kiosks.

"What about you? What's been keeping you so busy that you couldn't call me back in over a week?"

If there's one person I can talk to about my current romantic relationship, it's Avery. She's known all about my crush on Reid since middle school, and she's quite aware of "the curse."

"So, I might have started a little relationship."

"A little *relationship*?" she shrieks. "With who? Oh my God, wait, let me guess. Hmm . . . is it Jake? I know you can't get enough of his crab cakes, plus he's so yummy."

"Not Jake."

"Okay, I mean, that would have been a good match, but I can let that one go. Hmm, oh, how about Oliver over at the general store? He's so mysterious, always churning his ice cream but not saying much besides what flavors he's making. Have you gotten him to open up?"

Oliver *is* kind of a mystery.

"No, not Oliver. He's a little too quiet for me."

"Fair enough. Okay, give me a second. I'm trying to think of all the single guys in Port Snow. Well, it's definitely not Tracker because you've told me before that his man-whore ways aren't for you. Right?"

"Correct."

"Well, if it's not Tracker and . . . oh wait." A smile crosses my face, but she says, "Caleb, it's got to be Caleb."

Oh boy. Maybe she's not as in tune with me as I thought she was.

"Didn't he recently get divorced? Look at you, snagging him. He's super sexy behind that camera of his."

The local photographer, Caleb, shoots everything from scenic pictures of Port Snow to weddings to graduations to boudoir. He lives high up on a hill in a little cottage that overlooks a cliff, which he might turn into a wedding venue. I believe he told Mrs. Davenport, who then told everyone, that if he couldn't make his marriage work, he could at least help others make some happy memories.

"It's not Caleb." I slow my pace, taking in the little shops on Main Street. I pass the local art gallery and peek inside the window, where I spot Beck, Port Snow's new artist and curator. I give him a quick wave, which he returns, and keep moving.

"Well, then I give up. Who else is there? I mean, yeah, there are some other singles hanging around, but none that we've talked about." She pauses and then laughs. "It could be a Knightly." More laughter fills my earbuds. "Yeah, like *that* would happen. Who's even left? Brig and Reid? Brig is way too—" She pauses, and I swear I can hear her mind working on overdrive. "Holy. Shit. Eve, are you seeing Reid Knightly?"

Why is it impossible to hold back a smile when I hear his name? Am I really that smitten?

"Might be him."

"Might be or *is*? I need some solid confirmation here because this is huge."

"Yes, it's Reid," I say quietly, making sure no one overhears me.

"Oh my God!" she screams. "You're dating Reid Knightly? Since when? For how long? Why did you not tell me right away? I'm so mad at you!"

"Settle down, okay? It's been a little over a week, and I honestly didn't really think it was the real deal at first."

"How did it happen?"

"Well, it kind of came out of nowhere. I think he's had feelings for me for a little while and decided to act on them."

"Of course he's had feelings for you—any person with eyes would be able to see that. So he made the first move?"

"Yeah, he likes to think I did, but it was totally him. It was the night of my dad's death anniversary; he was at the Inn and asked me to dance after he made me take a few shots."

"Nice. Got you all liquored up."

"That's what I thought, but I never really felt drunk. And the dancing, Avery, we're not talking about ballroom stuff; he was grinding up on me, and it was so freaking hot."

"Oh God, was he hard?"

"Yup."

"Ah! Then what happened?"

"I brought him back to my place because the roads were impossible to drive on. He came back, and well, I might have taken my shirt off."

"You hussy. I love it. So obviously you've had sex. Are the rumors true about Reid's assets?"

I knew she was going to ask. It's why I love Avery so much: she has no filter. "Let's just say he lives up to the legend."

"Oh damn. I'm fanning my face right now. Of course he lives up to it. The Knightlys are their own breed of man." I can't disagree with that. "So, this is kind of amazing. Are you giddy?"

"Maybe a little," I answer honestly. "He's just—God, Avery, he's the same guy who's always teasing me, but there is this other side of him, this relationship Reid, that makes me absolutely swoon."

"Aw, I'm so happy for you. Not at all jealous. Not even the slightest. No jealousy whatsoever."

"You're a little jealous."

She exhales. "It's Reid freaking Knightly. God, he's so sexy." He is, especially with all his clothes off. "All right," she says. "We need to change the subject before I turn green. How's school?"

"I'm in my last semester, and I just got done with midterms, which I aced, so I'm going to celebrate with some fudge."

"That's my girl. Last semester? I'm so proud of you. You impress me, Eve."

"Stop it—I should have gotten this degree years ago."

"But instead you chose to let your brother pursue his dreams while you worked at the Inn, took care of your mom and dad day in and day out, and studied every waking moment while taking online courses."

Though I barely even admit it to myself, Avery's right. My life *is* incredibly hard and time consuming, but it's worth every second I committed to my parents and to my studies. Back when I was taking care of my mom and dad, there were times when a few people from town would lend a hand, especially the Knightlys, but for the most part, I was on my own, keeping them company, making sure they were comfortable, showing that they were loved and appreciated.

"You are impressive," she continues. "And don't try to tell me otherwise. This is huge, and I couldn't be more proud."

"Thank you, Avery. It means a lot to me." I arrive at the entrance to the Lobster Landing and step to the side, near the giant lobster bench. "But hey, I should get going; the fudge is calling."

"Get the walnut!"

"As if there's any other kind. I promise not to go another week without talking to you."

"You'd better not. Love you, girl."

"Love you too." I hang up and take out my earbuds. I stick them in my purse along with my phone and open the door to the Lobster Landing, where I'm immediately greeted by the delicious smell of baked goods and fudge. There's a private door for locals in the back, where you can buy what you want and skip the crowds, but since it isn't tourist season, I take the opportunity to use the main door and take in the view.

The Lobster Landing is split into two sections—one is devoted to food, with a small bar and old-fashioned cash register, and the other is the souvenir side, where the Knightlys sell Port Snow–themed apparel and the kinds of lobster goodies that anyone visiting Maine would want to get their hands on. One thing I love about the store is that none of their stuff is cheap crap that people end up throwing out the second they get home. They sell quality items like oven mitts, T-shirts, hats, and wooden lobster spoons. They also have blueberry-flavored everything in the back. Pancake mixes, syrup, bread . . . beer. It's a blueberry paradise. Avery always asks for blueberry-flavored white-chocolate-covered pretzels for her birthday, and it's become our tradition that I send them to her every year.

No one is at the fudge counter, so I make my way there first, taking a moment to peruse the multitude of flavors. I play with the idea of going with something new, but in the end, I always end up with walnut.

"Eve, how nice to see you," Jen says, stepping up to the counter. There is a huge smile on her face, and I know exactly why.

"Go ahead, get it out of your system."

Flying around the counter, Jen rushes toward me with her arms held out. In three seconds flat, she has me wrapped up in a giant hug and is squeezing every last ounce of air out of me. "Oh my gosh, I can't even contain how excited I am that you and—"

"Shhhh," I say before she can say Reid's name. "It's not public knowledge."

"Oh." She laughs. "Sorry. I'm just so excited." She pulls away and cups my cheeks. "I can't believe you're going to be my sister-in-law."

"Whoa." I pull her hands down. "It's been a little over a week. Let's cool your tits for a second, Jen."

"Please." She waves a hand in front of her face. "You two have been meant to be since you were ten years old. I just can't believe it's finally happening. I think we need to celebrate."

I hold up my hand. "Please don't. I beg of you. No Knightly party. He's a little skittish as it is. I think a party would throw him."

"Reid, skittish? Are you kidding me? That boy has been floating around the store today. Yes, *floating*. He's in such a good mood it's throwing us all off."

"He's here?"

In that moment, two strong arms wrap around my waist, and a familiar pair of lips presses against my cheek.

I sink into his touch even though warning bells are going off in my head, reminding me that we're in public, where anyone can see us.

"Yes, I'm here." Reid's deep voice sends a chill right down my spine as he spins me around to face him. "What are you doing at the Landing? Looking for some eye candy?"

Reaching up, I quickly run my hand up his scruffy jaw and then pull away, remembering where we are. "Just getting some fudge."

He doesn't let me get far because he pulls me in close again and tips my chin up. He presses the softest of kisses against my lips, and I swear I melt right there on the spot.

So much for being able to keep this a secret.

"Oh my God, you two. I can't even." We both turn to face Jen, who has her hand clutched to her chest, the other pressed against the fudge counter. "The cuteness is overwhelming."

I push Reid away, but he treats me like a yo-yo and pulls me right back in, grinning.

"What happened to keeping this a secret?" I whisper as he presses another kiss to my temple.

He groans. "Fuck, I forgot." He glances behind us, but the shop is pretty desolate—a rarity I'm grateful for. "Coast is clear; let's make out."

"Stop it." I push at his chest, putting a good two feet between us.

"You have to watch out for that one." Jen points to her brother. "He's horny. As a teenager he would never leave his room; it was—"

"Can we not? Christ, Jen."

I grin. "Your teenage years are no secret to anyone, Reid. Sorry to say, but your one-handed escapades are public knowledge at this point."

"Fantastic," he says.

"I want to say it's sweet, but I mean . . . it's really not." I laugh, which only makes Reid roll his eyes.

"So, you want fudge." Smart man that he is, Reid quickly changes the subject and leads me over to the fudge counter before stepping behind it. "Since I know you're not an avid fudge eater and only buy some when you're celebrating—what's the occasion?"

I haven't really told anyone except for Avery about my classes. After staying back in Port Snow to help my parents, I realized quickly not to overshare, especially not with anyone in town. When I started going back to school, I wasn't even sure how far I'd make it, and the last thing I wanted was to become the town's resident failure—the girl who tried but never earned a degree. So I kept it a secret, only letting Avery and Eric know.

It's a big deal, though—I know it is—and I'm so close to actually having a degree. So do I mention it to Reid? Technically he's my boyfriend, and this is something I would tell him, something I should be proud to tell him.

But for some stupid reason, I'm nervous.

I glide my finger over the fudge counter's smooth top. "Uh, just celebrating midterms."

"Midterms." When I glance up at him, there's a crease in his brow. "Like *college* midterms?"

I bite the side of my cheek and nod.

"You're going to college?"

"Yeah," I answer. "I've been taking online classes." Jen apparently has no problem listening in on our conversation because she leans against the wall, turning her head back and forth between Reid and me.

"Since when?"

"For a while now, about seven years. I'm in my last semester, actually."

"Seriously?" Reid adjusts his signature Lobster Landing ball cap. "Shit, Eve, how come you never said anything?"

I shrug. "Didn't really tell anyone. Avery and Eric know, and that's about it."

"So you've been taking online classes this entire time in secret? Babe, that's . . . amazing." His face lights up, and he comes back around the counter to give me a hug just as Jen interjects, a finger pointed in the air.

"Um, he called you *babe*; I think I might go cry into a fudge pan— that's so adorable."

"Not now, Jen," Reid huffs, placing a kiss on my head. "Eve, I can't believe you've been getting your degree this whole time. I'm truly . . . wow, I'm amazed. What are you majoring in?"

"Business." I try to tamp down the blush I feel creeping on my cheeks. "Since I've been managing so much at the Inn, I thought it was a good fit. And surprisingly, I really enjoy it."

"Well, damn. I'm proud of you."

And that's the second time in thirty minutes someone has said that to me. It feels good. I'm not one to fish for validation—I know how well I'm doing—but ever since my parents passed . . . well, I'd be lying if I said I didn't miss hearing those four words.

I'm proud of you.

Those are the words that justify my years of hard work, and they mean more to me than anything else.

"Thank you."

He squeezes me again and walks behind the counter, a giant smile on his face and awe in his eyes. "So what do you mean, you're celebrating midterms? Are they over? Did you get your grades back?"

"Yes and yes. Aced all of them."

"Damn." Reid whistles and then elbows Jen in the boob—she grasps her chest and scowls. "My girl is a genius. Did you hear that? Aced all of her midterms."

"I heard it. You didn't need to puncture my boob to tell me."

Not even a little bit apologetic, Reid turns back to me. "I'm guessing you're going with the walnut?"

"Yes, please. Just a quarter."

Reid cuts the fudge but keeps looking up at me and smiling. It's adorable. He wraps the fudge up in a signature white Lobster Landing box with red-and-white string and then hands it over to me.

"On the house, babe. Congrats."

"No, I can't do that. Let me pay."

He and Jen exchange glances and laugh. "You're dating a Knightly," Jen says.

"And along with amazing sex, I come with free fudge and treats," Reid cuts in, eliciting another scowl from Jen.

"Don't talk about sex."

"Yes," I agree. "Please don't talk about sex in front of your sister."

"We're an open family. Aren't we, Jen?" Reid pulls his sister into a hug and rubs his knuckles against her head. She swats at him and attempts to push him away, but he has at least a good fifty pounds of muscle on her, making escape impossible.

"Reid, quit it." She cocks her arm back, but before she can hit him square in the crotch, he releases her, and she flips her head up, her long brown hair a complete mess. Anger in her eyes, she takes off toward the back of the Landing, muttering something I can't quite make out.

"Real mature," I say as he turns to me with a huge grin.

He shrugs and leans on the counter, his eyes like pools of blue shining from beneath the bill of his hat. "Besides fudge, what do you have planned for tonight? Want to celebrate with me?"

"From the glint in your eyes I'm going to guess you want to get naked."

"Is there any other way to celebrate?"

I hold the fudge up. "Yup, with confectionary sugars."

I take a few steps backward as he says, "Your place, after your shift tonight. I'll be on your bed, butt-ass naked, legs spread, showing off the goods."

A laugh pops out of me, and I shake my head, still headed for the exit. "Please don't have your legs spread."

"Oh, they're going to be spread so fucking wide that you won't know what to do with yourself."

"That's terrifying."

"Get ready to celebrate, Eve. The party starts in our pants."

"I hate you right now. That is so lame."

Griffin steps out from the back of the store and pats Reid on the shoulder. "Party in your pants, bro? That's lame."

Reid shrugs him off. "No one asked you. This is a conversation between me and Eve."

"Listen to your brother," I call out when I reach the door. "And think of some better lines." I give him a quick wave and then head outside, the bell ringing above me as I tuck the fudge under my arm.

This shift at the Inn is going to be the longest of my life. Even though the whole *legs spread* thing is kind of weird, I can't deny the excitement that's bubbling up inside of me at the thought of seeing Reid naked in my bed when I get home.

My phone buzzes in my pocket, and without looking at the screen, I know exactly who it is.

Reid: No kiss?

Smiling, I text him back.

Eve: You did enough kissing in there. I'll be shocked if there isn't a write-up about us tomorrow morning.

Reid: Wouldn't be the worst thing in the world, especially since I'm suffering now, being deprived of your lips.

Eve: Pretty sure you'll survive.

Reid: No way I'll be able to wait until tonight. You looked so fucking good.

On a whim, I turn back to the shop and text him back.

Eve: Trying to get on my good side?

I open the shop door and spot Reid leaning on the counter, looking down at his phone. When he glances up, pure joy spreads across his face. He rounds the counter and quickly pulls me into an embrace. Lifting my chin up, he presses his lips against mine, his hold strong, his mouth desperate, but before we get too lost in the moment, I pull away.

"You're a fucking tease."

"You said you wanted a kiss, so there you go, Knightly. I'll see you tonight, and for the love of God, keep your legs closed. You didn't lose the key I gave you?"

"Never, babe. You're getting the full show when you get home."

Why is that terrifying and thrilling all at the same time?

CHAPTER ELEVEN

REID

"There you are."

I shut the fridge, and my dad appears on the other side, wearing his classic black-and-red buffalo plaid flannel shirt tucked into a pair of dark-washed Wranglers. Seeing him in anything other than plaid and Wranglers means either someone's getting married or someone passed away.

Guess I should be glad he's wearing plaid and Wranglers right now, especially with the irritated look on his face.

I take the Tupperware of chili to the counter and start serving myself a decent bowl to heat up. "What's up, Dad?" I place a paper towel over the bowl and nuke it for two minutes.

"Did you get my text the other day? That I want to talk to you?"

"Yeah, I did." I put the Tupperware back in the fridge, carefully avoiding eye contact.

"Were you going to respond?"

"I was, but I've been a little busy."

Dad crosses his arms over his bulky chest, his posture as familiar as my own. Tall and broad, my brothers and I all inherited the Knightly physique, but we're not nearly as sensitive as my dad. Intimidating as he is on the outside, once you get to know Clint Knightly, you soon realize you could make him cry at just the mention of his grandchildren or children. He's a giant teddy bear who spends his days coming up with fudge flavors and spoiling everyone he loves—me included.

It's why when he crosses those arms I don't cower. I know it's just a front.

"Heard you and Eve Roberts have become close."

Of course he has.

"Who told you?" I ask as the microwave beeps. I reach in, grab my bowl, and take it to the dining table, where Dad joins me with a basket of cornbread and a bowl of tortilla chips.

"Doesn't matter who told me."

"Dad . . ."

Chuckling, he leans back in his chair and drums his knuckles on the table. "It was Brig."

"Fucking idiot," I mutter and take a bite of the chili. "I swear he can't keep anything to himself."

"In his defense, he was so excited that he had to tell someone."

"Oh, I'm sure he did. He doesn't have any self-control."

"He's just a romantic like your father." Dad plucks a chip from the bowl, scoops some of my chili, and pops it in his mouth.

"At least you know when to keep a secret."

"That I do." He clears his throat. "So, think you can carve out some time to talk to your old man?"

"What's it about?"

"Your future."

Those two words make my entire nutsac shrivel up. *Your future.* How many times has my dad had this conversation with me? More than I can count, and every time it consists of him trying to get me out of my "rut," as he likes to say. I know he's worried, and for a good reason—I'm not the same guy that I was a few years ago. My drive is gone, and I just can't bring myself to look for more in my life. But all his "talks," all his worries . . . all they do is push me further and further away from my old dreams.

"Spare me the lecture, Dad. I'm not interested."

"This isn't a lecture."

"No, it's you expressing your concerns. I get it. I'm not like my brothers—I don't have a thriving business to call my own. I'm not like Jen—I don't have a family to come home to. I'm a fuckup who lives on a houseboat with nothing to his name besides a few hundred in the bank account. We can't all be perfect, Dad."

"I'm not asking you to be perfect."

"Not outright, but I can see it in your eyes. I'm an embarrassment to the family. The black sheep, the one child who has literally nothing going for him except a girl who seems to have lost her mind and decided to date him. But trust me, I'm sure I'll fuck that up too." What is she even doing with me in the first place? The girl is so goddamn ambitious. For the past seven years she's been earning her college degree in business, on top of working full time and everything else she's gone through. Isn't she afraid I'll hold her back? Because I am.

It wasn't until she told me about going to school that I really saw the vast difference between our lives. She's thriving and I'm stagnant. Will she realize I'm not good enough for her?

I'm the Knightly who's not going anywhere. Why would anyone want to attach themselves to that?

"Now listen here." My dad's voice grows angry, but I don't give him time to finish.

My spoon clanks against my bowl as I push back from the table and make my way down the hall to the front door.

"Thanks for the chili, Dad, but I've lost my appetite."

"Reid, I'm trying to talk to you," his voice booms from behind me.

"How many times have I told you that I don't want to have that conversation?" I yell back. "Just let me be. Let me be the family fuckup.

I'm fine with that as long as everyone just stays out of my goddamn business."

"Reid."

The door shuts behind me before Dad can get in another word. There's no doubt in my mind that I'll be getting a call from Griffin later about disrespecting him, but I'm not going to worry about that right now. I just need to get far, far away.

Carve some time out for him. Like I really want to fucking find time to hear about my mistakes all over again. I'm well aware of where I've fallen short. I don't need a reminder—I live with my failure every damn day of my life.

◆ ◆ ◆

"Why are you sitting in the dark?" Eve asks, stepping into her apartment and switching on the light before tossing her things to the side. "And why aren't you naked, on the bed, legs spread?"

I don't answer. Instead I sip my beer and stare out the window from my spot on her couch. Numb. It's how I've felt ever since I left my parents' house. I debated even showing up at Eve's tonight but knew that if I didn't, she'd be coming to the houseboat, and I didn't want her to drive down to the harbor after a long shift.

"Hey, what's going on?" She sits down next to me on her couch and takes my face in her hands, tilting my head toward her.

"Rough day."

She studies me, her beautiful hazel eyes searching for any kind of clue. "Am I missing something? Last time I saw you, you couldn't not smile. What happened in the last six hours?"

"Nothing I want to bother you with." I let out a deep breath and, trying to pull it together, put my arm around her and ask, "How was work?"

"No way, not happening. You are *not* going to deflect. Talk to me, Reid."

I drag my hand down my face. "I really don't want to get into it, okay? It's just going to ruin the night."

"Well, that's already happened since you weren't naked." She crawls onto my lap and faces me, the warmth in her eyes starting to thaw the icy walls I threw up the minute my dad tried to get serious. "Talk to me."

I run my hand up her thigh, wishing she didn't have pants on right about now. "How about we skip the talking and strip instead."

I reach for the zipper on her jeans, but she stops me. "Or we can talk, and then you can do whatever you want to me in the bedroom."

"Whatever I want?" I ask, brow raised.

"Within reason. I have some hard nos."

I think it over. I mean, anything I want. I think I can suck it up for that particular reward.

"Remember, we were friends first, which means you used to tell me things. Don't stop now that you can get in my pants."

I chuckle. "You're so fucking eloquent."

"I pride myself on it." She tugs on my shirt. "Come on. How about for every thing you tell me, I'll take off a piece of clothing. How does that sound?"

"Promising," I answer, my hands slipping under her shirt, my mood already lightening. "How about we start with this." I lift her shirt up and over her head, revealing a purple lace bra. Damn. I don't think I've ever seen more perfect tits on a woman. Not super huge—just two perfect handfuls.

Needing more, I reach for the front clasp of her bra, but she quickly swats me away. "I gave you a shirt, so now you give me some details about your day."

"Fine," I huff. "My dad wanted to, as he put it, *carve out some time to talk*."

"That doesn't seem so bad. What did he want to talk about?"

I shake my head. "Pants. I want the pants off before I answer."

Sighing, she stands and strips out of her jeans, revealing a matching pair of lace boy shorts. God, those are hot, and see through. She proceeds to sit back on my lap, where I'm sure she can feel my growing excitement.

"First he mentioned how we were dating. Brig told him," I say. Eve rolls her eyes. "Tell me about it. Apparently Brig just *had* to tell someone else."

"Great. So you talked about us, but that can't be why you're so upset."

"Nope." I reach up and pop the front clasp of her bra. Her tits spring forward, and my mouth waters. Fuck, I'm not going to be able to sit here without touching her for too long.

She shrugs off her bra and squeezes her boobs together with both hands before giving them a little nipple tweak.

"What the hell are you doing?" I ask, the zipper of my jeans starting to cut into my hard-on.

"Trying to hurry you along."

"Christ, Eve, don't play with your nipples."

"Mmm, but it feels so good." Her head rolls back.

"Future!" My voice cracks. "He wanted to talk about my future. This wasn't the first time he's talked about it, and I know it won't be the last. He's not happy with my life, and he's always trying to fix it, which just reminds me of what a loser I am, of how I've fallen short." The words rush out of me so fast that I can barely remember saying them.

She lifts her head and meets my gaze. "You haven't fallen short."

"Don't." I shake my head. "Let's drop it, okay?"

"Reid, don't shut me out. If you're upset, let's talk about it."

I groan and press my palms to my eyes, wishing I'd never started this conversation. "The last thing I want to do right now is talk about this shit—not when you're almost completely naked on my lap."

"Then I'll get dressed." She moves to pick up her clothes, and I quickly slide her down on the couch, trapping her beneath my body.

"You're not getting fucking dressed."

"Well, you're not fucking me until we talk about this."

"Why? Why the hell do you want to talk about this? It's only going to make you want me less. Do you really think I want to talk about my shortcomings with you only wearing underwear?"

"Do you really think I'm that shallow?" she shoots back.

"No, but I do know you could be with anyone you want, and I'm just the lucky asshole who happened to hit on you at the right time during a blizzard."

"So you admit you made the first move?" Her eyes light up.

I lean down and press a kiss against her nose. "I'm admitting to liking you a lot and not wanting to spoil that with talk about what I'm doing with my life."

"I understand that." She presses her hand against my cheek, and I lean into her touch. "But I've known you for a long time, Reid. I know all about your life. If I didn't like it, we wouldn't be together. So share with me, because it's not going to change my mind about you."

"It might."

"It won't," she says fiercely. "I understand if you don't want to talk about it. I wish you would, but I get it. You need time to trust me."

"What?" I furrow my brow. "I trust you, Eve. I trust you just as much as my family. I just . . . fuck." I breathe out heavily, hating every second of this. "I don't open up much—or at all, really. I don't with my family, and I never really did with Eric. Emotion has always meant weakness for me—ever since culinary school, when we didn't have time to feel emotion. Back then we were trained to just react, to feel nothing. So it's going to take me time to adjust to opening up."

"Okay." She smiles, but I can see the sadness in her eyes, and I hate that I caused it. I hate that I made her think she's not important enough or that I don't trust her. I don't want to talk about my life because I have no idea what the fuck I'm doing with it. Ever since that night in New Orleans, I've been trapped in this standstill, this purgatory, with no end in sight. Cursed or not, I have to start over, and I have no idea where to begin or how to do it, but I know I need to do it alone.

"I'm sorry," I whisper, shame hitting me hard in the chest.

"Don't be. It's fine. Can I just say one thing?"

"Sure."

She runs her hand through my hair, starting at my brow and moving down to my ear. Her touch sinks into my bones, easing the self-loathing I've been storing there.

"Don't shut out your family," she says. "I've lost two parents, and I would give anything at this point to get one more lecture from them, one more conversation about my life. Or just to hear their voice, listen to their wisdom. I know you're hurting, Reid, but also remember—your family is your heart. They're a part of you, and you never know what might happen. Your dad loves you and only wants the best. Give him a chance, and honor that love by listening to him."

Well. Fuck.

"Eve, I'm so sorry; I wasn't thinking. I have no right to complain."

"Don't apologize. You don't need to. Just give it some thought, okay?"

I nod, already resolving to call my dad tomorrow. Eve's words sink in, reminding me of the devastation etched across her face the day of her dad's funeral. I promised myself then that I'd make a conscious effort to be closer to my family, to appreciate the fact that I still had them in my life.

That was then.

I've forgotten that promise. Looks like I just needed a little reminder.

CHAPTER TWELVE

EVE

"Hey, stranger."

A tall figure looms over me as a smooth, seductive voice pulls me from my work. Only one man can make my entire body light up with excitement with just the sound of his voice.

I look up to find Reid standing in front of me, wearing his worn-out jeans and Lobster Landing shirt, looking absolutely perfect.

"Hey, you." I can't hold back my smile. I've spent my day off in Snow Roast, our local coffee shop, trying to get some studying in— and hoping Reid might stop by. I did mention my study plans to him, after all.

Yeah, I dropped subtle hints, and I'm not ashamed of it.

I'm so glad he took those hints, because seeing him does more than just tip up the corners of my mouth—it puts me at ease, shows me that this man is mine.

"This seat taken?" he asks, pointing to the empty armchair beside me.

"All yours."

Coffee in one hand and a paper bag in the other, he sits down and says, "I didn't get you any coffee, since I saw that you already have some, but I did bring some scones from the Landing."

"And Ruth is okay with that?" I ask, worried that the coffee shop owner might take offense to having outside food in her establishment.

"Yeah, she's good—right, Ruth?" Reid shouts across the shop, holding up his bag.

She winks. "All good, Knightly."

"See?" Reid turns back to me. "We have an understanding. I buy copious amounts of coffee from her every week, and she lets me bring my girl a scone while she's studying."

"Your girl, huh? Did you tell her that?"

"Nah." He leans back in his chair and pulls out a blueberry scone. "But she knows we're friends. Plus I told her the other day that I wanted to try her new blueberry coffee while eating a blueberry scone, *and* I promised to bring her one so she could try it too."

"Ahh." I put my pencil behind my ear and set my book down. "Bribing the shop owner. Makes sense." I lay out a napkin on my lap and place the scone down before breaking off a piece and popping it in my mouth.

God, it's so good.

It's no secret that the Lobster Landing has not only the best fudge in town but the best baked goods as well. Ruth doesn't even bother serving anything but muffins and breakfast sandwiches in her shop because there's no point competing. Although she has started carrying some of the Lobster Landing's baked goods for people who don't want to walk the two blocks, and she sells out immediately.

But the scones, they're my absolute favorite. They remind me of the scones my grandma used to make before she passed. I didn't get much time with her, but the time we did have was spent in the kitchen making apple-cinnamon scones. Of course that's where Eric caught the cooking bug, from our grandma, and why he's so good at not just cooking but baking too. Dare I say that our scones are even better than the Knightly recipe?

These are a good second option, though.

"How's the studying coming along?"

"Good. I can't wait for school to finally be over. I'm kind of sick of it. For a tiny moment, I considered going for a master's, but I chucked that idea right out the window the minute I started this last semester. I think my bachelor's is good enough for now."

"I don't think I could ever go back to school."

"No?"

He shakes his head and sips his coffee. "Nah, I was never good at that shit."

"Wasn't culinary school all about studying and taking tests?"

"Yeah, but in a different way. It was more challenging than anything, and I enjoyed that." He looks out at the coffee shop, and I wonder if he's thinking about all the fun he used to have making things, coming up with new recipes, and testing them out on friends and family. That was the Reid who would come up with the craziest concoctions with Eric and then sit me down at the Knightly dinner table just so he could force me to try out their "latest and greatest" recipe. Some dishes were surprisingly delicious given the unheard-of combinations, and some made me run to the bathroom faster than I could put my fork down. I miss that Reid; he was so full of life, so excited.

Don't get me wrong: I like Reid the way he is, but there was a certain spark in his eye when he was in the kitchen. It was where he belonged, where he still belongs. I just wish he would find his way back.

Clearing his throat, he nudges my foot with his. "So, I texted my dad this morning—told him to pick a time and place so we can meet up to talk."

"Really?" He took my advice. My heart warms at the thought.

"Yeah, really. You were right."

"Wow." I sit up in my seat and hold out a pen and paper to him. "Can I get that in writing so I can use it against you in the future?"

He chuckles, the sound rumbling over me. "Never, Roberts."

"Figures." I cross my legs. "So what do you think he's going to talk to you about?"

"I don't know. Probably wants me to work with his friend up in Pottsmouth again. He suggested it a year ago, and I refused."

"Who?"

"Willy Kneader." Such an unfortunate name. "He runs a fishing company up there. Dad said I would make more money if I had better gear and a boat that didn't threaten to sink every time I took it out to sea, but I don't want to be working for someone else. I like my hours. Plus I enjoy being on my boat by myself. I like the solitude. The last thing I want is to hang out with a bunch of guys I don't know while they bro out. I'm good. But I'll hear what my dad has to say, let him know why I don't want to work with Willy, and leave it at that."

"Willy Kneader . . . was he the one with the daughter who asked that famous football player to prom, and he said yes?"

"Yeah. Gabby Kneader. He wound up taking out all their friends in a stretch limo. Rogan was so jealous. I think he told Harper at the time that she should have pulled the same stunt just so he could meet Joe Garrison."

"That's right. He was whoring his own girlfriend out for his personal gain. I remember that. Harper was so mad because Rogan made it seem like the football guy was more important than her."

Reid leans forward and looks over his shoulder before saying, "I think at the time Rogan would have taken Joe over Harper."

"No way." I shove him back in his seat. "Rogan was so in love with Harper. Even though I was just a sophomore watching them as seniors, I knew what infatuation looked like, and Rogan couldn't ever take his eyes off Harper. I remember wishing a guy would look at me like that one day."

"Yeah?" Reid asks, staring me down. "Am I looking at you like that right now?"

"Oh yeah, and it's giving me all kinds of butterflies," I deadpan. "Please stop. My heart can't take it."

"Sorry, babe. Can't help myself when I'm with you."

"Shut up." I nudge him with my foot. "It wouldn't kill you to be more romantic."

"You don't think I'm romantic?" His eyes widen. "What do you call the way I sucked on your clit last night? If that's not romantic, I don't know what is." He crosses his bulky arms and huffs.

"Say it a little louder next time," I whisper, glancing around. "And that's not romantic—that's being a sexual deviant."

"Sexual *deviant?*" A hearty laugh pops past his lips. "If I'm a sexual deviant, then you're Satan's mistress after the blow job you gave me this morning."

"Reid," I hiss.

"What?" He shrugs. "That was some good sucking, babe. Nearly sucked me to my knees."

"Oh my God." I go to pack my things, but the devil of a man grabs my wrist and pulls me onto his lap, right in front of everyone in the coffeehouse. A few people turn, watching us with wide eyes; others just ignore us altogether. "What the hell are you doing?" I whisper out of the side of my mouth.

He cups my cheek and draws my face close to his. "Trying to make it into the newspaper as the most romantic guy in town." He presses just a whisper of a kiss across my mouth, teasing me, taunting me. He knows how much I get lost in his kisses, and he's using that to his advantage.

When he pulls away, I run my tongue across my lips, tasting his blueberry coffee. And even though we're in public, in goddamn Snow Roast no less, I can't seem to pry myself off his lap, not when he makes me so completely happy.

"You're not playing fair, Knightly. You can't kiss me like that and think I don't want more."

"Do you want more?"

"You know I do."

"Then take it," he says, challenge in his voice.

"People will take pictures, sell them to the newspaper. We'll be the talk of the town. Tales will be spun about us, and an innocent kiss in Snow Roast will quickly turn into a sexual encounter on the espresso machine. You know how things get out of hand."

"As long as they make my penis seem even bigger than it already is, I'm cool with anything." His free hand wanders up the back of my shirt, his warm palm pressing against my spine.

"Do you know how juvenile that sounds?"

"Hey, if you want, I can put in a good word for your boobs. Instead of mosquito bites, I can ask them to make some embellishments."

"What?" I pinch his side. He squeaks and laughs at the same time. "I do *not* have mosquito bites. Last night you practically gagged on them."

"Look who's twisting the truth now. You're hanging out with me too much, Roberts."

"Yeah, maybe I should do something about that. Maybe call off our little get-together tonight. Not sure I'll make it to the houseboat."

"What?" He pouts. "But I bought sexy candles. They smell like man."

"As appealing as that sounds, I think I'll have to pass." I rub my thumb over his jaw and down his neck as he leans in for another kiss.

"Come on, I'll bring the good tongue action."

"Oh, the good tongue action. What have I been getting then? Mediocre?"

"Slightly above average. I have some tricks up my sleeve I've been meaning to show you."

"I don't believe you."

He shifts me on his lap so I can feel just how excited he is to have me there. Men. They're impossible.

"Fine, don't believe me." His hands slide to the waistband of my pants, and his fingers slowly inch beneath it.

I stop him quickly.

"Don't you dare."

"What?" His smile is wicked. "I'm just trying to get my fill since you won't come over tonight."

He slips his hand farther down.

"Reid. I'm warning you. Not here."

His grin widens. "Are you shy, Eve?" A few more inches. "You didn't care when I had my hand down your pants on the dance floor. So why now?"

"Reid . . ." He tickles my backside, and I nearly fly off his lap while laughter spills from him, filling the coffee shop. "I hate you so much."

"No you don't." He continues to laugh, pinching my chin with his forefinger and thumb, lowering my mouth to his. "Just say you'll come over tonight, and all of this will be over."

"Blackmail."

"I'm not ashamed. Come over tonight. I want to show you how twisted my tongue can get." His tongue flicks out against my lips, and my legs clench together from the sheer thought. Ugh, how I wish he didn't have this effect on me.

"Fine," I mutter, giving in way too easily. "But if there's no twisty tongue action, I'm leaving."

"Trust me, babe," he whispers. "There will be so much twisty tongue action that you'll be screaming my name, begging for release."

A girl can only hope.

◆ ◆ ◆

"Reid, please," I moan, my hands strapped above me, my legs spread across the bed, and Reid's head between my thighs.

"Mm, I love when you beg." He flicks his tongue across my clit and then pulls away, watching as my body writhes up and down, almost thrashing as I try to ease the ache pounding through my very core.

"I'm so close. I need to come."

His hand presses against my stomach. "I understand that, babe, but I'm just going to hang out here for a second."

Reid wasn't kidding when he said *twisty tongue action.* For the past five minutes, he's been swirling his tongue in all different directions, applying pressure to my clit, giving me the best buildup to an orgasm I've ever experienced.

Sparks of pleasure shoot up my limbs as excitement builds and builds at the base of my spine to the point that tears are welling in my eyes.

Breasts heavy, nipples taut from his continuous pinching, I'm past aroused and ready to tip over the edge into the oblivion any second.

Why I thought tying my arms to the headboard was a good idea I'll never know, because I have zero control. But God, does it feel so good.

Spreading my legs even wider, I thrust my pelvis toward his mouth, but he simply presses sweet kisses up and down my inner thighs.

"I can't take it any longer," I say, losing my last vestige of cool. "Please, Reid."

"Patience, Eve. I love seeing you like this, and I want to soak it all in."

"You're tormenting me. I'm so fucking ready, Reid. Please. I'm wet, throbbing, aching for your cock. Please, just fuck me." The words fly out of me.

He growls and reaches to the nightstand, ripping open a condom and sheathing himself in a matter of seconds.

Thank God.

On his knees, he leans forward and takes one of my nipples into his mouth while he enters me.

Yes.

He's so amazing.

Everything about this man makes me ache. His voice, the way he walks, the way he can just reach out and tweak my nipple without even thinking about it. He's confident in the bedroom, protective but also commanding with every one of his movements. There's a reason I crushed on him for so long.

As he slides, smooth as velvet, inside of me, I watch as his well-defined abs ripple with each inch he takes until he's fully inside. He abandons my breast and lifts my hips up off the mattress, holding my bottom half in the air as he pumps into me.

Slowly at first, he develops a mind-numbing rhythm that teases me, builds on the throbbing ache in my core. And then, his pace picks up; his hips swivel into mine, sparking a spot inside me that shoots a bolt of lightning right up my spine.

I clutch my bound hands together and thrust up as he thrusts in and hits that spot again.

"Yes, oh fuck, Reid, right there."

Again, he pounds into me.

And again.

And again, until a wave of raw bliss sweeps through me. My mouth is open, but no sound comes out as my body shakes in Reid's hands. I grind against him, my orgasm possessing me, as he comes too, his body stilling, his grunts spurring me on.

It feels like our orgasms last forever until we both slowly float back to reality, small spasms here and there racking through the both of us. Reid reaches up and unties my hands. I quickly wrap my arms around him and bury my head in his warmth, seeking solace from the insane ride my body just went through.

All at once I feel like crying, cheering, and doing it all over again. What the fuck is wrong with me? With my emotions running haywire, I hide in his shoulder, not ready to face reality—or him.

Gently, he rubs my back, his body still connected with mine. "Hey, are you okay?" His voice is soft, soothing.

I nod against him.

"Are you sure? I didn't push you too hard, did I?"

I shake my head, not able to voice anything.

He lifts my chin and forces me to meet his gaze. I can feel the tears that want to spill over. I try to count to ten, holding them back, not wanting to seem like the lunatic girlfriend who cries after really intense sex.

"Hey, what's going on? Did I hurt you?"

"No," I squeak.

"Did I upset you? I'm sorry if I—"

"Everything was perfect." I press a kiss against his lips. "Just perfect."

"Okay," he drawls out. "Then why are you so upset?"

"I'm not upset. I just . . ." I take a deep breath to prevent any stammering. I need him to know what he means to me, what this means to me. "I just . . . I really like you, Reid."

Satisfaction curls his mouth as he snuggles in closer, his large, sinewy body enveloping me. His voice blissfully happy, he says, "I like you a lot too, Eve."

And with that, I fall asleep in his arms.

CHAPTER THIRTEEN

REID

ALERT: NEW LOVE IS BLOOMING IN THE SNOW

Reid Knightly and Eve Roberts—a couple?

There have been mumblings of a possible romantic romp between the second-to-youngest Knightly and his best friend's sister, Eve Roberts, but that's all they were, mumblings among our town's finest.

Rare sightings, here and there, of them talking closely.

A playful fight in the snow.

An unreliable and drunk source reported that they danced at the Lighthouse Inn one snowy night. But there's been nothing concrete until now.

That's right, Port Snow. Hold on to your loins and find yourself a comfortable surface to swoon onto. We have it on great authority that Eve Roberts (26) and Reid Knightly (26) have been spotted at the very popular Snow Roast, not only canoodling but also making out with intensely wandering hands. Let's just say Reid Knightly was fishing for more than just lobster.

We're not sure how long this little tryst has been going on, but we do know the hens around town have their eyes open for any future sightings.

We can honestly say that this is one coupling we are very happy about. After all, who doesn't love a little friend-to-lovers, best-friend's-sister romance?

But does this mean the infamous curse has been lifted for the once aspiring chef turned sexiest fisherman in Port Snow? Only time will tell.

Shaking my head, I fold the article and stick it in my back pocket as I let out a low chuckle. Eve was right; it's absolutely ridiculous. And "aspiring" chef? Pretty sure I *was* a chef.

Fucking Port Snow and the nosy bastards who live here.

I check the time on my phone and then stare down the hall of my parents' house toward the front door. I parked it at the dining room table, not just so I can keep an eye on the entryway but so I could also enjoy a nice piece of leftover cherry pie. My dad isn't the only one who knows how to bake—my mom makes the best pies ever.

Dad wanted to take me out to eat and talk, but I told him meeting at the house was fine. Honestly, I think he wanted a public setting so I couldn't walk out on him again, but I wanted neutral ground in case he said something that pissed me off.

I remember Eve's words and resolve to have an open mind about what he's going to say—and to be grateful for his love and support. I'm going into this meeting with the best attitude I'm capable of mustering.

It helps that right before I left for my parents' house, I had Eve up against the wall of her apartment. Her moans are still fresh in my ears.

That fucking woman. I swear to God, being inside of her is something magical. I've never experienced anything like it. The way she claws at me, her moans, her unbridled passion. It's like I'm drunk on her, and yet I can't quite get enough.

She likes me a lot, and fuck if the sentiment isn't returned in full force. I have a feeling I like her too goddamn much.

I shovel a scoop of pie in my mouth and shoot her a text. The girl is always on my mind.

Reid: I can still smell you on me.

The Inn must not be busy because she texts right back.

Eve: Good or bad?

Reid: Really good. What's your perfume?

Eve: It's called Sex Addict.

Reid: Really?

Eve: No, LOL. It's Ralph Lauren.

Reid: I mean, I wouldn't mind if you wore a perfume called Sex Addict. I would be cool with that.

Eve: So glad you approve. If we're exchanging confessions, I can still feel the burn of your scruff on my inner thighs.

Reid: That's hot.

Eve: Please don't tell me you're texting me this in front of your dad.

Reid: He's not here yet. My mom had some leftover cherry pie that I've helped myself to though.

Eve: Happen to pack any up for your girl?

Reid: I can. Want some pie, babe?

Eve: Yes, please. XOXO

The front door opens, and my dad comes bursting in, shaking his coat off his shoulders as he strides into the kitchen, grumbling about the chill in the air. It's still cold for the time of year, but that's the unpredictability of Maine weather. One day it's beautiful, the next day you're freezing your nipples off.

Pocketing my phone, I push my now-empty plate to the side, making a mental note to grab a slice for Eve before I leave, and give my dad a wave as he approaches.

He adjusts the sleeves of his flannel. "Christ, it's cold out. I don't think my old bones can take the weather. I'm going to become a snowbird, and that's final."

I laugh and shake my head. "Yeah right, Dad. You would never leave Port Snow for more than a week. This town makes your blood pump."

He takes a seat and plops his beefy forearms on the table. "Why the hell does it have to be so cold?"

"Maybe because you live in one of the northernmost states. Could be worse, though. Could be Alaska."

"Thank God for small miracles." He sighs and nods at the empty pie plate. "Your mom outdid herself."

"So fucking good. Promised Eve a slice."

"So things are still good with her? I heard some rumblings from the elders this morning down at the general store about you two. They were saying you were being indecent at Snow Roast. Getting a little handsy?"

Chuckling, I nod. "Yeah, we might have gotten 'handsy' at the coffee shop and outed ourselves." I play with the fork on my plate, moving it over a pile of leftover crumbs. "I hated being quiet about the whole thing. I know she wanted to keep it between us, but hell, keeping anything secret in this town is basically impossible, so I just went for it."

"How did she react?"

I think back to that night, the way she writhed beneath me and what was probably the most intense orgasm of my life—of both our lives.

I can't help but smile. "She reacted well. Was a little nervous at first but then fell into it."

"Good, good." He drums his knuckles across the table, and I know things are about to get serious. "So about the other day."

I hold up my hand. "Before you say anything, I want to tell you I'm sorry for walking out. I shouldn't have done that. Things have just been tense for me lately, and I hate talking about my future because honestly I have no idea what I'm doing."

"I can understand that," he says, voice sincere. "But I didn't want to harp on you. I actually wanted to talk to you about an opportunity."

"Dad, I love you, but I really don't want to work with Willy."

He hesitates, blinking a few times. "It's not with Willy, Reid; it's an opportunity to work with me."

"At the Landing? But Griffin's in charge."

"Not at the Landing. This is a new opportunity."

"New? What are you planning on doing? Opening a restaurant?" I laugh, but when his face grows serious, my stomach somersaults on itself.

"Yes."

"Wait, what?"

"You know the warehouse right next to the Landing? Where we used to make our T-shirts before we outsourced them? I want to do something with the space, and the best idea I could come up with is a restaurant. It's the perfect location, looks over the harbor, and the Landing's right next door, so people can get treats and souvenirs after. It's at the center of town and is big enough for a gourmet industrial kitchen, a bar, and a good amount of seating with the possibility of extending into the water with some outdoor seating as well. I've already had an architect look at the space and draw up some initial blueprints for renovation."

I don't think I would be more shocked right now if my dad came out and told me he's not my real father.

Or if he ripped off his flannel and started belly dancing.

Or if he told me he's prone to wearing titty tassels to bed because he likes to bedazzle himself for a good night's sleep.

A restaurant? He can't be serious—can he?

The space is kind of perfect if I truly think about it, but extending into the water?

"You have blueprints?"

"Initial ones, so things can still be moved around. I want an experienced eye to look over them, and that's where you come in."

"You want me to consult on the space?"

Lowering his head, he chuckles. "I want you to run the restaurant, Reid. Cook, design, plan. I want to be a silent partner and eventually have you take over the entire thing."

Holy.

Shit.

I lean back in my chair, stunned.

This was *not* the direction I thought this conversation was going to take.

Never in a lifetime would I have thought my dad was going to want to open a restaurant . . . with me.

"But I don't cook anymore."

"Yeah, and it's about damn time you stop with that bullshit." He clenches his fist and then pounds his thick finger into the table as he enunciates every word. "I didn't let you get your GED at seventeen and then work my rear end off to put you through culinary school just so you could tell me that the best chef I know doesn't cook anymore. That's bullshit and you know it."

"Dad—"

"No." He slams his fist on the table, anger quickly taking over. "I refuse, as your father, to sit back and watch you waste your life doing something that doesn't feed your soul. This is your *life*, Reid, and you only get one. And sure, you failed once. Doesn't mean it won't happen again, but it sure as hell doesn't mean you quit your passion. Failure should not define you, but it sure as hell should motivate you."

"I gave that up," I reply. The words fall past my lips, though I don't know if I really believe them. I gave up cooking, but that doesn't mean the urge to pick up my knives doesn't still burn in my bones.

"You hung up your apron, but you didn't lose your God-given talent. It's time you set aside your pride and try again."

I drag my hand through my hair, my thoughts racing at having another shot at what I thought was supposed to be my calling. "But what if I fuck up this one? This isn't my money; this is yours. I can't do that to you and Mom. You're both retiring soon."

"First of all, we're fine with our retirement, so don't worry about us. Secondly, you won't fuck this up because you're going to hire people I trust, people I know will make this restaurant thrive. And that brings me to this—there's one condition to my proposal." I should have known. There's always a condition when it comes to my dad. "You will not be doing this alone."

"So are you saying you'll be the world's loudest silent partner?"

He shakes his head. "No. The only way you're going to be putting together this restaurant is with Eric."

"What?" I ask, sitting a little taller. Eric, as in Eric, my best friend? The guy I've barely spoken to in almost three years? The one who helped bring down the first restaurant? "Why?" I ask, thoroughly confused. "Why would you take a chance on two guys who basically let their restaurant go up in flames? Why take those chances?"

He looks me straight in the eye. "Because I believe in you. I believe in the partnership you two created. I believe in your food, and I sure as hell believe in your vision." He holds my gaze. "You two had the hottest new restaurant in Boston, not just in a small town but in *Boston*. Your food was brilliant and brought people in from all over. Your talent is incomparable, and I want that for my restaurant."

"Dad . . ." I sigh as my mind rages with possibility and doubt. "I . . . fuck, I don't know."

"What's keeping you from saying yes?"

I shuffle my fork around the crumbs some more, like it's a zen garden, but it's not doing much to calm my nerves. "The possibility of taking a handout, failing again, disappointing you . . . disappointing myself."

"First of all, this isn't a handout—this is a serious business opportunity that I've been thinking about for a long time, that I've dreamed of, and it just so happens that my son is a brilliant, trained chef. Secondly, failure is what makes us stronger. Without failure, we would never succeed. You failed big time in Boston, but instead of quitting, you need to learn from your mistakes and make sure you don't repeat them. Failure is an opportunity to grow, not a chance to give up."

I know he's right, but it still doesn't stop me from feeling sick to my stomach.

"But I haven't really talked to Eric in years. He has a job. He's not going to want to leave it."

"Looks like you need to plan a trip to Boston then and do some convincing."

There's no doubt in my mind that my dad has ulterior motives here. He's always hated that Eric and I had a falling-out and knew it was like I'd lost a fourth brother.

"I don't know, Dad." Emotion wells up inside me. Fear, excitement, the chance for something new—it's all-consuming, and before I know it, I find my dad sitting right next to me, hand on my shoulder as my throat starts to close and fucking tears well up in my eyes. What the hell is happening to me?

"Talk to me, Reid."

"I'm . . . I'm scared," I admit, head turned down, unable to look my father in the eyes. "That restaurant was everything to me; I worked my ass off to open it. I put every last penny I had into that place, and then it was just *gone*. One night, one person, that was all it took. My dream was stolen, and I had nothing to fall back on. I don't know if I can go through that again." A tear falls from my eye. "I don't think I can put that much hope and love into something again, not when I'm constantly worried we're going to fail. I can't do that to you either."

He lifts my chin, his finger rough against my skin. "I won't let you fail, and I won't let you stop chasing your passion. Cooking, creating, that's what makes you happy. You're alive in the kitchen, Reid; it's where your heart beats, where your mind soars. You belong there, and I'll be damned if I leave this earth with the knowledge that you aren't doing what you're meant to do. You're a chef, always have been, always will be."

More tears stream down my face, and I'm grateful it's just my dad and me. I'm not sure if I've ever had a moment like this with him, not even after everything crashed and burned with the restaurant. I pushed everyone away, so this time with him and these tears are long overdue.

"Tell me this—do you miss it?" he asks.

I nod. "Yeah, I do. It's like a piece of me has been lost since I quit, and I've been too scared to even go looking for it. Too scared to try again."

"Then say yes. Take a leap of faith; know your skill and your ability. You know you can do this."

I wipe the tears from my cheeks and think about it. I could really do this; I know I could. This could be my second act, my chance to do things differently—to be cautious where it counts but daring where it pays off. This could be my chance to bring all the flavors I love back to life.

But will Eric want to work with me again?

"I don't think Eric will do it," I say honestly. "We didn't end things on a happy note. The only time we really talk right now is on each other's birthdays, and it's a quick text. Things are strained between us. And then . . . fuck." My stomach drops.

"What?" Dad asks, his hand gripping my shoulder.

"What about Eve?"

"What about her?"

"Eric doesn't know. I don't think he'll like the fact that I'm seeing his sister. He's always been protective of her, and when we were young, he made it quite clear where my feelings should stand with her: just friendship. When I wasn't speaking to him, I didn't think it would be an issue. But if I have to work with him, then what the hell do I do?"

"Work it out. That's all I can say—you just need to work it out."

I look up at my father, feeling dizzy. "You kind of flipped my world upside down."

He chuckles. "Yes, but in a good way."

"I don't know. Give me some time to think about it, okay?"

"You have a week, and then I'm moving on to someone else."

"You would really hire another chef?" I ask, surprised.

"Yeah, I would. Like I said, it's been a dream of mine to have a restaurant connected to the Landing, and just because I can't get my son to work with me that doesn't mean no one else will."

I nod again. "Ahh, I see what you did there."

"Good. Now stop being a moron and make the right choice."

The water is a little more restless than normal on my houseboat, which is only fitting because it matches the churning in the pit of my stomach.

A fucking restaurant.

My dad wants me to open a restaurant with him.

Of course, there have been rumors about a possible Lobster Landing–affiliated restaurant circulating around town for years. But I always thought that was all they were: rumors. In a small town, the gossip tends to be outrageous at best, and I never wanted to even consider the possibility.

But here it is.

My dad wants me to open a restaurant with him, and a huge part of me is screaming *yes*. It was almost like my dad wafted a huge breath of fresh air into my lungs and awakened me. I didn't realize how dead

I've really been over the past few years, until my dad just up and made me this offer.

I want to do it. I can feel the urge to pull out my knives right now simmering in the marrow of my bones. But reconnecting with Eric? Putting everything at risk again? Possibly killing my dad's dream like I killed mine?

The pressure is already building, and I haven't even said yes.

I stare down at my phone, needing someone to bounce this off of. My first thought is to dial Eve's number, to talk to her about my worries and fears but also about the small excitement that's brewing inside of me—but I don't want to get her involved. At least, not yet. Not when I have no fucking clue what I really want.

Which leaves the group. Before I can stop myself, I shoot off a text.

Reid: I need to talk about something serious.

It doesn't take long to get a response.

Griffin: What's it about?

Rogan: If your pee burns, get it checked.

Brig: Are you proposing?

Yup, I probably should have just texted Griffin.

Reid: Dad had a talk with me.

Brig: Did you ask for mom's ring?

Rogan: Oh shit, Eve's pregnant.

Griffin: You idiots, it's probably about the restaurant.

Rogan: Is it?

Brig: No proposal?

Reid: No proposal. Jesus, Brig. And yes, it's about the restaurant.

Just as I hit "Send," there's a knock on my door. I glance up as all three of my brothers barge in, their arms overflowing with beers and wrapped-up meatball subs from our favorite Italian place in town, Moretti's. I would know that shape and size anywhere.

After they come piling in, making a scene by tackling me and throwing off their jackets and shoes, I finally catch my breath. "You couldn't have just texted that you were right outside?"

"Where's the fun in that?" Rogan asks, rubbing his hand over my hair. Even though we're in our twenties, he still treats me like we're kids.

"I love the dramatics of it all," Brig says, handing me an opened beer. "But seriously, were you thinking about proposing to Eve?"

"No!"

Rogan yanks on Brig's arm, forcing him down onto one of the dining table chairs they moved across from the sofa. And then like the good oldest brother he is, Griffin hands out the subs with napkins. Italian sauce and spices waft through my house as we all unwrap the subs and take large bites.

With his mouth full, Griffin asks, "So, Dad told you about the restaurant, huh?"

I swallow and nod. "Yeah. Did you all know?"

"I didn't." Brig primly pats his mouth with his napkin like a dipshit. I swear he does stuff like that just to get a reaction from us. "Apparently Dad didn't want me spilling the beans. But I can keep secrets."

We all stare at him for a few beats before shaking our heads.

"He asked me for investment advice," Rogan chimes in. "I'll admit I didn't think it was the best idea, since you've been such a bastard over the past three years, but after talking to Dad again, I think it could work."

"You do?"

"Yes," Griffin adds. "I think it would be good for you, for both of you. Dad has always blamed himself for what happened with the first restaurant. He thought that if he'd made you stay in school longer or helped you with the gritty details of running a business, you and Eric might have made it."

"So this is a pity ask?" My stomach aches at the thought.

Rogan shakes his head. "No, it's not. This was a well-thought-out decision on Dad's end. He considered going with someone else, but in the end, he knew he wanted to work with you. According to him, you're the most brilliant chef he knows, and he wants brilliance for this restaurant. His words."

Brig claps a hand over his chest. "He really said that? Hell, I wish Dad would say something like that about me. Do you think he thinks I'm the most brilliant mechanic he knows?"

"Not about you, Brig," Griffin mutters. "And Rogan's right: Dad spoke to me about his choices as well, and when it came down to it, you were his number one pick. Not because he felt bad or because you're his son but because he truly believes you will turn that empty space into the best restaurant in Port Snow."

"Shit," I say, laughing and taking an uncomfortable swig of beer. "That's a lot of pressure."

"The best kind," Rogan says with a nudge of his elbow. "Soak in the challenge, and come out swinging. You can kill this, Reid. We all know you can."

"Is that why you're here? Dad sent you along with meatball subs to convince me?"

"No," Griffin says, taking another bite. "He wanted us to check on you, so we came here as a group to make sure you didn't let your fear make a bad decision. Face it, Reid, you haven't been happy since you've moved back here. You need this in your life, and like Dad always says, do what feeds your soul. This is it."

"Yeah," Rogan chimes in. "So make the right decision, and don't be a goddamn idiot."

I stare down at my sub. "He'll only give me the job if Eric comes along for the ride. Which means I'll have to face him."

"Do I smell a road trip?" Brig asks, rubbing his hands together.

"No," I answer, dead serious.

"Come on, I'm a good time, and you don't want to drive all the way down there by yourself."

"I really do."

"So you're going to go down there?" Rogan asks. "Maybe take Eve with you. I'm sure she'd like to see her brother."

"Oh yeah, great idea," I say, my voice dripping with sarcasm. "Let me bring his sister—the girl I'm fucking—down to convince him to come back to small-town Port Snow to start another restaurant with me."

"It's not a terrible idea." Rogan shrugs.

"Rogue, it's a horrible idea. Now that I'm involved with Eve, the whole situation is exponentially more complicated. I wish Dad asked me to do this before I started seeing Eve."

"Why?" Griffin asks. "Because then you wouldn't have made a move?"

"No, probably not, because I would have known what an awkward situation that would be. It's not like Eric is just her brother—he's her twin. They were attached at the hip growing up. It's only been since their dad passed and we lost the restaurant that Eric has been distant with her. There's so much shit between them, so much unsaid crap, that bringing me into the mix just overcomplicates everything." It burns to admit that. But even though I know my relationship with Eve just adds another level of complication, I still want to be with her. I still *need* to be with her. She's special. It isn't just about the sex with this woman or the way she keeps me on my toes; it's about how she makes me feel. It's like she parts the dark cloud that hovers over my head and helps me see my true self.

I don't want to lose that.

But will I still have to?

"So what are you saying?" Brig asks, growing serious. "Are you going to break up with Eve?"

"No," I answer quickly, my chest aching at the thought. "I mean, I don't want to."

"But if you have to?" Rogan's brow pinches together.

"Fuck, I don't know." I set my sandwich down and grip the back of my neck just as there's another knock at the door. Is Jen joining the party? "Come in!" I shout.

The door opens, and it's a girl all right, but it's not my sister. It's Eve. Speak of the devil. As her eyes sweep the room, she winces and stays in the doorway.

"I'm sorry, I didn't know you were all here. I can leave."

"Nah," Griffin says, standing up quickly. "We were just heading out."

"Oh, yup, we were leaving." Rogan stands too, his bad leg giving him a bit of trouble before he escapes the deep, old cushions.

"What?" Brig looks around, confused. "I wasn't done. We were just getting to the good stuff. I want to know what—"

"Unless you want to walk home, we're leaving," Griffin says in his big brother voice, which used to terrify us. Now it's barely a blip on the radar—but still effective because Brig stands, grumbling something under his breath, and puts his jacket and shoes on with Griffin and Rogan. Half-eaten sandwiches in hand, they all give me a quick wave and take off up the dock to their parked car, leaving me alone with Eve, who's biting her lip, confused.

As the door closes behind my brothers, a pang of regret hits me all at once. Here I am with this woman who has practically taken over my brain, and I was just talking about her as if I could let her go. What was I even thinking?

"They didn't have to leave. I'm sorry, I didn't mean to interrupt whatever you were talking about."

"It's fine." I beckon her with my finger. She takes off her coat and walks over to me, and with a tug, I pull her down on my lap and cup her jaw. "Hey, you."

"Hey," she answers with a furrow to her brow.

"What's going on?" I ask.

"Just concerned, that's all. I mean, I haven't heard from you all day, and then when I come over, all your brothers are giving you what looked like an intervention. Is everything okay? Are we okay?"

"Yeah." I swallow hard. "Everything's fine." The lies flow before I can stop myself.

"What did your dad want to talk to you about? Was it a Willy proposition?" She smiles, but it barely reaches her eyes. Mine barely reaches as well.

This was the moment I've been dreading ever since my dad and I talked—and why I've been avoiding Eve all day: I just can't decide if I should tell her about my dad's proposition, especially since my answer is still up in the air. Not to mention the fact that her brother is involved as well. And now, confronted with her uncertain gaze, I realize that even though we're together, this is something I don't think I can talk to her about. Not right now—not when I don't even know what I'm doing yet.

So I stroke her back and say, "Just some new investment he's doing—he wanted to get my opinion." Not entirely a lie, just not the full truth. "The boys came over because they wanted to share a meatball sub. We haven't had one together in a while." I hold up the sub to her. "Want a bite?"

She studies me, and in her eyes I see the questions starting to brew, the suspicion that I'm holding something back. She glances down at the sub and then takes it.

I can feel the moment a small fissure fractures the space between us, born from my little lie of omission. She knows it; I know it—I just hope it doesn't do too much damage.

"I love a good meatball," she says before taking a bite, but her voice isn't the same; her excitement isn't there. She knows me too well, knows that what I just told her isn't the full truth.

The question is, Will she ever call me out on it?

I sure as hell hope not.

CHAPTER FOURTEEN

EVE

"He's lying to me," I say, falling back on my bed and looking up at my apartment's cracked and chipped ceiling.

"What?" Avery says, her voice over the phone scratchy from the early hour.

I haven't been able to sleep the past few days, not since Reid had his conversation with his dad. He was off that night, and though I could tell he was trying to be normal, his laughter wasn't genuine, and his attention was never completely there.

And we didn't have sex.

He said he just wanted to cuddle instead.

Sweet, I know, but that's not Reid. He's stripping me down every chance he can get. Even when he visits me at work, he tries to take me to the back to do naughty things—as he likes to say. He's rabid when it comes to sex, so when I started to peel off my clothes for him, and he just pulled me in close, claiming he wanted to hold me instead . . . that was my first major warning sign.

From there, it's gotten worse. A claim that he was too busy to meet up, missed text messages, and a quick phone call last night, telling me he was going out of town and that he would *hopefully* see me when he gets back.

Hopefully.

As if maybe when he gets back he won't see me.

What the fuck is that about?

"Reid," I say, trying not to panic. "He's lying to me."

Avery gasps, alert now. "Did he cheat on you? I swear I will fly up there and cut his dick off; then he really will be cursed."

"He's not cheating on me." At least not that I know of . . . no, I mentally shake my head. Reid isn't like that. The Knightlys aren't like that. And if Reid did cheat on me, I'm sure Avery wouldn't be the first one in line to chop his dick off. First his mom, then Jen, then I'm sure his dad, followed up by all his brothers. If anything, the Knightlys are the most loyal clan I've ever met. If you're in with them, you're in for life. It's why even when Reid and Eric were in culinary school and doing their restaurant thing, and I was back home taking care of my parents, the Knightlys would check in on me, offer up little deliveries of fudge. They did what they could and are a huge reason why I don't think Reid would ever cheat.

"Okay, well, that's good, because chopping off penises just doesn't seem like something fun to do. Not to get gory, but do you use a meat cleaver? Pruning shears? An axe?"

"It's too early for that kind of questioning."

"Hey, don't you give me sass—you're the one who called me. I was having a wonderful dream about the choreographer I take tap lessons from. You should see his thighs, Eve. Bigger than my head. I want to know what they feel like wrapped around me while I blow him, and I was just getting to the good stuff when you called."

I rub my hand across my forehead, my patience wearing thin at the visual—those massive legs encircling my friend's head. "That's a little too much for me to handle right now." The man calves are hairy. I take a deep breath, banishing them from my mind. "I'm sorry for interrupting your dream, but I really have no one else to talk to about this. All my girlfriends here are kind of tied in with Reid somehow."

"Then tell me everything. We can dissect it."

"Well, he had a conversation with his dad and said it was about some sort of investment but didn't go into any more detail. I could tell it shook him because he was acting weird that night. I didn't push the matter, though, because I'm still trying to get to that level of trust with Reid."

"He doesn't trust you? That seems pretty fucked up. You've known each other for such a long time. At this point, you should be one of the only people he trusts."

I can't deny that she's right.

"I know, but this is also a different kind of trust. It's the boy-friend-girlfriend trust. We've been friends, but we've never explored our feelings until now. And if I've learned anything over the last few weeks, it's that Reid really doesn't tell anyone anything. He holds everything in. Even when he and Eric were close, I don't think he spoke up much."

"Yeah, I can see that. But maybe you could be that person for him, the one he confides in."

"I want to be, but I'm just not sure he wants that."

"Why? Hasn't he been all over you since you two got together?"

"Yes, he has. It's been really great, and I'm not just talking about all the sex." Avery sighs dreamily at that. "He knows how to comfort me," I continue, "take care of me. It's the little things, like bringing me scones, candles, checking in on me after a long day, helping me study. We've been so involved in each other's lives, and then something shifted after he talked with his dad. I can feel that he's starting to pull away, but I have no idea why."

"Do you think his dad warned him away from you?"

"No, Mr. Knightly wouldn't do that. I even saw him around town the other day, and he stopped to whisper to me how happy he was that I was with Reid."

"Yeah, you're right, that man is an angel in plaid. Then I wonder what he said."

"Whatever he talked about has thrown Reid for a loop. I haven't seen him since that night; his texts are lackluster . . . then he told me he's leaving town, and do you know what he said?" I pull on a strand of hair, my frustration needing an outlet.

"What?" Avery asks, the edge in her voice telling me she's about ready to pounce.

"That when he gets back, he'll *hopefully* see me."

"Hopefully? What the hell does that mean? Did you tell him he damn well better see you?"

"I didn't respond. I didn't know what to say. *Hopefully* is such a weird way of putting things. Like, is he going to get eye surgery and maybe it will go wrong? Is there a chance he might not literally see me?"

"I don't think that's it, but nice try there."

I groan, sit up from my bed, and reach for my water bottle, taking a long pull from the straw. "I thought I would give it a try. Ugh, I don't know what to do, Avery. I wish I could be that girl who plays it aloof, gives him the silent treatment, and shows him what he'd be missing, but I don't think I can."

"Here, I can be that girl for you. Forward your phone to mine; I'll tell him a thing or two about *hopefully* seeing you when he gets back."

"You would destroy him. I don't think I want that. Not at this point at least, but I'll keep the offer in my back pocket."

"It's always there."

I chuckle. "Reid has always required a little more patience than his brothers, and if he's going through something difficult right now, the last thing he needs is for someone to shut him out."

"But that's what he's doing to you."

"Reciprocating bad behavior doesn't make it better."

"It's disgusting how mature you are."

"I'll try to be more childish in the future."

"It would be appreciated." She claps her hands, so I know I've been on speakerphone. "Okay, so what's the plan? We need a plan. Do we need to take nude shots of you and send them to Reid, remind him what he's pushing away?"

"You should know better than anyone to never suggest nude shots, given your profession."

"Hey, they're not of me. I know better than to send nudies to people, but I mean . . . you can."

"No!" I gasp, and she chuckles in response. Even though Avery hasn't been too helpful in the solution department, I'm still glad I called her. She's eased the weight that's been pushing down on my chest ever since I walked into Reid's houseboat. "I think I might just keep trying to talk to him. You know? Let him know I'm here if he needs me."

"God," Avery breathes out. "That man is so freaking lucky to have you—no joke. You are one of a kind, Eve."

"Hey, so are you."

"Yeah, because I dream of giant man thighs wrapping around my neck."

I can't argue with that.

Eve: Hey, I just wanted to let you know I'm thinking about you.

I send the text, not really expecting anything back, so when my phone starts ringing and Reid's name flashes across the screen, I'm truly shocked. Water sloshes around me as I sit up in the tub, the bubbles barely covering me up. I set my glass of wine on the floor and answer.

"Hello?"

"Hey," he says, his voice smooth, calm.

"Hey, you. I wasn't expecting a call."

"Why not?"

"You've just seemed a little distant, that's all. But I'm glad you called. It's nice to hear your voice."

"I needed to hear yours."

The hairs on the back of my neck rise. "Is everything okay?"

"Yeah, just long fucking day. What are you up to?"

"Taking a bath."

"I wish I was there with you."

I can't deny the relief that fills me at those words.

"If you were, you wouldn't fit in this tub. I think you've forgotten, but my apartment isn't exactly a luxury villa."

"You could sit on my dick—then we would have plenty of room."

"I should have seen that coming."

He laughs, the sound dangerously sexy. "You fit best on my dick, Eve. You should know that by now."

"How could I possibly forget? Hmm . . . maybe because you left without showing me your dick last time." It's supposed to come out as a joke, but I can hear an edge to my voice.

"Yeah, I'm hating myself for that." He hesitates for a second, but when he speaks up again, his voice holds a hint of raw emotion I wasn't expecting. "Hey, babe, I'm sorry."

Four simple words, but they're all it takes for tears to well in my eyes. The true regret in his voice—*this* is why I didn't shut him out. I know that he's going through something, and the last thing he needs is drama from me.

"Sorry for what?" I ask, still wanting some specificity.

"For being weird lately. I'm just . . . trying to figure some crap out. It has nothing to do with you, with us, but I know it's affecting what we have, and I want you to know I'm sorry. I'll get it straightened out. I won't be gone much longer."

"I know you will," I say. "And when you do, I'll be here for you."

"You're so goddamn amazing. I really . . . fuck, I really like you, Eve."

A stray tear falls past my cheek, and I have no idea why I'm crying. Why I'm so emotional. Maybe because I just got my period, maybe because this man has taken my heart by storm, maybe because I can feel the hurt that's deep in his bones and the struggle he deals with, trying to find his self-worth. I went through the same thing after my dad died, but I'm finally on the right track; I know what I want. I just hope Reid can find the same clarity, and I want to be by his side, to help him look for it. Then again, I can only be that person if he allows me to be. You can only poke a brick wall so many times until your finger starts to go numb.

I want to ask him more questions, get down to the real issue here, but knowing Reid's personality and how closed off he is to pretty much everyone, I remind myself to take things slow, to let him open up in his own time. I just need to be patient.

"I really like you too, Reid."

"And you know I mean more than friends, right? Like . . . *lovers.*" The way he says *lovers*, in a pseudosultry way, has me laughing out loud.

"Lovers, huh? What a grown-up title." In a different, slightly deeper voice, I say, "Hi, I'm Eve, and this is my lover, Reid."

"And then I whip out my dick for a handshake, or *dickshake*, if I may."

"You may not." I chuckle. "Your dick is not for handshakes; it's for me only. And why did I think of a milkshake when you said *dickshake?*"

"Because my dick has deposited some pretty impressive milkshakes inside of you."

"Ew! Reid. What the hell is wrong with you?" He's laughing so hard I don't think he can hear me. "Don't ever say that again."

"Are you complaining about my milkshakes?" he chokes out, still laughing.

"And we're done. Have a good night." I hang up before he can talk about his "milkshakes" any longer.

Seriously, men are so disgusting.

I'm about to toss my phone to the side when it starts ringing again, Reid's name lighting up the screen.

"What do you want?" I answer, a smile creeping across my face.

"Hey, you're using too much salt right now; tone it down."

"You called back to lecture me?"

"No. I called back to say I miss you."

Well . . . damn it.

"Don't say shit like that when I'm trying to be annoyed at you."

"I wish you were in my arms right now with my lips pressed against your sweet neck."

I nibble on my bottom lip, practically feeling his lips on me. "Stop it. You were just talking about dickshakes."

"I wish I could taste your lips right about now, the sweetest pair I've ever kissed."

"Laying it on thick."

"You want something thick?"

Poof, the romance is gone.

"Oh my God, Reid! Seriously, you need help."

"I wasn't talking about my dick, Eve."

I roll my eyes, shifting in the tub. "Sure, okay, then. What were you talking about?"

"My thumb. Want to sit on it?"

"Night," I groan, then hang up again.

Seriously, he's absolutely impossible. I haven't had any intimate conversations with the other Knightly boys, but I would bet on Reid's "thick thumb" that he's the most pervy of them all.

And for some reason, some sick and demented reason, I like it. Maybe that makes me a little pervy too.

My phone rings again, and of course I answer it. "This better be good."

"Just wanted to tell you good night properly. I miss you, Eve."

I sigh, dropping my fake annoyance. "I miss you too, Reid."

"I'll be back soon. Can't wait to have you in my arms again."

"I can't wait either; it's my favorite place to be. Good night."

"Good night, beautiful."

I hang up and stare down at the dissipating bubbles of my bath. Everything is going to be okay. If I learned anything out of that phone conversation, besides confirming just how perverted Reid is, it's that we're going to be okay.

CHAPTER FIFTEEN

REID

"Are you nervous? I'm nervous. My legs are shaking. It's like long-lost lovers being reunited."

"Can you shut the fuck up? Christ, man."

Why I brought Brig with me to talk to Eric I have no idea. I was having a weak moment, and after he asked to come for the tenth time, I finally gave in.

The drive to Boston is only about four and a half hours, so I could have easily done it myself, but the thought of having company was appealing at the time. Now I'm wishing I was alone.

Although I have to admit, all the sightseeing we did yesterday was kind of fun. Instead of jumping right into bombarding Eric, we decided to take a day and walk around Boston. I showed Brig all my old stomping grounds and brought him to some of my favorite pubs, and then we spent the night in a fancy-as-shit hotel because Brig "has standards." Though those standards somehow involve sharing a king-size bed.

And I'm fucking tired this morning because he gabbed the entire night like we were two tweens at a slumber party. He kept telling me about this girl who he thinks is the one. Cue the eye roll. That's what he says about every girl. But I know for sure she isn't the one because she was a random woman we saw passing by on one of those drink-and-bike tours. He didn't even talk to her—just glimpsed her for about a half second. He said if they were meant to be, the universe would pull them together again.

I think at this point everyone in the family hopes Brig finds someone to spoil and fawn over—and soon. Because his tireless pursuit of love is starting to drive everyone crazy. Myself included.

Maybe if he stopped trying so hard, it would just fall in his lap. But I know better than to tell the lovesick puppy that.

"I'm going to act like you're not really angry with me but just lashing out from nerves. Do you want to talk about it?"

"No, I want you to stop talking."

"I understand you're getting anxious about seeing Eric again, but that doesn't mean you need to pick fights with me. I'm not going anywhere, bro. I'm here for you, no matter how hard you try to push me away."

Jesus. Christ.

I reach into my pocket, pull out my wallet, and, just like when we were kids and I wanted him out of the way, take out a twenty and hand it over. But he doesn't bite. No, he just stares at it and then back up at me.

Voice rising, he says, "Are you trying to tell me that I came all this way—"

"It was four hours."

"Four and a half," he corrects. "I came all this way, pumped you up, helped you practice what you were going to say—"

"We did not fucking practice."

"Uh, I asked you what you were going to say, and you said you didn't know."

"That's not practicing," I reply, exasperated.

"It is in my book—don't take that away from me." Pushing me in the shoulder, he says, "I helped you practice and prepare. I listened to you cry and wiped your tears." Oh, for fuck's sake. "And you're not going to let me—"

"Reid?"

At the sound of Eric's voice, we both swivel around to find him stepping outside of the restaurant's back entrance, wearing his chef's coat and a confused look on his face.

Tall, maybe an inch taller than me, with broad shoulders and the same eyes as Eve, Eric stands there like he's frozen in place, disbelief etched in his features as he takes in two blasts from the past.

I stuff my hands in my pockets, feeling awkward and wishing Brig wasn't here to soak up every moment of this "reunion." "Hey, Eric. How've you been?"

He takes a step forward, expression still dazed. "Uh, good." He looks around. "Are you hanging out back here for a reason? Are you looking for someone?"

I'm about to answer when Brig pipes up. "Yes, you. We've been waiting for you."

I pull on Brig's shoulder, trying to tamp down the excitement that's basically pouring out of his mouth like a rainbow, and step in front of him. "Do you have a moment to chat?"

"Yeah, I'm on my break." Eric's brow crinkles. "Is everything okay?"

I nod and swallow hard. "How much time do you have?"

"Half an hour." He looks between us. "Want to go to the pub?" He tilts his head to the side.

"That works." Turning to Brig, I say, "Give me half an hour."

He leans in and whispers, "Promise to tell me everything?"

"Yes, now beat it."

Like the good brother he is, Brig reaches out to Eric, takes his hand, and gives it a good shake. "Good seeing you again, man. Have fun."

Once he takes off, heading back around the building, probably hoping that he'll run into bike-tour girl, Eric and I head on over to the pub next door. We slide into a booth in the far back, where we both order waters and a plate of nachos to share. I'm glad we're in a secluded spot, just in case things get heated.

Hopefully they won't.

In no time, the nachos are placed in front of us, and after we each grab a chip and take a bite, Eric asks, "What brings you to Boston?"

"You, actually. I wanted to talk to you."

"You still have my phone number, unless you deleted it. You could have called."

"This isn't a phone call kind of conversation." For a brief moment, I consider starting the conversation with *So, I've been banging your twin sister* out of sheer nerves . . . nerves and guilt. Despite our falling-out, I still have a sense of loyalty when it comes to Eric, and I've been breaking that loyalty, being with his sister. Then again, I've been there for her when he hasn't, so maybe I've earned the right to call her my girlfriend, to call her mine. There's a war of right and wrong raging in my head over what to do, but thankfully I hold my tongue and cut right to the chase. "My dad is starting a restaurant in Port Snow."

Halfway through chewing a chip, Eric pauses and stares back at me, blinking a few times.

Damn, I should have started out a little softer. Maybe given us time for a little catch-up. Then again, I don't have much time, and we have to flush out a bunch of bullshit between us.

"He's starting a restaurant?"

I nod. "Yeah, the old warehouse next to the Lobster Landing where Dad used to make the T-shirts."

"When he 'hired' us to help?" Eric asks, using air quotes.

I laugh, thinking back to when my dad thought paying us under the table to do random tasks was a good idea. It definitely wasn't, because all Eric and I would do was fuck around. "Yeah. I guess it's been a dream of his to have a restaurant by the Landing. People can get something to eat and then go and shop."

"Like Cracker Barrel," Eric suggests, eyebrows raised.

"I guess so. Didn't think about it like that, but yeah, similar vibe."

"Okay, so what does this have to do with me?" Eric doesn't beat around the bush either.

I grip my glass of water, the condensation running over my fingers as my nerves eat me alive inside. I just need to fucking say it and get it over with. "He wants me to partner up with him, develop the restaurant, the menu, everything . . . and he wants me to do it with you."

"With me? Why?"

"He can't think of a better duo."

"Does he have amnesia? Does he not remember what happened to our last restaurant?"

"Yeah." I rub the back of my neck. "I mentioned that, and he said something about how failure is a stepping stone to success. Either way, he wants us, and it's not a pity ask. He really thinks we're the best guys for the job. He's always loved our food, our style. He wants what we can offer—our classic New England cuisine with a twist." I smile nervously. "He has an architect already working on the building and is planning for indoor and outdoor seating, as well as a short menu and take-out window. He's moving forward, with or without us—he just offered the job to us first."

"So why don't you just take it?"

This is where it gets awkward for me. I turn my glass, my hands refusing to stay still. "It's either both of us or neither of us."

"Wow," Eric says, looking to the side. "That's pretty ballsy of your dad."

Chuckling, I nod. "Tell me about it. But I agree with him. It's taken me a bit to come to the realization, but I was good because you were always there, pushing me to be my best."

"Bullshit." He pops a chip in his mouth. "You're a good chef—"

"*Was* a good chef. *Was* is the key word there. I don't cook anymore."

"What do you mean, you don't cook anymore?" Even through the tense air between us, there's definite concern in Eric's eyes. "Cooking was your life. Are you telling me you gave all that up?"

"Yup." I lean back in the booth and drum my fingers against the table. "I snag lobsters now and pick up shifts at the Landing. I don't even cook myself meals anymore. Ever since we lost the restaurant, I haven't been able to do much more than make ends meet."

"Shit." Perplexed, Eric unbuttons the top of his chef coat. "How come you didn't say anything to me?"

"Uh, in case you haven't noticed, our relationship hasn't exactly been great. When I got back from New Orleans, and we realized we lost the restaurant, too much shit went down between us. I wasn't about to dump all my woes out on you, especially since you'd just lost your dad a few months earlier."

"But you're my best friend. Even with everything that happened, you could have turned to me."

I shake my head. "No. Too fucking ashamed. Still am. The only reason I'm here is because I felt a tiny bit of excitement at the idea of starting over again." I drag my hand over my face, hating that I have to admit all of this, but I might as well—what do I have to lose? "I've been lost, man. I've felt like the loser brother, the one that can't seem to accomplish anything, and I hate that. I hate that I've let myself get to this point." As the confession leaves me, the meaning behind it builds with each second.

The loser Knightly.

The one who failed.

The brother who couldn't amount to anything.

"Yeah, I'm not quite where I want to be either. A line cook at a three-star restaurant who lives with three other guys in a two-bedroom apartment . . . that doesn't scream wild success either. But this gig pays the bills, and after everything we lost, I can't be a risk-taker anymore." He glances up at me, his meaning clear in his hazel eyes.

"I get it." He doesn't have to say it out loud; the writing is on the wall: starting another restaurant is too big of a risk—and one I don't think he's ready or willing to take.

"It's nothing personal." He says that, but it feels incredibly personal. "I'm barely surviving as it is, and I can't afford to not have a job, to lose everything again."

"Who's to say we would?"

"We couldn't get it together the first time," he says. "What makes you think we can get it together this time?"

His words sting, but they also ring true. What was I thinking, coming here?

"Forget I even asked." I know that it's over, that our dream isn't going to happen.

"I'm glad you did," he says, looking just as dejected as I'm sure I do. "But hey, you need to get behind the burners again, man."

I shake my head. "Nah, I'm good. Fishing makes a living, especially during tourist season." I check my watch. "You should get going. I've taken up too much of your time."

"Okay, yeah." The plate of nachos hardly touched, we both stand, and Eric holds out his hand. I give it a good shake as he says, "Don't be afraid to reach out again."

"It goes both ways." I give him a sad smile.

After we say our goodbyes, I go out to the truck and text Brig, letting him know I'm ready to get the hell out of here. I should have known this was going to be a waste of my time. Yeah, it may have been nice to see Eric again, but there's still so much shit between us. Too much shit. And even though he said he didn't want to take the risk, I think that what he really meant was that he didn't want to take the risk with me.

◆ ◆ ◆

I pull into the harbor, the salty sea air doing nothing for my goddamn mood. We got back to Port Snow last night, but instead of calling Eve to see if she wanted to hang, I went straight to bed and woke up early this morning to hit the waves. I made a good catch, but the solitude I normally crave has only put me in a worse mood.

I know why—it doesn't take a psychologist to break it down. There was a glimmer of hope at the end of this monotonous tunnel I've been trudging through ever since we lost the restaurant. And with one sentence, Eric squashed it all.

He didn't want to take the risk . . . with me. That simple, sickening truth circles through my head.

Brig did a number on me in the truck, trying to get me to tell him what happened, what was said, but I kept silent until he gave up, leaving me to focus on the road. But it didn't stop him from texting the whole family—including Dad—that I was in a shit mood, so they probably all know what happened.

This morning, Brig said that Dad would maybe want to work with just me but wanted to see if I could patch things up with Eric first. Even if that were the case, I don't want the job. I wasn't lying when I said Eric was the one who made me great. He pushed me, helped me think outside the box. And after three years of staying far away from the food industry, I really don't think I could do it without him, and really, I don't want to.

Which leaves me here, fishing for fucking lobsters.

The prospect of working with Willy popped into my head last night, but I tamped that down immediately. I don't want to fish forever. Which means I need to figure out what else I want to do with my life.

I started a list last night.

Accountant. That's safe but requires school.

Permanent Lobster Landing employee. I fucking hate tourists, so that's out of the question.

I have a knack for candle sniffing. Maybe Sticks and Wicks is hiring.

I also know how to be a jackass to people. I wrote that down as an option. Professional jackass. People pay me to be an asshole to friends and family so they don't have to. I could create an app for it . . . because I know how to do that—insert eye roll.

Christ. It all feels hopeless.

This morning Jen said I could start giving cooking lessons at the community college up in Pottsmouth. No fucking thank you.

Griff told me to become a firefighter since they're always looking for more help. I mean, I'm not a wuss by any means, but walking into burning buildings and dealing with terrified people doesn't really speak to me.

Rogan said I could help him renovate houses. I turned that job down just as quickly as I did the first time he offered. I appreciate it, but home improvement gives me zero stirrings in my groin.

And of course there's Brig, with his grand idea of going into business together. He uses the backyard of his garage for events, and business has been booming. He wants an in-house caterer, which is a good idea but not something I'm remotely interested in doing. Going from a five-star chef to caterer . . . I'd rather be out on the sea.

So I'm back at square one.

I dock the boat, lower the anchor, and tie up before turning toward the lobster cages. Instead of taking these to the Inn today, I told Harold over at the Lighthouse Restaurant to come pick up what he wants, and then I'll sell the rest to Jake, since he's started making lobster rolls on the weekends.

"Hey."

Startled, I turn to find Eve standing before me on the dock, arms crossed over her chest, a very unhappy look on her face.

"Hey, what are you doing here?" I ask, blocking the rising sun with my hand as the boat sways in the harbor.

"Well, I hadn't heard back from you, but I heard from everyone else that you were back, so I figured I should come see for myself." She shifts her stance, anger dripping from every word. "Why didn't you come over last night?"

"It was late." I turn toward the cages and start making short work of them.

"When has that ever stopped you?"

"It did last night," I answer in a short, clipped tone, one that she notices right away.

"So I haven't seen you in days, and now you're going to be an ass?"

See, that paid-asshole job would make me a shit ton of money.

"I have to get these lobsters to Harold, Eve. I don't have time to discuss whether or not I came over last night to fuck you."

She's silent, the weight of the moment pressing down on my shoulders. That was a shitty thing to say, but my mouth has a mind of its own right now. My back is still to her, and I wonder if she's left—until I look over my shoulder and find her staring at me in shock, mouth agape.

"Is that what you think this is? You just fucking me? Because I was under the impression that we were much more than just fuck buddies." I meet her gaze, and her eyes—so similar to Eric's eyes—are like ice.

Fuck.

Sighing, I take a seat on an empty lobster cage pushed up against my boat and rest my head against the old, worn-out Plexiglas side. "We are more than fuck buddies, Eve. I'm just going through some shit right now, and I don't need you harping on me. Okay?"

"I'm not harping on you, Reid. I'm trying to find out if my boyfriend, who I care a great deal about, is okay or not. You're being so hot and cold with me. Warm and loving one minute and then distant and frigid the next. All I want to do is help, but every time I talk to you, it's like a different Reid shows up to the conversation. Two nights ago you were telling me how much you miss me, how much you wish I was in your arms, and right now you can barely even look at me. What's going on?"

"It's because I can barely look at myself in the mirror!" I shout, my hand flying out to the side. "I despise everything about myself, so why would I want to be near someone who thinks I'm worth their time?" I take a deep breath and stare at my feet, trying desperately to calm down. "You need to leave before I say something really stupid. Please, just fucking leave."

I brace for her comeback, ready for fiery, feisty Eve to make an appearance. But when I look up, I'm greeted with nothing but her retreating back, and an astronomical amount of guilt hits me in the chest.

Good job, Reid, keep pushing away every single person who cares about you. See how that works out for you.

CHAPTER SIXTEEN

EVE

"You're quiet today," Ruth says, sitting down next to me at Snow Roast, a rare lull in the crowd giving her some time to take a break.

"Yeah, not having the best day." I shut my textbook and stare out the window toward the harbor.

"I'm sorry." Ruth reaches out and presses her hand against mine. "Is there anything I can do?"

"I don't know—do you have a secret decoder in the storage room that tells you exactly what the Knightly boys are thinking?"

She chuckles and leans back in her chair, folding her hands over her stomach. "If I did, I'm pretty sure life would be much easier . . . for all of us."

"Still crushing on Brig?"

Ruth's eyes pop open as she glances around the empty shop. Rylee, the romance novelist, is the only one left besides us, but she's tucked into her usual corner, headphones on. She can't hear anything.

"What did I tell you about that?" Ruth whispers. "That was a drunk slipup, and you are not to repeat it to anyone."

"Oh, Ruth, I'm pretty sure Brig is the only one in town who doesn't see it."

"Is it that obvious?"

"Pretty sure heart beams shine from your eyes whenever he walks in here to get coffee. It's quite obvious."

"Great," she says, her cheeks reddening. "That's so embarrassing."

"It's sweet."

"It really isn't. I'm sure I'm the laughingstock of this entire town."

I wave my hand through the air. "No, I think that would be me. Thanks to Reid's lovely public displays of affection, the entire town knows about us, and they must think I'm absolutely delusional. Besides the curse that everyone's obsessed with for some godforsaken reason, Reid is the most temperamental, unpredictable, and surly Knightly. No one in their right mind would even attempt dating him, even with all the rumors about his unspeakables. I'm the laughingstock—not you."

Ruth blushes even deeper. She knows exactly what I'm talking about. "So I'm going to take it things are rocky with you two?"

"Yeah, you could say that. And he won't talk to me. We were doing so well, like really, really well, and then he goes and has a talk with his dad—"

"About the restaurant."

"Yeah about . . . wait, what?"

"The restaurant that Mr. Knightly's starting." At my confused look, Ruth's face blanches. "Oh dear, oh no, he didn't tell you, did he?"

Does this look like the face of a girl who knows anything about her boyfriend? Nope.

A restaurant. That's what this is all about, and he decided not to tell me.

How many other people know?

Am I the joke of the town?

I run my tongue over my teeth and shake my head. "No, he didn't, but now everything's making way more sense. Why he's basically in crisis—and so hot and cold with me all of a sudden. Can I ask you something?"

"Sure, I'm sure my big mouth would repeat it anyway."

"Don't be upset at yourself," I assure her. "Any sane person would have assumed a boyfriend would tell his girlfriend about this. But lucky me, I'm dealing with Reid, the most closed-off person in Maine."

"He does seem like he would be difficult to talk to, but he also has a sensitive side, and I'm sure it's lovely to be around." Ruth is so sweet, always trying to see the best in everyone, while I'm about to go on a warpath.

"It is," I admit, humoring her. "It's so nice. I don't mind his asshole tendencies. I grew up with that, but when I get to see the sensitive side . . . God, Ruth, it does something to me. Like I can't get enough of him."

"I can understand that. So what's your question?"

"Do you know if Mr. Knightly asked Reid to help with the restaurant?"

"I don't know much, but Ren did mention that Mr. Knightly was looking to go into business with Reid."

"I see." I look away, not wanting Ruth to see the hurt in my eyes. I can't believe he didn't tell me. He was presented with this opportunity, this huge opportunity, and it's clearly tormenting him, but he didn't think he could discuss it with me.

What does that say about our relationship? I know he says we aren't just fuck buddies, but in this moment, it feels like we are.

This is a huge piece of his life, but he kept it from me. Does he not value my opinion? Does he not trust me enough to confide in me?

The feeling of being discarded eclipses me once again, just like when Eric didn't come to me when Bar 79 closed. Reid is treating me the same way, keeping me in the dark and not letting me help.

If I know one thing, it's this: I feel damn foolish for being patient and not pressing him for details now that it seems like the entire town knows.

And where the hell did he go the past few days if this was the reason he had to leave town?

Millions of questions float through my head as the gravity of this omission hits me.

"Are you okay?" Ruth asks, pulling me from my thoughts.

I nod but start packing my things. "Yeah, thanks for being honest with me. I really appreciate it."

"You're upset. I upset you. I'm sorry. Please, let's talk about this."

I pause my packing and look her in the eye. "This isn't on you, Ruth—this is on him. I have to get going."

"I don't like that you're going to leave upset. I feel terrible."

"Don't." I pat her hand. "You actually helped me."

"You're not going to break up with him, are you? You two are so cute together."

"No, I'm not; I don't think I have that in me, but he owes me an explanation. That's for damn sure."

I give her a quick hug and take off for my apartment right as I shoot off a text to Reid.

Eve: My place, tonight. We need to talk.

CHAPTER SEVENTEEN

REID

Dead man walking.

Yup.

Whenever your significant other texts the words *We need to talk,* it's never fucking good.

Ever.

With the way Eve stormed off the dock and has been ignoring my texts, I can feel our relationship's impending doom. And to be honest, I don't even think I'm going to fight her over it. She deserves better; she deserves more. Not some guy who's fucked up in the head with no future to speak of. She deserves a man who can actually communicate and who's going to be there for her when she needs a cheerleader or a shoulder to cry on. She doesn't need a man who's going to test her limits—or keep secrets.

I lean against the hood of my truck and stare at the small basement apartment window that faces the parking lot. My breath floats like a white cloud into the air as I let out a long sigh. Hell, maybe I *am* cursed with broken love. Here I was, lucky as shit to even have Eve look my way, and then I fuck it all up because I can't seem to get my head on straight.

She's so goddamn perfect—from her personality to her intelligence to her fine-ass body and beautiful eyes. She's my dream woman, the person I've had a crush on for over a decade, but when I finally get the chance to be with her, I go and push her away.

I'd never admit this to Brig—or either of my other brothers for that matter—but I can't seem to write off the notion that something truly happened to us in New Orleans, that perhaps some cosmic force did strike us in the hearts, dooming our chances at love until we screw our heads on straight.

Or I'm just the world's biggest dumb-ass, the guy who pushed away the woman he's been pining after for years—and all for a job that won't work out anyway.

My heart in my throat, I push off my truck and head to her apartment. It almost feels like walking the plank, but instead of man-eating sharks, my fate involves Eve ripping out my goddamn heart.

I have no one to blame but myself.

Nerves completely shot, I lift my fist to knock on the door—just as it opens. Eve stands on the other side wearing a pair of silky red shorts, a black tank top, and a smile.

A smile?

I almost expected her to be wearing a black turtleneck and a menacing scowl powerful enough to shrivel up any pair of balls that gets in her way.

"Hey." I can barely get the word out before her arms are wrapping around my neck and pulling me into her warm apartment while her lips find mine.

What is . . . fuck, her mouth is so amazing.

Warm and soft, she kisses me, shuts the door, and pushes me up against it. This feels familiar but with roles reversed. Her hands run from my shoulders down over my pecs to my stomach, where she starts to undo my pants.

What the hell is happening right now? Not that I should really care—Eve is trying to take my pants off. Now is not the time for questions.

An instant later, my jeans fall to the ground, and one of her hands shoots into my briefs, cupping my already-hard cock.

"Fuck," I say against her lips. She squeezes, and a hiss falls past my lips as she pumps her hand up my length. "Eve, what—"

She silences me with her mouth, her tongue diving in deep, dancing with mine, matching my strokes. She's aggressive, needy, and I find myself feeling the same exact way.

Getting myself together, I pull down the front of her tank top and take her breast in my hand. I roll her nipple between my fingers, enjoying her moan, which I capture with my mouth. I move over to the next breast, yanking down on her top even more, not caring in the slightest if I rip the damn thing.

Needing more, I lift her up, and her legs wrap around my waist, my cock rubbing against her backside. My mouth falls to her tits, and I suck one in as her head falls back, exposing her beautiful long neck. Shit, I need to be inside her now, more than anything I've ever needed in my life. There's no time for going to the bedroom or even the couch for that matter. I drop down to the floor and make quick work of my clothes as she does the same.

We're frantic, we're frenzied—we're a pair of uncontrollable addicts looking for their next fix. She sprawls on the ground, pulling me on top of her and rubbing my cock along her slit.

"Fuck, you're so wet," I mutter, shutting my eyes at how goddamn amazing she feels.

In response, she guides my cock to her entrance.

"Condom, babe."

"I'm on the pill," she says right before slipping me inside.

"Fuck," I growl. "Shit, Eve."

Without a word, she flips me to my back and fully fills herself as she sits down on my lap, her hips rocking back and forth, starting a rhythm I'm not quite ready for as my cock swells inside of her.

"Eve . . ." She grinds against me. "Fuck, Eve, I'm going to come if you keep doing that."

"Good. I want you to come inside of me."

Jesus Christ, what has gotten into her? I don't have much time to think about it as she leans forward, angling her hips and sending herself into overdrive, her pace picking up as her hands roam my chest. I keep my grip planted on her thighs and enjoy the way she rides me, drawing out her own pleasure.

I watch, fascinated, as her face morphs, filling with an all-consuming passion that takes over her body. Her hand floats through her hair as her boobs bounce with her rhythm—the sexiest thing I've ever seen.

"Yes," she says softly, grinding down hard. "Yes," she says a little louder as her mouth falls open. "Oh God, yes." Her hips rock even faster, and her pussy clenches around me. I'm a fucking goner. There's no holding back. My orgasm hits me square in the balls as I rock up into her, groaning, just as my name falls off her lips, and she comes right along with me.

She collapses onto my chest and very gently continues to rock her hips until she's completely sated. I press a light kiss across her forehead and wrap my arms around her, holding her tight, soaking up every goddamn second of her.

As we lie there in each other's arms, I finally get a chance to think everything over. On my way here, I thought it was the end—that I'd have no choice but to walk away tonight and never get another chance to kiss Eve.

That's not the case.

At least that's not what it seems like.

I rub my hand over her back and whisper, "Are you okay?"

She presses a kiss to my chest, her lips lingering as she nods. "I'm perfect. I needed this, needed you." She looks up into my eyes. "I needed to feel you inside of me, be truly connected with you, because it's felt like we've been drifting."

"That's my fault, and I'm so fucking sorry. I'm not good at this shit."

"I've gathered that." Her hand cups my face as she leans forward and presses another kiss to my lips. "Let's get dressed and talk."

"Good talk or bad talk?" I ask, my stomach turning in knots again. This girl can truly make or break me with a few words.

"A *let's clear the air* kind of talk."

"Do we need food?"

"I have some mac and cheese in the oven right now. Should be ready soon."

"You cooked me dinner?"

"Yeah, and if you judge it with your fancy palate, I'm going to smack you in the balls."

"Babe," I chuckle, "I eat SpaghettiOs out of a can. My standards are pretty low at this point, and anyway, I bet your mac and cheese is amazing."

"It is." She winks and stands up. I take a second to admire her naked body before she starts putting her clothes back on. As she covers her beard-burned breasts, she nudges me with her foot. "Get dressed. I'm not going to be distracted by your nakedness."

"But my dick likes the fresh air."

"Well, tell him to take a deep breath because you're putting your pants on." With that, she walks off toward the kitchen.

I quickly put my clothes back on, sending an apology to my penis, and then help her out with the plates, bringing them to the table with two sodas. In all honesty, her mac and cheese looks fucking amazing as she pulls it out of the oven and dishes it out.

"Are those crushed Doritos on top?"

"Nacho Cheese," she says, proud of herself. "The only way to eat mac and cheese is with crushed Doritos on top—or Fritos. Depends on how I'm feeling."

"Skipped the bread crumbs?"

She raises an eyebrow. "Why use bread crumbs when you can use freaking Doritos?"

"You have a point." I laugh and take a seat. Wasting no time, I dive my fork into the mac and cheese and take a big bite.

Creamy and crunchy from the Doritos. This very well might be the best mac and cheese I've ever had.

"Did you make a roux?"

"Yup, used three different cheeses as well." Her mouth opens wide as she takes a big bite. Shamelessly I watch her lips work over the fork, all the blood in my body rushing straight to my cock once again. That's all it takes with this woman, watching her eat freaking mac and cheese.

I clear my throat and look away. "Well, it's really fucking good."

"You're not just saying that?"

I shake my head. "Why would I lie? You just put out, so no need to butter you up."

That garners me some good old-fashioned side-eye.

"Well, aren't you a charmer."

I plop another huge bite in my mouth, already thinking about seconds. "I like to think so."

"Well, Mr. Charmer, why don't you tell me about the restaurant your dad wants to start with you?"

Errr . . .

Fork halfway to my mouth, I stare back at her. How the hell did she find out?

Did Eric call her up and tell her? Was it spread through town gossip? Was it Brig?

That fucking nimrod probably told pretty much everyone at this point.

"Who—"

"Ruth. Not that it really matters at this point, because I should have heard it from you."

"Wh-what, uh . . . what exactly did she tell you?" I tread carefully, wanting to find out how much she really knows. Like, does she know about Eric and my trip down to Boston? I can't imagine that going over well if she did.

"That your dad is starting a restaurant and asked you to head it up." Okay, so she doesn't know everything. "Why didn't you tell me? That's huge, Reid, and I feel like that's something you should talk to your girlfriend about." She moves her fork along her plate, avoiding my gaze. "Do you know how embarrassing it was to find out about the restaurant from someone other than you?"

If I were in her shoes, I would be pretty fucking pissed.

"I'm sorry, Eve, but it's a little more complicated than that."

"Really? Seems pretty easy to tell me. You just say, *Hey, Eve, guess what?*"

"Not when I don't think I'm going to do it." I push back from the table. "There's more to it. One, I don't cook anymore. Two, I've already lost a restaurant—I can't lose my dad's dream. I would never forgive myself." *And the fact that your brother doesn't want to take a chance on me again pretty much justifies every fear I have.* I keep this last part to myself, though.

"But with help, it could work. I'm getting my degree in business, and you guys will need a manager. I could—"

Knock. Knock.

We both turn our heads toward the door and then look back at each other.

"Expecting someone?" I ask, raising my eyebrows.

"Only you." She stands from her chair, tosses on a sweatshirt over her tank top, and opens the door.

A gasp falls from her lips, followed by, "Eric, what are you doing here?"

I shoot up from my chair and stand as far away from the table as I can get, as if that's going to make things look innocent.

I'm pretty sure he's the last person either of us expected to show up at her apartment.

Jesus. Thank fuck we have our clothes on. I can't even imagine what Eric would think if I was sitting in his sister's apartment shirtless.

"Hey, sis," he says, stepping inside and pulling her into a giant hug. "I thought I would come pay you a much-needed visit. I have some—" He notices me and stands straight, eyeing me from over Eve's shoulder. "Reid, what are you doing here?"

"Hey." I wave my hand awkwardly. "Good to see you, man. I, uh, was just catching up with Eve." I stick my hands in my pockets, unsure how to act. *Deny, deny, deny*—that's what's on repeat in my head. "But I should get going. Early morning on the boat tomorrow." I walk toward the door and quickly slip my shoes on and grab my coat. I reach out and shake Eric's hand. "You look good." I pat him on the back and give Eve a parting glance. "Thanks for dinner, Eve. See you around."

Before I can hear her response, I'm out the door and headed straight for my truck, my lungs barely functioning as my mind whirls with what the hell he's doing here.

Whatever it is, I don't think it's going to be very good on my end.

CHAPTER EIGHTEEN

EVE

I blink a few times, almost as if a ghost is standing before me. I can't remember the last time I saw my twin brother. It's gotten to the point that I don't even see him on holidays. We barely talk on the phone. We shoot each other random texts on occasion, and that's the extent of our interaction. After Dad died and Eric lost the restaurant, well, things have been seriously strained between us.

And the strain becomes all the more obvious when Reid leaves the apartment like his ass is on fire, and the only way to put it out is by getting in his truck.

And the worst part is that Reid barely spoke to Eric, someone he hasn't seen in almost three years. Instead, they exchange a handshake, and he's gone.

"So are you going to welcome me?" Eric asks, looking a little confused by Reid's abrupt retreat.

"Yeah, sorry." I stand there, blank and shaken. "I'm sorry, I'm just surprised to see you."

I let him in and shut the door behind him as I hear Reid's truck pulling away. I hope this doesn't scare him off, that he doesn't put even more distance between us—I'm pretty sure that would just about destroy me. And right when I was about to tell Reid how much I care, how much I want to be there for him . . . Eric decides to come waltzing back. I swallow down my annoyance.

Eric strolls into the kitchen. "Do you have dinner with Reid often?"

Eyeing the place settings, I bite down on the side of my cheek. Should I tell him that I'm seeing Reid, that I've been seeing him for a while now? Would the truth make Eric angry? He shouldn't really have a say at this point since he's been out of our lives for so long. Then again, judging from the way Reid sprinted out of my apartment, I'm guessing he's not ready to let the cat out of the bag. But I don't think I am either, in all honesty. Eric has kept so much from me; the last thing I want is for him to storm back out the door the minute he arrives because he's pissed about my new relationship with Reid. I want to know why he's here; I want to hash things out with him. I want to fix our relationship, and then I can ease him into the new development. So instead of telling my brother the truth, I say, "Um, not really, just on occasion to catch up."

"Huh, okay. Mind if I fix a plate? I'm starving."

Well, that was easy.

"Sure, have a seat. I'll grab you one."

As I'm dishing out the mac and cheese, I notice how Eric takes in my apartment. It hasn't changed since the last time he's seen it. I don't make enough money at the Inn to even consider changing anything up. Every piece of furniture is a hand-me-down from our parents' house, torn and tattered; it all does the job but isn't even close to being visually appealing. I wince internally at my worn sofa—its tears covered by an artfully arranged blanket.

I set a full plate down in front of Eric, along with a fork, and whisk Reid's plate away, leaving it in the sink. Even though I love my brother, I would rather be sitting across from Reid right now, going over everything I wanted to talk to him about, but it seems like that will have to be put on hold . . . for a while.

"So, what brings you to Port Snow?" I ask, sitting across from him, though my stomach is so knotted I don't even consider finishing my meal.

"To see you, of course." His answer falls flat.

"Come on, Eric. I know you better than that. Something big had to have happened for you to come back home. You didn't even return for Dad's death anniversary."

"I had to work."

"You and I both know you could have gotten out of it if you tried, so don't pull that with me."

"Fine. I wasn't ready to come home. Is that what you want to hear?"

"If it's the truth, then yes, that is what I want to hear."

"It is." His voice is empty, emotionless. "I didn't want to return to a bunch of people who know me and know what I've become."

Sounds a lot like Reid. Both of them too proud to start a new chapter, so they keep writing the same one over and over again.

"So why are you here now, then?"

He shovels a scoop of mac and cheese in his mouth. "I need to talk to you."

Fear runs through my body. "Is everything okay?"

"Yeah, everything's fine," he says. "But I kind of was offered an opportunity . . . wait, you probably already know about it."

"Why would I know about it? I haven't spoken to you in a while."

He thumbs toward the door. "Because it's with Reid. I'm sure he told you."

With *Reid*?

What the hell is going on?

My neck burns with rage as a wave of heat creeps up my back. Why on earth do I keep getting news about Reid secondhand when I should be hearing it straight from him?

I take a guess. "About the restaurant?"

"So he did tell you." He smirks. "Was he over here trying to convince you to convince me to do it?"

I smack my lips together and shake my head. "Actually, I have no idea why you're even involved; this is news to me."

"Oh." His brow pulls together. "Well, shit. I for sure thought he would have told you if he was over here."

"Well, why don't you enlighten me?"

"He came down to Boston two days ago." Eric scratches the side of his jaw. "Told me Mr. Knightly is starting a restaurant, and he wants both of us to run it, to create the entire thing from scratch."

"Really?" I ask, dragging the word out, my fists clenching on my lap. Why wouldn't he tell me Eric was involved? Why would he drive all the way to Boston to visit my brother and say nothing about it?

I think I'm about to blow a gasket.

"Yeah, apparently Mr. Knightly wants both of us or neither of us."

Ouch. I do feel a sliver of pity, despite myself. That couldn't have felt good for Reid to hear.

"What did you say?"

"No." Well, Reid's mood makes sense now. He's presented with an amazing opportunity, and with one word, my brother kills it. My anger simmers rather than boils now as everything starts to connect in my head. "But now I don't know," Eric continues. "I think I might actually consider it."

"Like, you would move back to Port Snow and start up another restaurant with Reid?"

"Maybe." He scratches the side of his jaw. "We were fucking unstoppable, Eve. Our restaurant was quickly climbing the ranks in Boston; we were getting press from all over the place. But one wrong move, hiring someone we didn't really know to handle the books, ruined everything." He bows his head. "I lost everything. All the money from Mom and Dad, your college money, everything they put toward making my dream a reality . . . we lost it."

"You didn't lose it, Eric. Janelle stole it from you."

"And I was the one who convinced Reid to hire Janelle when he started struggling with the business side. It was my fault."

I can't help it—I laugh.

"Why the hell are you laughing?"

"Because you two idiots keep taking the blame for the restaurant instead of moving on. It's probably the most infuriating thing I've ever had to deal with."

"That's easy for you to say—you didn't live it." Excuse me? I didn't live it? He can't be serious. "You didn't—"

"I lived it!" I shout, my anger spilling out. All the lies, the omissions, the neglect, the sacrifices—they all come surfacing at the same time. "I was the one who put my life on hold so you could go and chase your dreams. I was the one who put off college so I could take care of our sick parents. I was the one who stayed back in Port Snow, found a way to pay the nursing home bills so you could take the money from Mom and Dad's house and open a restaurant. And when it was time, you were supposed to bring me out to Boston so I could go to college, pursue my dreams too. We shook on it. You first, me second, and I was okay with that, Eric. I was okay with making that sacrifice because I love you, and I knew you were going to succeed. So don't tell me it's easy for me to say. You're not the only person who lost something that day. I lost too. I lost more than you could ever imagine."

Tears spring to my eyes, and I take a deep, shaky breath.

Eric turns his tortured eyes on me. "Eve, I'm . . . fuck, I'm sorry. I know everything you did was for me, for us. I didn't mean—"

"Save it, Eric. I'm just so sick of the two of you playing the *woe is me* card." I motion around my apartment. "Do you think I like living here? In a moldy apartment below a guy who likes to save his toenail clippings as a hobby? No, but it's what I can afford while I put myself through school and work at the Inn. I didn't give up when life took everything away from me. I pushed forward. I made lemonade out of lemons, and yeah, it's been fucking hard. I've had some really bad days, but I know by the time I graduate this semester, it will all be worth it. All the hard work and the tears will be worth it. I didn't give up, so why did you?"

He shakes his head, taking a pause as I watch him absorb every last emotion I spilled between us. On a gulp, his eyes flash up, and barely above a whisper, he says, "I'm not as strong as you, Eve. Never have been. I still have no idea how you could spend every free moment you had with Mom and Dad while they were dying, watching them deteriorate every day. I don't know how you've been able to carry yourself with such poise, such strength, after everything we've been through—and still be a goddamn inspiration. It's one of the reasons I haven't come back. I've been too fucking ashamed to show my face around you, knowing how much I've let you down in almost every facet of our lives."

I stare him down. "Then don't let me down anymore."

"What do you mean?"

The wheels in my head are turning, sifting through the possibilities of Reid and Eric's new opportunity. "Take the job with Reid. Create something even better than Bar 79. Prove to yourself and to Reid that even though you failed once, you're not going to do it again. Stop hiding, and be the person I know you can be."

"Eve, I don't know . . ."

"And take me along with you," I say before I can chicken out.

"What?" His brow creases.

Here goes nothing.

"You admitted it yourself—both you and Reid are bad at business. I'm sure Mr. Knightly is going to want a business manager for the restaurant. I'm about to graduate with a bachelor's in business, and I've been managing the Inn for the last two years. I'm qualified, and I have a bunch of fresh and new ideas, ones I can't act on at the Inn because they're so set in their ways. Let me be a part of *this*. Let me help you finish what you started."

"You want to manage the restaurant?"

"Yes, I do, and I want you to make it mandatory that I'm a part of it."

I might be overstepping, but I don't care. I'm so sick of these two morons sulking around and not making true use of their God-given talent. They need someone to push them, to guide them down the path to success, and I have the tools to do that. Mr. Knightly won't hire Reid without Eric . . . well, guess what, Eric is going to come with a plus-one as well. If they're not going to take advantage of this amazing opportunity, then I'm going to make them . . . I'll guilt them if I have to.

I have zero shame.

"I don't know, Eve. That's asking a lot."

"You owe me," I say, catching him off guard. "You owe me this. You owe it to Mom and Dad as well."

"Eve . . ."

"Do you not trust me? Do you not trust in my ability to manage a restaurant?"

"This isn't my choice to make," he snaps back, hand to his chest. "I can't just say you're hired when it's not my goddamn restaurant."

"Then convince them why I would be great for the job. They want you, so make them see why they should want me too." I catch my breath. "You even said it yourself, years ago—once I got my bachelor's, you'd go into business with me, and we'd take over the restaurant industry. What happened to that dream, Eric? That was *our* dream."

"It was."

"Then help create another. I love you, Eric, and I'm so glad you're back in town. Stay this time. Not just for me, but for Mom and Dad. You left me and our plans back here in Port Snow, so help make them a reality." My voice cracks.

He leans back in his chair, my words hanging between us.

Then I see the tears in his eyes. "Shit, Eve," he says. "I didn't come here to fucking cry."

I chuckle and toss my napkin at him. "But you came here for some sisterly advice, and here it is: You belong here, you were meant to cook with Reid, and you're supposed to be doing something great with your talent. The opportunity is there, so snatch it up before you let it slip through your fingers."

He smiles, eyes shining. "Looks like I need to set up a meeting with Mr. Knightly."

CHAPTER NINETEEN

REID

Reid: Fuck. FUCK! Eric Roberts is back in town.

Griffin: Oh shit! Is he taking the job?

Rogan: Does he know about you and Eve?

Brig: If he does, I didn't tell him so don't go blaming me.

Reid: No idea if he knows. He stopped by Eve's last night when we were having dinner, but I bolted so fast I couldn't even tell if he was suspicious.

Rogan: That couldn't have been more obvious.

Griffin: But what about the job?

Brig: I just asked Tracker if he heard anything about Eric being in town and he said no. You still might be safe, bro.

Reid: No idea about the job. I was fucking blindsided last night, and now I feel like I'm about to lose my damn mind. What the hell do I do?

Rogan: What are you worried about?

Reid: Eric finding out about Eve and me. And fuck, I don't even know what's going on with us. I've been so all over the place that I'm surprised she even wanted to see me last night.

Brig: Yikes, sounds like trouble in paradise.

Rogan: Yeah, you're kind of in a sticky situation.

Griffin: This is why you don't date friends' sisters.

Reid: Wow, you are all so fucking helpful. Thank you.

Brig: Not a problem.

Rogan: Any time.

Griffin: We are here to serve.

Reid: Fuck all of you.

Brig: ^^^ don't take that personally, boys. He's just projecting the anger he feels about his own decisions onto us.

Reid: I will pop all of your goddamn tires.

Brig: Now that's just low, going after my cars. That's so beneath you.

Reid: At least something is beneath me, unlike you . . .

Rogan: Oh damn.

Griffin: Ha, he's talking about how you haven't had sex in a really long time.

Brig: Thanks, Griffin. Wasn't sure I got that (note the sarcasm). I'm saving myself for the woman I'm going to marry.

Reid: Either that or the curse passed over all of us and landed only on you.

Rogan: Ooo, that's not going to go over well.

Griffin: [Homer Simpson backing into bushes GIF]

Brig: You mother FUCKER! You know how hard I've been working to cleanse my goddamn aura. Don't be throwing that around if you don't mean it.

Reid: Who says I didn't mean it?

Rogan: Dude, you're going to make him cry.

Griffin: And then I'm going to have to pick up the pieces.

Brig: I'm dying ALONE!!!!

Rogan: Good job, Reid.

Reid: At least I'm not the only miserable one now.

◆　◆　◆

Dad: Meet me at the restaurant at four. Be sharp.

I stare down at the text message and then back up at the restaurant . . . or at least the space that my dad wants to make into a restaurant. I have no idea what he wants. All I got from him was this text and nothing more. I haven't heard anything from Eric or Eve either. I sent her a text a few hours ago, asking her how she was and apologizing for bolting last night, but I haven't heard anything back.

Why do I feel like I'm about to get bombarded?

Heaving a deep sigh, I scan the warehouse beside the Lobster Landing. Dad has kept up with its outward appearance, making sure it isn't a sore thumb on the end of Main Street, but it serves no real purpose. With its white siding, its pitched roof with Cape Cod–style windows, and the giant LOBSTER LANDING sign painted on the side with an arrow pointing to the entrance, the building is used more for Instagram pictures than anything.

Pocketing my phone and trying not to let my nerves get to me, I make my way to the restaurant and pull open the door. A loud creak echoes through the hollow space, pulling the attention of three figures standing near the expansive windows that overlook the bay. From the sunlight pouring in, I can't quite make out who the shadows are until I walk across the sealed concrete and step up next to them.

The first person I see is my dad, followed by Eric . . . and Eve?

"Reid, glad you could join us," my dad says as he gestures to the space. "Won't this be beautiful once it's all done? They've already started on the floor plan, sectioning things off and putting in the proper wiring for what we need, but the design is still slightly up for debate. All I know is the kitchen and bathrooms have to be on the left."

Err . . . did I miss something? Did I black out at some point and am now just waking up?

"Yeah, okay." I look between Eve and Eric and then to my dad. "Uh, what's going on?"

"Didn't they tell you? They're on board." My dad claps his hands, grinning.

"They?" I ask, swallowing hard.

"Yes, Eric and Eve. Eric will be joining you in the kitchen, and Eve will be handling all the business. She has quite the impressive résumé, even without the bachelor's degree she's about to earn. I have a design meeting set up for tomorrow, and from there, you boys will take it over. I'd like to be updated on all developments at the end of every week, and then there is the focus of what I want this restaurant to be."

What the hell is going on? I'm still reeling from the thought of all three of us working together. As in me, Eric, and Eve . . . the girl I'm seeing and Eric's twin sister. This won't be fucking awkward at all.

"What were you thinking cuisine-wise?" Eric asks my dad, folding his arms over his chest, his *let's get down to business* face on. I've seen that expression so many times. It means he's ready to listen and then dream big. Happens every time. The man's ideas are huge, and I've always been the one to bring him back down to earth.

"Well, I'd want the atmosphere to be casual and cool. Hip and modern, nothing stuffy, but food everyone would enjoy. You know, street eats, things you would get from food trucks, but slightly elevated and for a sit-down place," Dad says. "I don't want to step on anyone's toes in town, so no crab cakes or lobster bisque, things restaurants are already famous for around here, but I also want to bring a New England flair to our menu and remind tourists where they're dining."

I may still be in shock over this change of events, but even so, a part of my brain, the one that's been lying dormant for years, can't help but turn on. Recipes and ideas start developing in my head.

Deconstructed clam chowder.

A flight of lobster.

New England street tacos.

"That's a great idea," Eric says. "I'll hook up with this guy"—he grabs my shoulder—"and we'll see what we can come up with. I'm already seeing flights of food, tapas, soups with special dipping breads. We can completely change the face of Port Snow cuisine."

Feeling like I'm in a catatonic state, I just let everyone else do the talking as I attempt to wrap my head around what's happening.

"Perfect. I'll leave you to it, then. Feel free to start drawing up plans. I'm heading back home. Have fun and make it great." My dad claps me on the back and heads right out the door, leaving me completely stunned.

Silence fills the warehouse. Without a word, Eve starts walking around, checking out the space, as Eric and I stand there, facing each other. The tension is thick between us—tension from the past, from what's been said, from why he's here, why Eve's here.

I need answers, and now.

"What the hell just happened?" I ask.

"I decided to join you," Eric answers, rocking back on his heels as if it's the easiest decision he's ever made.

"That would have been great to know before you went and spoke with my dad. Who says I want to do this now?"

"Don't be a dick, Reid. You know you want to be a part of this."

No . . . sort of . . . okay, maybe.

"I really don't fucking know, actually." I push my hand through my hair. "I don't know if I want to be back in the kitchen. And when the fuck did Eve get involved?"

At the mention of her name, she whips around, her face a mask of rage. Well, there we go. This just confirms what I already suspected: I have a spot on her shit list.

"I don't want to fail again, so I want to do this with someone I trust," Eric says.

"You don't trust me?" I ask incredulously.

"I don't trust either of us with the business side, and your dad was going to hire someone new to manage everything. So I suggested Eve.

191

Because if anything, I know she's not going to fuck me over. She's just as invested in this as I am."

"Well, I'm glad you two figured everything out because I'm having a hell of a time wrapping my head around this. Do you really think it's a good idea for all of us to go into business together? Did my dad?"

"You thought it was fine going into business with just Eric and your dad," Eve says, walking back over to us. "That's why you went to Boston, right? To get him on board?" Shit. "So why does adding me to the mix make everything so hard to understand?"

For one, I'm fucking you.

Two . . . we're dating.

Three . . . I like you too goddamn much to let this restaurant come between us.

But I don't say that.

Instead, I say, "It just seems . . . complicated. That's all."

"Well, it isn't," Eve shoots back. "You two take care of the menu and the design, and I'll handle the business. Simple. We'll stay out of each other's way so things don't get too *confusing* for you, Reid."

Shit, she's mad. Really fucking mad. Make that place number one on Eve's official shit list.

"It'll be good," Eric says, the happiness palpable in his voice. "I have so many recipes rolling around in my head—and the desserts, we could have an entire dessert bar. A *make your own hot chocolate* menu for the kids and *design your own beer* for the adults." Always the dreamer—this is the Eric I used to be friends with. He's transformed into a completely different man since I talked to him in Boston. What fucking jolly pole got stuck up his ass, and can he tell me where to find one? "I have to head back to Boston and quit, pack my things and whatnot. I can stay on your couch—right, sis?" That won't make things even more uncomfortable.

"Of course," she says.

"Awesome." He gives Eve a quick hug. "I'm heading out. I'll be back for the design meeting tomorrow, and then, Reid, let's start working up a menu. I'll think of some ideas. See you tomorrow." That's it? No hashing out our problems, our trust issues, all the shitty things we've said to each other? He's just going to act like everything is fine and fucking dandy between us? He strides away and, with a wave, shuts the door behind him, leaving me alone with a not-so-happy-looking Eve.

"Eve—"

"Don't, Reid." She holds up her hand. "Just don't." She starts for the door, but I stop her, gripping her wrist at her side. She glances down at my hand and then back up to me. "Let go."

"I'm sorry, Eve. I'm really fucking sorry."

"Sorry for what?" She faces me now, our bodies so close that I can practically feel the anger rolling off of her. "Sorry for lying to me? For not trusting me? For insulting me and my ability to add something valuable to this project?"

Well, that pretty much sums it up. I've dug myself quite a hole, and honestly, I have no idea how to fix it besides apologizing.

"I'm sorry for everything. I really am. I just don't do relationships, and I've never been good at them." Not my best apology, but I've certainly had worse.

"You don't need to be an expert dater, Reid. You just need to be a decent human being. Ignoring me, pushing me aside, not trusting me with what you're going through . . . that's not the kind of man I want to be with."

"I know, and fuck . . . you deserve better. So much better, Eve."

"I do. I want someone who's going to stand next to me, hold my hand, be a partner in life." She shakes her head, disappointment bleeding into the gesture. "What do you even want from this?" She motions between the two of us. "What do you want from me?"

"I . . ." I push my hand through my hair. "I don't know."

"You don't know?"

"This is all new to me, Eve."

"Don't." She waves her hand, clearing the space between us. "Don't keep using that excuse. That you don't do relationships. Jumping into this, you knew what we were getting into; you knew what I wanted from you. We talked about it. Well, now it's time to get real. What do you want from me?"

Her eyes bore into me, waiting for an answer as her arms cross over her chest. The empty space fills with tension. If I want this woman in my life—which I know I do—I'm going to need to man up.

"I want you, Eve." My tongue swipes across my dry lips. "I want you."

She looks out toward the harbor. On bated breath, I wait for her to say something, anything, to ease the nerves rolling in my stomach.

Finally, she turns back to me, a firm expression etched on her face. "And I want you, Reid." She can't be serious—after everything I've said, after everything I've done? My shoulders slump as relief washes over me. She jabs a finger at my chest. "But I want you to be better with me. Do you want that? Do you want this?"

More than I think she'll ever know.

I nod and pull her even closer, pressing my hand against her cheek. "I want you, Eve, and I don't want to lose what we have, but it's about to get a whole lot more complicated. Eric is going to be living with you. We're all going to be working together, and he doesn't even know about us."

"We can make it work. I just need you to want to work at it, to trust me and tell me things. No more hiding." She presses her hand to my heart. "Let me be a part of your life and everything about it. Please don't keep me in the dark."

She still wants me. How is that even possible? Eve Roberts is a goddamn saint; any other woman at this point would have flipped me the bird and walked away. But there is patience in Eve, patience for me and for the relationship that's blooming between us.

I wrap my arms around her and press a kiss to the top of her head as relief floods my body. "I don't know why you like me—or how I could snag you—but what I do know is I don't want to lose you."

"You're lucky I'm crazy desperate." She laughs. "There aren't many choices in Port Snow."

A low laugh rumbles through my chest.

"Are you saying I'm the best choice out of the worst pickings?"

"Pretty much." She stands on her toes and presses a kiss to my chin. "Just promise you'll talk to me, Reid. Promise me."

"I will," I say, grateful for this incredibly understanding woman. "Just continue to be patient with me because I'm bound to keep fucking up."

"Just remember to get me walnut fudge every time you screw up."

"Done." I press another kiss to her lips. "Will you come over tonight? We can talk about how we're going to make this work."

"Will you be naked?"

"With my legs spread." I wink, making her laugh.

"Fine, but you're required to make me dinner. You're a chef, after all, and you need to dust off those knives."

"You drive a hard bargain."

She shrugs and pulls away. "Naked, legs spread, and a homemade meal. I think you can handle it."

CHAPTER TWENTY

REID

"I can't believe you're really naked."

"Not naked." I tug on the strings of my apron. "I have this fella on." And thank God, because my spaghetti sauce has already splattered, and I can't imagine what that would have felt like on my sensitive man skin.

"Your entire ass is on display."

"Would you rather I wear it like a cape so you can see the frontal goods while you eat?"

She laughs and sips from the wine I poured her the minute she got here. "I don't know which is worse."

"You mean which is better, babe. Which is better." I wink and finish plating the dishes with a small garnish, adding some green to the overall appearance. I wipe the sides, making sure the presentation is on point, and then I bring dinner over to my girl.

Not going to lie, I stumbled a bit around the kitchen while making dinner. I made some mistakes, simple errors, but since it's been three years since I've actually cooked something, I was kind to myself.

It felt good, though—odd but good.

"Spaghetti and meatballs." Eve glances up at me with a smile. "You remembered my favorite meal."

I sit down in my chair, the cold wood surface making my balls want to retract up into my body. "I remember everything about you, Eve."

She glances over her wineglass. "You make it seem like you've liked me for a long time."

"Just doing a little bit of flirting," I say instead of admitting to my almost-lifetime crush. "Trying to prove that I can be the man you deserve."

Her features soften as she reaches out and rubs her thumb over the back of my hand. "I know you are." I bring her hand to my lips and give it a gentle kiss before picking up my fork. I feel her eyes on me for a few seconds longer, studying me. "How did it feel, cooking again?" she asks.

"Different, good, weird. To be honest, I stood in front of the ingredients for a while, asking myself if I could do it, revisit something I haven't done in so long."

"Were you naked while you stared at the ingredients?"

"Of course." She laughs, and I can't resist adding, "Those meatballs might be a little jealous, having my balls to compare themselves to."

"Oh my God, what is wrong with you?"

"I tried to do mirror images for you, but I'm out of practice. Don't worry, babe, I'll get it right one day, and you can finally say you've had my balls in your mouth."

She shakes her head and takes a bite, her eyes fluttering shut before she smiles. "You know, you are the biggest pervert I know, but damn it, Reid, you are such a freaking good cook."

I glance down at my plate. "You don't have to go over the top with the compliments. I'm going to do the restaurant."

"I'm not going over the top. I wouldn't do that. You know I tell the truth, and right now, the flavors that are exploding in my mouth are pure magic. One bite—that's all I need to know that you're doing what you're supposed to be doing: cooking."

"That means a lot, Eve. Thank you." I sit back in my chair and let out a long breath. "Fuck, I'm feeling emotional, and I don't want to look like a tool bag in front of you."

"You don't want to cry in front of me—is that what you're saying?"

"Yeah, and I sure as hell don't want to cry while naked either. It would be way too much of a vulnerable moment for me."

She pushes her chair out, and coming to my side of the table, she sits on my lap and loops her arms around my neck.

"Be emotional with me; tell me what you're feeling, how it made you feel to be in front of the stove again. I want to know all of it."

This is what she wants: the truth, the vulnerability. And even though I'm not the type of guy who divulges shit like that, I need to show her this side of me and show her just how desperate I am to keep her in my life.

"I hate myself—that's what it comes down to."

"What do you mean?" she asks, a crease to her brow. "Why do you hate yourself?"

"Because the last few hours have been some of the best hours of my life over the past few years, you excluded." She smiles. "Yeah, I stumbled around—I fucked up on the pasta a few times, had to remake the dough—and I was a dipshit and forgot the egg in the meatballs at first, but I felt energized. I couldn't stop smiling. Tasting, testing, challenging myself to push for the flavors I developed so many years ago. Perfecting every last inch of the plate. It was like finding my home again."

"Then why do you hate yourself?"

"Because the happiness I thought I'd lost has been right in front of me this whole time, but I was too much of a stubborn ass to realize it—or to give in. I thought that if I never cooked again, I would be doing the world a service, but in reality, I was slowly eating away at my soul." My throat tightens. "I fucking missed this, Eve, and I honestly can't believe I'm getting another chance at my dream."

She cups my cheeks, and those hazel eyes bore into me. "You are bound to do great things, Reid. I know you don't want to hear this, but sometimes we face adversity so we are directed down a different path. The town may be thriving, but it still needs you. It needs Eric, and it needs your flavors. Your dad has a vision, and you're helping make that come true. You're giving him one of the greatest gifts you could ever give him by making the restaurant real. You need to realize that this isn't just for you. This is also for him. This is for Eric . . . this is for me. The dream may have crumbled the first time, but we're dusting ourselves off, and we're moving forward."

My hand moves up to the nape of her neck as I rub my thumb across her skin. "This really matters to you."

She nods. "More than you know. I gave everything up so Eric could pursue his dreams. I stayed back and cared for our parents, I put my schooling on hold, I put my life on pause. And slowly, I've built myself up, I've educated myself, I've worked my ass off at the Inn so that one day I could go back to Eric and tell him I was ready to pursue the dream we had. That's what it was supposed to be all along: me managing his restaurant. But I gave that up for our parents. Now that the chance is here, I'm not going to let go of it."

"Shit, Eve. You never told me that. Eric never said anything."

"Because I told him not to. I knew when the time came he would bring me on board. That time is now. This restaurant is so much more than an opportunity or a vision; it's a moment in time that will define us."

And this is why I can without a doubt say I love this woman.

I fucking love her.

Because she looks past my bullshit, my unruliness, my bastard-like tendencies and sees the good in me, the good in everything. She's been dealt a shitty hand, and yet she pushes forward, finding the positive in every situation. It's why she's perfect for me, why I want her in my life . . .

why I need her in my life. She lights up every aspect of my existence, and above everything else, I need her at my side.

"You amaze me, Eve Roberts."

"You give me butterflies, Reid Knightly." She leans forward, and as she gently presses her mouth against mine, all I can think of is the fact that she does the same for me. She gives me an onslaught of butterflies every time I get to hold her in my arms.

◆ ◆ ◆

"Let's go over the rules."

"Are you serious right now?" I look down between us and then back up. "Babe, I'm so fucking deep inside of you and ready to come. We're not discussing rules."

She shifts on my lap and wraps her legs around my waist, stuffing them between the couch and my back. "Then make it quick," she says, her voice breathy.

"Literally all my blood has rushed to my cock. I don't even know what you're saying right now." She rocks her hips back and forth, and I grind my teeth together. "Fuck," I drawl out. "Eve, either move faster, or I'm taking charge."

"Rules, Reid."

"Eve."

"Reid," she says with more force.

"God damn it, woman." I press both hands against my face. "Fuck, fine." My balls pulse as my legs start to tingle, letting me know that my impending orgasm is right there when I'm ready to take it. "No kissing in front of Eric."

"That's a terribly obvious rule."

"Blood to the cock, babe. Blood to the cock."

"Ugh, men." She moves her hands to her breasts and starts tweaking her nipples. Her head falls back, and fucking hell, that's all it takes for me. Screw the rules: I need to finish this.

I grab ahold of her hips and start to vigorously pump up and down. Her surprised gasp turns into a moan as she falls forward and holds onto my shoulders.

I move both of our hips until her pussy clenches around my length, and she screams out my name. I follow closely behind, my cock swelling right before I come inside of her. There is seriously nothing better than filling her up and watching her mindlessly thrash in passion.

When her hips slow down, she flips her head up and pushes her hair out of her face. "That wasn't fair—we were talking."

"You were . . . torturing," I say, still trying to catch my breath. "If you want to talk about rules now, fine."

"You can't always get your way, you know. It's not fair."

"And when your pussy is pulsing around my dick, snuggling in so damn tight that I'm about to blow my load, I will always take what I want. And that's you."

"Fine." A small smile curls her lips. "Let's talk rules. This might not be the most mature way to handle things, but given the abrupt appearance of Eric, I think it might be the best way to handle our relationship around him. I want to be respectful to him, but I also don't want to bombard him with what we have between us. So, no PDA in front of Eric, no secret smiles, no touching, and no inside jokes. Keep it professional, and no grabbing my boobs in front of him."

"That would fall under the no-touching rule."

"Just wanted to clarify."

"What about when we want to see each other? He's staying at your place, so that means no sleepovers."

"We'll just have to be creative, that's all." She slips off my lap and walks toward my bathroom, her pert ass swaying before disappearing inside.

"I can be very creative," I call out. "I've been known to be super creative."

She leans out of the open bathroom door. "You better only be creative with me."

"As if I could handle anyone else. You're it for me, babe."

"Damn right. We just have to be honest, and once we get through all the early stages of the restaurant and things start going smoothly, we tell Eric. We will sit him down and respectfully let him know. And at that point, we'll be able to say that if we got through the early processes of putting together a restaurant while dating, then we for sure can get through opening and beyond."

"Prove to him that we can do both." I nod, thinking about her plan. It very well might work, and I really don't have any other suggestions on how to handle the situation other than walking up to him and telling him right now, which I know will blow up in not only my face but also everyone else's. It would be putting a lot of dreams on the line, and I can't fathom doing that right now. My dad's face flashes in my mind, the excitement he had in his eyes when talking about the restaurant; yeah, I can't fuck this up for him. "You know, that's going to be a huge fear of his, the two of us being able to work together, because Janelle screwed him over, screwed us both over. I'm not sure he's going to be okay with mixing business and pleasure."

"This isn't business and pleasure." Eve walks back into the living room wearing one of my shirts, which hits her midthigh. "We're in a serious relationship with the promise of a future, and we also happen to be working together toward a common goal. This is completely different from him and Janelle. We'll just have to help him see the distinction."

That makes sense. And it is different. I'm not just fucking Eve; I'm falling for her . . . hard.

"We can do that, but in the meantime, we can find secret places to do it." I wiggle my eyebrows.

She smothers my face with her hand and laughs. "Seriously, five minutes, Knightly. Five minutes without talking about sex."

"That was like ten."

"Ha, okay . . . nice try." She curls up on me and pulls a blanket over the both of us as she rests her head on my shoulder.

"What about the town?" I ask, just remembering that we live in a place that put out a freaking news article about our budding relationship.

"Damage control. Hit up the biggest gossips in town; let them know to spread the word."

"Spread the word about what?"

She glances up at me. "Spread the word about keeping this a secret."

"You think that's going to work?"

She nods. "You have to know the right people. I can hit up Franklin and Mrs. Davenport. Use them to our advantage for once. Within an hour, everyone in town will know. They work fast."

"What do I do?"

"Tell Brig—he'll work his side of the gossip train."

I chuckle, half in disbelief, half in awe. "You're unfortunately right. I already told my family to keep their mouths shut, but I'll reinforce it with Brig and have him spread the word."

She tilts up and kisses my chin. "Perfect."

Perfect is right.

I snuggle into her and hold her tight. It feels like everything is going right in my life. But even in the midst of all this happiness, part of me is fucking terrified. Because when everything goes right, the ball is bound to drop at any second.

I just hope I can hold everything together when it does.

CHAPTER TWENTY-ONE

REID

Reid: Heads up, Eve and I will be secretly dating now, spread the word.

Rogan: Okay, good luck with that.

Brig: Secretly? How is that possible in our town when everyone already knows you're dating?

Griffin: You know I hate agreeing with Brig, but I'm kind of with him on this.

Reid: We are being discreet. Acting professional with each other around Eric, and when we're ready we're going to tell him.

Rogan: Truth is better than deception, bro.

Brig: Haven't you watched any Lovemark movies? This idea ALWAYS goes wrong.

Reid: I don't make decisions based on frilly romances. This is real life. We can be adults about this.

Griffin: Smells like a bad idea.

Jen: As a lady, I would like to interject and say it can be done if handled properly. It's usually the man who screws everything up . . . according to Lovemark.

Brig: Not FUCKING true. In Trotting for Turkey Love, Isabelle was the one who broke Kent's heart by not being honest about the turkey-carving contest. It's not always the man.

Reid: You are seriously disturbing. Why do you know their names?

Rogan: He's watched each movie at least five times.

Griffin: He recorded the turkey one on my DVR and watched it at my house at least twice.

Jen: Twice at my house.

Rogan: Once at mine.

Brig: Four at mine, OKAY! We get it, I like the damn movie. There's just something about watching Isabelle's tits jiggle while she's carving that turkey with a motorized knife that gets me every freaking time. And then the heartache Kent feels when she cheats him out of the win. God, I feel it in my bones.

Reid: . . .

Rogan: I . . . oh hell.

Griffin: Jiggling tits? Come on, man.

Jen: Not that I ever want to defend Brig (I think we're all on the same page when it comes to that) but I must say that Isabelle IS stacked and her boobs do jiggle a lot. Brig played it for me in slow motion a few times. I can see the appeal.

Brig: THANK YOU. **Drops Mic**

Griffin: I really need to remove myself from this group text.

Rogan: Jen, you're better than that.

Jen: **Shrugs** They were jiggly. I'm not sorry.

Reid: Jesus Christ, can you all just promise me to be cool and not mention anything about me and Eve dating. Any help is appreciated.

Brig: I don't ever want to hide love, but I'll suck it up and do this for you, bro . . . because I love you.

Griffin: Seriously, removing myself right now.

Rogan: Why do you always have to make things weird, Brig?

Jen: It's sweet.

Reid: Jen!

Rogan: Jen!

Griffin: **Figuring out how to remove myself**

Brig: Jen—you, me, Oliver's ice cream and April Showers Brings May Man Powers this Friday. You in?

Jen: Oddly, I think I am.

◆ ◆ ◆

"Got some more fudge," Dad calls out as he enters the Lobster Landing's kitchen.

I've been packaging and blocking yesterday's fudge for the past hour, painstakingly making sure everything is the way Griffin likes it. He's very particular about how we present our products. And I get it, because if it was my restaurant, the rules would be the same.

"Did you bring more chocolate raspberry?" I ask. "Griffin's been going insane since we ran out."

"Brought two batches, so he can pull his undies out of his ass."

I chuckle as I set a dozen blocks to the side and help my dad pull the rest of the fresh fudge out of the coolers. "What's this?" I ask, holding up a pan of pink-and-orange-swirled fudge.

"Sherbet. Don't tell your mother, but I slipped that one in last night. Thought I'd try something new in preparation for summer."

"A new flavor without the family taste testing it first? Do you think that's smart, Dad?"

He waves his hand at me. "I know when fudge is good, and this is good."

"You think?" I take off the clear plastic cover and flip the block over on the table. With my metal scraper, I slice off a piece and take a taste. I'm immediately hit with an overwhelming wave of sweet that nearly rips my tongue in half.

"Good, right?" Dad is nodding as I run to the fridge for water.

"Dad, that was . . . oh fuck, that was gross. You need to get your taste buds checked."

"What?" His brow furrows as he reaches for a bite. He chews and then grimaces before letting out a deep, throaty chuckle. "Well, that teaches me to make fudge while drinking beer. Let's just chuck that slab, huh?"

"Good idea."

While I'm clearing the sherbet fudge from the counter, Dad says, "You know, I'm glad I have you for a second. I wanted to talk to you privately."

"Is it about bombarding me yesterday?"

"Maybe." He smiles and leans against one of the stainless steel countertops that stretch along the side of the kitchen. "I could read it all over your face that you were shocked, to say the least. I was, too, when Eric and Eve approached me without you, but I had to admire them. Eric insisted that I'd either take on him and Eve together or neither of them. He stepped up for his sister, told me why she would be perfect for the job and why all three of you would be perfect for the job. His parents would have been proud."

"He said all three of us?"

He nods. "And he said that Bar 79's success didn't come from either one of you but from the chemistry you two had in the kitchen. I couldn't agree more. With Eve at the helm managing everything, I know that this is going to be successful. I did mention to Eve that while you two are working out the details of the menu, I'd want to put her through some vigorous training during the little spare time she has. She said she was ready for it and will do anything to make this a success. Those are the kinds of things I want to hear."

"This means a lot to her," I admit. "It means a lot to us, Dad. I don't really know what to say about the chance you've given all three of us, but I feel like I'll forever be repaying you."

He shakes his head and pushes off the counter, stepping closer and placing his large hand on my shoulder. "Don't you realize, Reid, that I'm not doing you a favor? You're actually helping me out. You're bringing a dream of mine to reality, and for that, I'll always be grateful to you, son."

Fuck.

What's with the emotions I've been having lately? You'd think I was a pubescent tween. It's been getting goddamn annoying.

But there's something that happens to you as a man as you get older and watch your parents age, especially your dad. There is this innate need to help him, to impress him, to garner his forever respect, to make sure you turn out to be the man he's always dreamed you'd be. But after the restaurant crashed and burned, I gave up hope of being much more than an embarrassment.

Now, though, there's hope—a whisper in my mind that I'm on my way to becoming the man he raised me to be, and that means more than anything.

This is the man who put his faith in my talent, who took a chance on a young punk who wanted nothing more than to cook. He invested in me, cheered for me, and stood by my side when the worst happened. He's picked me up when I've been down, he's lifted me up when no one else would, and he's trusted me with his dream.

In this moment, I make a silent promise to myself. I will do everything possible to make sure this restaurant is not only a true success but also a legacy.

I reach out and pull my dad into a hug, and we take the moment to pat each other on the back, a silent exchange of appreciation passing between us.

"I'm really excited about this, Dad," I say as we pull away. "The design meeting is going to be amazing, and I actually cooked something for Eve last night."

His brows shoot up. "You did?"

"Yup." I decide to leave out the cooking-naked part. "Made spaghetti and meatballs. It felt really fucking good too, like I was breathing again."

He breaks out into a grin. "That makes me happier than you could ever imagine. And I think it has to do with the woman you were cooking for."

I couldn't agree more.

"She's everything to me, Dad."

"I can see it in your eyes." He pauses. "Eric doesn't know yet, does he?"

A wave of anxiety hits me, and I shake my head. "Because of Janelle and what she did to us, we thought keeping things quiet right now might be a good idea. We plan on telling him but want to prove to him how well we can work together first. Are you going to be okay with that?"

He looks to the side and lets out a heavy sigh. "Not really, but I also get why you're holding back. My suggestion to you, son, is to tell him sooner rather than later. Prove yourself early on—both of you, prove your investment in this, and then tell him. Because the longer you wait, the worse it could be."

"I know. We just need a little time. Like you said, prove ourselves and then come out with it. After everything Janelle did to us, after leaving him with our money, I know he's not going to trust any kind of workplace romance, even if it's between his best friend and his sister."

"There's history there, but if any two people can do it, I know it's you."

CHAPTER TWENTY-TWO

EVE

Want to know what's incredibly sexy?

Watching Reid in his element, speaking with such confidence and conviction. It's taking every last ounce of strength to not reach out to hold his hand or cup his junk. Yeah, I have an urge to reach out and just cup him through his pants, make my hand a penis hammock. It's an odd urge, one that I'm not entirely proud of, though it's there. But in front of Mr. Knightly, Eric, *and* the architect—my little fantasy is wildly inappropriate.

"So you don't want to expand into the harbor?" Giselle, the architect, asks as we all study the wall that runs parallel to the water, charted out on the blueprints spread out atop the table we're hovering around.

"No." Reid shakes his head. "Not if it's going to take five months. We can still have an indoor-outdoor space using the square footage we have." He waves his hand through the air. "We could bring the ware-house wall back six feet, which would give enough room for a small patio. Then line the entire wall with pocket doors so they can slide open on a nice day. Line the ceiling with heaters that point inward for those chilly nights so patrons can still feel like they're outside but not freeze their asses off. And on the outside, silent fans to deter flies and insects from coming inside the restaurant."

Huh, who knew fans could do that?

"Good idea," Eric says, his eyes lighting up. "The safety rail can be glass so when you're sitting, the view isn't obstructed, and if people want to take pictures, they can."

"Exactly. But have all the seats under the roof, nothing actually on the patio."

Eric nods. "And with the color motif from the Landing as inspiration, it's going to be perfect."

Reid came to the meeting with a palette of colors and a layout of all fixtures, floorings, and woodwork he wants to see. How he did it all in one night is beyond me, but then again, he did have the Lobster Landing to model everything after. The goal is to create a sense of cohesion between the two buildings, meaning the walls will be covered in white shiplap with natural wood accents in the tables, flooring, exposed beams, and countertops. The chairs will all be teal with basket-wrapped bottoms for extra texture. Iron details will be worked into the light fixtures, pocket doors, window frames, and fans, as well as in the exposed kitchen. They want it out in the open so patrons can watch their food as it's made. Red accents will be added with the logo, just like the Lobster Landing, and the plating will be red while the glassware will be tinted teal.

I'm beside myself with excitement. I can see it all: the industrial yet beachy theme, the bright reds, teals, and whites, the enhanced loft where the office will be, the subtle hints of rope, the ironwork, the long wall of pocket sliding doors for the view. It will be absolutely breathtaking.

The boys both pause and turn to Mr. Knightly. His arms are crossed, and one hand cups his chin as he stares down at the plans.

"What do you think, Dad?" Reid asks quietly.

He doesn't answer right away. Instead he pushes a few visuals from the design board around and then looks up at his son, a tear rolling

down his cheek. "It's absolutely everything I could have dreamed of."
He pulls Reid into a hug. "It's perfect."

He did good.

He really did, and all in a short time frame. This is how good
Reid is, how amazing his visions can be. He's spent enough time at the
Lobster Landing to know how to bring the atmosphere into a restaurant
setting while still embracing the industrial look.

When Mr. Knightly pulls away, Reid says, "And the outside, red
corrugated panels, the logo ten by ten and painted directly on the wall
with white paint. It will go perfectly with the Landing but also stand
out as a separate building."

"I love it," Mr. Knightly says, his arm still wrapped around Reid's
shoulders. "I absolutely love it. I couldn't have thought of anything better. And using the loft space for offices—you've really thought of it all."

"I have to agree," Eric says, amazement in his eyes. "If I wasn't a
part of this, I would be incredibly jealous because this is everything Port
Snow's been missing. Casual family dining that feels modern but still
has a hint of nostalgia. I'm really impressed, Reid."

The smile—the pride—that crosses over Reid in a matter of seconds
almost brings me to my knees. I don't think I've ever seen him so happy,
so in his element. It might have taken a lot for him to get to this point,
but I can see the life start to spark back in his eyes.

He's finally found his purpose.

Giselle looks over everything again. "Well, let's get started, boys.
I can have the men start tearing down walls tomorrow and demoing
anything that needs to be taken out." She hands Reid some red tape.
"X everything you want gone. And if you want to help to move along
the process, please feel free to show up at seven tomorrow morning."

Reid takes the tape. "I'll have a hand in everything—that's if Griffin
can find someone to cover my shifts at the Landing." He looks over to
his dad, who laughs.

"We can surely find some backup."

"Good," Giselle says, collecting the design boards. "I'll find samples of everything you want and bring them in over the next few days. I think we can have this place up and running in a few months. The bones are here, and since you're keeping the layout open and exposing the natural architecture, there won't be much we have to do building-wise beyond making everything pretty. Permits are set, so now you just need to settle on a name."

"Any ideas?" Reid asks as his dad nods slowly.

"Knight and Port. Knight for the family, Port for the town. It's a combination of the two things I hold closest to my heart."

Knight and Port—I can see it.

I press my hand against Mr. Knightly's arm. "I love it. It has so much meaning but feels modern. It's perfect."

"Yeah, it is, Dad." Reid glances around the space, unable to contain his grin. "Looks like we have a menu to create."

"And I have just the place to start," Eric says, pulling a notebook from his back pocket. "Let's get to work."

One hundred items.

One, zero, zero—that's how many things the boys have on the menu. At least that's how many they had when I left.

A little prolific when it comes to the ideas.

I don't even know how they could think of that many recipes, though they kept reassuring me they were going to pare everything down.

With a headache looming, I cash out the bar at the Inn and bring the money to the back, thankful it hasn't been a busy night. I'm exhausted from the sleepless night I had with Reid. He wanted to get in as much sex as possible before Eric came to crash on my couch, and after all the excitement and planning today, I can barely move one leg in front of the other.

I crash into the office chair just as my phone rings. I dig it out of my pocket to find Harper's name crossing the screen. I answer quickly.

"Please tell me you have a masseuse at your house and are inviting me over for a rubdown."

"That's one way to answer the phone." She chuckles. "I don't have a rubdown ready for you, but I do have some wine and the biggest charcuterie board you'll ever see. Rogan is out for the night, and Ren is coming over—thought you could help us take down the cheese and crackers I overindulged in."

"Sounds amazing. I'll come straight there if you tell me I can borrow a shirt and sweatpants."

"Done. Hurry up, we're waiting."

That puts a pep in my step. I shoot a quick text to Eric, letting him know the apartment is his for the night, and then finish up my business in the office.

It's officially Eric's first night back in Port Snow, and yeah, maybe I should spend it with him, but then again, I need some girl time. It's been a while since I've seen Harper and Ren. Eric will be fine on his own.

I'm out the door in record time, and Walter, one of the town's Uber drivers, is waiting for me out front. During the drive, he drones on about the town gossip floating around—Franklin has a mole he's getting checked out, Caleb's seeing some girl over in German Town, and Tracker had an apparent pregnancy scare with a tourist—but I couldn't care less. I tune Walter out and text Reid, letting him know I'm hanging with the girls and reminding him just how sexy he looked during the design meeting today with his backward hat and tight jeans.

The man has been my fantasy for longer than I can even remember. It's still a bit surreal, being able to text him things about his tight ass and how I wanted to stick my hands down his pants. He's always been a pipe dream kind of guy—someone who could never see me as more than a friend. But with each encounter, each interaction over the past few years, something was growing between us until finally he made a move, right on the dance floor. Probably one of the most epic moments of my life, having Reid Knightly look at me as more than just a friend, more than just his friend's sister—as someone he couldn't keep his hands off of.

These past few weeks with him have had their ups and downs, but I wouldn't trade the roller coaster for a steady carousel any day because the ups and downs have helped me come to the realization that I love this man. He's it for me.

My phone rings again, and I see it's Eric.

"Hey, what's up?"

"You're really not coming home?" The whine in his voice makes me laugh.

"Are you lonely?"

"A little." We both laugh.

"Work on the menu. I need some girl time."

"What about some bro time? We have three whole years to make up for. I know you like to say that things are cool with us, but I can still detect some tension, Eve. Are you trying to avoid me tonight?"

Yes, there's tension and maybe a little bit of awkwardness, but that will go away with time. The more we work together and mend the open wound in our relationship, the more we'll get comfortable again. After all, we're family, and family always sticks together.

"I'm not avoiding you, I promise. Harper just offered me wine, cheese, and crackers. What can you offer?"

"Nothing, because that's what you have in your fridge. Absolutely nothing."

"Looks like you should take a trip down to the general store then. Maybe say hi to Oliver. You two were friends growing up."

"Until his boating accident. After that happened, he pretty much sequestered himself to his shop."

"Well, reach out. He might need a friend. I'll be home later. And don't go snooping in my things; you never know what kind of vibrating objects you might find."

"Jesus, Eve." I laugh, hard. "That wasn't necessary."

"It really was. Talk to you later, bro."

When I hang up, Walter looks up into the rearview mirror with a brow raised. "Vibrating objects?"

Shit.

Of course Walter overheard *that* tidbit.

I can count on my little comment being broadcast around town within an hour. Reason number one for never answering my phone while getting a ride from Walter: whatever you say is guaranteed to get spread from one mouth to the other like a kissing virus.

But his eavesdropping gives me an idea.

"Say, Walter, did you happen to hear—"

"That you don't want anyone exposing your relationship with Reid to your brother? Yeah, that's old news."

I smile to myself. For the first time since I can remember, I actually appreciate the gossip in this town.

"I don't think you'll be getting these pants back." I flop onto the couch and rub my hand over my leg. "This is the softest fabric ever. Where did you get them?"

"Rogan got them for me. I think he likes the way it feels when he runs his hands up and down my legs."

"Sounds about right. The Knightly men seem to all have one thing in common, besides those devastating blue eyes—they're all horny."

Ren snorts as she sips her wine. "Yeah, that's one way to describe it. Did I ever tell you about the first time Griffin and I had sex?"

"No," Harper and I say at the same time, leaning in.

"It was after we went on a camping trip with everyone. Brig and Reid were doing everything in their power to keep us from having sex, and Griffin was so frustrated. We made an excuse to go back home with one thing in mind . . . doing the deed. But then Griffin was pulled away by his family, cockblocking of course, and then my parents showed up just as Griffin and I started to get handsy. He had to sneak out the back of my house with the biggest boner ever and trudge across the neighborhood to his house. That night, we met up on the beach—"

"Oh my God!" Harper says, slamming her hand on the couch. "Hold up. That rumor of you two doing it on the beach is true?"

Ren slowly nods.

"Wait, you did it on the beach in Port Snow, where anyone could catch you?" I ask.

"Yup, see? Horny men, all of them."

"Rogan is the same way; it's like he's reliving our teenage years again, trying to sneak it in wherever he can. I can't even tell you how many times we've done it in the manor at this point. Poor Gina, she must regret being Rogan's assistant. I'm almost positive she's heard us at least a dozen times. I told Rogan she needs a raise."

"What about Reid?" Ren asks. "I'm guessing he's just as bad."

"Worse," I answer. "Not only are his hands always all over me, but he's also so perverted, constantly making sexual innuendos."

"Yup, sounds about right," Harper says and then turns to Ren. "That boy has always been sexual, ever since I've met him. Didn't he lose his virginity at like thirteen?"

"Sixteen," I correct, hating that I know such an intimate detail. I remember the day he bragged about it to Eric—I was so heartbroken. "It was with Kelsey Littleton. I got to hear all about it when he told Eric."

"Oh, that must have been fun." Ren sips her wine.

"Especially since you were crushing on Reid big time, right?" Harper says.

"You were?" Ren asks.

I nod, reaching over and grabbing a few cheeses and grapes. "Oh yeah. Typical brother's-best-friend crush. I was infatuated with him, but he was clueless."

"Eh, I wouldn't say that," Harper says. "I remember the way he used to look at you back then. It was puppy love."

I shake my head. "No, because if that was the case, he wouldn't have gone after every other girl in our grade until he went off to culinary school."

"Who knows—maybe he was too nervous to take things to the next level with you."

"Okay." I laugh. "I'm pretty sure that wasn't the case at all. But it doesn't matter at this point, now that we're together."

Ren and Harper exchange looks before Harper says, "Do you love him?"

I raise my glass of wine to her. "I should have known this invite was going to be a shakedown for information."

"Oh please," Harper counters. "You were up my ass when it came to Rogan. It's only right that I do the same with you and Reid."

It's true. I was relentless when she was thinking about getting back together with Rogan after so many years of being apart. But that's what best friends do, right?

"Can't fault you for that," I say and twist my wineglass by the stem as it rests on my leg. "Yes, I do. I love him, and it's scary and exciting and consuming. I'm not sure if he feels the same way, but what I do know is that he's working really hard at being the man he thinks I deserve."

"Gah, my heart. Oh, Reid. Look at him, all grown up." Harper clasps her hands over her chest.

Suddenly, the front door whooshes open, and in come the four Knightly men, all looking as handsome as ever. Rogan leads the group, followed by Griffin and Reid, with Brig bringing up the rear.

When Reid sees me, his smile stretches across his face, and we stare at each other, savoring the moment. I love that smile so much, that look in his eyes whenever he sees me. Talk about butterflies: they're constantly floating in my stomach when he's around.

"Hey, I thought you were all going out," Harper says as Rogan plops down beside her on the couch.

"Brig was bringing us down, so we thought we'd come back here and make him even more depressed," Rogan answers before planting a kiss on her lips.

With both hands on the armrests of Ren's chair, Griffin bends at the waist and gently kisses her on the mouth. I watch them for a moment before my own Knightly scoops me up and sets me on his lap, his arm wrapping around my stomach, his lips connecting with the side of my head.

"Hey," he whispers before tugging on my earlobe with his teeth.

Shivers roll up my spine, and goose bumps spread across my skin.

"Hey," I answer back, feeling a little shy.

"Well, isn't this just fucking lovely," Brig says, standing in front of all of us, his arms crossed. Sarcasm drips from his voice as he looks over each couple. "None of you fuckers were looking for love, and there you are, all smiling idiots with a girl in your arms, while I'm over here, tit-less, with no prospects in sight."

"Maybe because you're calling yourself *tit-less* rather than single," Griffin points out.

"Whatever. I'm texting Walter. I'm getting out of here. I don't need to be thrown down a well of depression because you're all insensitive to my struggles." He turns and heads out the door, slamming it behind him.

I try to hold it back, but I can't. And neither can the rest of the group—we all burst out laughing. Oh, poor, poor Brig.

"Maybe if he stopped trying, love would find him," Ren says.

"He's too sensitive about what happened in New Orleans. He's on a hunt to make sure the curse is broken, and there's no stopping him," Griffin says.

Harper scans the room. "You can't *possibly* think that thing is real."

None of the boys answer. Instead, Griffin stares down at his fingers, examining his cuticles with more intent than a man should. Rogan's eyes seem to find the ceiling quite intriguing at this very moment, and Reid, well, he cuddles closer, making it impossible to see his reaction. Unbelievable.

"Want to get out of here?" Reid whispers, breaking the silence.

"Well, I was *supposed* to be having a girls' night."

"Have a girls' night with my dick."

I turn to face him. "Are you telling me your penis is a woman?"

He cringes. "I guess that didn't come out right, did it?" I shake my head. "Then let me be more clear. My dick wants to play with your vagina, so please let her come out and have a good time."

"Did Reid just ask your vagina to come out and play?" Harper butts in.

"Hey, no one asked you to listen in on our conversation," he snaps back, as if she were his very own sibling.

"Hard not to when you're breathing heavy like that."

Rogan squeezes her leg. "Good one, Harp."

"You *are* breathing pretty loudly," Griffin points out. "It's getting weird, dude."

"I am not. Fuck all of you." Before I know what's happening, Reid stands, still holding me in his arms, and walks to the door. "Say good night to your friends—you're coming with me."

"Reid, my clothes," I call out, just barely able to snag my purse from a side table.

"We'll get them later. We're going to show these old farts how to have a good time."

"Are you going to record it for us?" Rogan calls out.

Reid throws up a middle finger in response before hurrying through the night air to his truck and setting me in the passenger seat.

"Where do you think we're going?" I ask after he hops in and settles himself behind the wheel.

"To my place."

"What if Eric gets bored and decides to visit you? Might not be the best idea."

Reid's hands clamp around the steering wheel, his knuckles turning white with frustration. "Damn it. Uh, okay, let's go to the Point." He roars his truck to life.

"The make-out spot for high schoolers?"

"Why not?" He smiles wickedly. "Could be fun."

CHAPTER TWENTY-THREE

REID

Shit.

Fuck.

Ahhh . . .

"Babe, I'm . . . fuck, I'm going to come." My hand is tangled in Eve's long brown hair while she's bent over the console, sucking me off.

Talk about every childhood fantasy come true. When I decided to bring Eve to the Point, it was on a whim, but now I'm the most grateful motherfucker ever. After I felt up and sucked her tits for a good twenty minutes, I fingered her to completion, and she went ahead and returned the favor. She's had her mouth on my cock for five minutes, and I'm already about to explode.

Instead of moving her mouth, she sucks harder and grips my cock tighter at the base, shooting all my blood to the tip.

Her tongue swirls; my balls tighten.

Her tongue flicks; my hips thrust up.

Her tongue swirls again, and with one last suck, I'm gone. I'm coming so hard that white spots start to impede my vision and a low, long groan explodes out of me.

"Mother . . . fucker." I breathe as I release my hand from her hair, realizing I was gripping it rather hard. "Ah, shit, babe. Are you okay?"

She nods as she looks up at me, her eyes watery but happy.

"I didn't mean to pull on your hair like that." I massage her scalp. "I kind of lost control."

She works her way up my body, pressing kisses against my bare chest and then across my lips. "It was hot, Reid. I kind of liked it."

"Yeah?" I ask, brow raised. "Got a little kink in you?"

"Maybe a little. So keep that in mind when you want to start getting creative."

"Christ, I think you just made me hard again."

She rolls her eyes and adjusts her shirt so her tits are securely back in place. Despite my dick wanting to hang out longer, I stuff it back in my jeans and buckle up before turning to watch Eve smooth out her hair.

She's the same girl I've always known, the girl I crushed on for so many years, but somehow even more beautiful. Her strong-willed personality and intelligence turn me on, and add that to her insatiable need for me every time we're around each other, and I'm just a man head over heels in love.

No doubt in my mind. I just need to find the right time to tell her. And inside a truck right after she's blown me is not that time. I want something that's going to make her swoon and leave her with no choice but to say the words back.

"Oral at the Point . . . can't say I've never done that before."

"What?" I ask, whipping my head around, making her laugh.

"Oh God, that was too easy. You had this dreamy look on your face, and wiping it off was just hilarious."

"Real funny, now who was it?"

"No one. I was only kidding."

"Don't joke about giving oral to other people. As far as I'm concerned, my dick is the only one that's touched your lips."

"Okay, keep telling yourself that."

I will.

I really fucking will.

"Come here." I pull on her hand and drag her over to my side until she's sitting on my lap and resting her head on my shoulder. I kiss the top of her head and squeeze her tight, not wanting to let go, not wanting to have to drop her off at her apartment.

"What would your ideal date with me be?"

She nuzzles in even closer. "Well, besides giving out blow jobs at the Point?"

"Yeah." I chuckle. "Besides that."

"An ideal date with Reid Knightly, hmm . . ." She thinks about it for a few moments, then: "Fishing."

"Fishing?" I ask, surprised. I was thinking more along the lines of taking her up to Bar Harbor or somewhere just as romantic, but fishing?

"Yes, fishing. We would go out on your boat looking for the best lobsters or crabs or fish, and once we had the catch, we would take it back to your house and cook it together. You'd stand behind me and show me all your culinary expertise while casually dropping seductive kisses on my neck. Music would be playing in the background, those yummy candles would be lit, and there'd be wine available for whenever we wanted a sip. Maybe while we're cooking, you'd spontaneously pull me into a dance and then dip me and slowly press a kiss against my lips."

"That's doable, babe. Let's plan for it. The night before the restaurant's soft opening, let's celebrate by going out on your perfect date."

"That's a few months from now."

"Worth the wait, don't you think?"

She pulls away so we're facing each other, her face barely visible in the darkness. "Think we'll still be together a few months from now?"

"If I have anything to do with it, we will." I bring her head back down to my chest and run my fingers through her locks.

The words are on the tip of my tongue: *I love you.* I want to say them, put them out there, let her know this is something special; this is more than me just liking her. I want to tell her about my crush, about how I'm pretty sure a small part of me has been in love with her for a long time, but it took me forever to realize it. But I stop myself. I think I'll hold out for her perfect date.

I actually couldn't think of a better time.

Stepping out of the shower, I wipe the fog off the tiny bathroom mirror and lean on the counter. I'm beat. Since I'm skipping out on some Lobster Landing shifts—not all of them, but a good portion—I went at it hard this morning on the boat, bringing in enough lobster to keep my bank account afloat.

But hell, it feels like every muscle in my body is aching, and it probably doesn't help that I spent the last night trying to figure out the best way possible to have Eve in my truck. My back and my ass are sore where the long gearshift kept poking me. On the actual butt cheek— not inside, you perverts.

My phone beeps on the counter, so I wrap the towel around my waist and check it.

Griffin: Wow, are they tearing down the whole building over there? It's really fucking loud.

Chuckling, I type back.

Reid: Only for the first two days. Demo won't take very long and then it's a matter of putting everything together.

Brig: I could hear it from the garage.

Rogan: You also said you could hear it while getting coffee, and insisted it was so loud you couldn't concentrate on your order.

Brig: I have supersonic ears, like a rabbit. When you fools don't think I can hear you talking about me, I do.

Reid: It's because we talk loud enough so you can hear what we're saying.

Brig: So you're being rude, just to be rude? How did we grow up in the same household?

Rogan: I ask myself that same question every day.

Griffin: Did Dad like the plans?

Reid: Loved them. He actually cried. It was weird but also felt really good.

Brig: You made Dad cry? How did you hold it together? I would have been bawling like a baby.

Griffin: We know.

I'm about to respond when there's a knock at my door. I set my phone down and look out the window and around the corner, catching a glimpse of Eric. Grateful it's not a curious neighbor, I keep a firm hold on my towel, walk over to the door, and open it.

"Hey," I say as a greeting, but it barely falls off my lips as I take in the pure rage marring his features.

Oh.

Shit.

"Is it true?" he asks through his teeth, seething as he bursts into my house.

I shut the door quickly. "Is what true?" Because why not stall a little bit longer?

From his back pocket he pulls out an old newspaper clipping, the one announcing my official relationship with Eve. The same article I was chuckling over just a couple of weeks ago.

Fuck.

Brandishing it in front of me, he repeats himself, "Is it true? I found this in Eve's kitchen when I was cooking."

I can't hold back the wince on my face or ignore the feeling of being caught red-handed, so I just come out with it.

"It is."

He crumples the newspaper and starts pacing the floor. "And when were you going to fucking tell me? Never?"

"No, not *never*. We were waiting."

He shakes his head and turns on me, jabbing his finger in my face. "End it. End it right fucking now."

"What?" I take a step back. "I'm not going to end it with Eve."

"The fuck you aren't. Do you not remember what happened the last time? You don't mix business with pleasure, Reid. I would have assumed you would take your own advice, the advice you gave me over three years ago."

"This is different," I snap back.

"Because it's you?" He shakes his head. "It's a distraction—for both of you. I love my sister more than anything, and I want to see her succeed. You're a moody motherfucker who can flip at the drop of a hat. You need to focus on the restaurant, and she needs to focus on the business, on school, on becoming the woman she has been working so goddamn hard to become. She doesn't need you and your drama and impulsiveness getting in the way."

"Wow, good to know you think so highly of me," I say, crossing my arms over my chest. But despite my stance and the strength in my voice, Eric's words instantly start to eat away at my resolve.

Since Eve and I have been together, I *have* been moody, unpredictable, a bastard at times, and she's always been forgiving, understanding, and patient. How much more can she take, though? This restaurant won't be easy—there will be really hard days, arguments—and I'm probably going to take it out on her. Will I push her away like I did before? I can't guarantee I won't. And strong as she is, I know my moods affect her. I can hardly admit it to myself, but I know it's true. I love her—so much—but what if Eric is right, and I end up derailing her entire future?

Then there's the issue that's been plaguing me ever since Eve came into the Lobster Landing looking for fudge: she's driven and hardworking; she knows exactly what she wants in life and has taken the steps to accomplish it despite every speed bump and roadblock life has thrown her way. She doesn't give up. But I do, and I could see her finding that a huge weakness—one I'm not sure I could ever overcome.

"End it. Today," Eric says.

"And what if I don't?"

His eyes narrow. "Then I'm out. And you and I both know you don't want to do this without me."

I fucking hate that he's right.

I run my tongue over my teeth and meet his gaze. "It's not a fling for me, Eric. She's more than that."

"And she's been dicked over by guys in the past—even guys who cared about her. I would know since I was one of them. She needs this, this job, this opportunity. And you need this. What's going on between the two of you is a distraction that none of us need. You saw what happened last time with Janelle. Relationships blind you; they muddy the waters, affect your decision-making, and we can't have that. But if you won't end it for us, end it for your dad. We can't fuck this up for him." And there it is, the one thing—besides Eve—that will bring me to my damn knees: mentioning my dad. "End it before it goes any further. It's better this way, and I know my sister. She'll act like a professional and move on."

That's what I'm afraid of. I don't want her to move the fuck on. Because I sure as hell won't be able to.

Then again, everything Eric has said has been completely, painfully true.

I'm not the most levelheaded in the family, and even though I don't want to admit it, I can see myself distracting Eve, pulling her away from her tasks to help soothe whatever bullshit my head is putting me through. That's what these last few weeks have been, so why would that change all of a sudden?

When my dad approached me about the restaurant, I shut down immediately, leaving her in the dark, taking off without saying goodbye. And when I got back, I snapped at her on the dock when she was just making sure I was okay. My problem was a blip in the road in the grand scheme of things, but I almost lost Eve over a blip. That night, when I went to her apartment, I thought she was going to break up with me, but somehow I managed to find the most forgiving woman on the planet.

And when I blew up at her after she and Eric announced they were going to be a part of Knight and Port, I managed to not only insult her but also put our entire relationship on the line after just another blip.

What happens when things don't go right in the restaurant? When I lose my shit again? Is she going to be just as forgiving? Should I even let her be? How many times can I really dick her around until I should let her go?

At this point, I think I'm pushing my luck.

"Fuck," I breathe out, my hand pushing through my hair. "Fuck."

"Do the right thing, Reid. Don't fuck us over like I did."

My mind races, wrestling with the possibilities.

My heart nearly breaks my rib cage with how hard it's pounding.

And an overwhelming sense of dread washes over me as I realize I don't really have a choice in the matter.

The stakes are so much higher now. It isn't like Bar 79 when Eric and I lost everything; there are more people involved, more hearts on the line.

Not only is this a second chance for me, a chance to find pride in myself again, but this is also a second chance for Eric, an opportunity for Eve she deserves more than anything, and lastly, a long-overdue dream of my dad's coming true.

This isn't just about me; this is about everyone around me. My siblings, my mom, Eve, Eric, the town . . .

I need this to be a success.

I need this to be more than just an average restaurant in town.

I need this to be a complete win, an empire, something that is passed on from generation to generation.

Which brings me to the hardest decision of my life.

I love her. I know deep in the marrow of my bones that Eve is the very match to my broken soul, and I would give anything to make her happy, even if it means taking a step back so, for once in her life, she can put herself first and accomplish what she's been working so hard to achieve. I can't fuck this up, no matter how much losing Eve is going to break me. I refuse to let anyone down ever again.

Eric starts to leave, but before he makes it through the door, I call out, "Don't be home tonight after her shift."

"Thank you," he says without turning around. And with that, he takes off.

When the door shuts, I crumble to my couch and press my head into my hands. *End it.* Two words that are going to change my entire life, and not for the better.

CHAPTER TWENTY-FOUR

EVE

As I wrap my coat around me—guarding against Maine's early-spring cold—and make my way to my apartment, all I can think about is how I wish I could be wrapped up in Reid's arms right about now, lying in bed together while watching some kind of mindless show, his hands playing with my hair, my hands stroking his bare chest.

Instead, I have to go back to my apartment, to my brother, who is not going to cuddle with me and push his hand through my hair—not that I would want him to. Why I thought it was a good idea to have him stay at my place is beyond me, but it's apparently a good form of torture given his incessant need to take up all the space in my living room with his bags and recipe books and notes. He's messy, loud, and constantly trying to talk my ear off about all the new ideas that keep coming to him. I love the guy, but sometimes it's nice to watch a show without hearing about the latest searing technique he's learned.

The wind blows my hair off my shoulder, and I pull my coat a little tighter as I crest the small hill that leads from the Inn to my apartment. I make quick work of the distance, not wanting to hang out in the dark by myself for too long. It's a small town, but there are still creeps. There always are.

Head tilted down, I'm almost at my apartment when I glance up and spot Reid's truck—and then Reid, leaning against the hood, arms crossed, staring me down.

What the hell is he doing here? I scan the parking lot; Eric's car isn't here, which means he isn't either, but that doesn't mean he won't be coming home soon.

"Reid, what are you doing here?" I say, hurrying over to him.

Not quite looking me in the eye, he says, "I need to talk to you."

"Here? Now? Eric could be home any moment."

"He's with Brig. They're out for a bit."

"Okay." I study him, the droop in his shoulders, the tension in his neck, the uneasiness vibrating off of him. Something's wrong. "What happened?" I press my hand to his arm. "Is everything okay?"

He pulls on the back of his neck, and a vein stands out on his forehead. Whatever happened is causing a lot of stress. "I . . . uh, I've been doing some thinking."

"Okay," I drawl out, taking a step closer, trying to ease the tension that's holding him captive. "Is it about the restaurant?"

"Sort of, yeah. You know it's a big project, and my dad's relying on me."

"Yes, but in just a few days you've already painted a beautiful picture of what's to come. It's going to be amazing, Reid."

"Yeah, thanks." He looks over my shoulder, still not meeting my eyes. "So it's a lot of work. I've had a hard time in the past trying to keep it together during a project like this, and I don't think I can handle it all."

"What do you need help with? I'm here for you."

I reach for his hand, but he takes a step back. And that's when the hairs on the back of my neck rise, a shiver of anxiety passing through me.

"That's what I need to talk to you about." He lets out a deep breath, sticks his hands in his pockets, and stares at the ground. "I think we should, you know, maybe take a break or something."

My heart hitches in my chest, and my entire body goes still. Did I just hear him correctly? Take a break? That can't be right. Just last night we were making promises about the perfect date before the soft opening. What happened between then and now? What's made him do this about-face?

"A break?" I glance around. "Is this some kind of weird joke you're playing on me? Because I really don't find it funny."

"Fuck," he mutters, turning away. "It's not a joke. I need to focus on the restaurant. I won't have time to spend on you, and you should focus on yourself too. Finish up school, get Knight and Port ready, train with my dad. There's no time for us."

"There's time if you make time. It doesn't need to be one or the other."

"I can't have both." He turns back around, his jaw firmly set. "I can't manage both, and in the end, I'm just going to disappoint you—like I've *been* disappointing you."

"What are you talking about?"

"Come on, Eve," he says, his curt, condescending tone lashing me right in the heart. "You can't say our relationship has been easy."

"It's not supposed to be easy," I shoot back. "If a relationship is easy, then you haven't broken the surface of the emotions that make someone the person they are. We've had our ups and downs, but every relationship does; that's what makes you stronger."

"It's only going to get worse. Don't kid yourself."

"Why? Why do you think it's going to get worse? Because you're taking on a new responsibility? Because you're starting something new? Of course it's going to be stressful and hard at times, but that's why you have me—to lean on."

"I know you think I can be a better man, the man you deserve, but I know that's bullshit," he snaps. "People can't change. I can't change."

Caught off guard at his abrupt confession, I take a step back, my feet aching from my long shift. "I don't want you to change. I like you for the man you are."

A sarcastic laugh pops out of him as he looks down and shakes his head. "You're delusional then."

"Excuse me?"

He doesn't answer; instead, he jumps to the last thing I expected to hear tonight. "Might as well end it now before I fuck up the restaurant and hurt you even more."

"End it? Now we're breaking up? I thought you just wanted to take a break."

"They're the same fucking thing." He tosses his hand up in frustration.

"So." I take a deep breath. "You're breaking up with me because you think that's what's best . . . for the restaurant."

"Yes, and for you. For everyone. This way we're not sneaking around; we're not getting distracted. You focus on your shit—I'll focus on mine."

"Oh, how nice. Should we high-five in passing too? Just drop all the feelings we've developed, and go back to just being friends?"

"Sure," he says, the sarcasm starting to build in his voice. "If that's what you want, I'll hand out a high five here and there."

I push at his shoulder. "Don't be an ass. Don't use that to push me away right now."

"I'm not using it—it's who I am. You should know that by now. You've known me for over a decade. What you see is what you get."

"That's a lie." I step closer to him, my breath misting through the air between us. "That's a lie, and you goddamn know it. You're not the irritable prick you like to make yourself out to be, the one you showcase for the world. You're a beautiful soul with a loving heart and a caring mind. This guy who's standing in front of me, he's not the Reid I know. He's just a placeholder for the man I love."

His eyes widen right before he shakes his head and casts his eyes down again. "You don't love me, Eve."

"Don't tell me how I feel." I step closer, giving him no choice but to meet my eyes. "If I say I love you, then I freaking love you, and you need to accept that."

He runs his tongue along his lips. "I think you need to accept that, yeah, we know how to fuck, and that's been good, but in the long run we're not compatible." I reel back from the verbal slap to the face he just delivered.

We know how to fuck? Yes, the physical chemistry has been a huge plus when it comes to Reid, but it's not why I chose him, why I still choose him, why I love this man standing in front of me, the one purposefully trying to break my heart.

I love Reid because he challenges me, because he's a roller coaster. He gives me highs and lows, he keeps me guessing, he shows me that life isn't about walking around wearing rose-colored glasses. There's defeat, there's sorrow, and there are moments of utter clarity that mold you.

And even though I don't truly want to admit this, and I would probably never say this to Reid, I sense his need, like he needs my spirit, my thoughts, my mind. I took care of my parents, and even though it was devastating to watch them slowly fade away, it filled a hole in my heart I never knew I had: the urge to take care of someone. Reid considers himself a burden on me, but he isn't—in fact, he fills a part of my soul that's been gaping ever since I lost my parents.

"How could you say we're not compatible? Don't you see how well we fit together?"

Growling, he rakes both his hands through his hair. "This is over, and the sooner you understand that, the better."

Like a knife to the chest, his words stab me, cutting me to my very core. "You don't mean this. What about last night; what about our plans? What about me being the girl for you? Where did all that go?"

He casually shrugs. "Sometimes you can't have it all."

He takes a step back, and my heart lurches. "Reid, don't do this. Talk to me."

"Nothing to talk about, Eve. It's over."

"Just like that? You're just calling it?"

He reaches for the door handle of his truck. "Someone has to be smart about this."

"You think you're being smart? Okay, genius, tell me how you expect us to work together with this heartbreak hanging between us?"

He glances at me, his blue eyes flashing with confidence, though not for him . . . but for me. "You're a professional, Eve. I know you'll be able to handle it."

With that, he gets in his truck, and it roars to life. Without a backward glance, he takes off, leaving me and my bruised, battered heart in the parking lot of my apartment building.

◆ ◆ ◆

You're a professional, Eve.

That's what I keep telling myself over and over again as I stand next to Reid, the scent of his cologne hitting me in the gut, the warmth of his arm so close to mine that if I step an inch to the left, our skin will be touching.

And my eyes can't help but wander over his body as he speaks to Giselle, directing her and the construction manager, Dale, with precise detail.

When his arm lifts to point, I take in the definition of his forearm, the indent on the inside of his biceps, the shapeliness of his shoulder and how it used to feel wrapped warmly around me, cocooning me into his body.

When he speaks, I close my eyes as I listen to the deep baritone of his voice floating around me like a warm hug, remembering all the times he would gently whisper into my ear when he was deep inside of me.

And when he stands there, listening intently to everyone present at the meeting, I can't help but stare at the dark scruff that lines his jaw—the same scruff that left delicious beard burns up and down my legs—or the way his backward hat seems to intensify his eyes somehow, lending them the same fire that would smolder in them whenever I walked into a room.

It's been one week, but every time I look at him, my heart feels like it's being ripped out all over again.

That night . . . I don't think I've ever cried as hard as I did after he left. I fled to my apartment, locked myself in my room, and buried my head in my pillow. The grief, the anger, the confusion—all of them poured out of me at once. The next day when Eric took in my appearance and asked if I was okay, I just nodded and told him the spring allergies were getting me. I don't think he believed it, but he didn't ask any other questions.

Every night after that, I've done the same thing: I've gone straight from work to the apartment, barricading myself in my room and insisting to Eric that I need privacy to study—though I have yet to open a textbook since Reid broke things off.

And Reid thinks this is for the better? Maybe for him. In a cruel twist of fate, he actually looks hotter, seems more confident, and exudes nothing but excitement as he checks over every last detail of the restaurant.

Then there's me, the walking dead. I'm pretty sure I have mascara on only one eye today, I can't remember the last time I brushed my hair, and I know for damn sure that my socks don't match. This breakup most definitely hasn't made my life any easier.

And the loss is starting to eat away at me. At my confidence, at my energy, at my ability to focus—hence why I can't take my eyes off his pecs right now.

"What do you think, Eve?" Eric asks, snapping me to attention.

"Um, yeah, great," I answer, not quite sure what the hell we're talking about.

"Then we all agree," Reid says. "I look forward to seeing how it all turns out." He glances at his watch. "Have a shift at the Landing. Got to go. I'll catch you two later." He gives us a quick wave, and just to be an ass, I flutter my fingers at him. I'm tempted to toss him a middle finger as well but hold back.

Giselle and Dale take off toward the kitchen, continuing the conversation and leaving me alone with Eric, who stares at me, his arms crossed over his chest.

"So that went well," I say, studying the air above his right shoulder.

"Do you even know what we talked about?"

"Yeah . . . things."

"Eve—"

"You know, as much as I want to explore that disappointed look on your face, I'd rather not right now. I'm going to go hit up the library and do some studying. See you tonight. You're cooking." As if I need to say that. He's been cooking every night, testing out new recipes and dishes for the restaurant. He wants to tell Reid that my mac and cheese with Doritos should be featured on the menu, but Lord knows how that will go.

Oh, Eve's recipe, gross, ew, I want nothing to do with her—said in a snarky, ugly voice.

That's how Reid sounds in my head right now, despite the fact that I kept wanting to lick his neck today. Straight up lick the man's neck, claim him as mine, let everyone in Port Snow know that even though we're on a break / broken up, he's still mine. I've spent a week in a semidazed state, trying so hard to keep it together, but now I feel myself teetering on the edge of control.

Leaving Knight and Port, I make a left instead of a right, hoping Eric doesn't catch me. It's a good walk, one that should help me clear my mind, but instead of taking in the tall ponderosa pines on either side of the street and marveling at their beauty, I'm stewing, my ball of anger growing bigger and bigger with each step. Striding away from town, I'm grateful for the distance from all the prying eyes and running mouths.

I should breathe in the fresh sea air, but instead I'm huffing like a bull, stomping my feet into the ground, ready to charge.

And instead of waving happily at all the locals, greeting them with a friendly hello and accompanying wave, I'm giving them an easy view of the horns growing out of the top of my head and the fire blazing in my eyes.

By the time I reach my destination, I toss the door open and call out, "I hope you have pants on because I'm coming in."

Harper is standing at the bottom of Snow Vale Manor's grand staircase, clipboard in hand, paper half-lifted, her eyes wide as she takes me in.

"Good God, woman, who enters a building like that?"

"Do you have booze?"

She points toward the den, where her office is. "Scotch in the desk drawer."

"Good." I huff my way across the newly refurbished floors, too angry to really appreciate the beauty of the manor, which Rogan painstakingly restored as a testament to his love for Harper.

See, isn't that romantic? Restoring an old manor in the name of love? That's what men should be doing: romantic gestures. Not offering up high fives like you're bro-ing out in a locker room.

No woman wants a goddamn high five!

I rip the desk drawer open, the force shaking the pen cup balanced on top, and spot the scotch. In one swoop, I bring the bottle up, uncap it, and take a big swig.

"Whoa, what happened to you?" a very familiar voice says from the armchair behind me.

Spinning on my heel, I point my finger at a man who has the same eyes as the dipshit I happen to be in love with.

"I hate you."

"What?" Rogan's eyes narrow as he sets down the tablet he was working on. "What the hell did I do?"

"You're related to Reid, correct?"

"Last time I checked, unfortunately I am."

"Then I hate you. I hate everyone connected to him."

"Uh, does that include me?" Harper asks as she steps inside and sits down in her desk chair, looking over what seems to be a checklist. Ever since Rogan opened the manor to the public, they've been booking out months in advance for events, and Harper is in charge of all of them. She loves her job, loves her man, loves her life.

How freaking perfect.

"Yes, because you're happy—I can see it in your eyes even if you're trying to hide it. Don't try to trick me. I can smell happiness, and it's oozing out of your every pore."

Harper sets her clipboard to the side. "You seem a little hysterical, maybe on the verge of a mental breakdown. How about you take a seat and we talk this over."

"Oh no, I'm not sitting down." I pace the room, bringing the bottle up to my lips for another swig—guess who's calling in sick to the Inn tonight? This girl.

Rogan cuts in. "I'm going to take one guess that this has to do with my idiotic brother?"

"Yes, mm-hmm, that's correct. Sir Reid 'the Moron' Knightly. He's the cause of this lunacy."

"What did he do this time?" Rogan asks, sounding exasperated.

"Oh, you know, just broke up with me. That's all."

"He *what*?" Harper asks as Rogan mumbles something unintelligible to himself and drags both of his hands down his face. "He broke up with you?"

"Yup." I slump against the wall and let my ass hit the floor, feeling like every last ounce of air has been knocked out of my lungs. "He broke up with me a week ago—in my apartment's parking lot. It was a real fairy tale. A moment every girl dreams of. Flickering streetlamp, total eye contact avoidance, a mumble here and there. I don't think I could have dreamed of something more enchanting."

"Did he say why?"

"Oh yeah. He told me we need to focus on the restaurant, that he can't handle both things and in the long run he's going to end up hurting me, so we should just break up now. Mind you, he said *take a break* at first, and I thought he was totally Ross-ing me for a second, but he changed his tune really quickly to *breakup*. Probably didn't want to get into that whole *we were on a break* argument."

"Okay, rewind," Harper says. "What did you say to him?"

I take another gulp of scotch, savoring the intense burn singeing down my throat. "Oh, this is the real kicker. He said he wanted to break up with me, and do you know what I said?"

"Please don't tell me it involved three words," Rogan says, wincing.

"Oh yes it did." I nod. "Told that backward-hat-wearing motherfucker that I loved him. I proclaimed it to all the cars in the parking lot. *I love Reid Knightly*, and then he told me I didn't. Which, God"—I turn to Harper—"isn't it so wonderful when men tell you how you're supposed to feel? There's nothing better than a human with a dick coming up to you and saying, *That's not how you feel, peasant woman*." I pat my chest. "Really makes your nipples hard, doesn't it?"

"Umm, sweetie, maybe we shouldn't drink so much. I love you, but you're really starting to sound a little crazy."

"Oh no, I'm just getting started." I take another swig, regaining some strength in my legs, and pace the room again. "I've had the absolute worst crush on that stupid man for so long that I can't even remember the last time I didn't compare another man to him. He's always been my gold standard. Reid Knightly. He's the most irritating asshole to ever cross my path, and yet I'm that idiot girl who thinks she can make him feel, make him change his ways and fall head over heels in love with her. And just like the idiot girl in every other movie and book, I come up short."

"It doesn't make sense." Rogan pulls on the back of his neck. "He was almost Brig-level infatuated when he told us about you two getting together. He was really happy."

"Yeah, well, he got what he wanted, and now he's walking away. And *working* with him is exceptional, just an absolute dream come true. But the worst part of it all is that it's like, in his mind, we never even dated, he's never seen me naked, and he's never taken"—I hold my hands out wide and thrust my pelvis in the air—"that giant cock of his and shoved it right up my ma-moo." I jab my finger in the air. Harper looks positively disgusted.

"What the actual fuck is a ma-moo?"

I wiggle my finger at her crotch. "Vagina."

"For the love of God, just say *vagina*. No one wants you saying *ma-moo*."

"I don't know, I kind of liked it," Rogan says with a smile. "Does your ma-moo want to play with my pee-pee when we get home?"

"And you just made my nipples shrivel up, thank you." Harper shivers.

Rogan chuckles, the sound almost identical to Reid's. It's infuriating.

"Why can't Reid be more like you?" I say, feeling deflated. "When you two got back together, it was—?" I pause and stare directly at Rogan. "Oh my God, if this has to do with that stupid, idiotic curse you four believe in, I am going to become one ax-wielding, pencil-snapping psychopath, and when I say *pencil*, I mean *penis*." I throw my hands out to the side. "I will chop off all the penises."

"I don't think this has to do with the curse," Rogan says quickly. "Although his curse could technically be in his head. Self-sabotage."

"Oh my God, I will scream."

"Okay." Rogan holds his hands up. "Okay, just take a deep breath. I'm sure there's a reason behind whatever Reid did, stupid as it might be."

"Which means," Harper cuts in, her eyes blazing, "you get to make his life hell."

"What do you mean?"

"Remember when Rogan was being a dick to me, back when I first came back to town?"

"In my defense," Rogan says, "I was so goddamn in love with you I didn't know how to control my emotions." Harper melts just a little at that. Stepping out from behind her desk, she walks up to him, sits on his lap, and presses a quick kiss to his lips before turning back to me.

"When he was being awful," she continues, "you told me that it was time to make him jealous, remind him of everything he was missing out on."

"Wow, Eve. Thanks a lot," Rogan deadpans.

"Whatever, you got the girl." I roll my eyes at him and lean forward. "Tell me more."

Harper eyes me, her gaze sweeping over my knotted hair and rumpled clothes. "Well, look at you. You don't look like the cool and confident Eve I know—the Eve who can take down any man with one bat of her long, pretty lashes. You look like a disheveled bag lady who got dressed in the dark. And do you have mascara only on one eye?" I solemnly nod. "That's what I thought. You need to pull it together, woman. You are better than this. You are stronger than this, and you know it. Yes, Reid broke your heart, but I bet you anything he's just as unhappy as you are."

"Yeah, okay. Trust me, he didn't look at all heartbroken today. He's probably glad he lost the old ball and chain. He was practically glowing today."

Harper shakes her head. "I don't believe it for a second. He's good at putting a mask on—you should know that by now. And do you know what you have to do to strip that mask off? Stride in there with every ounce of confidence you have, do your job like the amazing woman you are, and show him that he's the one who is missing out; he's the one who should be hurting."

"I really like that plan," Rogan says. "I love my brother, but he needs to get some sense knocked into him, and I couldn't think of a more perfect person to do it. He's always thought he had to sacrifice everything for his dreams—that he could never have love and success. Show him that he's missing out by not trying."

Slowly, realization dawns on me. Yeah, I *should* show him what he's missing. He thinks he can't change, that we're not compatible, that Knight and Port is more important than the bond we share? Well, fuck him and fuck that. If there's anything I'm certain of, it's that Reid made a huge mistake breaking up with me, and after this little pep talk from Harper, there's no doubt in my mind that he's going to realize that.

"So I need to torture him, basically. Be a boss lady. Graduate, do my job, date someone, show him just how great I am, and make him weep himself to sleep."

Rogan laughs. "Please, please fucking make him weep. He needs nothing more than a good dose of reality."

"You know what? You're right." I glance down at myself. "I'm not this girl, the one who shows up to meetings looking like a complete disaster. I'm not the girl who gets hung up on a guy. I'm not the girl who forgets about her dreams or why she's pursuing them. Damn it, I'm better than this." I reach up, pull my ponytail holder out of my hair, and fling it across the room as if I'm making a grand statement, declaring a new day. "Listen up, you two. From this point on, you're going to see the old Eve back in action. Hold on to your loins, people, because I'm coming in hot!" Feeling like myself for the first time in a week, I stride out of the office and toward the manor's front doors.

"Might want to take a shower first!" Harper calls out after me. "Because your hair hasn't moved since you took it out of that ponytail."

"Well aware, Harper, well aware."

I shut the front doors and race off toward Main Street with one thing on my mind: getting my life back in order.

CHAPTER TWENTY-FIVE

REID

Rogan: And the dumb ass award goes to **Drum roll**

Griffin: [Michael Scott Drum Roll GIF]

Jen: Oh I'm positively excited to find out.

Brig: **Crosses fingers** please don't let it be me, please don't let it be me.

Rogan: Not this time, bro. It goes to your older sibling, Reid.

Brig: That's a relief.

Jen: What did he do?

Griffin: Has to be really dumb for Rogan to be talking about it.

Rogan: He broke up with Eve.

Jen: What?!?!

Griffin: Uhh . . . why?

Brig: My heart just plummeted. **Whispers** The curse.

Rogan: Heard from Eve, just waiting for Reid to chime in.

Griffin: Care to share, bro?

Jen: Curious minds want to know why you're an idiot.

Brig: My heart can't take this rollercoaster of emotions.

Rogan: Reid . . .

I toss my phone to the other side of my living room couch. The last thing I want to fucking do right now is talk to them—not that I can anyway because they all seem to have a connection to Eve. And anything I say about the breakup will most likely get back to her. I can't have that. Not when I'm barely hanging on by a thread.

It's taken every ounce of energy left in my body to not drive up to the Inn and just stare at her from the bar.

Working with her, oh yeah, a real fucking treat—note the sarcasm. Seeing her, acting like everything is cool . . . it's fucking killing me. A slow, torturous death.

But after just a week, I have to admit that we've all been working well together. Eric and I have been pairing flavors, figuring out a menu. Construction is in full force, and we really couldn't ask for more.

Well, I could.

There's a knock at my door, and before I can say, "Come in," it opens. I don't bother to look up, knowing full well it's Eric, come to do some taste testing.

"You look like shit," he says in greeting, taking a seat across from me at the table where I have everything set up.

"Yeah, well, when you force me to break up with your sister, this is what happens." Even I can hear the bitterness in my voice.

"Don't do that, Reid. If roles were reversed, you would have asked me to do the same exact thing."

"Or you're just trying to be a dick because I was a dick to you years ago."

Eric sits back in his chair, slaps his notepad on the table, and crosses his arms over his chest. "So this is how it's going to be? You're not going to be able to be a mature adult about this? I didn't ask you to break up with her because I was trying to be a dick. I asked you to break up with her because she's a business partner. You and I both lost everything we ever wanted because I mixed business with pleasure, and it clouded my judgment. Even back then, you warned me against dating a coworker. I'm just installing the same guidelines here so that this time we can succeed."

My jaw works back and forth as I stare down at the covered plates in front of us. The difference between the two of us, though, is that I fucking love Eve, I was with her before the opportunity came about, and restaurant or no restaurant, I don't know if I want to wake up another day without her in my arms.

With every day that goes by without a text from her, without seeing that contagious smile or hearing her sharp tongue, I realize more and more just how attached I am to her. And every time I see her at Knight and Port, I wonder if I made the right decision. We're working seamlessly right now, but we were beforehand too. Did I make a gigantic mistake and let go of the one thing in this world that truly made me happy?

In all honesty, I don't think I'm good enough for someone like Eve—someone with so much damn confidence and drive. I may not be good enough, but what I do know is that she's good for me.

But before I can say any of that, I swallow my pride and lift the cover off the first plate.

"A classic take on the baked bean sandwich. French toast bread, grilled and buttered, baked beans, crispy applewood bacon, cheese, and thinly sliced Granny Smith apples."

"French toast bread? Like this is actual french toast?"

I nod, the previous conversation vanishing the minute we start talking food. "The idea came to me the other night when Griffin was going on and on in a text message about Ren wanting breakfast for dinner, french toast in particular. Since baked bean sandwiches are such a New England staple, I thought it would be fun to have a breakfast-for-dinner take on it."

Eric picks up the sandwich, examines it with a sniff and a cautious eye, and then takes a large bite. The crispy bacon crunches against the soft beans and tart, fresh apple. I know it's fucking good. I spent most of the afternoon perfecting it.

I push a small dish toward him. "Dip it in the bourbon-pecan glaze."

"Oh, dude." He smiles and dips the sandwich in the glaze before taking another bite. I swear his eyes roll into the back of his head as he slowly chews. And for a brief moment, I forget about my deep-rooted pain at the loss of Eve. And instead, I'm transported back in time to when I used to test new dishes and flavors with Eric. We spent so many long nights in the kitchen, trying to top one another with secret ingredients like on *Top Chef*, throwing each other off, and reveling in the challenge.

"This is damn good. Fuck, it's really good."

"Thanks."

"This has to be on the menu, no question about it." He picks up his notepad and starts writing down the details about the sandwich.

"Would you change anything? I wasn't sure if I should add nutmeg or not."

He shakes his head. "I wouldn't change a damn thing."

With a surge of pride, I uncover the next dish and pour the sauce on top before he picks it up. I didn't want the bread going soggy.

"This is a take on a meatball sub. I made lobster balls with panko and egg as a binder with some lemon seasoning, and the sauce on top is a cheesy clam chowder, all on a New England bun, buttered and toasted."

"Cheesy clam chowder sauce? Where the hell did you come from?"

I chuckle. "It's something I've been dreaming about for a while. But I never tried to make one because, well, I wasn't cooking. So there it is. Let me know what you think."

I hold my breath while he takes a bite, and as a slow smile creeps across his face, I know I have another winner on my hands.

My heart might be broken, but at least my cooking talent isn't.

◆ ◆ ◆

"Here." I plop a plate of cider donuts down on my parents' empty dinner table and then take a seat.

My mom comes over to my chair, grips both of my cheeks, and plants a kiss on my head. "There's my favorite chef. What are these?"

"Cider donut bites." I pop one in my mouth. "Eric and I had a competition to see who could make a better one, and he won. He's always had a way with the sweet stuff. So we're going with his recipe. Now you get to eat the rejects."

"How thoughtful." She reaches out and takes a small bite. "Wow, these are amazing; if these are the rejects, I can't wait to taste the winners."

"He does something fancy I still can't pinpoint." I shrug and drum my fingers on the table.

"Can I just say"—yup, I knew this was coming—"I'm so proud of you, Reid, for taking another shot at this. Dad's been telling me all about the progress you've been making over the last month, and I took a sneak peek in the restaurant the other day. I can't believe the transformation. The crew is working really hard."

"They are, and I'm impressed, actually. They think we'll be able to do the soft opening in just two months."

"Seriously? Just two more months?" Mom's eyes widen. "That's . . . soon."

"I've been putting in some work, and so has Rogan."

"Well, he *is* the renovation expert in the family. That's so wonderful. I can't wait to see how everything comes together. Your dad is positively giddy."

"Yeah, he's been hugging me a lot lately. I'm guessing that's his way of silently thanking me."

"That and he's a little heartbroken about you and Eve."

"Jesus. So glad my siblings can keep a secret. Was it Brig?"

Mom brushes her graying hair off her shoulder. "He came racing into the house, looking for matches, the night he found out. Everything was closed, and he said he needed to light a *cleansing candle*."

"Such a douche." I chuckle, thinking about Brig's panic and worry, his unwavering belief in the curse. I don't think my breakup with Eve has anything to do with the curse, other than bad timing and falling for the wrong girl . . . at least that's what I'm telling myself.

"He's concerned, honey. We all are. You seemed to be so right for each other. What changed?"

I pat my mom's hand. "Nothing you need to worry about."

"What doesn't she need to worry about?" my dad asks, coming into the kitchen, freshly showered, his thinning hair combed to the side.

"What happened between him and Eve."

"Oh, it's quite the talk of the town, how they're no longer a couple, especially since Eve went out the other night."

I freeze, lungs seizing. Did I just hear that correctly? "What? She went out? Like girls' night or out on a date? With who? Do you know who it was?"

A knowing smirk crosses my dad's face as he reaches into the fridge and pulls out a water bottle. "Not quite sure about the details, just that she went out on a date."

Of course he doesn't know the details but has no problem dropping a bomb like that without any sort of additional information. If you're going to make a man keel over, at least have the decency to provide some details.

Was it a casual date? Someone I know? Someone I don't like? Did they kiss?

Did they fuck?

I have an urge to punch a wall and throw up at the same time. Wow, that's a new sensation.

"You might want to wipe that stricken look off your face because she's going to be here any minute."

"What? Why's she coming here?" My heart rate kicks into overdrive as I try to grasp this barrage of new information.

The doorbell rings, and I swear to Christ, my balls jump up inside my stomach. She's here, and I'm supposed to act normal?

"She's here for training," Dad calls over his shoulder as he walks down the hall. I hear the door open and then, "Eve, come on in. We'll hang out in the kitchen."

"Sounds great." Her sweet voice echoes down the hall.

I attempt to stand, but Mom digs her claws into my leg, pushing me down. I love my mom, but I'm pretty sure she's working for the devil. "Tell me, sweetie, what kind of spices did you use in these donuts?" She barely gets the words out before Dad and Eve walk into the kitchen.

She looks so goddamn beautiful it hurts in a pair of tight-fitting jeans and a green sweater that highlights her hazel eyes. Her hair is styled in waves, loosely hanging over her shoulders.

I can feel my mouth gape open at the sight of her. It's not like I don't see her every week at the restaurant, but lately, she's been showing up either after or before me. We've been skirting each other, and I haven't been in the same room as her for a while.

Why the fuck did I have to bring those donuts to my parents' house? Because seeing Eve now, looking positively breathtaking . . . well. It's unraveling any resolve I had left in me.

"Hey, Reid," Eve says casually as she follows my dad to the table and takes a seat beside me.

"Uh, hey, Eve. How's it going?" This is painful. Painful to watch, painful to be a part of.

"Great. Thanks. Oooh, are these Eric's cider bites?"

"Reid's, actually," my mom says. "Apparently not as good as your brother's."

Eve pops one in her mouth, and her nose crinkles as she nods. "Yeah, definitely not as good."

Well . . . damn, they're not that bad. They're not as moist and fluffy as Eric's, but they're still pretty tasty.

"Are you staying for training?" Eve asks me as she starts to set her notebooks and pens out on the table.

"No, just dropping off donuts."

"Oh, Clint, before you get started, can you help me with something in our bedroom?" Mom asks.

"Can Reid help you?" Dad replies, bringing Eve a water bottle. "Eve and I have a lot to go over."

"No . . . it's . . . in the *bedroom*."

"Oh." He chuckles, so oblivious sometimes, and then takes my mom's hand as they go up the stairs, leaving me alone with Eve.

Needs help with something in the bedroom—yeah . . . okay, Mom. Insert giant eye roll here. She just wanted us to be alone, and guess what? I'm going to take advantage of it.

Spinning in my chair, I waste no time. "You went on a date the other night?"

From a little pouch, she takes out a pen and clicks it a few times before saying, "Yup."

Wow, not even going to dance around it.

"So just like that, you're going to start dating people?"

She tips her head to the side and gives me a slow once-over. "Well, we aren't dating, so that means I can date anyone I want."

"And who is this someone? Is it Tracker? I will fucking kill him if it's Tracker. Is it him?"

"Reid, this shade of green really isn't attractive on you."

"Just tell me if it was fucking Tracker."

"Frankly, it's none of your business." She must hear me grind my teeth because she adds, "But just to ease the little tic in your jaw, it's not Tracker."

That does nothing to ease the tic—it only makes me wonder who else it could be.

"Oliver? Jake? Krew?"

"Krew? Over at the hardware store? No, but he *is* one tasty dish."

"Eve," I warn.

"What's wrong, Reid? Weren't you the one who wanted to split up? You can't possibly be mad about this, right? Because that would be absolutely ridiculous."

I lean toward her. "Are you dating to get under my skin? Is that what this is all about?"

She rolls her eyes. "I have better things to do with my life than try to get under your skin. I have a life, Reid, and unlike you, I plan on living mine to the fullest." She puts on a smile. "Now, is there any business you want to go over before your dad and I start training? Any pressing restaurant matters that need to be addressed?"

No, she's taken care of everything because she's so goddamn perfect. The promo—including all graphics—the budget, the early start on staff interest, the tedious paperwork: she's been on top of every single task that's been put in front of her. But instead of pointing that out, I say, "Yeah, new policy: while the restaurant is being put together, we all have to be celibate."

She laughs, her head dropping back a few inches, exposing her neck. "Okay, Reid." She slaps me on the back as if we're old pals rather than exes. "Good one."

Heat scorches my face, lighting up my cheeks as I lean in closer and whisper, "Are you having sex?"

Before she can respond, my mom and dad walk into the kitchen hand in hand with giant smiles on their faces. I glance over at Eve, who has the same smile passing over her seductive mouth. Great. Glad everyone is so fucking happy around me because I'm pretty sure I'm about to jump into the harbor—with weights on my legs.

◆ ◆ ◆

"Why do you keep looking out the window?" Brig asks. "I didn't even invite you over, and now you're ignoring me. That's fucking rude, man."

He knocks me in the arm. "Your soup is getting cold, and I worked hard on that shit."

"You put too much salt in it," I say, still peering through the blinds.

"The fuck I did. Your snobby taste buds just can't stand the fact that I'm actually good at cooking."

I snap the blinds shut and look over my shoulder. "You made a kale-and-bacon soup from scratch. It's actually really gross. I was being nice with the salt comment."

He shakes his head. "You will just take any chance you can get to cut me down, won't you? Trust me," he says, jabbing his finger on the table, "if I showed this to Eric, he'd be asking for the recipe."

I turn back to the window. "Give me a Tupperware full of it, and I'll pass it along."

"Oh, nice try. You would tamper with it before he even got a shot to try. No fucking way. I say we have a blind soup-off. My kale-bacon soup against your vegetable soup that you think is so goddamn delightful. See which one people like better."

"One hundred percent mine without a doubt, no questions asked. Don't embarrass yourself, Brig."

He huffs behind me and mutters something I can't quite make out, but I really don't care. I'm on watch. I heard from Rogan, who heard from Harper, that Eve was going out on a date tonight, two weeks after her last one—first guy must not have been a winner—and they were going to go to Franklin's for a sandwich. So fucking lame. Taking Eve Roberts out on a date to Franklin's, who does—

Holy shit.

Of course they'd go to Franklin's. It's the town's gossip cesspool, accompanied by deli meats and cheeses . . . and one of the best mustards I've ever had.

And how convenient that I have the perfect view of Franklin's from Brig's apartment on top of his garage. And Harper just happened to slip up with the date info? I'm smelling a setup.

I whip around to Brig. "Did you all plan this?"

"Plan what?" He slurps up a huge spoonful of soup. My spine quivers. Seriously, that soup is positively vile.

"Getting me here, giving me the perfect view of Franklin's—is this all a setup?"

"I have no fucking clue what you're talking about, but I hope you're gone by nine because *The Bachelorette* is coming on, and I swear to Satan himself that if she gives that motherfucker Tag a rose, I am going to scream like a lady. Straight up scream."

"Jesus. Christ," I mutter, turning around. I have no idea how we share DNA. I part the blinds and try to peer through the glass again, but a layer of grime makes for a foggy view. "Why don't you get your windows washed every once in a while? It's almost impossible to see anything past the dirt and water spots."

"Sorry that I don't make it a habit to creep on people."

"That was a passive-aggressive apology."

"It was meant to be." *Slurp.* Shiver. "What the hell are you looking at anyway?"

"You really don't know?"

"No, I don't, and if someone doesn't tell me what's going on"—Brig's voice rises—"I'm going to scream—"

"Enough with the screaming. You know that threat does nothing to scare me and only makes you look like a douche."

He sighs. "Just tell me. What is it?"

"Eve. She's on a date."

"What? Again?" Brig jumps from his seat and digs through a cabinet until he pulls out something that looks like a stick of incense. Lighting it and waving it around his apartment, he makes circles near me, wafting the smoke near my crotch and then up around my head.

Naturally, I smack him away.

The whole scene is absolutely ridiculous. Here's this man—a grown-ass man—who's built like me and my brothers, with muscles as big as

Rogan's. He works on cars for a living, for Christ's sake. And yet he's waving around a tiny stick of incense and mumbling some sort of chant.

He's completely lost his damn mind.

"What the hell are you doing?"

"You're bringing all kinds of bad vibes into my apartment. I don't need your negativity soaking into every surface, cursing me with your bad luck."

"I don't know why I hang out with you."

He gestures toward the window. "Apparently for good access to Peeping Tom locations." After he's done filling the air with what I can only describe as a rank shoe smell, he puts out the incense and comes up next to me, peering through the blinds as well. "Where is she?"

"They must be sitting in the back because I can't see them."

"Damn it. Should I text Franklin and ask for the deets?"

"Christ, no. Are you insane? If Franklin gets a text from you asking about what's going on with Eve, he's going to know I'm behind it."

"Ah, yeah, you're right. That's totally obvious. Want me to use the Hen Line?"

"What's the Hen Line?"

"It's an anonymous call-in where you can put in a request for info, which is texted out to everyone who's signed up. Text backs are posted to the Hen Line app, so you can find all your answers there."

"You've got to be fucking kidding me. That really exists?"

"Where do you think the newspaper gets all its information? The Hen Line is life. Dude, you have to read it. Some of the greatest things are posted in there. Just yesterday, Crazy Old McGwen up on the hill, he was caught outside, sipping coffee in nothing but a polo and a jockstrap—his bare, wrinkly ass just hanging out. There were pictures, and I'll be honest, I did a shit ton of squats yesterday, thinking of that wrinkly ass the whole time, praying mine stays firm and taut for my future wife."

I stare blankly at Brig. "You need a life."

And with that, I grab my things and take off. This visit was a complete waste of time.

I'm halfway out the door when Brig calls out, "Sure, just leave. No thank-you for the soup, for the access to my window, for the cleansing of your aura." His voice cracks. "You're a user, Reid. A user."

Sighing, I turn back and grip the doorframe, plastering on a fake smile. "Thank you, Brig, for being such a generous host, feeding me swill, giving me access to your dirty-ass window, and almost setting my dick on fire with your gross incense."

He crosses his arms over his chest and lifts his chin. "See, was that so hard?"

Jesus.

Christ.

I slam the door shut and jog down the steps from his apartment to my truck, thinking over everything we talked about, as the gray of spring clouds the sky. The Hen Line? Who even comes up with something like that? Most likely Franklin. He'd do just about anything to beat Mrs. Davenport to the town gossip.

I don't even know why I went to Brig's apartment in the first place.

Maybe because I'm desperate to find out anything about Eve and her life beyond Knight and Port.

Maybe because I'm hopelessly in love with a woman who is now dating other men.

Maybe because I'm beginning to realize I made the biggest mistake of my life by letting Eric convince me to break up with his sister.

◆ ◆ ◆

"Have you heard anything from the Hen Line?"

Yup, I've cracked. I'm sinking to a new low, but holy fuck, I can't go another day without hearing at least the smallest bit of information about Eve and her new dating life. I'm desperate.

"Ha! I knew it! And it took you a whole week to break—I'm impressed. I thought it was going to be a lot sooner."

"Just fucking tell me if you've heard anything," I say, growing annoyed.

Brig slides out from under the car he's working on and takes a rag from his pocket as he sits up, wiping his hands before picking his phone up from the ground beside him.

"Let's see." He's getting way too much fucking joy out of this. I can tell from the way his eyes are lit up. I almost didn't come. I talked myself out of it quite a few times, but after seeing Eve this morning, decked out in leggings and a low-cut sweater, I snapped.

I need to know if anyone else has been inside her sweater. I need all the information, and there is only one person to turn to—though I know he'll never let me live this down.

"You know, you could always ask Harper. I bet she knows everything since she's one of Eve's best friends."

"She would never tell me anything. Girl code." I also asked her a few days ago, but she laughed in my face and then walked away. When I asked Rogan to help me out, he basically said he liked sex and wanted to make sure he always got it. He wasn't about to cross Harper. So much for bloodlines.

"True, those girls are really close." He taps around on his phone and then pauses, reads something, and barks out a laugh, the sound echoing off the walls of the open garage. "Oh fuck, I think this is the best thing I've ever seen on the Hen Line."

Dread instantly fills me. I just know it has something to do with me. "What?"

"So I anonymously called, asking for information on Eve's new fling, and it was posted . . . and all the comments are basically telling you to get a life."

"What?" I rip the phone from his hand and scan the comments.

Nice try, Reid.

259

If you're so concerned with who Eve's dating, you should never have broken up with her.

I guess the Knightly curse really is true, but I thought it doomed you to broken love, not to becoming a complete and total idiot. #TeamEve

"Team Eve? Seriously?"

"Keep reading." Brig laughs.

He might have the biggest penis in Port Snow, but he definitely has the smallest brain.

"Hey, that one is fucking rude," I say.

Brig peers over my shoulder and pats me on the back. "At least they're saying you have a big penis. Read two down from that one."

I read it out loud. "'Who are you kidding, Reid? You totally got Brig to post this and are probably bugging him to find out the answers. Leave Brig alone. He's one of us, and we protect our own.'" I shake my head and hand the phone back to him. "I stand by my statement: the Hen Line is idiotic."

"Don't hate because you were called out. Respect the gossip; respect the game."

"I'm seriously going to emancipate myself from you."

"What?" he calls out as I walk away. "That's not even a thing!"

I glance around the manor, taking in the CONGRATULATIONS banners, the smiling faces, and the pink decorations—all for the one girl I can't seem to stop looking for.

Eve graduated.

And instead of taking her out to dinner, celebrating just the two of us, I got a secondhand invitation from Harper to attend her graduation party. Talk about a blow to the heart. I know how hard she's been working to earn this degree, and I can't even celebrate the way I truly want to. I can't spoil her; I can't make her a special meal and spend the night making love to her, letting her know just how proud I am of her.

And I only have myself to blame.

To top it all off, it seems like everyone in town is here, making my pursuit to congratulate Eve that much more difficult.

Graduation presents are stacked off to the side, a buffet of food made by Eric flanks the far wall in the ballroom, and music is lightly playing through the new speaker system Rogan had installed when he was renovating. It's everything I would have planned for Eve if she were my girlfriend, but Harper planned the entire event instead—without an ounce of help from me.

I don't think I could possibly feel worse about myself at this point.

"Hey, when did you get here?" Griffin says, sidling up next to me, drink in hand.

"A few minutes ago." My eyes continue to scan the ballroom. "Have you seen Eve?"

"Yeah, and she looks damn good. Ren helped her get ready earlier." Griffin pats me on the back. "I love you, bro, but you're a goddamn idiot for breaking up with her."

Can always count on my big brother to make me feel so much better about myself.

"Well, you're a fucking ray of sunshine," I say, looking him up and down. "If you want, I can whip my dick out and you can stomp on that too—put me out of my misery."

"You know, there's just something about stomping on another man's dick that doesn't appeal to me, but want me to ask Rogan if he's interested?" Griffin jabs a thumb behind him.

"Fuck off." I start to walk away when Griffin chuckles and pulls on my shoulder.

"She's over in the kitchen, talking with Avery." Shit, Avery's here? When did she get into town? I'm sure Eve has filled her in on every idiotic move I've made over the last few months. "Don't say anything stupid," Griffin adds, probably seeing the way the wheels in my head are turning.

"Pretty sure I've said way worse at this point."

After shucking my brother off me, I head toward the back of the manor and into the beautifully renovated kitchen. Marble counters, white Shaker cabinets, industrial-grade appliances, everything top of the line. I wouldn't mind cooking in there. When I peek around the corner, I find Eve leaning against the counter and chuckling at something Avery just said. Her hair hangs around her shoulders in sultry waves, and she's wearing a bright-red, flowy dress and a matching red lipstick that makes me ache for her lips.

I'm not surprised in the least that Avery is here. Even though their friendship has been mostly conducted over the phone now that Avery's living in New York, they still make a point to talk to each other at least once a week. I know this because one time I'd just given Eve a mind-blowing orgasm, but her phone rang, and she took the call, insisting she couldn't miss a call from Avery.

From the disapproving glance Avery just gave me, I'm going to guess I'm not on her list of people she wants to catch up with.

I wish I was a smarter man, one who made decisions based off of confidence and facts rather than fear and uncertainty, because if I was smarter, I would be standing next to Eve right now, my arm draped over her shoulder, laughing right along with her while sneaking in little kisses here and there, showing Avery that I'm man enough to be with a woman like Eve.

As I approach, Eve looks to the side and spots me. Nothing in her face changes, no sign of excitement or disappointment—instead she gives me a small wave.

Taking that as an invitation, I step forward, hands stuffed in my pockets to keep myself from reaching out to touch her.

"Hey, Eve." I smile at Avery. "Hey, Avery, it's nice to see you again."

Hard eyes take me in, a chastising purse to her lips. "Well, hello, Reid." Yup, definitely on her shit list.

"How have you been? How's New York?"

She sneers. "Yeah, no thanks. I don't want to do this catch-up thing." She leans in close, her voice just above a whisper. "Thank your lucky stars we're surrounded by family and friends, or else the heel of my foot would be implanted in your scrotum right about now."

Wincing, I try to curl my lips up in a smile. "Pleasant. Always nice to see you."

Smiling sardonically, Avery clears her throat. "I'm going to go see if Harper needs any help with the food." She excuses herself and leaves me alone with Eve—but not before shoving past me, her shoulder bumping into mine rather violently. Damn, someone has been hitting the gym. That fucking hurt. Tempted to rub my shoulder, I hold back, not wanting to reveal just how strong the girl is, while Eve stands there confidently, a brilliant smile on her face.

"Hey, Reid, how are you?"

Terrible.

Lovesick.

Desperate to feel your lips on mine again.

A little shaken from the minibrute who just blew by me.

"Okay." I shift on my feet. "Uh, congratulations on graduating. Huge accomplishment."

"Thank you. It feels good to have it all over with."

"I bet." I swallow hard, trying to manage the regret roaring through my body. "The party is—"

"Oh, there's Krew and Jake; I'm going to go say hi." She lifts off the counter and presses her hand to my shoulder. "Thanks for coming. Have some food, mingle."

Excuse me? Krew and Jake take precedence over me?

Before she can get too far, I say, "Your present . . . it's, uh, in the works. Sorry I don't have it with me."

She turns to me, hazel eyes bright. "You didn't have to get me anything, but thanks, Reid. Have a good one."

Looking positively radiant, she takes off toward Krew and Jake and wraps them in big hugs. Hugs I wish I received, hugs I would give anything to have at this point.

Fuck me.

◆ ◆ ◆

Remember when I said I hit a new low? I was wrong. This is absolutely a new low for me.

This is probably the lowest, dumbest thing I've ever done in my entire life, but I'm fucking desperate. I struck out big time at the graduation party two weeks ago, and I need to make another move. We open in a few weeks, and I have yet to find out anything about Eve's dating life. Whatever happened to the loose lips in this town? Just last week I heard about Mr. Thornton getting a bone spur removed and Dr. Bruin throwing up in the toilet once Mr. Thornton hobbled away.

Is that information you think I want engrained in my brain? No, but it's there.

There has to be some sort of town-wide loyalty pact to Eve because no one is speaking up about her. I need to take matters into my own hands.

And before I get judged, I would like to state for the record that I have used every conventional tactic to find out information, including but not limited to the following:

Asking her.

Casually asking Eric.

Asking Harper.

Asking Rogan.

Embarrassingly asking my dad.

Scouring the town's newspaper.

Peering out of Brig's apartment.

Downloading the Hen Line app on my phone—but quickly deleting it.

And I struck out every single time. So here I am, reaching my new low, which consists of sitting at the Inn, incognito, at a table directly across from the bar so I can oh-so-casually watch Eve as she works.

See? I said it was bad.

But it's not like I had anything else to do on a Friday night. I've put in weeks of late nights in the kitchen, and if I make one more blueberry-and-bacon compote I might chop off my own fingers. I needed a rest. Knight and Port is smoothly coming together. Between the two of us, Eric and I have come up with one hell of a menu. Construction has been seamless too, probably because Rogan has stepped in as well to oversee things with me, which I don't mind—he's an expert, after all. He's well respected in town, so people work hard for him. Eve and my dad are handling the entire business side, and I still can't quite believe that we're almost up and running. But despite all the work we're getting done, I haven't really seen Eve at all. She's been doing her thing, and I've been doing mine. It's brutal and wearing on my sanity, but I can't help but think about what life would have been like if we'd had this team the first go-around.

Then again, if we'd had a team like this in Boston, I wouldn't be in this delightful situation, hunkering down behind a newspaper, wearing a fisherman's hat, sunglasses, and the fakest mustache I've ever seen— but it was the only thing available at the Pottsmouth dollar store. Who wouldn't want this life?

"Can I get you anything else, sir?" Jessica, the waitress, asks.

In a high-pitched voice—because that's *so* believable—I answer, "Good," on a squeak.

As she walks away, I look behind me to see if I dropped my balls on the way in here. They must be in the parking lot.

I ordered a bunch of food off the menu to make it seem like I was a hungry tourist coming in from a long day of sightseeing and definitely not a pathetic guy who's hoping to catch a glimpse of any men hitting on his ex.

The food at the Inn is okay. It's not great, and it's nothing compared to what we have planned down at Knight and Port, but for someone staying at the Inn, it's a pretty good option.

Their biscuits are a little dry, their soup a tad salty, and their steak slightly overdone. It's the little mistakes here and there that add up to a subpar experience at a restaurant—little mistakes I'm determined not to make at Knight and Port. It's why Eric and I are perfecting every last recipe, why we're making sure the construction work is inspected every night. We are building a legacy, not just a restaurant. After all, we have the Lobster Landing's quality to live up to.

Lowering the newspaper just slightly, I peer over it and perch my sunglasses on the bridge of my nose so I can have an unobstructed view of Eve over at the bar. She's striding around flawlessly, delivering drinks and food while chatting up every person who has a seat at her bar. She's an absolute professional. Her work ethic is impeccable, and her drive is a huge turn-on for me. Juggling her duties at the Inn and Knight and Port until the soft opening—she's impressive with how she's able to accomplish everything.

Not to mention how goddamn beautiful she is. I swear she's doing something different just to torture me, but I can't put my finger on it. It's not her hair or her makeup; it's almost like her aura—as Brig would say—is different. The smile doesn't leave her face. Is she happy without me—glad that I cut ties?

And that's not even taking her confidence into account. She's always been a ball buster and extremely self-assured, but this new level of confidence has brought her hot factor up to inferno levels.

Also, she's been wearing a lot of low-cut shirts, showing off her perfect tits. She wears them a lot to Knight and Port, and she's even wearing one now. I know I'm not the only guy here who's watching her bend over. It makes me want to go around the restaurant with a can of wasp spray and blast any person who even glances in her direction right in the eye—teach them to never check out my girl.

Yeah, my girl.

Sure, I get it. I'm the moron who broke up with her, but for good reasons. After all, just look at Knight and Port; things couldn't be going more smoothly, and it's because we all know our place, we all know what we're supposed to be doing, and there are no distractions—excluding my night incognito.

Maybe Eric was right, and our breakup was for the best—though I can't stop wondering what life would be like if Eve and I were still together. I sure as hell wouldn't be hanging out with my parents as much as I am right now. It's so bad that I voluntarily sat between them last Friday night, watching *A Star Is Born* as they both cried, each of them clutching one of my hands. In that moment, I couldn't believe that was what my life had come to: my parents crying on my shoulders while I listened to Lady Gaga sing.

No man wants that life.

And now, I'm dressed like a chump, peering at my ex over a table of mediocre food . . . Jesus.

I tear my gaze away and stare down at the lobster mac and cheese in front of me as I press my hand to my brow. What the hell am I doing? This isn't me. I don't stalk women. I don't dress up in cheesy mustaches and order subpar food just so I can pretend I'm not pining over someone.

And I sure as hell don't download small-town gossip apps on my phone either.

I need to get—

"Reid, what are you doing here?"

Eve.

Fuck.

My body stills as my stomach drops to the floor in pure mortification. With my head still down, I say in my high-pitched voice, "No Reid here. Wrong person. I'm Cleatus. Food's good. Thanks." I give her a little wave and continue averting my eyes as she stands over me.

My hat is torn off my head, and when I reach for it, Eve bends down and rips off my mustache.

"Ouch," I say, rubbing my upper lip. "I stuck that on with a glue stick."

"What the hell are you doing?"

Looking around, trying to see who's paying attention, I sit up and place both hands on the table after lifting my sunglasses. "Well, thanks for blowing my cover, Eve."

"Everyone in this building knew it was you—it's all the kitchen staff can talk about. Don't be surprised if you're in the newspaper tomorrow."

Great. Real fucking great.

"You didn't have to come over here and turn this into a grand reveal. Have a little respect for a man's privacy."

"Why are you here?"

"Isn't it obvious?" I wave toward the abundance of food on my table. "Scoping out the competition." I don't mention that the *competition* has nothing to do with the restaurant industry and everything to do with her heart. "And you just spoiled that. Good job, Eve."

From the suspicious lines at the corners of her mouth, I'm guessing she doesn't buy it.

"If that's the case, you could have just come in and eaten food—no need for the pathetic disguise."

She holds up the mustache that's stuck to her finger. I quickly tear it off and stick it in my pocket. "It's not a pathetic disguise. I thought it was creative."

"You looked like a fool."

"Well, since we're no longer together, how I look isn't your concern."

Her lips quirk to the side. "We might not be together, but you're my business partner, and I don't need you scaring away customers before we even open the doors."

"Why don't you worry about the paperwork and the press, and I'll worry about how I look and what we serve, huh?"

"How you look is part of my job. How you act is part of my job. Everything you do is my *concern*. So stop dressing up like Tom Selleck's estranged brother who was lost out at sea for two years, and act like the five-star chef that you are."

"Ah, you think I'm a five-star chef?"

I don't think her eyes could roll any harder. "I'm leaving."

"Hey," I call out before she can get any farther. When she looks over her shoulder, I casually say, "So . . . are ya dating anyone?"

Chuckling, she shakes her head. "You're so transparent, Reid."

"Transparent enough that you'll come to my place tonight and try some food?"

"No."

Damn it.

◆　◆　◆

"I can't take it anymore," I declare, barging through Brig's apartment door, scaring the piss right out of the poor guy.

He jumps out of his desk chair and swears under his breath. Shirtless, with an online dating profile open on the computer behind him, he clutches his chest and lets out a long breath.

"Holy. Shit. I think I just had a heart attack." He glances at me and laughs. "Man, I think you just jump-started my soul—I feel alive."

"That's great." I wave him off and flop down on his couch. "But we need to talk about me."

"Shocking. When are we not talking about you?" Brig turns off his monitor and joins me, taking a seat on the chair opposite me, his spread legs giving me a front-row view down his shorts.

"Dude." I hold up my hand. "Why don't you have underwear on?"

"Because I'm in my apartment and wasn't expecting my older brother to come crying to me for help . . . again. You should be counting your blessings I wasn't feeling like a naked night, because I have those. Shut the curtains, turn on some good music, and let the dong fly as I dance my ass off."

I blink a few times.

"Please don't tell me you actually do that."

"I'm not ashamed. You're not living until you feel your dick slap your legs to a good beat."

I physically can't take the fact that Brig is the one I have to rely on when it comes to all this Eve crap. But Griffin, Rogan, and Jen are too close to her, and that leaves me with the helicoptering dancing queen.

"Can we focus, please? I need your advice."

"Fine. What's on your mind?"

I'm surprised that he gives in so quickly—I almost expected him to gloat. "Breaking up with Eve was stupid."

Took me far too long to realize it—endless nights staring at the ceiling of the houseboat, wishing she was lying next to me, wishing I'd been at her side during her graduation party, and yearning for the excitement we could have shared over the restaurant coming together so flawlessly—all things I've missed, all things I wanted to share with her.

Watching her in her element, working her ass off, not letting one ball drop, it made me realize how much I doubted her, doubted what we had. I never should have listened to Eric; I never should have given in to his threats, his concerns, because all it did was fuck me in the head and make me lose out on a strong pillar that's held me up for so long. That's what she does: Eve lifts me up and helps me be a better man.

"Well, yes, I think the entire town knows that by now."

"It was stupid, but there's something you don't know. Uh, Eric came to my house, knowing all about the relationship, and asked me to end it."

"*What?*" Brig sits a little taller. "Why would he—ohhh, because of what happened with him and Janelle, huh?"

I nod. "Exactly. He was terrified of what the relationship could do—not only to a brand-new restaurant but his relationship with me, with Eve. And he didn't want my insecurities and issues to distract Eve from her goals."

"I can see where he's coming from, but he never even saw you two together. You never brought her down—she stood strong, because that's the kind of woman she is, and helped lift you up, make you better."

"Yeah, I know." She was the reason I had the confidence to step back into the kitchen. "I've been doing well handling the restaurant since we broke up, but Christ, Brig, I've been miserable otherwise—and spending way too much time with Mom and Dad."

"Mom told me. Said she wept on your shoulder while watching *A Star Is Born* . . . on a Friday night."

"It's getting pathetic. I don't want to be home because I swear I can smell her all over the houseboat, and I'm too damn afraid to run into her while she's on a date, so I go to Mom and Dad's. That's not a life I want."

"Then what kind of life do you want?"

"One with Eve."

"Yeah?" he asks, brows raised. "What are you saying?" He clasps his hands together and leans forward. "Please, please tell me you're going to try to get her back."

I stare up at the ceiling. "I don't think I have any other choice. The restaurant is smooth sailing at this point. The menu is almost done and perfected, everything has been ordered, and all the marketing is underway." I take a deep breath, my resolve solidifying. "I understand Eric's concerns, but you're right: he didn't see us together; he doesn't know how well we work together. And if Dad thinks we can handle being together while working at Knight and Port, then that's all the validation I need."

"Fuck, I'm so excited. So, how are you going to do it?"

"Get her back?" I ask. Brig nods. "That's where I need your help. When we broke up, she told me she loved me, and I pretty much destroyed that love. I think I need to build it all back up. Not just the love but the trust—"

"The friendship. That's what you need to focus on. That's where you two thrived, and from there, when you think you're truly in a good place again, that's when you make your move. Do something grand, something that will take her breath away."

I have the perfect idea for something grand, but I'm definitely going to have to work up to it.

"Don't doubt yourself," Brig says, growing serious. "Remember what the palm reader said—the curse won't be broken until your mind has matured. Understand your self-worth, what you can offer her, and allow yourself to be the man she deserves."

Well, shit, when did he become so profound? I sit up and stare, but he just smiles and shrugs.

"I've done a lot of reflection, and I know you better than I think you know yourself. You're notorious for digging yourself into a hole with all your self-doubt, and from there, you sabotage everything around you. Don't let that happen with Eve. You messed up three years ago, but you can't keep letting the past affect your present—learn from it instead. You've grown, Reid. Acknowledge that and keep moving forward. Eve is the girl for you. We all know it. Now you just have to go win her heart back." He hops to his feet and fist pumps the air.

Jesus.

Painfully romantic antics aside, Brig has cleared away the confusion that's been clouding my head. I might not think I'm good enough for Eve. And I still have a lot of growing up to do. But one truth rings clear through my whole being: no one is going to love her as much as I do, and I want to spend every day of my life showing her just how much that is.

I'm not going to jump right into it, though. I can't. I need to ease her back into my life until I think she's ready, and then . . . oh fuck, and then I'm going to blow her away.

CHAPTER TWENTY-SIX

EVE

"These floors are gorgeous," I say, running my toe along the old, refurbished hardwood, which is stained in the same light-blond color as the Lobster Landing's. "I can't get over how perfectly imperfect they are. And the chairs with the basket weave seats pop against the white and red. Seriously, this place is an absolute dream." I turn to Giselle as we walk through Knight and Port and glance down at my clipboard. "What else on the list needs to get done?"

"The kitchen still has some appliances to be installed, the tiling in the bathrooms needs to be finished, and all the fixtures need to be put in, but we're getting close. Three more weeks and we should be ready to open."

"I seriously can't believe how hard and fast you worked."

She smiles. "Mr. Knightly had an opening date set for the beginning of the tourist season, and he paid to make it happen."

"I'm so impressed. And the loft—is the office ready?"

"Almost. We're installing a few ceiling fans up there to push around the air, and the built-in shelves are almost finished, being sanded as we speak. Construction should be done in two weeks, and then you'll have a week to make sure everything is in place."

"Great. Wow." I squeeze my clipboard to my chest. "This is . . . this is just so amazing. Thanks for meeting with me, Giselle."

"Not a problem." She takes a look at her watch. "I have to go meet Rogan at another property. I'll be in touch, though."

I give her a firm handshake, and we stride out of the restaurant. But as she walks to her car, I make my way toward the general store. The weather is starting to really warm up, and we're at the precipice of tourist season, when hordes of people come flooding into our small town for fudge, harbor tours, and the little shops up and down Main Street. The soft opening looms before us, three weeks from today, and it will be our chance to work out all the kinks. I've been working really hard at getting a trio of highly sought-after restaurant bloggers to come and taste the food. It's a long shot, but if I do manage to bring them to Knight and Port, it could be a huge boost to our presence. In the restaurant world, they're as good as the Midas touch—whatever they recommend turns into pure gold. I haven't told any of the guys yet because I don't want to get their hopes up, nor do I want to make them nervous, so I'm keeping it to myself until I know for sure that they're coming.

I step into the store, which boasts a small but diverse range of groceries if you need something quick and can't make it up to Pottsmouth. I head to the back, knowing exactly where to look for the man I'm searching out.

Standing by the ice cream case, stocking his homemade ice cream, is Oliver—handsome as ever, with a bit of mystery behind those dark eyes of his. I wave as I approach. He smiles and closes the cooler door. When I reach him, he pulls me into a hug. "Hey, what are you doing here?"

"You said you made blueberry-buckle ice cream. I'm going to need some of that."

"You know I don't start selling it until five o'clock sharp."

"Can't you make an exception for me?"

He looks toward the cooler, considering. "I don't know. You didn't let me pay for dinner the other night. I'm still kind of mad about that."

"Stop," I say, pushing his shoulder. "You know—"

"What's going on here?" a voice asks. There's curiosity in that voice but an edge too. I don't have to turn around to know exactly who it is. Reid.

Plastering on the same fake smile I've learned to keep on my face whenever I'm around him, I turn. "Oh hey, Reid. How are you?"

He looks between me and Oliver, blue eyes keen. "Fine." He wiggles his finger back and forth. "You two look chummy."

Not even being subtle about it.

"What do you want, Reid?"

"Besides a word? Nothing else." He nods toward the restaurant. "Have a second to chat?"

I glance down at my watch and wince. "Not really, just stopping to get some of the ice cream Oliver was telling me about, and then I'm on my way."

"It's not five yet."

"He's making an exception for me." I give Oliver a wink as he reaches in and hands me a fresh pint of blueberry-buckle ice cream.

"Want to make an exception for me too?" Reid asks, batting his eyelashes.

Staring blankly at Reid, Oliver answers with one word: "No."

Reid's face falls flat, and then his eyes narrow, issuing a silent warning.

Needing to break the tension building between all of us, I say, "Okay, Reid, bye."

"What?" His brows shoot up to his hairline. "Are you dismissing me?"

"Yeah, I was having a private conversation with Oliver. So if you could leave us alone, that would be nice."

The corner of his jaw pulses right before he spins on his heel and stomps away, basket of groceries in hand. When he's out of earshot, Oliver leans down toward my ear and says, "That was uncomfortable."

I turn back toward him, feeling bad he got mixed up in that. "He's going through things."

"Does he think we're dating?"

"Probably." I chuckle; I can't help it. "Apparently, he's been running around town trying to figure out who I'm going out with, and it looks like you've just become his prime suspect. He's gonna be so mad when he realizes we're just friends."

"He's still so hung up on you."

"Yeah, I know." I sigh. "It's a shame that he ruined it."

"There's no second chance for him?"

I glance toward where Reid walked off. "I really don't know at this point."

I was expecting a good amount of applications to work at the restaurant—but not this many. Holy cow, a *lot* of people want to be a part of Knight and Port, and I don't blame them. The buzz around town about the restaurant has been absolutely amazing. The restaurant committee approved the menu, which is an important step, especially in a small town. No one ever wants to step on anyone's toes, so to see the overwhelming support for what the boys created is a huge win.

Now to hire some people.

Two weeks out. Interviews have been conducted, and now I have to make the final decision. Mr. Knightly had a few candidates he really wanted to hire, the boys picked a couple of chefs to help out in the kitchen, and now I have to fill in the holes.

On Friday, Eric and Reid are making all the new hires a buffet of the entire menu so they can test everything and know how to talk about it with customers. Since the kitchen isn't quite done, Mr. Knightly said he would hold a cookout at his house as a celebration for Knight and

Port. I stare at the mountain of applications on the kitchen counter, knowing I only have a few days to make some decisions.

I'm shuffling through some applications as my apartment door opens. Expecting Eric, I say, "Please tell me you got the orange chicken."

"I didn't, but I'm sure hoping Eric did."

Still staring at the applications, I try not to let myself get excited at the sound of his voice. "What are you doing here, Reid?"

"Such a nice greeting." He shuts the door behind him and takes a seat at the table with me. When I still don't look at him, he lifts my chin, forcing my gaze to his and creating a crack in my usual confident veneer. I miss lying in bed with him and staring into those eyes. I miss the little jokes, the teasing, the command he held when buried deep inside of me.

I miss all of him.

He's wearing his classic worn jeans and a tight black shirt that clings to the boulders of his arms, and his hair is styled into an almost fauxhawk. Dangerous and compelling, his self-confidence in this moment has me light headed.

"There she is," he says and then pulls away. "What are you up to? Besides waiting for Eric to bring you orange chicken."

I stare at him for a few beats and then clear my throat, pulling myself together. "Uh, I'm looking through applications for the restaurant. I have a few waitstaff positions to fill before Friday."

"Need some help?"

"No." I shake my head. "I'm good. I can finish this up later." I push the applications to the side. "Why are you here?"

"What, am I not allowed to come visit you?"

"Not really."

His brow pinches together. "But we're friends."

"I don't know what cheery boat you stepped off of today, Reid, but we're not friends. We're business partners, and that's about it."

He lets out a deep breath. "Listen, Eve, I know I hurt you."

"Hurt me? You think you just hurt me?" I shake my head. "Reid, you destroyed me." The stiff upper lip I've had about our relationship loosens as my bottled-up feelings surface. "Do you realize how close we were? How close we were to having it all, to . . . to . . . love? I was there, right there, handing you my heart, and you didn't take it. You didn't just hurt me; you broke me."

"I . . . fuck, Eve, I was—"

"Save it." I hold up my hand. "I don't want to get into this right now. It's been months—I've moved on."

"So I noticed," he bites out. "How is *Oliver*, by the way?"

"That's none of your business, and you have no right to use that kind of tone with me. Unless you have something to say about the restaurant, I suggest you leave."

Regret flashes over his face. "I want to be friends," he says, looking me dead in the eyes.

He must really be losing it if he thinks that's an option.

"Never going to happen. There's too much between us, too much hurt, too much that went unsaid. You completely blindsided me, Reid. That's going to be very hard to get over."

"Try," he pleads, leaning forward. "Try to be friends."

I shake my head just as the apartment door opens, and Eric walks in. I see it the minute he takes us in, the question in his eye. "What's going on in here?"

Reid stands and sticks his hands in his pockets. "Had a question about the applications. Thanks for taking care of it for me." His voice sounds distant, strained, and it pains me to know I'm the one who put that tone there. "I'll catch you two later."

He takes off and shuts the door behind him, and I'm left wondering if I was too hard on him. But then again, he's the one who did this to us.

He wants to be friends? I don't think that's ever going to be possible. How can I go back to friendship when the love I have for him still runs deep in my bones?

Morning-catch day is the worst. I begged Barb to take care of Reid's payment this morning, but she just glanced at me and snorted. Have I mentioned she's the absolute worst?

With a deep breath, I open the back door to the Inn kitchen and keep my chin high as I come face to face with Reid.

Not wearing his fishing gear this go-around, but still standing next to his full cooler of lobsters, he actually seems approachable—not like he would smell like this morning's catch.

I haven't spoken with him since he left my apartment a few days ago. He shot me a text later that night, apologizing for upsetting me and ruining everything between us. As tears streamed down my face, I realized I didn't have it in me to text him back. I knew that if I did, I would probably crumble and ask him for another chance.

I can't be the one to break, the one to give in. He did this to us, and if he wants to have any other kind of relationship with me beyond the restaurant, then he's going to have to figure it out himself.

Keeping things neutral, I stare down at the catch and say, "Wow, you caught a lot this morning."

"Had a little help from Brig."

"And he didn't fall off the boat?" The joke slips effortlessly from my mouth before I can rein it in.

The tone in my voice must lift his spirits because he smiles and takes a step forward. "I didn't say that."

"Wait, *did* he fall off?"

"Yup." He laughs, the sound so sexy that I have to will myself not to fall into his arms. "When he was pulling up a cage, the boat caught a wave and lifted him up and overboard. He fell in and started flailing around like an idiot."

"Oh God." I laugh, picturing the whole thing. "I wish that was on camera."

He pulls his phone from his pocket. "I didn't get it on video, but I did get a few good pictures." He steps toward me and holds the phone out. I take it and immediately start laughing when I see Brig's arms flailing about in the water and a panicked look on his face.

"Poor Brig. You must have scarred him for life."

"Let's just say he sat in the corner with a space blanket wrapped around him for the rest of the trip. I don't think he'll be going out with me again anytime soon."

"Why did he go to begin with?" I ask, handing back his phone, careful to make sure our fingers don't brush.

"I wanted some advice, and the only time we could talk was early in the morning. Don't worry, I bought him breakfast after and promised coffee from Ruth's on me for the rest of the week."

"That's a good brother." I toe the ground. "What kind of advice did you need?" I don't know why I asked, really. Except that maybe, despite wanting to keep him at arm's length, I also want a little more time with him.

His long lashes flutter open, and he tilts his head, studying me. "Romantic advice."

My stomach falls to my toes, and nausea creeps up my throat. Is he going to start dating? I don't think I would be able to handle watching Reid date someone else. And that's when it hits me: maybe this is how he feels, hearing all the rumors about me seeing someone. That's all they are, rumors, but he doesn't know that, and I did nothing to ease the anxiety that must be raging through his mind about me dating.

"Oh. Starting to date again?" My breath catches in my chest as I wait for his answer. Honestly, Reid could date anyone in this town if he wanted to—despite what people say about the curse. If he asked someone out, they wouldn't even blink before saying yes. He's the whole package.

"No." He shakes his head and chuckles. "How could I possibly date when I'm still hung up on you?"

"Wh-what?" I stutter in surprise. "But you broke up with me. If you were still hung up on me, why would you do that?"

He drags his hand over his face. "At this point, I don't even know. But what I do know is that I want what we had."

He can't be serious. I don't think I've ever met a more confusing man.

I shake my head. "You can't keep running so hot and cold with me, Reid. Don't you see how messed up that is? You want me, and then you don't, and now you do? My heart can't deal with that kind of indecision. This isn't figuring out which spices you should put in a recipe—this is my heart you're dealing with."

"I know." He takes a step forward, and I move back, letting him know to keep his distance. He stops, understanding, and says, "I'm going to make it right, Eve."

Not sure what to say, I reach into my pocket and pull out some cash. I quickly do some math in my head and then hand him his payment for the lobsters. "That should be the right amount," I say. His hand grazes mine as he takes the cash, lighting up a part of me that's gone gray and dull.

He lingers and I let him. "I *will* make this right," he says again, this time with more force. He pockets the money and goes back to his truck. "I'll see you later, Eve."

Lord help me, I don't think my heart can take another roller coaster from Reid.

◆ ◆ ◆

"Eve, is that you?" Reid calls out over the racket of the kitchen installation as I step into the restaurant. I look up and see him in the loft, hanging over the railing and waving frantically, as if he didn't just see me yesterday. "Come up here—I want to show you something."

Applications in hand, I head up the stairs that lead to the loft, marveling at the iron handrail and the open staircase, which leaves the space feeling airy rather than like a big block of stairs. When I reach the loft, which I'm surprised to find is much quieter, Reid greets me with a big smile, his large body blocking the view of what will soon be my permanent office space.

"Close your eyes."

"Why?"

"Duh, because I have a surprise for you."

"Did you really just say *duh*?"

Chuckling, he nods. "Humor me and close them."

"I don't know my way around the space with my eyes closed. What if I fall over the railing?"

"It's insulting you think I'd let that happen. Here." He takes the applications from me, sets them to the side, and then wraps his hands around mine, his large palms eclipsing my small ones. "I got you. Now close your eyes."

Lost in the feel of his hands holding mine, I don't remember to argue before I'm closing my eyes and allowing him to guide me through the loft space. My feet shuffle against the hardwood before my steps soften, and I realize we're walking over a rug now. The smells of fresh paint and new furniture surround me, and with them, there's a hint of Reid's familiar, fresh scent.

"Okay, are you ready?"

"I'm warning you—if I open my eyes and find you naked, I'm kicking you in the crotch and leaving."

I'm wrapped in his deep laugh. "If I was naked, I wouldn't be cooking—I'd be a magician who could disrobe while holding someone's hands. That's a million-dollar Vegas show."

"Or a quick ticket to jail."

"Or that." He chuckles. "But rest assured, I'm not naked. So go ahead, open your eyes."

My eyes flutter open, and the first thing I see is Reid's excited face, smile stretching from cheek to cheek, eyes sparkling with pure joy.

The next thing I see is the space.

My heart rate picks up as I take it all in. Large white desk with a matching white desk chair. Plush gray, white, and teal carpet, large built-in shelves and cabinets behind the desk with gold hardware. A brand-new Mac sitting pretty on the desk's glass top, and a nameplate in gold and white staring back at me.

MISS EVE ROBERTS.

"Happy graduation. Do you like it?"

I don't answer right away; I can't. Instead, I walk around the desk and drag my fingers over the cool surface. It's . . . it's perfect. A bouquet of fresh peonies rests on the shelves, pictures of me, Eric, and Reid are framed and perfectly placed, a large wooden sign with the words **BOSS BABE** inscribed on it is hung on the wall to the left.

It's more than I could have ever dreamed of.

Tears fill my eyes as I finally look up at Reid. "It's so perfect, more than I deserve."

"You deserve more, but this is what I could put together at the moment. We can add to it once you get familiar with the hustle of the restaurant, but I figured this is a good start for now. And that empty frame over there is for your diploma."

"This is a perfect start. This is so thoughtful and wonderful."

He points to the computer. "Everything you're going to need is downloaded and set up. The Wi-Fi password is *ReidIsHot*. Unfortunately, that can't change."

I smile, tears still brimming in my eyes. "All of this is really for me?"

He nods. "Yup. I talked to my dad and told him that since you're the brain of the business, you should have a comfortable space, especially if we're going to lean on you for everything. He agreed. I worked on the loft this week. I wanted to make sure it was ready before opening."

"You did all of this yourself?"

"Well, Rogan helped. Even though I like to think I know how to build things, the shelving turned out to be trickier than I expected. I went up to Pottsmouth yesterday to pick up the desk and saw that sign at an art gallery up there and had to have it. You're our boss babe. A strict but fair boss and one hell of a babe." He winks, and a smile pulls at my lips.

"I can't believe you did this." I look him in the eyes. "Thank you, Reid. This means a lot to me. It's truly a dream come true."

"Well, happy graduation and congratulations on the new job." He falls silent for a second. "I really wish I handled everything differently between us, but I realize I can't go back and change that—all I can do is move forward and try to make things right." He gestures around the office. "I wish I'd known this was what you wanted when we first started dating. I wish I'd known more about your dreams, about where you wanted to go with your life. But now that I do, I want to be there to support you. I know you're going to do amazing things up here, Eve."

With my throat dry and tight, my emotions heightened, I try to be grateful, but all I can muster without bursting into tears is a small smile and a nod.

"Well, I have to go. Meeting Eric to go over the kitchen installations. I'll catch you later."

As he starts down the stairs, I tell myself to call out to him, to pull him back up to the space so I can give him a hug, a proper thank-you, but I'm frozen in place, frozen in awe, in pure appreciation of what he's done.

This is the nicest thing anyone has ever done for me, hands down, and it was all Reid.

He said he was going to make things right. Well, this was a giant leap in that direction.

◆ ◆ ◆

Knock. Knock.

I glance at my door and then the time. Ten o'clock. Did Eric lose his key? He was going out on a date with some girl he met on a dating app. I love my brother, but I also know him well enough to assume he probably won't be coming back to the apartment tonight, not when his nerves are taking over. We are just over a week away from opening, and he's getting jittery. When he's like that, he needs to get his energy out somehow—and that means going home with his date.

So who else could be at my door?

As my suspicion builds, I set my notebook down and open the door to find Reid standing on the other side. He's leaning against the doorjamb, holding a bag, and sporting a heart-melting grin.

"Hey."

I give him a once-over: casual Adidas Joggers, a tight-fitting, long-sleeve T-shirt, a backward hat—casual but yummy.

"What are you doing here?"

He holds up the bag. "Late-night delivery. I heard you were working hard on final preparations and thought you might need some fuel."

I cock my head to the side. "Are you trying to butter me up, Reid Knightly?"

"Yup," he answers unapologetically before stepping over the threshold and making himself at home. He kicks off his shoes and heads straight for my kitchen, where he pulls down two plates.

Two.

Not just one but two. Which means he plans on staying, at least for a little bit.

I walk up behind him and try to peer around his shoulder to see what he brought, but he boxes me out. "Watch it—it's a surprise, so why don't you go sit down and chill while I get everything ready?"

"Get everything ready? It's not just something you pull out and eat?"

"Not necessarily. Now go sit, maybe turn on some music or something so we don't have to awkwardly listen to each other moan when we have this tasty little dish."

"I don't moan when I eat."

He glances down at my crotch. "You sure as hell moan when *I* eat."

My face flames, and heat rushes through my body as images of Reid between my thighs strike me all at once in a flood of naughty memories. Damn him.

Laughing, he nods toward the table. "Go on. Put on some of that Shawn Mendes shit—he's catchy and upbeat."

"You've been hanging out with Brig too much."

"That's what happens when I fuck things up with you. I'm forced to hang out with other people and pick up their bad habits."

Rolling my eyes, I go to my phone and look through my Spotify playlists. "Yeah, I heard you've been having some movie nights with your parents."

"Jesus, are there no secrets in this town?"

"Nope."

"Let me guess, Harper told you?"

I pick a simple crooner playlist that's a mix of Louis Armstrong, Doris Day, and Frank Sinatra. "I keep my sources to myself."

"It was Harper." He looks over his shoulder. "Are you ready for this?"

"If you're amping it up, it better be good."

"Be prepared to get your tits blown off, babe."

I would be laughing at his statement if I wasn't so caught off guard by his term of endearment. *Babe.* I don't have much time to think about it, though, as he spins around and holds out a little tray full of fresh apples, what look to be cake bites, and donuts. In the center is a pot with two sticks coming out of the top. In his other hand he carries the plates.

All that was in his bag?

He sets the tray down, and the smell of warm blueberry caramel floats in the air.

"You brought me fondue?"

"Not just any kind of fondue but a special recipe I plan on using to shock the hell out of your brother tomorrow, as a final add-on to the menu. Donut holes made from scratch along with the pound cake bites and, well, the apples. I just sliced those, but I sliced them myself."

"Impressive," I joke. "And the caramel?"

"My secret recipe. Blueberry caramel as an ode to Maine, with a rich, sweet texture. It's really fucking good, and since I maxed out my parent-time quota this week, I thought I'd share it with you."

"I wasn't your first choice?" I ask, teasing, but his face grows serious.

"You know you're always my first choice, with everything."

And I believe that. After what he showed me yesterday, the space he created for me, I know that's the truth, and accepting it chips away another piece of the wall I erected around my heart the night he broke it.

Needing to take the conversation in a less intense direction, I ask, "So you're surprising Eric with this tomorrow? You should wait until Friday and have it at the Knight and Port gathering—really shock him."

"I thought about it." He hands me a skewer. "But then I didn't want to throw your brother off completely in front of all of the new employees. He's not keen on surprises, so I figured I'd have it on the table when he comes over tomorrow. But I want your approval first—let me know it's good enough."

"My approval, huh? Well, I'm not going to take it easy on you. I'm going to tell it like it is. If this is crap, I'll let you know." I skewer an apple slice, then dip it and bring it to my mouth. "I don't want you selling—" I take a bite. "Oh heavenly mother." I chew. "Oh my God, what the hell is in this caramel? Crack?" I look him dead in the eyes. "Did you put crack in this?"

Laughing, he shakes his head. "Lots of butter and the freshest blueberries."

I dip my apple and take another bite. "Seriously, this is so good."

Brow furrowed, he looks at the caramel pot and then back up at me. "You just double-dipped."

"So?" I shrug, dipping again.

"You contaminated it. Now I can't have any."

"Oh please." I roll my eyes as I chew. "Your tongue has licked the back of my throat. You'll survive."

"Yeah, but I don't know where that mouth has been," he teases.

"Nowhere since you broke up with me," I shoot back, picking up a donut and popping it in my mouth. Just as good. Seriously, he's a genius.

"Wait, what?" With a donut halfway to his mouth, he stares at me, shocked. "I thought . . ."

"You thought wrong." I pop a soaked piece of pound cake in my mouth and nearly drool. "This very well might be my new favorite thing. Seriously, Reid, be prepared to make a lot of this."

"Wait, can we go back to what you were saying about the dating thing? I thought you were with Oliver?"

"We're just friends. Do you really think I would be out dating people right after we broke up?"

"Shit." He blows out a rough breath and then pulls on the back of his hat. "That . . ." He chuckles. "That makes me feel a whole lot better."

"Why?"

"Because that means I won't have to fight anyone to get you back."

"Not true," I say, glancing over at him. "You have to fight yourself, and that will be the biggest battle of them all."

CHAPTER TWENTY-SEVEN

REID

"Do you need any help?" my mom asks, placing her hand on my back and looking over one of the buffets of food that stretch across five six-foot-long tables spread across the house.

"I think we're good." I stand back and scan the appetizer table, hands on my hips. "Shit, do you think we have enough food?"

"Oh, I think there's plenty. You're only having thirty people over."

"But do we have too many options? These are just the appetizers, and there are fifteen different options."

My mom studies the table. "I'm not quite sure I can answer that for you. I love options, but you're the expert here. I'm sure you have the perfect amount." She gives me a bright smile before strolling away.

It's the perfect mom answer but not the brutal honesty I was looking for. When I was paring down the menu with Eric, I pushed to make more cuts, but he was adamant about keeping everything. Now that I'm looking it all over, I'm having second thoughts, especially since we barely managed to prepare all the food today.

"It smells amazing in here," Dad says, coming up next to me. "I might have snuck some of those Dorito mac and cheese bites when you weren't looking. I'm not even going to apologize for it. Where did you come up with Doritos as the bread crumbs to fry everything in?"

"That was Eve, actually. It's her mac and cheese recipe with a twist. We turned them into bites. In her recipe, she drenches the top with Doritos, so we used it as the batter."

"That girl is smart. We need to keep her around, keep her happy."

"Yes we do," I answer, looking over the appetizers one more time as my dad bumps his shoulder against mine.

"That means you. You need to keep her happy."

"Working on it, Dad."

"Really?" he asks, looking pleasantly surprised.

"I hope so." Needing to confide in someone other than Brig, who is far too emotional about love, I say, "I'm actually kind of scared of it all. I mean, I want her, Dad. She's it for me, and I know that now. Breaking up with her was the dumbest thing I've ever done, but now that we're about to open the restaurant, I still have to wonder if I can do it all. Can I be the man she deserves while running a kitchen and training a staff at the same time?"

Taking me by the shoulder, Dad guides me to the dining table, and we both take a seat. He leans back and says, "When we were opening the Lobster Landing, I had the exact same fears and doubts. I wasn't sure if I would be able to handle it all, and there were many nights that I lay awake, anxiety eating me alive. I was putting everything we had at risk. When I asked your grandpa Clark for your mom's hand, I promised him that I would always take care of her. The Landing was a gamble, and if it didn't work out, I would be breaking that promise. I knew we had something special, but I didn't ever believe it would get to this point, where my children are taking it over and helping expand the brand into so much more."

"But you didn't have a failure on your résumé."

"I wish I did."

"What?" My brow pulls together. "Why would you?"

"Because failure is what makes you grow, become better. I was laying it all on the line with no experience, with no one telling me my idea needed tweaking, needed massaging. I was going in blind, and that was terrifying. And trust me, I had my failures along the way, some that threatened my marriage. It wasn't easy, but with each speed bump, I grew stronger and stronger." He leans forward and grips my shoulders. "It's good you're afraid because that means you care. I would be concerned if there wasn't that underlying fear driving you to be the best."

"And what about Eve? She's so—God, Dad—she's perfect. She's so strong, so confident, and most of the time I don't think I could ever be enough for her."

That garners a full-on laugh from my dad as he shakes his head. "Boy, the apple doesn't fall far from the tree. I was the same way with your mom. She's simmered down since she's had you kids, but when I first met her, she was a firecracker. Always busting my balls, challenging me. And I liked it because she pushed me to be a better man. That's what Eve is to you: your counterpart in this life, the one who is going to help lift you up when you need it and ground you when your head is in the sky. You're a dreamer like me, son. Deny it all you like, but you need a levelheaded woman to tame your wild soul."

"And you think I can handle it all—being there for Eve and the restaurant?"

"If I didn't think you could, then we wouldn't be having this conversation. But there's one thing you need to realize, Reid. You are better with her. Being with Eve isn't going to hinder you; it's going to enhance your life."

I glance toward the front door as our new employees start filtering in. Eric is greeting them like the good guy he is. This all started with him, with his insistence that a relationship would kill the restaurant. But I think there was something he was missing, something he didn't quite understand when he asked me to stop dating Eve. He doesn't know how much his sister enriches my life with her sharp tongue, intelligent mind, and thoughtful words. As I watch him shaking hands and chatting, I realize I need to show him just how much I need her if I'm going to be the best version of myself.

I turn back to my dad. "Thank you, for everything."

"No need to thank me when I can see it in your eyes. Now go greet our employees. We have some food to eat."

◆ ◆ ◆

"I think that's the last of it," Eve says, coming up beside me and leaning against the counter.

"Shit, you scared me. I thought you left with Eric."

Eric left half an hour ago and took all the extra food to Snow Roast, where Ruth was kind enough to let us have an impromptu gathering for a few friends who wanted to sample the menu. I stayed behind to help my parents clean. I thought I was on my own, washing dishes as my parents retired for the night—but Eve just proved me wrong.

"I did. I helped him carry the food, but then I came back—wanted to help you clean up. Your parents were kind enough to host; I didn't want to leave their house trashed."

I rinse off the platter I've been scrubbing and stick it over on the towels I laid out to help dry everything. "Thank you, but I think I have it covered if you want to go back to Snow Roast."

She picks up a dish towel and starts drying one of the dishes I already washed. "Nah. Eric doesn't need me. He's having a great time catching up with everyone. I really think he's been in his element since he's moved back and started working with you again. I can't remember the last time I've heard so much happiness in his voice. I feel like he was barely living when he was in Boston, but being back here, with you, with me . . . it's reawakened his passion, and I can't tell you how grateful I am for that. Knight and Port means so much to him, and all he wants is to see it succeed."

"We all do. I have a good feeling about it. There's so much passion coming from all different directions, and when you have this many people working their asses off to put something together, only great things can come from it."

Pausing, she takes a second to study me. "That's not the normal, negative Reid I'm used to."

"People can change."

"I guess so." She smiles and picks up a delicate blue willow-patterned plate to dry. "Oh my gosh, your mom still has this plate?" Churchill China, a coveted "artifact" in the Knightly household, it's worth more than anyone would want to pay for a plate. There are five left in the house, and two of them have had to be glued back together.

"Yeah, and even though it keeps breaking over and over again, she finds a way to superglue it back together each and every time."

"I can still see the look in your eyes when we accidentally broke it. You, Eric, and I were fighting over who had dibs on a batch of cookies, right? We were all pulling on it and somehow dropped it at the same time."

"I can still hear the crash in my head. I thought I was going to puke when I saw it cracked on the ground."

She laughs, such a beautiful sound. "You went so pale that I thought you were going to puke too. And because your mom has supersonic ears, she came running downstairs to see what happened. The look on her face still scares me to this day."

"That's when Satan oozes from her pores—when someone fucks with her special Churchill China. They were my grandmother's, so she cherishes those things. And that day, I broke one. I really thought that was the end for me. Dead at thirteen."

"We didn't come over for two weeks—we were too scared she was going to slit our throats with the broken pieces."

Honestly, it's not that huge of an exaggeration. At the time, they were her most valued possessions, and I was shocked she let us use them for the gathering tonight. But when she handed me one of the plates, she insisted they've always brought good luck to those who served on them, and she wanted to make sure we had all the luck on our side.

"I'm pretty sure she was planning all of our deaths, even matched up our schedules with your mom so she knew when to strike."

"And she did, on Halloween."

I throw my head back and laugh. How could I have forgotten about that?

Eric, Eve, and I liked to trick-or-treat as teenagers because, honestly, we liked candy, and no one cared that we were too old. They were just happy we weren't getting into trouble somewhere else.

We would try to hit up all the houses in town and then go to the outskirts, where the houses are pretty huge and the families would hand out king-size bars. Only the brave went out to the woods since it was always so spooky, but it was worth it.

Since the houses were so far apart, we would bribe Griffin to drive us around in Dad's van and pay him in candy. He never complained since he and Claire would just hang out in the car and make out until we got back.

A few weeks after the plate incident, we were trick-or-treating, and after we made it all the way to the Carlsons' hilltop mansion, we went back to the van to hit up the next house. I reached for the door handle and opened it up, and out shot a screeching woman wearing a black cloak and a mask, who tackled all three of us to the ground as she leaped out of the car.

I don't think I'd ever been more scared in my life as the three of us tumbled down the hill, a screaming lady hot on our heels. We got all the way to the bottom, and I was on the verge of a serious mental breakdown when she started laughing. And that's when I heard her: my mom.

She laughed for a very long time, and so did Griffin and Claire, who'd helped her to plan the entire thing.

"Remember how we had a hard time opening car doors after that?" I ask.

"I wouldn't do it for so long, and my mom got really irritated with me. Of course she wasn't mad at your mom. Nope, she just said, 'Next time don't break one of Mrs. Knightly's plates, and she won't have to scare you out of your pants.' At least we learned a lesson. From then on, Eric and I only used paper plates."

"It was a smart move on your end. But there was something that stuck out at me that night—something I will never, ever forget."

"Eric's girly scream?"

"Well, yeah." I laugh. "But I also remember that as we were tripping and rolling down the hill, I was trying to grab onto anything that would get me away from the crazy lady, and I grabbed your boob for the first time."

She lets out a deep, hearty laugh. "Oh my God, you *would* remember that."

"It was the first time I ever touched Eve Roberts's boob—of course I remember it."

"You make it seem like you had a crush on me or something."

My smile falters. Does she really not know? It's been over ten years. We spent half of our childhood together. All of the sleepovers when I'd sneak over to her room and we'd talk after Eric fell asleep, all the times we'd stand up for each other, all of the times she caught me staring at her while we were at the beach. Does she really not know?

"Eve, I've had a crush on you for as long as I can remember. You were the epitome of my dream girl."

She shakes her head. "You don't need to lie to me. I remember our childhood quite vividly."

"Do you?"

"I do." She sets down a dish and crosses her arms before she props a hip against the counter and gives me a stare. "I remember every single girl you dated, from Kelsey to Lydia to Hillary. I remember the conversations you'd have with Eric about every single one of them. I remember the gossip that went around school about your conquests. The girls fawned over you, vied for your attention, scooped you up every time you were single for more than a second. It was a rotating door of girls. And then you got weird—you barely even looked at me after a while. So I know you're lying when you say you had a crush on me because if that was the case, and with your track record, we would have at least gone out on a date when we were juniors."

"But you were untouchable," I say, focusing on the dish in my hand as the truth pours out of me. "You were my best friend's twin sister, and one of my best friends. If I screwed things up with you, I screwed things up with Eric and everything we had planned. Just because I didn't make a move doesn't mean I didn't stare whenever I got a chance, that I didn't dream of you at night, that I didn't ever wonder what it would be like to press my lips against yours. You wonder why things got weird in high school, why I got distant? It was because I wanted you so damn bad but couldn't have you."

"Wait, are you serious right now?"

"Why would I lie about this?"

"I . . . I don't know. To get in my good graces again."

I turn off the water and face her. "Do you really think that little of me?"

"No," she answers quickly. "I'm just trying to comprehend it all. I mean . . . Reid, I crushed on you so hard, ever since Eric introduced you as his friend." She *what*? Excuse me while I try to comprehend this new little nugget. Eve Roberts crushed on me? "I would go to bed at night wishing you would look at me any other way than as just a friend."

"Trust me, I was."

She's silent for a second before slowly lowering herself to the floor, tucking her knees against her chest, leaning back against the cabinets beneath the sink. Unsure of what's going on, I do the same so our shoulders are touching, and we're both staring out into the kitchen.

"Then you finally made a move."

"Best idea of my life."

"So why ruin it all?" she asks. "We were so close, Reid."

"So close to what?"

She faces me, her features soft. "To love. We were so close to love, and then you broke it off." Her gaze falls to her knees. "I *loved* you, and I was just waiting for you to catch up to my feelings."

My stomach flips. "Loved?"

She presses her forehead against my shoulder and lets out a deep sigh before standing back up. I quickly join her, ready to confess everything. But when I face her, her expression has changed, her eyes have hardened, and I sense that she's raised her defenses again—and that after my little confession, she needs to keep me at arm's length.

"I should get going." She runs her hands over her legs. "We have a lot of prep to do tomorrow. And we're getting our first food delivery early in the morning."

She changes the subject seamlessly. Avoidance and deflection—I'm impressed. And since I'm not 100 percent sure what she wants, I go with it.

"Yeah, it's getting late. Do you need a ride back to your apartment?"

"No, I have Eric's car. Thanks, though. I'll catch you tomorrow. Good job on . . . all the food." She waves her hand about.

"Sure, thanks," I answer lamely as she walks away without a parting hug or even a pathetic high five.

That night, as I sprawl out on my bed and stare up at the skylight above me, I contemplate what I'm going to do with Eve. There are moments when she opens up to me again, when I'm convinced there's a chance we can have what we used to, but then she shuts down just like she did tonight, guarding her heart. I don't blame her. When she said we were so close, she was right; we were *so* close to having it all, and then I fucked it up.

CHAPTER TWENTY-EIGHT

EVE

Knock, knock, knock, knock.

Pause.

Knock. Knock. Knock. KNOCK!

I'm ready to really start pounding on the door just as it flies open, and I find a bleary-eyed Harper staring back at me, wrapped in a robe, her hair completely disheveled.

"Eve, what—"

"Sure, I would love to come in, thanks." I push past her and fling myself onto the couch just as Rogan appears from the bedroom, wearing nothing but a pair of sweatpants.

Damn. The Knightly boys really are the most handsome specimens I've ever seen.

He limps into the living room, a sigh of relief escaping him as he takes a seat, and I feel a twinge of guilt for pulling him out of bed. "Glad to see the incessant pounding isn't from an ax murderer," he says. "Just an inconsiderate friend who doesn't care how late it is."

"Hey." I point at him. "I wouldn't be here if it wasn't for your brother."

"Tea, anyone?" Harper asks. Rogan and I both raise our hands. "I'll put some water on."

"What did the idiot do this time?" Rogan asks, dragging his hand over his jaw.

"Oh, you know, just confessed to harboring intense feelings for me ever since we were young."

"You didn't know?" Rogan asks, looking surprised.

Harper joins us, taking a seat on Rogan's lap. He wraps his arm around her waist and pulls her close.

"No, I did *not* know that. I had no idea he even looked in my direction back then."

Harper rubs her eyes with the palm of her hand. "You know I love you, Eve, but I need to ask, Why does it matter if he liked you back then?"

"Because!" I shout, throwing out my arms. "It lowers my defenses; it makes me want to give in to his pursuit. It weakens my stance on not wanting to be with him and forces me to consider giving him a second chance."

"Isn't that what you want? To be with him?" Harper asks.

"No. I mean, maybe. I don't know." I stare Rogan down. "I blame you."

"Me?" He points to his chest. "Why me?"

I shrug. "You're the only Knightly in the room, and Reid's your brother. Therefore you get the blame." The kettle starts to whistle, and Harper hops up to grab it.

"Let me get this straight. You're mad at Reid because he had a crush on you when you were kids?"

"Yes, exactly."

"But why?"

"Didn't you just hear what I said?" I ask, as if it's not late and I didn't just wake him up. "He's weakening me."

"But don't you want to be with him?"

Harper takes that moment to pass us mugs of tea before sitting down next to me. From the scowl on Rogan's face, I can tell he's not happy about her choice in seating.

"Yes, but that's beside the point."

"Actually"—Rogan blows on his tea—"it seems like exactly the point."

Scowling, I turn to Harper. "This guy is making me mad."

"Well, you did barge into his house at eleven at night."

"Oh, excuse me, I wasn't aware you two are old farts and go to bed so early."

"We go to bed at a normal adult time," Rogan says. "That is, after we fuck all over this house."

Harper rolls her eyes. "Can you not say *fuck*? We don't fuck; we make love."

"Babe." Rogan looks her square in the eye. "What we did against the wall earlier today was not making love—that was straight-up fucking."

"Ughh," I growl. "Can you not shove your perfect relationship in my face? I'm dealing with an ill-tempered, terribly mannered asshole who can't seem to decide what he wants in his life, and for some god-forsaken reason, I'm in love with him. I need some advice."

"What do you want us to say?" Rogan asks, looking confused.

"I don't know, honestly. I really have no idea." I take a sip of tea, feeling deflated. "We could have had so much more, and I think that's what I keep coming back to. If we'd gotten together back when we were in high school, we could have been—"

"It never would have lasted," Rogan cuts in, shaking his head.

"Hey." Harper sits up, scowling. "Why would you say that?"

"Because I know my brother, and he wouldn't have been able to do long distance, not at eighteen. He would have driven her away when he went to culinary school. And even if he didn't, he would have for sure driven her away after the restaurant closed. He would have broken Eve's heart."

"Well, I have a broken heart now," I shoot back.

"But it's mendable," Rogan says. "You and I both know that. I see the way you look at him, the longing in your eyes. It's not over, Eve.

But the question you have to ask yourself is, How long are you going to hold out until you finally give in to what you truly want?"

"I hate how intelligent you're being."

He chuckles. "Sorry, Eve, I wish I could get on the *screw Reid* bandwagon—even though it's very appealing—but we all know what this really comes down to. It's not about his hidden feelings or about how insufferable he can be—it's about the fact that you truly love him for who he is. And he may not be perfect, but we all know that he's perfect for you."

"Ah, Rogue." Harper presses her hand to her chest. "That's so sweet. And true." She turns to me and takes my hand. "I've known you for a long time, Eve, and the happiest I've seen you has been when you're with Reid. And yes, he's difficult, he has his moments, but you're strong enough to help him through them, to help him see the kind of man he really is. You need the challenge Reid gives you, the excitement, the fire he lights inside of you."

Rogan nods. "That's true. You lift him up, Eve. I don't think he ever would have even considered Knight and Port if you two hadn't been together. You bring out the good in him, and he needs that. He needs you—just like you need him."

I do need him.

And he doesn't just challenge me. He brings out my softer side; he fills that hole that's been empty ever since I lost my parents. He gives me purpose, he challenges me, and weirdly, he brings my emotions to the surface, helping me feel and experience so much more than I ever thought possible.

Tears build up in my eyes, my friends' words hitting me hard. I've been so hurt about the way he broke things off that I've forgotten what truly matters. Reid is the man I will always love, no matter what, and if anyone can put him in his place, it's me.

"This is not the kind of conversation I was expecting when I came over here," I admit. "But it's what I needed. True honesty. Love isn't all roses and sunshine. There are some really ugly aspects to it, and right now we're living in an ugly moment. Maybe it's time to bring some beauty back to our love."

Harper claps her hands. "Oh my God, yes, please. Then we can go on double dates."

"Eh, I don't think I want to go on dates with Reid." Rogan winces. "Let's stick with Griffin and Ren. Reid's just going to tell you every embarrassing story he knows about me."

Harper smiles wide. "And that's exactly why I want to double date with him. There was a long lull in our love. I want to know all the dirty details."

Rogan groans as I start thinking about how to approach Reid, how to fix what went wrong between us. But maybe that's not my responsibility. Maybe I need to let him come to me again. But when he does, I'll listen to him with an open heart.

How does their stupid curse go? *Until your mind has matured, the curse won't be cured?* Maybe it's time to grow up and accept what this love really is: a combination of ugly and beautiful moments mixing together to create an everlasting bond.

◆ ◆ ◆

"The shifts look great," Mr. Knightly says from across my new desk, scanning the paper before handing it back to me.

It's my third day on the job, and I'm officially working full time for Knight and Port. Our soft opening is scheduled for tomorrow, and while I've always prided myself on keeping a cool head, I'm starting to get really anxious about all the fine details.

Did I schedule all the right people to work?

Did I send out enough invites?

Do we have enough food ordered?

Are the bloggers going to come?

The questions are plaguing me constantly—to the point that I can't remember the last time I had a full night's sleep.

"You're looking a bit pale. Is everything okay?"

"Yeah." I swallow hard. "Just nervous. I don't want to mess anything up."

Mr. Knightly is known in Port Snow as the man behind the town's success. A true patriarch and a bit of a mogul, he can be intimidating, though that's not the man sitting across from me right now. His features soften, and a faint smile passes over his lips.

"Eve Roberts, you are an intelligent woman with a great number of brilliant ideas brewing in that head of yours every day. Your skills and organization are impeccable, and your ability to learn on the fly and obtain knowledge is incredible. I could not think of a better person to be at the helm of Knight and Port." Emotions start to tighten my throat as he continues, "We're having soft openings for a reason—to work out the kinks—so even if things aren't as perfect as they should be tomorrow night, we'll iron out those wrinkles." He leans forward and places his hand on my desk. "We have the best team for this restaurant. I can't wait to see how well we do."

I nod, unable to voice my gratitude for his kind words.

Before I can start blubbering, someone ascends the stairs—but when I see that it's Reid, my heart flips in my chest, and my emotions skyrocket, putting me on the verge of sobs anyway, just at the sight of him.

"Sorry to interrupt," he says, holding his hand up in apology. "Dad, Mom's downstairs with some questions about the opening. Mainly what she should wear."

Rolling his eyes, Mr. Knightly laughs and stands up from his chair, his tall frame blocking the can lights in the ceiling. "Things she can do at home." He taps my desk. "You got this, Eve." With a parting wink, he takes off down the stairs, leaving me alone with Reid, who doesn't seem to get the hint that I want to be left alone as I stare down at my papers and shuffle them around. With every ounce of strength I have left inside of me, I try to hide the tears that are just starting to fall past my eyelids.

But when I hear him step forward, I know it's too late.

"Hey." He walks around to my side of my desk. Bringing his fingers to my chin, he lifts my head just in time to catch a few tears. "What's going on?"

I swipe at my face and push my shoulders back, trying to put on a strong front. But he sees right through it and kneels down in front of me, swiveling my chair to face him. All the nerves from the restaurant, all the feelings I have for this man, come crashing together at the same time, and before I can stop myself, tears stream down my face.

"Eve, talk to me," Reid says, placing both hands on my thighs and moving them up and down. The comforting gesture feels like an electric shock, lighting me up inside and confusing my emotions even more. "Did my dad say anything to upset you?"

"No." I shake my head with a quiet sob and take a deep breath before wiping my eyes again. "I'm sorry. I'm stronger than this." With another deep breath, I lean back and reach for a tissue on my desk. I quickly blow my nose and toss the tissue in the trash. "Okay." I shake my shoulders. "Sorry about that. Is there something I can help you with?"

"Yeah, you can tell me why you're crying."

"I'm not crying anymore, so no need to talk about it." Another tear falls, and I quickly wipe it away and plaster on a fake smile. "See, all good."

"Not buying it." He takes my hands, his thumbs circling over my knuckles. Everything about him is warm and comforting. "Talk to me, Eve."

Damn it. More tears start to fall. Isn't that always the case when you're trying to hold back the tears? You can keep them at bay until someone asks you what's wrong.

Knowing he won't let up on his questions, I look down at our connected hands and say, "Just nervous about the soft opening. This is big, and I don't want to screw anything up."

"Is that all?" He tilts my chin again to get a good look at my face.

I nibble on my bottom lip as I contemplate confessing to him. My conversation with Harper and Rogan has been festering in my head, building and building, driving me nuts, and creating almost a false sense of courage within me.

Even if he's not perfect, he's perfect for you.

That one sentence. It's been on constant replay in my head, becoming more and more true with each breath I take.

Can I take another chance on him? Throw my heart on the table one more time and risk him breaking it all over again?

I stare into his blue eyes, and I realize that, of all the risks that come in life, there's only one I'm not willing to take, and that's not giving us one more chance.

I look off to the side, my voice drifting off into a hushed whisper as I say, "You."

"Me, what?"

"Having you here, holding me. Your kind gestures, your surprises, your pursuit. It's all too much for me, Reid. I want to hate you, but . . ."

"But what?" he asks, leaning closer, anticipation brimming in his eyes.

"But I can't seem"—I pause and steady my shaking hands—"I can't seem to stop my heart from wanting you."

An irresistible grin passes over his lips. "You want me." The words are filled with his usual cocky attitude. My tears quickly dry up as I palm his face and push him away from me.

"Forget I even said anything."

"No way in hell." He stands and pulls me up with him as his arms loop around my waist. Seeming not to care about whoever sees us, he presses his forehead against mine. "Come over tonight. Let me make you dinner. We won't have time to fish and have the perfect date, but we can at least share the night before opening."

"I don't know," I answer, my protest sounding pathetic even to me.

"Please, Eve. Let me apologize to you properly; let me make this up to you. When I said I wanted to make things right, I meant it."

I said I'd listen with an open heart when he came to me, but it's a little harder than I thought to put aside how much it hurt when he broke up with me. The look in his eyes, that desperate plea to try one more time—this is why I'm bending, why I can't seem to turn this man away. No matter how cautious my brain is, my heart wins every single time.

"Tonight?" I ask. "I have plans." I smile.

"What are you doing? Washing your hair?"

"Close, shaving my legs."

He chuckles. "Come over, please. I promise it will be worth taking time away from shaving your legs."

"I don't know . . . I really treasure that time."

He pulls me into a hug and presses his lips to the side of my head. The rippling muscles beneath his thin shirt press against me and quicken my pulse. "It will be worth it. We're worth it."

And with that final dagger to the heart, I nod and agree to meet him for dinner.

Who was I kidding? My need for this man was going to win one way or another. I'm just surprised I was able to put up this much of a fight.

CHAPTER TWENTY-NINE

EVE

The door flies open, and Reid heaves a sigh of relief. "Ten minutes late—way to make a guy sweat."

Laughing, I step into his houseboat and take my shoes off right before he pulls me into his arms. "Sorry, Eric wanted to go over a few things before I took off."

"I thought you weren't going to show. I was about to drown my sorrows in some lobster bisque."

I pull away and look up at him. "Lobster bisque? I thought the Lighthouse Restaurant was the only place in town allowed to make that."

"Don't tell anyone." He winks. "Plus mine is better." He moves into the kitchen, and I selfishly take in his tight backside—that perfect, denim-wrapped butt. I stare at it for a few seconds before my eyes scan upward to the narrow cut of his hips and the breadth of his shoulders, where his traps stand out, even beneath his shirt. There's no doubt this man is one hot chef, and the way he hovers over his steaming pot as he takes a quick sip of his meal only makes him hotter.

"You really think yours is better? Those are big words, Knightly."

"Well, I have to bring in the big guns if I'm going to win you back."

"So your strategy is lobster bisque? You know the Lighthouse Restaurant's is my favorite. Do you really think you can compete?"

"I do." He reaches behind him and brings his shirt up and over his head before tossing it to the ground and facing me, topless and in all his beautiful, muscular glory.

I cross my arms over my chest and give him a slow once-over until I land on his cocky grin. "Nice try, but it's not about who serves it; it's about the taste." I take a seat at the table, unfold my napkin, and set it on my lap. I pick up my spoon and look him square in the eyes. "Your muscles will not alter my opinion."

"Damn." He laughs. "Tough critic."

"Don't try to woo me with your body. Woo me with your talent."

This time he's the one who gives me a once-over. "Pretty sure I've wooed you with my talent many times."

I give him an eye roll as he sets a bowl of soup in front of me. The smell alone is turning my stomach on, but the plating is also spectacular—not a drop of soup outside its bowl, a splash of green garnish to light up the dish, and a swirl of deep-orange sauce that blends beautifully with the creamy yellow of the bisque. This man may very well be the death of me, and this soup . . . my gravestone.

"Cheesy lobster bisque with some homemade ciabatta and honey butter."

Seriously, the guy made his own butter.

"How on earth did you get this all done?"

"Magic, babe." He winks. "I'm magic in the kitchen."

He's magic other places too, but to prevent any ego inflation, I keep my mouth shut and dip my spoon in the soup. I blow on it a few times and take my first taste.

Damn. It.

Don't close your eyes. I know it's good, but don't close your eyes.

Crap. I can't help it. My eyes close, and I savor the flavors as they bounce around my taste buds. Creamy, buttery, a hint of garlic, and all that cheese flavor. I really do think I've gone to heaven.

I don't have to open my eyes to know what I'll see across the table from me. Reid Knightly with a more-than-satisfied smile on his face, knowing very well that he just won the lobster bisque challenge. One spoonful, that's all it took.

"I won't gloat, don't worry. You can open your eyes."

Slowly, I part my eyelids to find Reid leaning back in his chair, looking as confident as I've ever seen him.

"You don't have to say it—it's written all over your face," he adds, arm draped over the back of his chair, his sculpted chest on full display.

"You don't have to be so arrogant about it." I take another spoonful, because I *need* another spoonful. It's so freaking good.

"Not arrogant, just pleased. And now that I won your taste buds over with my lobster bisque, I need to win back your heart. I can trust that you're open to hearing me out?"

"This lobster bisque might have helped you a little. Proceed with your groveling."

A low chuckle rumbles out of him before he sits back up in his chair and starts eating along with me. He butters two pieces of bread and hands me one right before taking a large bite. His jaw works up and down, chewing, until he swallows, and for some reason I'm both fascinated and shamelessly turned on by his mouth. Maybe because I know exactly what that mouth can do, and it's been far too long since I've experienced it.

"Groveling, huh? Do I need to get on my knees?"

"Maybe later, if you're lucky."

His brows rise, and that smile grows even wider—just as there's a knock on his door.

Groaning, he says, "Brig is coming over for some bisque. I told him I'd save some as a thank-you for his help. He's going to be annoying about us having dinner together, so just ignore him." Raising his voice, he calls out, "Come in, dickhead."

The door opens, and my spoon is halfway to my mouth when Eric walks onto the houseboat. He frowns, confused; his eyes first land on a shirtless Reid, and then they slide over to me. Pure rage flashes through Eric's gaze in a matter of seconds.

Oh crap.

Reid stands from his chair and puts his hands out. "Eric, let me—"

But before Reid can explain, Eric is charging him, cocking his arm back, and landing his fist right on his eye. Reid's body careens backward into the table, spilling lobster bisque all over the floor and chairs.

"What the fuck did I tell you?" Eric yells.

"Eric!" I scream, scared and confused at the same time. "What are you doing?"

He spins toward me, the veins in his neck popping, his fists clenching at his sides. "This doesn't concern you, Eve, so I suggest you leave." He turns back to Reid as he's picking himself up, lobster bisque and butter stuck to his backside. "I told you to end it with her."

"And I did!" Reid shouts back.

Excuse me? Eric told Reid to end things? When did he even know that Reid and I were in a relationship?

"Then what the fuck is this?" Eric gestures at our ruined dinner.

Chest puffed, eye starting to swell, Reid says, "I decided I wanted to win her back."

"You motherfucker." Eric charges Reid again, but I step between them, pushing my hand against Eric's chest before he can land another blow.

"Eric, stop. What do you think you're doing?"

"I knew it," he seethes through his teeth. "I saw all the warning signs but chose to ignore them. The glances you would give her, the times I would walk in on you two talking, and all the guilty looks. You two have been fucking behind my back, haven't you?"

"Have you lost your mind?" I ask as I feel Reid's bare chest come up behind me.

"What if we have? Would it have changed anything about the restaurant? Would it have made a difference? No, because I, unlike you, know how to separate the two."

"Fuck. You," Eric spits. "You know, I actually came here to talk to you, to make up for all our grievances in the past. I wanted to have an honest conversation with you, to start a new chapter before we open tomorrow. But you haven't changed since Boston. You're just as selfish as before. Never taking the blame, just placing it on others."

"I took the blame!" Reid shouts. "I took the fucking blame for what happened. I punished myself for years, and it wasn't until Eve that I actually started to forgive myself and try to start over. Don't tell me I didn't take the blame, because I wore that failure like a goddamn belt every damn day of my life."

"And yet you're making the same mistakes that I did." Eric shakes his head and stalks to the front door, throwing it open. "Here's to Knight and Port—let's hope it doesn't sink like Bar 79."

With that, he storms out into the night, the door slamming behind him, leaving me alone with Reid.

Shaken, angry, and hurt, I turn toward Reid. He reaches for me, but instead of falling into his grasp, I take a step back.

"Eve—"

I hold my hand up, a cold surge of anger gripping me. "Did you break up with me because *Eric* told you to?"

"It's more complicated than that."

"It's not. It's a yes or no answer. Did you break up with me because Eric told you to?"

"Eve, listen." He reaches for me again, but I take another step back and slide on my shoes.

"Yes or no, Reid."

He drags his hand over his face, his frustration clear. "Just let me explain."

"Yes. Or. No," I grind out.

"Yes, okay." He throws his hands out. "But there was more to the decision."

"I don't care if there was more. You let someone else decide your future rather than making the decision yourself. We were good, Reid, and you threw that away because what? Because Eric scared you? Brought up his past and Janelle? Wasn't I different? Wasn't what we had different?"

"Yes." Desperation laces his voice. "But I was a fucking idiot, okay? I was scared and didn't want to screw anything up again."

"So you chose the restaurant over me instead of fighting for what we had?"

"No, I mean, it seems like that, but—"

"Forget it." I open the front door, ready to run away, and collide with a brick wall. Glancing up, I see Brig's startled face.

"Whoa, sorry about . . . man, what the hell happened in here? Did you have wild sex? On my lobster bisque? Dude, I don't want your sex juices in my soup."

"Shut the fuck up, man," Reid snaps as I push past Brig. "Eve, wait."

"I'll see you tomorrow. Come prepared to cook your ass off."

I leave as a confused Brig calls after me to have a good night.

I stride away, fuming. He chose Knight and Port over me—that realization cuts deeper than I ever thought possible. But even worse, he gave up on *us*. And my brother, getting in the way? He'd better be ready because we're about to have a little talk.

Too bad he's not there when I get home, leaving me to stew in my own thoughts.

What a perfect way to spend the night before our opening.

CHAPTER THIRTY

REID

This is a goddamn disaster.

At least that's what Eric keeps saying as he stomps around the kitchen, handing out orders and practically pulling his hair out.

To say the tension is thick right now is an understatement.

I spent all last night not only texting Eve but also trying to get Eric to come back and talk things over before we opened. All I got was radio silence, though, until he showed up at Knight and Port, put on a big smile with the rest of us as we opened the doors, and then started cooking.

We're three hours into the soft opening, and we've already run out of supplies for three of our dishes. The local lager from the brewery down the road is out, and we're almost tapped out on two other microbrews. We have about six bottles of wine left, the waitstaff has fucked up three orders, and there is a line out the door that shows no sign of dissipating. To top it all off, I have one and a half eyes due to the swelling from Eric's punch.

It's kind of a disaster.

"Where the fuck are the eggs?" Eric whisper-shouts to the staff. "Don't tell me we're out of eggs." Just as he asks, a new wave of orders comes rushing in on the printer, announcing that there's no end in sight. I don't think we were prepared for this level of activity, and it's showing.

"Here," Alex, one of the sous-chefs, says, bringing Eric a carton of eggs.

I tried telling him a few times to chill, but every time I said anything, he just got more irritated. I stopped trying to handle him an hour ago and have stuck to what I do best: cooking.

Eve has popped into the kitchen a few times, looking frantic, delivering some plates herself and helping out wherever she can, even at the bar, but she hasn't spared a glance in my direction. Last time she came in, I stared for far too long and burned one of the baked bean sandwiches.

My head is not in it tonight, and it's one of the reasons I keep making mistakes, those little mistakes that add up to a subpar experience, like at the Lighthouse Restaurant. Missed salt here, bread on the grill for a little too long, caramel sauce not quite buttery enough. I'm producing, but it's not food I'm particularly proud of, and I know why: my entire world has been tilted on its axis.

Eric isn't talking to me.

Eve won't look at me.

And every time my dad checks in to see how things are going, I can feel his dream slowly slip from my fingers.

"Did you hear?" Alex asks, stepping up next to me with a bundle of veggies in his arms. "Terryn Bowers, the Foodie Fangirl, and Sir Wine-a-Lot were here."

My spatula pauses midflip at the mention of the three top food bloggers in the New England area. They were here? In Knight and Port? Eating our food?

Oh. Fuck.

I'm about to question Alex when Eric appears beside me. "What did you just say?" he asks.

"Uh . . ." Alex looks terrified. "Eve got the three best bloggers to review us for the soft opening."

"And she didn't fucking tell us? What did they order?"

Alex swallows hard. "I . . . I'm not sure."

"Dude, lay off," I say, pressing my hand to Eric's rapidly rising and falling chest. "Alex is just the messenger."

Eric swats my hand away. "Don't fucking touch me."

Before I can reply, he heads back to his grill and tends to his food, his presence like a ball of tension, while all of our new employees scramble around, trying to make sure they don't piss off the temperamental bosses.

Fucking great.

For the first time in five hours, I let out a long, pent-up breath and lean against the wall of the kitchen.

Holy fuck. That was a shit show.

Everyone is gone, staff and patrons, Eric is over by the grill, making himself something to eat, and I'm resisting the urge to walk up behind him and return the punch he landed on me last night.

He was a prick the entire night. He made the working environment unbearable and snapped at everyone who tried to help—even snapped at my dad once. Yeah, the entire night was stressful, and I don't think it was our best work, but it didn't call for this level of rage.

Knowing I need to confront him, I push off the wall and start to unbutton my chef jacket. "Congratulations on being the epitome of an asshole tonight," I say.

"Point that finger right back at yourself," he says, his back still turned to me. "You hold the title for asshole."

"What the hell are you talking about?"

Flipping the grill off, he faces me, arms crossed over his chest. "How do you think tonight went, Reid? Do you think it was a success? Because from my point of view it was a complete disaster."

"Yeah, you made that crystal clear," I shoot back.

"Because we were ill prepared. You fucked up so many times, burned so many dishes, that we ran out of food." Eve chooses this moment to step into the kitchen, but that doesn't stop Eric from shooting off, "We ran out of drinks, the waitstaff confused dishes, our ceiling fans stopped working at one point for God knows what reason, and we didn't have a quick enough turnaround, which meant that the line stretched out the door and down the street. And why do you think all those things happened?" He doesn't give me a chance to answer. "Because you two"—he gestures to me and Eve—"decided to distract each other rather than preparing for tonight. Sneaking behind my back, making me look like a goddamn fool." He rips off his chef jacket and tosses it to the ground. "We could have been so much goddamn better than this, but you chose sex over the restaurant."

"You're way off base," I say, stepping forward. "I did what you asked me to do—I broke up with Eve, and it fucking hurt—but I listened because I didn't want to fuck up the restaurant or our friendship, if you could call it that. Despite how much it hurt, I powered through and put together this restaurant—"

"Tonight was a joke. You're telling me you weren't distracted? That your head was fully in Knight and Port?" He turns to Eve. "And can *you* tell me you did everything you could to make this night a success? If you were more on top of things, Eve, you would have told us about the bloggers, we wouldn't have run out of food, we—"

"I put my heart and soul into this night," she cuts in, eyes blazing. "I brought the bloggers in and didn't tell you because I didn't want to make you nervous."

"And this is where experience comes in," Eric says. "If you actually had some experience in a five-star restaurant, you would know to always tell the chef who's at the tables. Always."

"Hold the fuck on—" I start, but Eve steps in front of me, chin up, anger pouring off of her.

"Excuse me? Are you saying that I shouldn't have this job? That I haven't worked my ass off to get where I am?"

"I'm not saying you haven't worked your ass off—I know what you've sacrificed," Eric replies, the edge in his voice softening slightly. "What I'm saying is, you don't have the experience, nor do you apparently have the ability to multitask with Reid between your legs."

And like a firecracker, I explode. In an instant, I'm on Eric, plowing into him, slamming him onto his back, and cocking my arm. I'm about to deliver one hell of a punch when my arm is restrained, and I'm yanked off Eric, my dad's voice bellowing through the entire restaurant.

"Enough!" He pushes Eric and me apart and then looks between all three of us. "That is *enough*." He takes a few breaths, calming himself, becoming the levelheaded man that I've always known. "Is this the kind of professionalism I should expect from you three? Beating each other up and tearing each other down?" Eric slouches, and Eve folds her hands in front of her as I keep steady eye contact with my father, knowing that's what he expects. "I did not hire you three so you can make a mockery of me and this restaurant."

"It wasn't the best night," Eric cuts in, but Dad shakes his head.

"That's where you're wrong. The night was a success, but you were too stuck in your head to even notice. All three of you were. Eve, you were upstairs crying for half an hour, apologizing when there was no need to apologize." Eve was crying? I search her face but don't see any signs of it. "I was the one who ordered the food, so I should be blamed for the fact that we ran out. But there's a learning curve here, and we shouldn't dwell on it. The bloggers were a huge win, Eve, and I'm glad you didn't tell the boys because it made their experience authentic—and contrary to what you believe, Eric, they gave us *rave* reviews."

Eric immediately deflates.

"As for the kitchen, an apology will be issued to our employees for the way they were treated tonight. I understand jitters, but acting like asses is uncalled for, both of you. The tension you two created didn't go unnoticed, and I suggest that if you both want to continue working here, you'd better air out your dirty laundry because I will not put up with another night like we had tonight." Standing proudly, my dad continues, "Tonight was a success in my book. Forget the small things, the details that you noticed, because not a single customer complained. Everyone praised Knight and Port—the staff, the atmosphere, the food. They had one hell of a night, and that's something we need to be proud of. That's something we need to remember moving forward. The small things we can fix—it's the big things that need to be addressed. You have until tomorrow morning. If you can't get over your egos and your past, don't bother showing up for our morning meeting."

And with that, my dad walks out of the restaurant without a backward glance, leaving all three of us in a monumental awkward silence.

There's only one way to break it.

I walk over to the open bar and grab a bottle of tequila and three shot glasses. I nod to Eve and Eric, who don't say a word but follow my lead. They sit at the bar across from me, and I pour each of us a shot. The sound of waves against the harbor rocks filters in through the open sliding glass windows, setting a peaceful mood for the conversation we need to have.

Together, we all take one shot and then set our glasses down. Hands pressed against the wooden bar top, I take a deep breath and break the ice. "I fucked up." I look Eric directly in the eyes. "I fucked up by not telling you about Eve and me right off the bat. I thought that if we could prove to you that we worked well together, if we showed you we could separate the business and our relationship, that you would accept it. I'm sorry for the secret. But I will never be sorry for pursuing your sister—that's something I won't apologize for."

He nods but stays silent, so I continue.

"As for Bar 79, we both failed, together." As the words flow from me, I feel myself accepting them, almost as if saying them out loud is what actually makes me believe them. "We were young, we were cocky, we thought we knew everything, and we were proven wrong. Bar 79 was our heart and soul, and the wound we have from losing it will probably never fully heal, but we can learn from it. We've learned that communication is one of the things we need to work on. Honesty is another. We have the talent, Eric. We just need a foundation."

Eric drags his hand over his face. "Fuck. I'm such a dickhead." Without another word, he spins in his seat and faces Eve, who's been silent this entire time. "I don't know what I was thinking, saying such horrible things about you, Eve. I was fired up, angry over the past and every little thing that went wrong. I was looking for someone to blame, anyone but myself, because I just couldn't shoulder yet another failure. And I took it out on you, my saint of a sister who's done nothing but support me. I'm so goddamn sorry."

He pulls her into a hug, and she wraps her arms around him, easily accepting his apology. If only it was that easy with me.

"You mean everything to me, Eve," he continues, "and I am so proud of everything you've accomplished and the strong, intelligent woman you've become. Please know I will never doubt that again. I'm sorry."

"You better not, or I'll use your own knives to chop off your fingers." She squeezes him tightly before pulling out of his hug.

"Noted." He chuckles before turning back to me, studying me with wide, earnest eyes. "Reid," he says. "It's hard for me to look you in the eyes and not feel a gauntlet of emotions ranging from happiness to rage to embarrassment."

"Embarrassment?"

"You warned me, man." He shakes his head. "You warned me to not go after Janelle, and I didn't listen. My pride was too strong, and I wanted to show you I could handle it. I couldn't. I let you down; I let us down. So when I found out you were with my sister, I just kind of lost it. All I could think of was Janelle and how much I fucked up. And I threw all of those feelings onto you. I was convinced that you were repeating my mistakes but that you were too proud to ever back down. I jumped to conclusions and gave you an ultimatum that I'm ashamed of, because if anyone could handle business and a relationship, it's my sister. And no matter what, I know she would keep you in line."

I laugh and turn to Eve, who hasn't cracked a smile. "You're right about that."

"I never should have interfered, nor should I have even had an opinion on the matter. Last night was a mistake I'll always regret, and my attitude today was despicable. Frankly I'm embarrassed and owe a giant apology to everyone tomorrow. But you get the first one." Looking me in the eyes, Eric says, "I'm sorry, man. You're the guy I need to depend on, not fight with. From here on out, I'll treat you like the brother you've been rather than the enemy I made you out to be in my head."

Rounding the bar, I hold out my hand, and he pulls me into a hug. As his arms wrap around me, a huge weight is lifted off my shoulders, and for the first time since that fateful night in New Orleans, I feel like I can actually breathe.

"I love you, man," I say, getting choked up.

"I love you too, and I'm so goddamn sorry about everything."

When we pull away, I grip his shoulders. "It's in the past; let's move forward. New slate, new chapter."

"New life."

We both nod and give each other one more hug. I've known this man since we were little boys playing by the harbor, chucking rocks out into the ocean, trying to make them skip across the surface. We've seen each other grow up; we've been there for one another during our teen years and when his parents died. I know everything about him, and after all these years, this feeling that we're finally on the mend breathes fresh air into my lungs. I never realized how much not having Eric in my life really weighed on me until this moment.

Patting my shoulder, Eric glances behind him. "I'll, uh, let you two talk now. I'm headed out to the Har-Bahr, so take your time." He presses a quick kiss to Eve's cheek and then takes off, his step lighter than I've seen it in months.

Once the door is shut and I'm left alone with Eve in the restaurant, I stuff my hands in my pockets and rock on my heels. "So, do you think we can talk?"

She stands from the barstool and smooths down her black pants. "I don't think that's necessary, Reid."

"I think it is. We need to get some stuff off our chests."

"No, I think I made everything quite clear the other night. You gave up on us, and that's fine."

"Whenever a woman says *that's fine*, it really isn't fine."

"Well, I mean it. It *is* fine."

"Don't do this, Eve. Don't put on a brave face and act like everything is okay. I know you."

"Yeah, you think you know me?" she shoots back. "Then you would know that I can't possibly be with someone who is so weak that he can't make decisions on his own. I've been through the wringer with you, Reid, ever since that night at the Inn. It hasn't been easy, but a part of me always believed that despite whatever was going on in your life, you would still choose to be with me over anything else. That was until I heard about Eric's ultimatum. If you were half the man I thought you were, you would have found a way to prove to him that I was worth the risk. But you folded. And I don't want to be with a man who folds so easily. I want to be with a man who fights."

"I'm fighting now."

"Well, you're fighting too late."

She pushes past me but turns back when she reaches the front door. "I will be professional, because this job means everything to me, but please, just leave me alone when it comes to us. It's over, Reid."

The door shuts behind her, leaving me feeling like a semitruck just crashed into my chest. It's over . . . but what if I don't want it to be over?

Until your mind has matured, the curse will go uncured—or some crap like that. I can't remember the damn curse verbatim, but what I do know is this is my fork in the road. I have two choices at this point. I can fold once again and act like the girl I love is just a colleague, or I can grow up, pull out my inner Brig, and romance the fuck out of her—show her just how far I'm willing to go for her.

My gaze sweeps across the restaurant, and despite my exhaustion, my pure heartache, I feel a fire igniting inside me, begging me to fight. I'm thinking option number two is the winner. Now to enlist some help . . .

CHAPTER THIRTY-ONE

EVE

"Are you really not going to eat any of these waffles I made you?"

I stare at the stack and shake my head. "I'm not hungry." I pull my legs in closer to my chest and rest my chin on my knees. "Stick them in the freezer. We can toast them in the morning."

"You never pass up my waffles. What's going on?"

Staring at the blank TV from my spot on the couch, I try to hold back the emotions that are bubbling up inside of me, but there's no use. When it comes to Reid, I'm an emotional wreck.

"I love him, Eric. I love him so much."

He's in the middle of packing up the waffles in a freezer bag when he stops and faces me. "What do you mean? Did you two not make up last night?"

I shake my head. "No. I mean, he wanted to, but I can't seem to let go of the fact that he chose the restaurant over me or that he so easily threw in the towel when things got complicated. That really hurt me."

Setting down the waffles, Eric makes his way to the couch and sits down beside me, pulling my feet over his lap. "You've been friends with Reid for as long as I have, and we both know he's the most loyal guy there is. Even after our falling-out, he still reached out, connected with me on our parents' death anniversaries, on holidays. He was always there. And he was there for you when I wasn't. But sometimes his loyalty goes too far. This was one of those instances. Instead of listening to his heart, he stayed loyal to me, honoring something I never should have asked of him. Don't punish Reid for that, for being loyal when he doesn't know any other way to be."

Furious at my own vulnerability, I swipe at my eyes and look away, but Eric catches my chin, turning me back toward him.

"If you still love him, then let yourself love him."

"What if he hurts me again?" I ask, my fears surfacing. "I've been broken twice already. I don't know if I can do it again."

He pulls me into a hug and holds me tight, letting me sink into the familiar feel of his embrace. "I can't promise you that he won't hurt you again, but what I can promise is that no matter what, he will always stand by your side because that's the type of man he is."

There's a knock at the door, interrupting my rebuttal. Standing from the couch, I wipe at my eyes again and open the door to find Brig standing on the other side.

What's he doing here?

"Eve, the fairest maiden in all of Port Snow, will you please accompany me outside?" He bows and holds out his arm.

From outside, I can hear Reid shout, "I told you not to fucking call her a *maiden*."

"You want her back, don't you?" Brig shouts in response. "Let me do my thing!" Turning back to me, he smiles widely. "Care to join me?"

Chuckling even as my heart kicks into overdrive, I take his arm. Despite myself, I'm curious to see what I'm going to find.

And whatever I could have imagined is nothing compared to what I see when I step outside.

Wearing an entire suit of armor and sitting atop a brown horse is Reid, looking incredibly uncomfortable and pushing back the visor of his helmet as it continuously falls forward.

Oh.

My.

God.

Standing at his sides are his other brothers, Griffin and Rogan, as well as Jen, Ren, Harper, and—how embarrassing—his parents.

I think I might just die from either laughter or embarrassment.

"What the actual fuck?" Eric whispers as he steps up behind me and then bursts into laughter.

Brig steps away from me and announces, "Cue the bubbles."

"What? Brig, I said *no bubbles!*" Reid exclaims as the horse starts pawing at the ground, getting antsy. "Whoa, buddy, settle down."

Jen pulls a toy lawn mower bubble maker from behind her back and starts moving it back and forth, producing a tiny stream of bubbles.

"Jen," Brig chastises. "I said *bubble maker*, not one of your kids' toys."

"You gave me an hour. This is what you get."

Groaning, Brig points to Rogan and Griffin. "Cue the music."

Rogan taps away at his phone while Griffin holds up a portable speaker barely the size of his hand. Taylor Swift begins to play, and Brig nearly has a conniption as he flies at Rogan and steals his phone.

"I said a live band, not Taylor Swift 2017. She's so angry. If you're going to play Taylor, go with 2008 Taylor."

With a few taps, "Love Story" starts playing on the speaker, and Brig points at his parents. "Unfurl the banner!"

Together, they roll out an old banner that says, **CONGRATS GRAD!** but the words are scratched out and **I'M SORRY** is written instead.

The only problem: it's upside down.

"For fuck's sake!" Brig hurries to his parents and rights the banner just as two confetti poppers go off, shooting paper into the sky and scaring the actual piss out of the horse, which rears up and knocks Reid right onto his ass with a loud *clunk*.

"Ahh fuck," he groans.

Harper and Ren stand motionless, confetti poppers in their hands, scared for their lives as Brig's face turns bright red.

"Those were supposed to be for *after* she accepts his love again. If you read my detailed email, you would know that." He pushes both hands through his hair and then throws them up in the air before walking over to his car and leaning against it, completely distraught.

We all stand there, unsure of what to do, while Griffin calms the horse and Reid tries to scramble up from the ground. But the heavy armor keeps getting in the way, and he thrashes around like a turtle turned over until his dad and Rogan lend a hand, righting him so he's facing me. Taking the helmet off his head, he steps toward me and runs his hand through his sweaty hair, an embarrassed smile stretching across his face.

"Uh . . . I'm supposed to be your knight in shining armor. The horse was supposed to be white, but we couldn't find one on such short notice." He takes another step forward until he's only a foot away, his metallic shuffling making each movement almost painfully awkward.

Behind me, Eric is chuckling, and I can't help but laugh as well.

Oh, Reid.

Beautiful, loyal Reid.

"Eve, I had these grand plans of making this enormous gesture to you this morning, and I enlisted Brig's help, knowing he would go above and beyond. I wanted to show you that no matter what's thrown my way again, nothing could ever stop me from being with you." His armor squeaks as he tries to adjust it. "Hitting on you was the smartest decision I ever made."

"Eloquent," Rogan says from the viewing party.

"So romantic." Jen chuckles.

"Swoon worthy," Griffin adds.

Brig is still pouting by his car.

Ignoring his family, Reid continues, "I've harbored a secret crush on you for so long that even when we were together, I thought it was too good to be true, that it would all disappear. And rather than live in the moment, I let my fears and doubts hang over me until I let them take over, and I made the worst decision of my life: letting you go. But I need you to know this: even though I pushed you away, you were always there, buried in my heart." He takes a deep breath. "I love you, Eve. I love you so goddamn much, and even if you don't want to be with me, I am going to spend every free moment of every day making it up to you, convincing you that you're what matters to me, *you* are what I want, what I need to be happy. Nothing else."

"Beautiful, son," Mr. Knightly says.

"Well said," his mom chimes in.

"I couldn't have said it better myself," Brig practically cheers.

Sighing, Reid whispers, "Kind of wish they weren't all here right now."

"But where's the fun in that?" I smile, letting the moment wash over me. All the doubt, the fear, it disappears as I stare into Reid's eyes. Eric's right—he's loyal to a fault. But I would rather have a loyal man than one I couldn't trust, and the love he has for me, the love brimming in his eyes, makes every moment of heartache worth it. Despite our ups and downs, I know that no matter what, Reid will always be by my side, and I would risk anything to have him there.

Getting our relationship back to where it used to be won't be easy, but then again, like my parents always taught me, love is never easy. Love is a foundation of challenges that stem from two souls colliding as one. There will be miscommunications and moments where we hurt each other, because we are human after all, but what truly matters is the realization that the person standing in front of you is the one person who makes you the best version of yourself.

And I can honestly say Reid is that person.

He challenges me more than anyone, keeps me guessing—never letting me settle but always pushing me instead. He helps me feel, helps me explore a gauntlet of emotions, and holds my hand on this roller coaster of life; even before we were together, he was there by my side. The intimacy I crave he gives me in spades; the hole I have for caring for someone he fills so easily by letting me take him into my arms. And most importantly, he puts me first.

It took me a bit to realize that, given the fact that I thought he was choosing the restaurant and Eric over me, but he wasn't. He was choosing my happiness, helping me obtain and reach my goals. He's always had me at the forefront of his mind. I come first, and for that, I will always love him.

"I love you, Eve. Please tell me we can work this out, that we can have the restaurant and the relationship."

"Well, that depends," I say, eyeing his getup. "Are you returning this armor to wherever you got it?"

"Do you want me to?"

"Desperately." I nod.

"Consider it returned," he says, a giant smile pulling at his lips.

I step toward him and stand on my toes as I loop my arms around his neck and let him pull me into a kiss, right in front of my brother, the Knightlys, and anyone in Port Snow who cares to witness the crazy show playing out in my apartment parking lot.

"I love you, Reid," I whisper, pressing my forehead against his.

"I love you, babe. Forever."

And as Brig cheers and takes pictures, his family clapping and hooting, I realize that not only am I holding the man of my dreams and listening to him pledge his love for me, but I'm also being accepted into a family, one that I've been missing for so long.

A line of support.

A line of love.

I have the job, the man, the family, the brother, the love. I don't think I could ask for anything more . . . besides some immediate private time with Reid and the "legend."

And I'm not talking about the curse.

EPILOGUE

REID

"Oh my God, *yes*! Reid, right there."

I flex my pelvis and push all the way inside of Eve, my teeth nearly shattering from how hard I'm grinding them together.

"Please, babe," I croak. "Fuck, I'm going to come."

"Me . . . too. Ah God," she groans and digs her nails into my back as her pussy convulses around my cock, spurring on my orgasm.

White-hot pleasure shoots up my spine as I spill myself inside of her.

No matter how many times I take this woman into my bed, it doesn't seem to be enough. It's been a month since we got back together, and I still can't keep my hands off her. It's distracting at work—but in a good way. She's not making me burn shit, but she does get me riled up when she walks into the kitchen, clipboard in hand and pen tucked behind her ear. She does it on purpose, knowing full well what the entire look does for me.

We always meet up at my house after work and fuck like crazy until we pass out and spend the rest of the night cuddling. It's perfection. Eric has grown to accept that Eve doesn't come home at night, which was fine until Eve went back to the apartment to get some clothes and came face to face with her brother's bare ass as he was doing some girl from Pottsmouth. They now text each other their plans. It's an image that's been . . . difficult for Eve to get out of her head.

Breathing heavily, I collapse onto Eve and kiss her neck as I try to calm my racing heart.

"God, I love you so damn much," I whisper.

Her hand sifts through my hair. "I love you too."

"Enough to say yes to my proposal one day?"

"One day," she says, giving me the same answer she always does.

I want to ask her, badly. I want to make her mine forever, but I also know that I have a lot to learn about love and putting it first, so I'm waiting until I feel confident enough that I can give her everything I have.

"And kids?"

"Two." She smiles against my skin.

"Pets?"

"A cat that only loves me."

"And a house?"

"Up on Wobbler's Hill with enough land that we can have our own greenhouse."

I rise up onto my elbows and kiss her lips. "And vacations?"

"Only ones where we can be fully naked for an entire week."

"That's my kind of vaca—"

The door to my houseboat bursts open, and a distraught Brig calls out, "Are you home?"

Eve squeaks, pulling a sheet over her even though we're up in the loft and Brig can't see her.

"Dude, try knocking," I say, scrambling to put on a pair of shorts.

Brig paces the living room below, his hands in his hair. "I don't have time for knocking—not when I'm the laughingstock of the town."

Oh Jesus. What now?

I hop down the stairs, bare chested, my hair a mess from Eve's relentless pulling, and go to the fridge. I grab a can of beer and toss it at Brig, but he doesn't even bother catching it, letting it land on the couch instead.

Okay, this can't be good.

"What happened?"

"I am going to die alone."

I've heard that before.

"If this is about the curse—"

"This isn't about the fucking curse," Brig says, looking really distraught. Oh crap. I drop the sarcasm from my voice and try to dig in deep.

"Okay, let's talk it through. What happened?"

Eve joins me in the kitchen, wearing sweatpants and a nightshirt, and falls into my automatic embrace, her arms wrapping around my waist.

Brig stares at us and groans before rolling his eyes and flopping on the couch. "You know how I've been trying out different dating apps?"

"Yeah, weren't you going on a date tonight?"

"Yup, and I did."

"Was the girl not who you expected?"

He sits up ramrod straight and stares me down, his eyes looking completely crazy. "No, *she* was not who I expected."

Uh oh.

"What happened?"

"I planned this great evening at Jake's Cakes. Share some crabs, watch the sunset, get to know each other better. When it started to get late, past when we agreed to meet, I thought she was going to stand me up. Well, until I saw a teal tissue box."

"Uh . . . what does that mean?"

"It was our symbol. We talked about all the Lovemark movies we liked and how sometimes we cried while watching them. We'd always joke about handing each other tissues, so we decided that would be our symbol, our way of showing each other we're the right person when we met up, since we didn't have pictures."

"Okay, so she showed up."

"No, Reid," Brig deadpans. "*He* showed up. Fucking Walter the Uber driver catfished me!"

Holy.

Shit.

I purse my lips, trying desperately to hold back the laughter that threatens to pop out.

"What?" Eve says, taking over—thank God—as I try to compose myself. "Walter wanted to date you?"

"No, he was making a mockery out of me. He gave me the tissue box and said it was for all the lonely nights I must have." Brig clutches his chest. "He catfished me and broke my heart. I thought he was the lady of my dreams."

I can't.

I'm sorry.

Don't judge me, but I laugh.

Brig's eyes narrow as he stands and adjusts his shirt. "I should have known you were going to be a dick about this. You know, I came here and bared my soul. The least you could do is give me a hug."

Eve pinches my side, wordlessly telling me to console my brother, the most gullible person I know. Wanting to make her happy, and also feeling a little bad for him, I walk over and pull him into a hug.

"I'm sorry you were catfished by a sixty-year-old Uber driver."

"Thanks," he says, burying his face in my neck. "This means a lot to me, Reid."

I grit my teeth as he snuggles closer. I'm not loving this warm, fuzzy shit, but I know this is what he needs.

"Do you think I'm going to die alone?"

Yes.

"No, not at all. The perfect girl is out there for you. Who knows? She might be right under your nose, and you just never noticed."

He sighs and pulls away. "I don't know, I think I'm going to go on a dating hiatus."

"You know"—Eve steps up and pats Brig on the shoulder—"whenever someone says they're not dating anymore, that's when they find the love of their life."

Brig perks up. "Shit, you're right. Classic movie meet-cute. Lovemark has done it at least a dozen times. That's it, I'm going on a dating hiatus," he announces. "Did you hear that, universe? I'm no longer dating. I'm celibate."

He's been celibate for a while . . . not by choice.

"Do you think I'll meet her tonight?" he whispers.

Eve smirks and shakes her head. "You have to actually go on a dating hiatus for it to work."

Sighing heavily, he nods. "Okay, sure. Fine. I will go on a dating hiatus." He walks toward the door but turns back. "Franklin, that motherfucker, took pictures of Walter and me, and I know they'll be in the newspaper tomorrow. Please, just tell people to be gentle—that's my heart they're messing with when they gossip."

"Sure thing, bro." I give him a curt wave. "Here's to the dating hiatus."

"May it bring me love." He clasps his hands together and then takes off. The minute the door shuts, both Eve and I bust out in laughter.

"Oh my God. Your brother, I just love him so much."

"Uh, excuse me?" I lift a brow.

"Not like that." She pushes my eyebrow down with her finger. "Come on, we have some cuddling to do."

She takes my hand and leads me back up the stairs, and as I stare at her ass on the way up, I can't help but think how far I've come—how, against all odds, I really have matured as a man. I might not actually know the truth about what happened in New Orleans, if we really were cursed, but I do know that I'm no longer threatened by the thought of broken love—because what Eve and I have will last a lifetime. From a secret crush to growing old together, it's the perfect love story.

ACKNOWLEDGMENTS

Going into Reid's book, I was nervous to explore him as a character because I really didn't know who he was. I remember talking to my agent about him, asking her, Who is Reid? And that's when we realized Reid doesn't even know who Reid is, so we took that knowledge and ran with it.

Out of all the brothers he was the most fun to write so far because it was rare when he had a filter, and I noticed quickly during edits how often I would snort or gasp at his ballsy reaction. I truly believe there is a little piece of Reid inside of me, that no-filter, obnoxious side, and I let it out big time in this book.

Kimberly Brower and Aimee Ashcraft, my agents, thank you for encouraging me while I wrote this book and having confidence in how fast I could write it. Aimee, huge thanks to you for being strapped to my back during this whole process and being my own personal cheerleader. Also, I think from here on out, the term *set the scene* will be permanently ingrained in my head.

Huge thank-you to Lauren Plude for having confidence in this series and my ability to deliver a manuscript that everyone will enjoy. Your support of my work will never go unnoticed. Thank you so much for putting up with my crazy and loving it.

To the bloggers and readers, thank you so much for loving these Knightly brothers and following their journey to rid themselves of their broken-love curse.

To my good friends who have clung to their phones, texting me back when deadlines were heavy and filling me with words of encouragement, Sara Ney and Meghan March, you make this journey easier. Thank you.

Jenny, you are the reason why I can just focus on writing. Thank you for keeping me in line and being my number one fan. I adore you.

And lastly, thank you to my wife, Steph. I will say this till the day that I die: you are my backbone, my soul mate, and one of the reasons why I am happy on a daily basis. I love you.

ABOUT THE AUTHOR

Photo © 2019 Milana Schaffer

USA Today bestselling author, wife, adoptive mother, and peanut butter lover. An author of romantic comedies and contemporary romance, Meghan Quinn brings readers the perfect combination of heart, humor, and heat in every book.